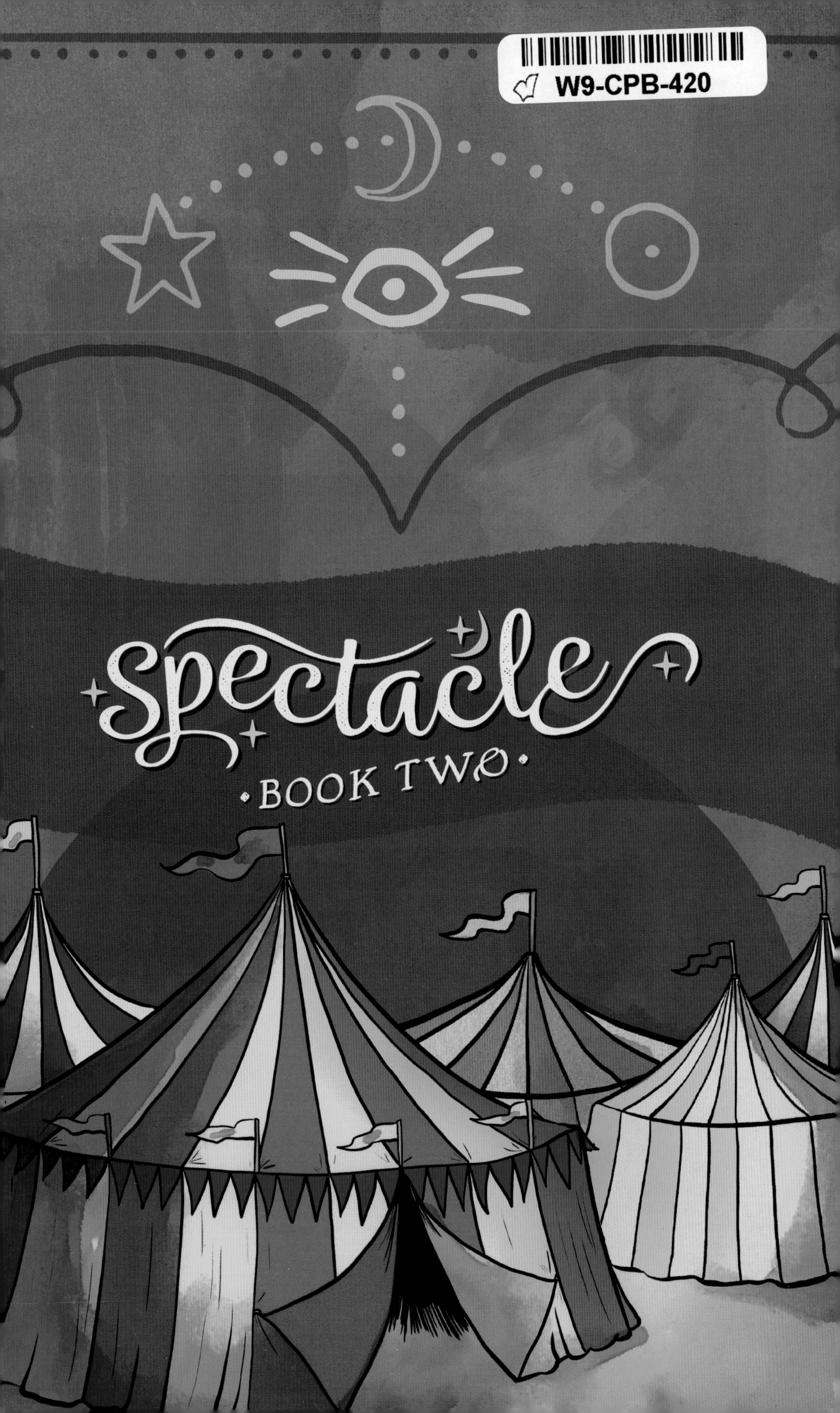
Spectacle
· BOOK TWO ·

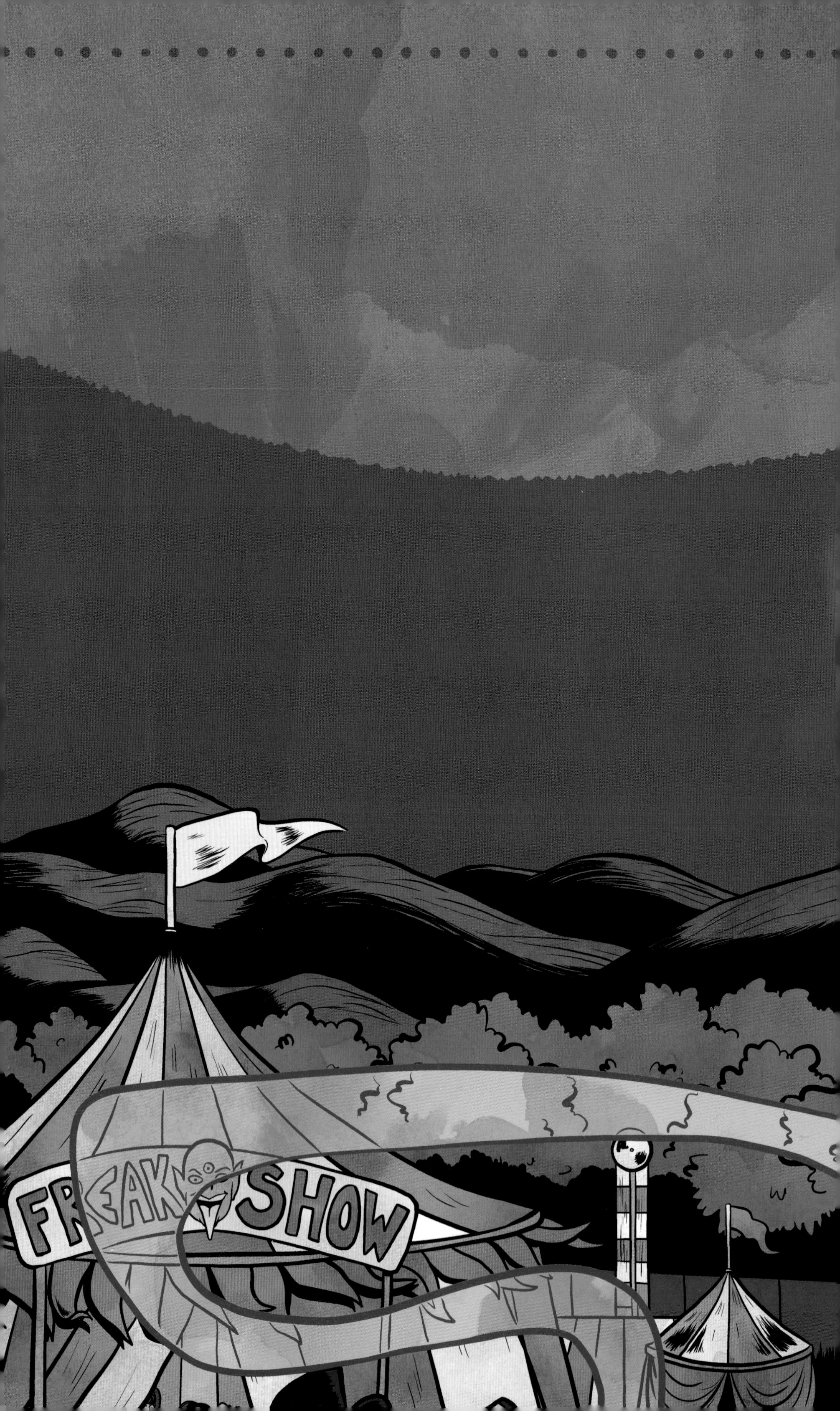
FREAK SHOW

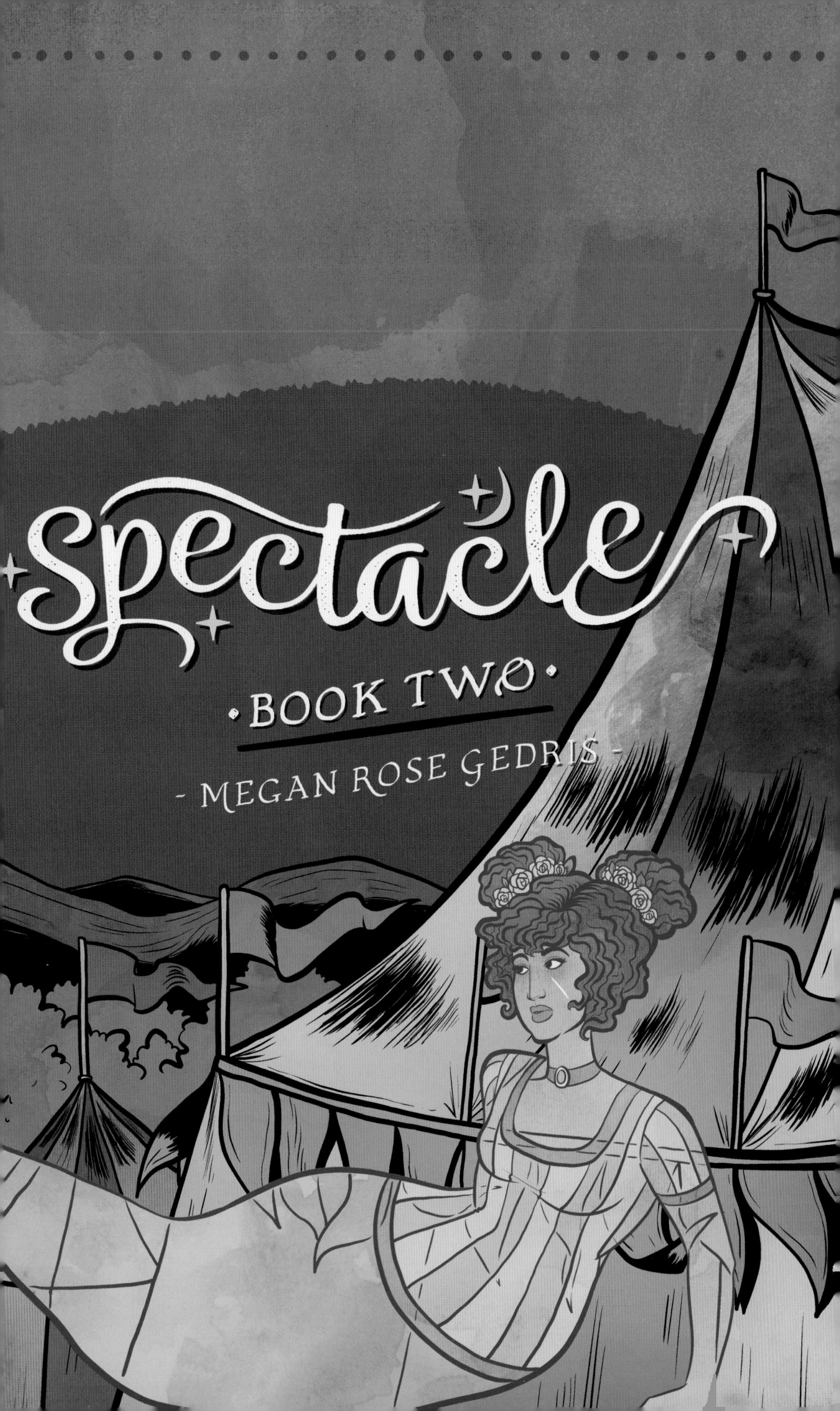
Spectacle
BOOK TWO
- MEGAN ROSE GEDRIS -

Designed by Hilary Thompson and Sonja Synak
Edited by Ari Yarwood

PUBLISHED BY ONI PRESS, INC.
Joe Nozemack, founder & chief financial officer
James Lucas Jones, publisher
Charlie Chu, v.p. of creative & business development
Brad Rooks, director of operations
Melissa Meszaros, director of publicity
Margot Wood, director of sales
Sandy Tanaka, marketing design manager
Amber O'Neill, special projects manager
Troy Look, director of design & production
Kate Z. Stone, senior graphic designer
Sonja Synak, graphic designer
Angie Knowles, digital prepress lead
Ari Yarwood, executive editor
Sarah Gaydos, editorial director of licensed publishing
Robin Herrera, senior editor
Desiree Wilson, associate editor
Michelle Nguyen, executive assistant
Jung Lee, logistics coordinator
Scott Sharkey, warehouse assistant

1319 SE Martin Luther King, Jr. Blvd.
Suite 240
Portland, OR 97214

onipress.com
facebook.com/onipress
twitter.com/onipress
onipress.tumblr.com
instagram.com/onipress

rosalarian.com
twitter.com/rosalarian

First Edition: May 2019
ISBN: 978-1-62010-599-3
eISBN: 978-1-62010-630-3

1 2 3 4 5 6 7 8 9 10

Library of Congress Control Number: 2018912758

Printed in China.

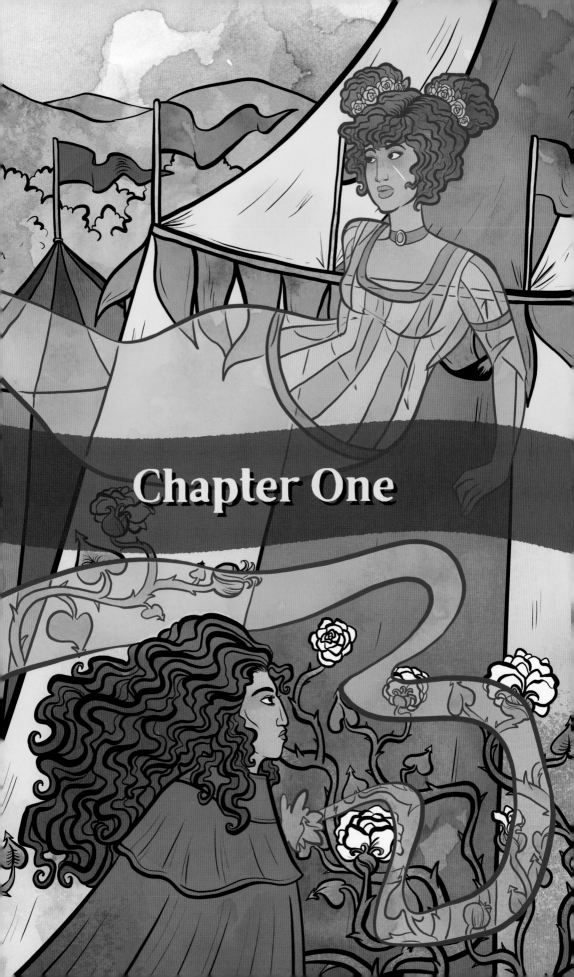

Chapter One

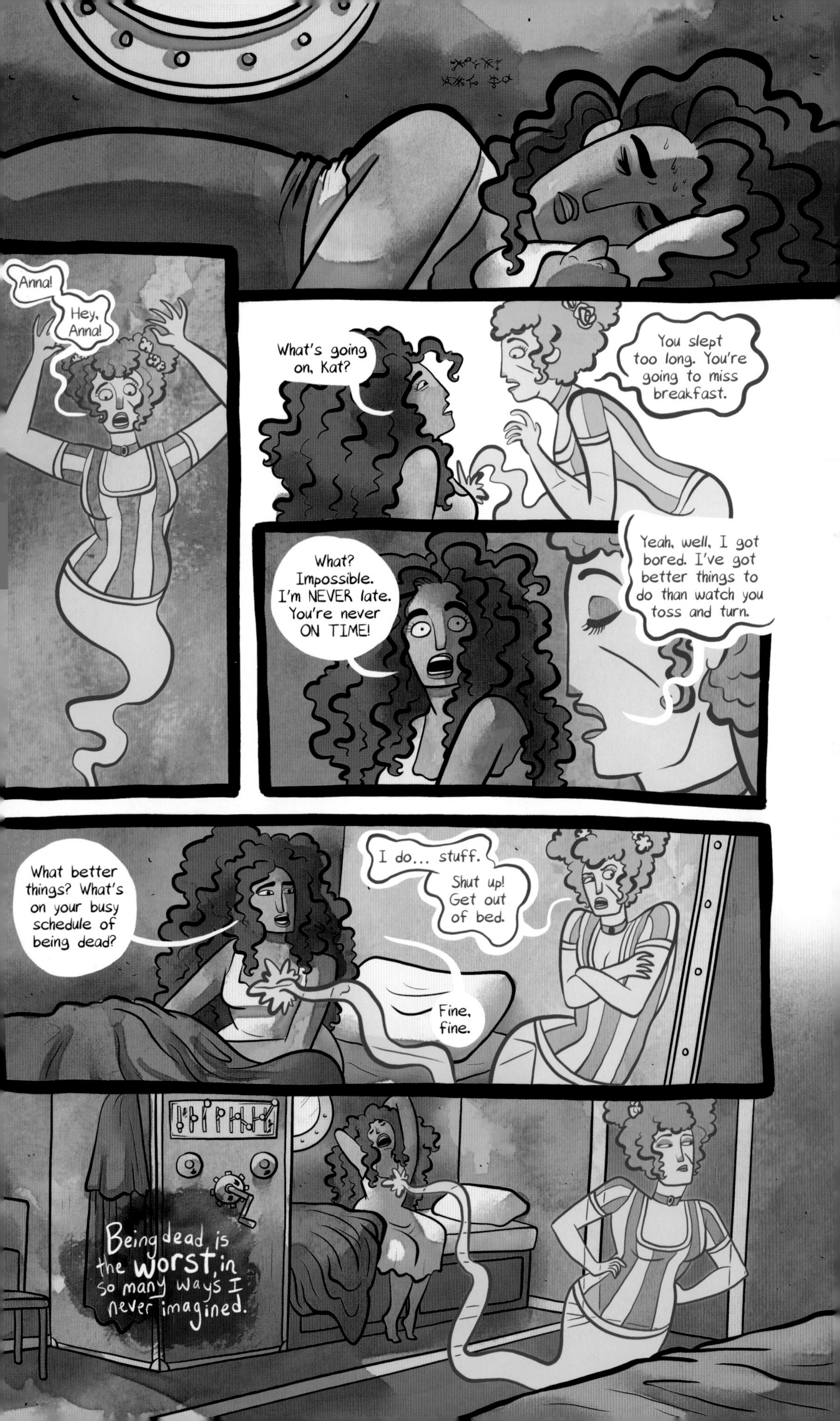
Anna!
Hey, Anna!
What's going on, Kat?
You slept too long. You're going to miss breakfast.
What? Impossible. I'm NEVER late. You're never ON TIME!
Yeah, well, I got bored. I've got better things to do than watch you toss and turn.
What better things? What's on your busy schedule of being dead?
I do... stuff.
Shut up! Get out of bed.
Fine, fine.
Being dead is the worst, in so many ways I never imagined.

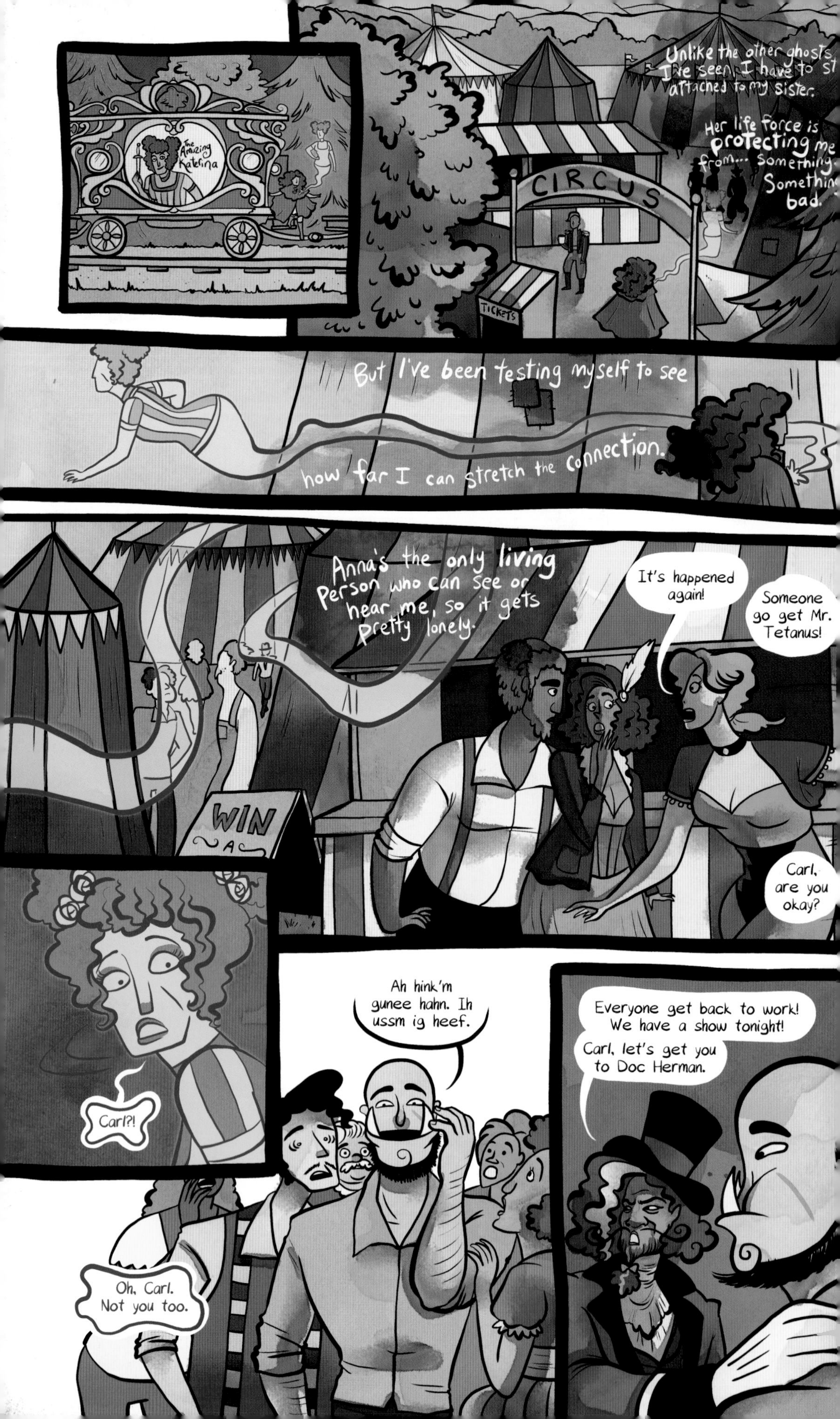
The Amazing Katerina
Unlike the other ghosts I've seen, I have to st attached to my sister.
Her life force is protecting me from... something. Something bad.
CIRCUS
TICKETS
But I've been testing myself to see how far I can stretch the connection.
Anna's the only living person who can see or hear me, so it gets pretty lonely.
It's happened again!
Someone go get Mr. Tetanus!
WIN A
Carl, are you okay?
Carl?!
Ah hink'm gunee hahn. Ih ussm ig heef.
Oh, Carl. Not you too.
Everyone get back to work! We have a show tonight!
Carl, let's get you to Doc Herman.

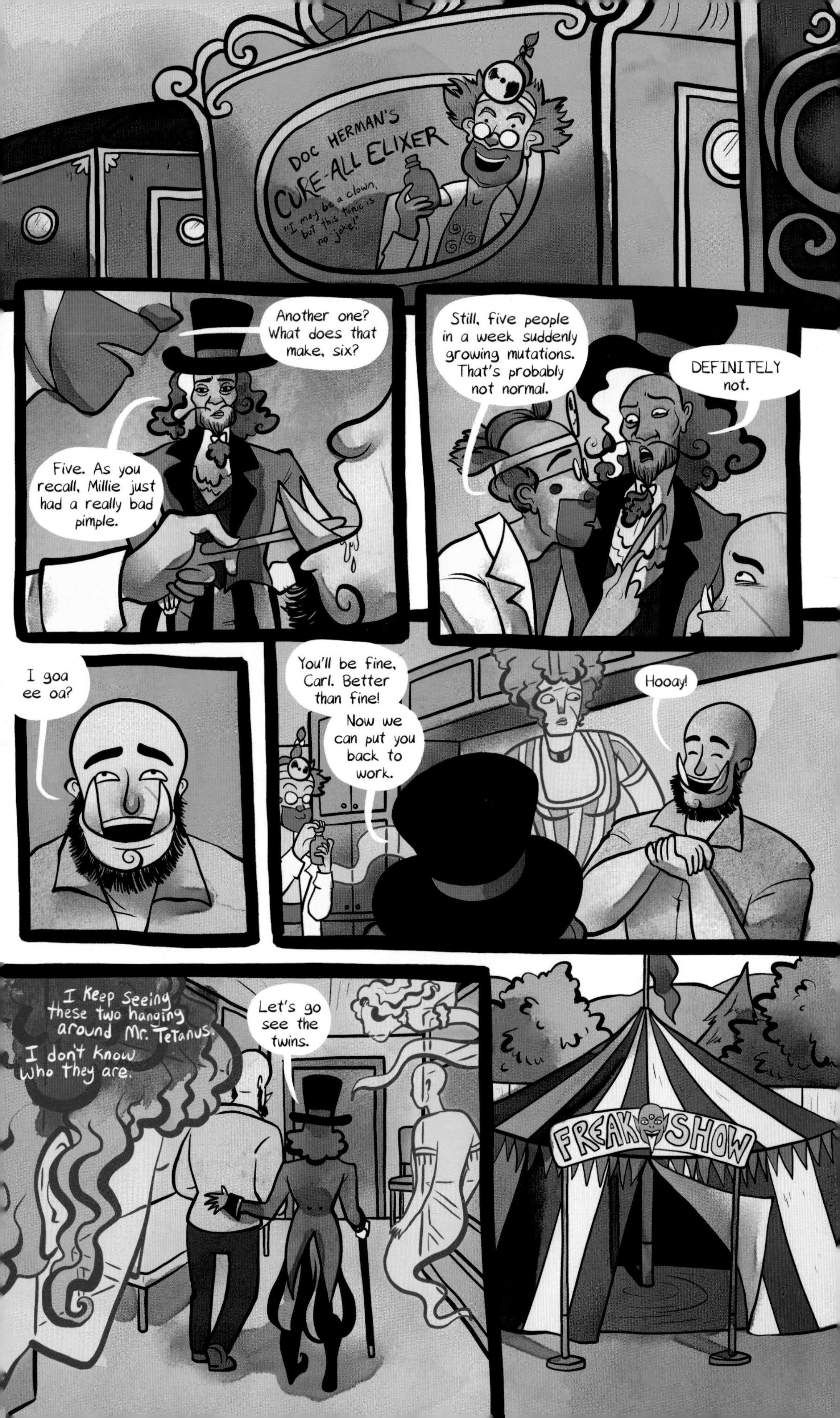
DOC HERMAN'S
CURE-ALL ELIXER
"I may be a clown, but this tonic is no joke!"
Another one? What does that make, six?
Five. As you recall, Millie just had a really bad pimple.
Still, five people in a week suddenly growing mutations. That's probably not normal.
DEFINITELY not.
I goa ee oa?
You'll be fine, Carl. Better than fine!
Now we can put you back to work.
Hooay!
I Keep Seeing these two hanging around Mr. Tetanus.
I don't Know Who they are.
Let's go see the twins.
FREAK SHOW

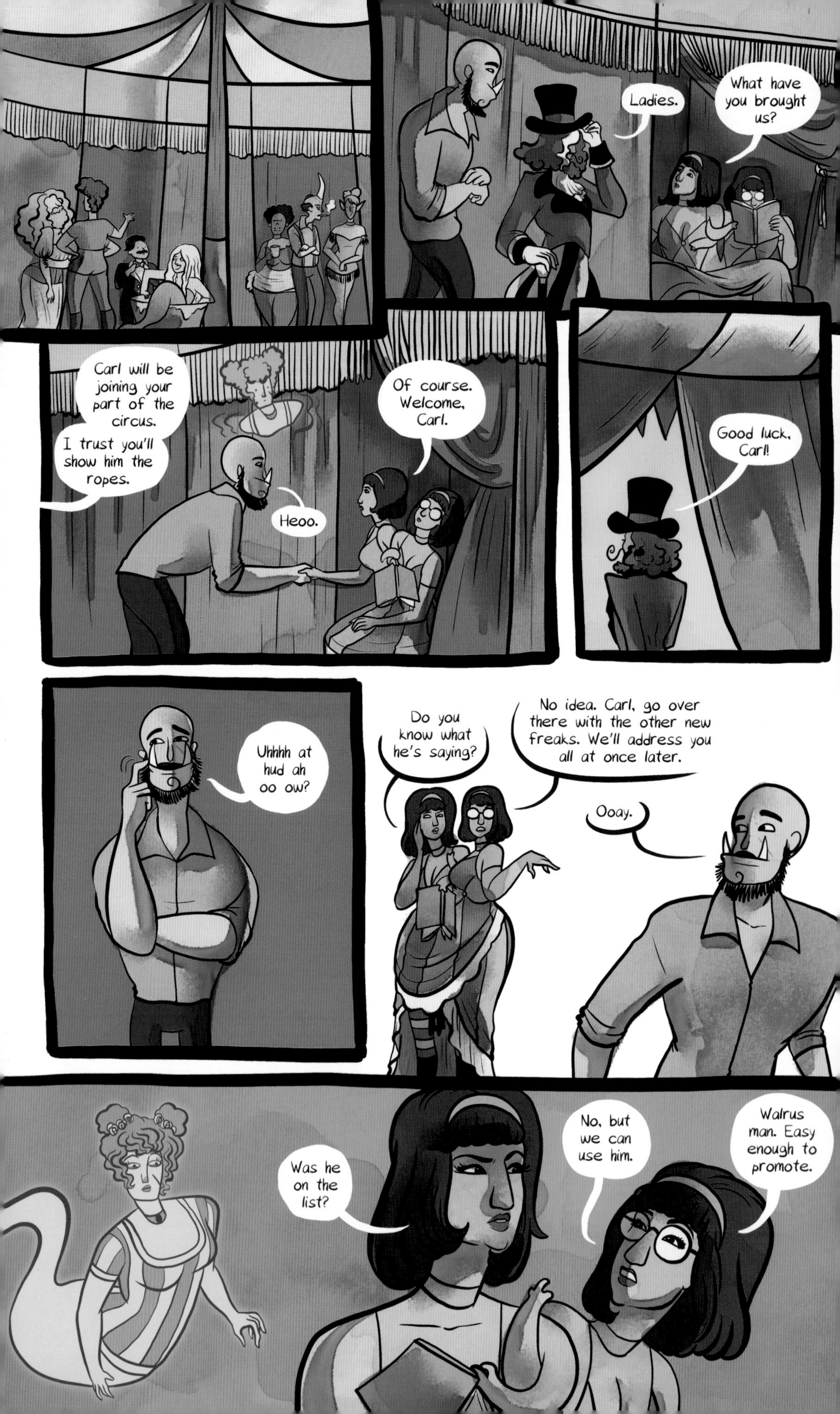
Ladies.
What have you brought us?
Carl will be joining your part of the circus.
I trust you'll show him the ropes.
Heoo.
Of course. Welcome, Carl.
Good luck, Carl!
Uhhhh at hud ah oo ow?
Do you know what he's saying?
No idea. Carl, go over there with the other new freaks. We'll address you all at once later.
Ooay.
Was he on the list?
No, but we can use him.
Walrus man. Easy enough to promote.

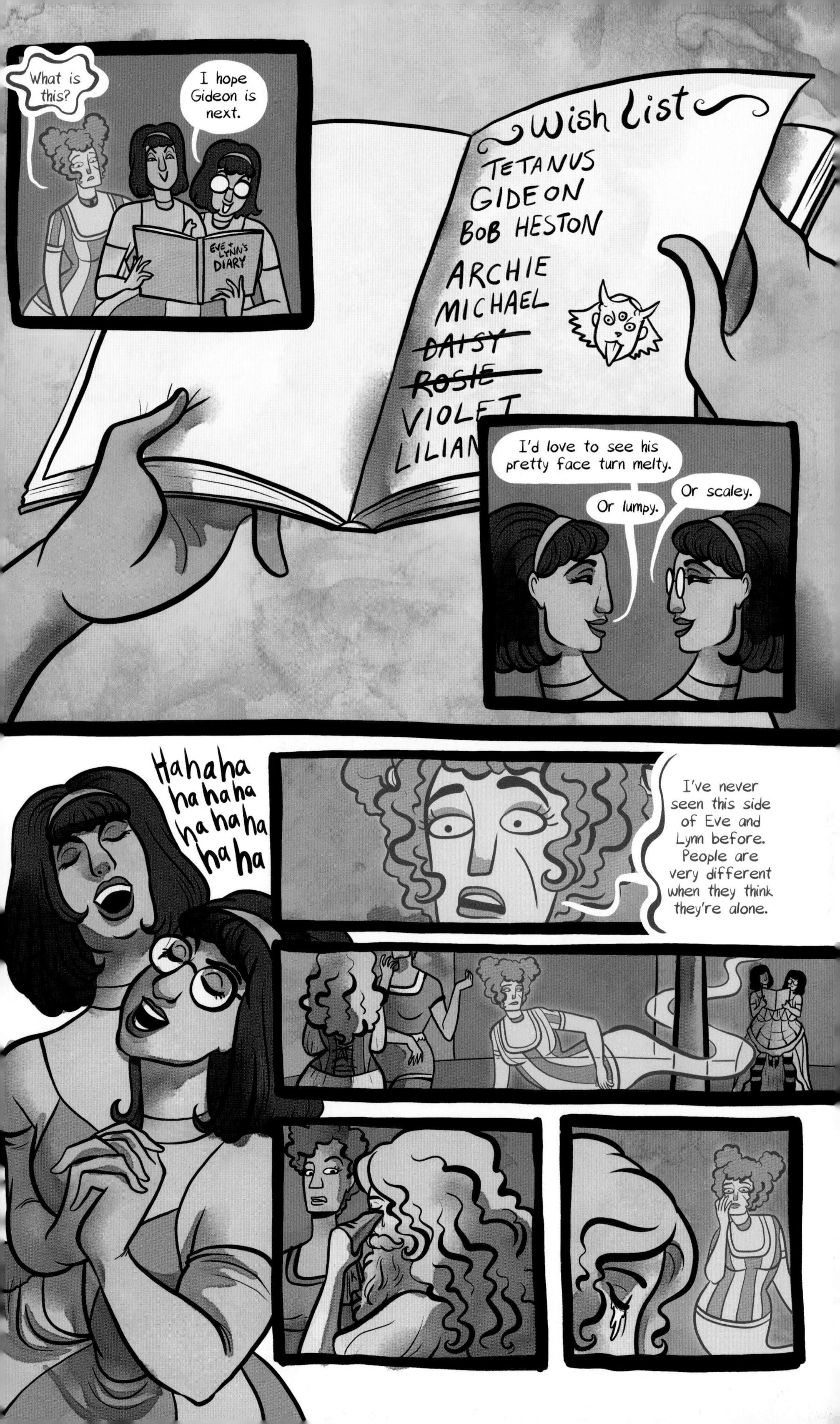
What is this?
I hope Gideon is next.
EVE + LYNN'S DIARY
Wish List
TETANUS
GIDEON
BOB HESTON
ARCHIE
MICHAEL
DAISY
ROSIE
VIOLET
LILIAN
I'd love to see his pretty face turn melty.
Or lumpy.
Or scaley.
Hahaha haha ha ha ha ha ha ha
I've never seen this side of Eve and Lynn before. People are very different when they think they're alone.

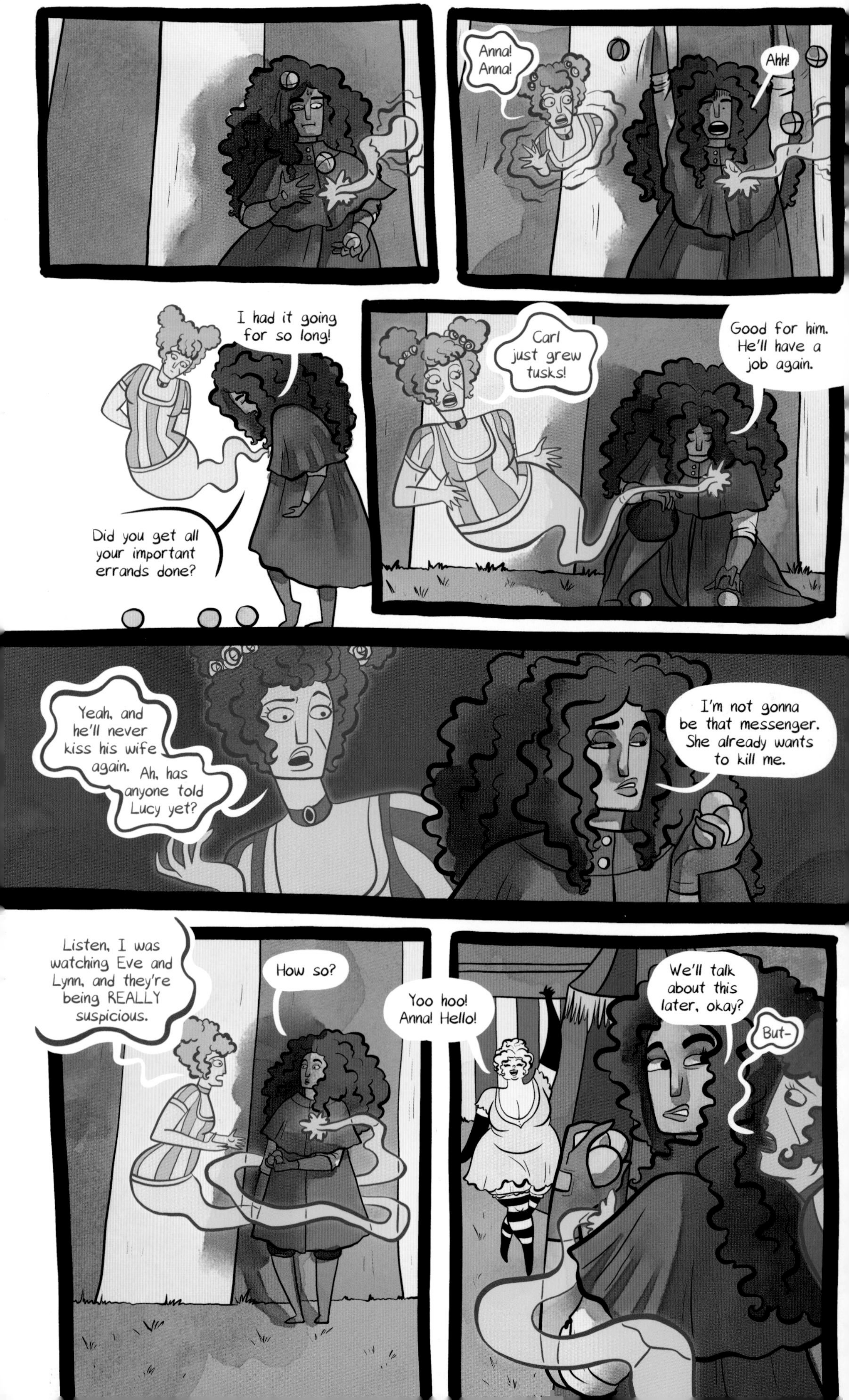
Anna! Anna!
Ahh!
I had it going for so long!
Did you get all your important errands done?
Carl just grew tusks!
Good for him. He'll have a job again.
Yeah, and he'll never kiss his wife again.
Ah, has anyone told Lucy yet?
I'm not gonna be that messenger. She already wants to kill me.
Listen, I was watching Eve and Lynn, and they're being REALLY suspicious.
How so?
Yoo hoo! Anna! Hello!
We'll talk about this later, okay?
But-

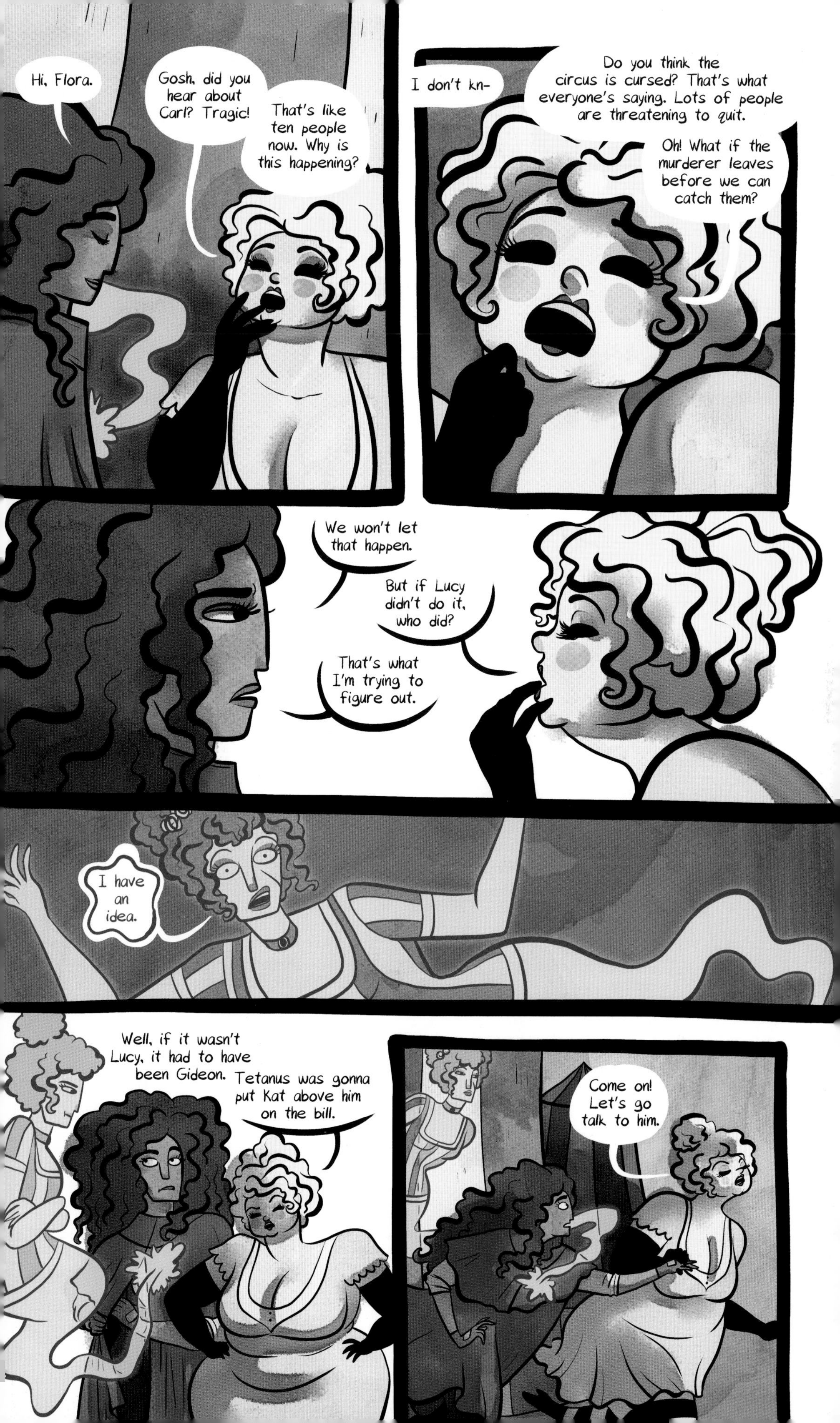
Hi, Flora.
Gosh, did you hear about Carl? Tragic!
That's like ten people now. Why is this happening?
I don't kn-
Do you think the circus is cursed? That's what everyone's saying. Lots of people are threatening to quit.
Oh! What if the murderer leaves before we can catch them?
We won't let that happen.
But if Lucy didn't do it, who did?
That's what I'm trying to figure out.
I have an idea.
Well, if it wasn't Lucy, it had to have been Gideon.
Tetanus was gonna put Kat above him on the bill.
Come on! Let's go talk to him.

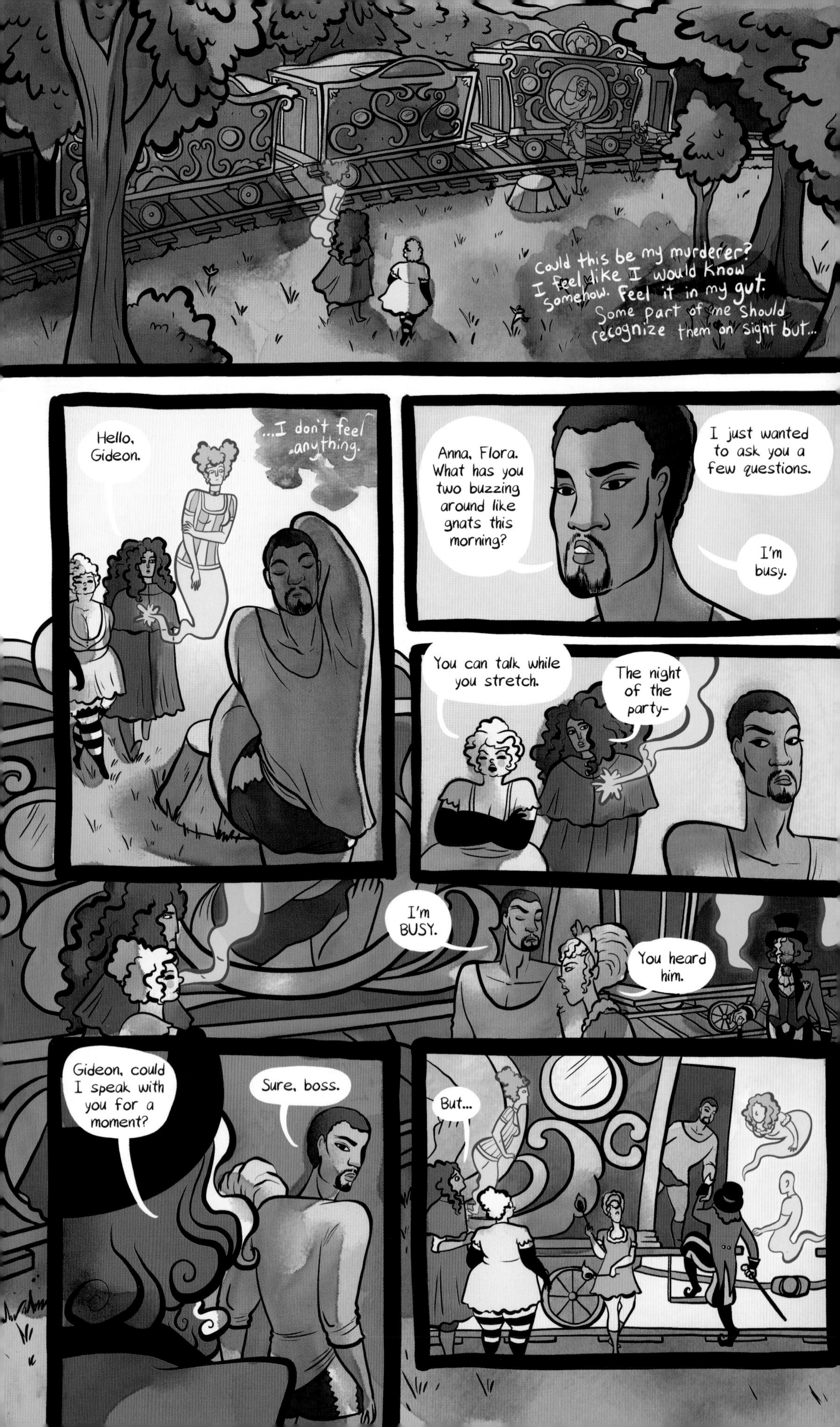
Could this be my murderer? I feel like I would know somehow. Feel it in my gut. Some part of me should recognize them on sight but...
Hello, Gideon.
...I don't feel anything.
Anna, Flora. What has you two buzzing around like gnats this morning?
I just wanted to ask you a few questions.
I'm busy.
You can talk while you stretch.
The night of the party-
I'm BUSY.
You heard him.
Gideon, could I speak with you for a moment?
Sure, boss.
But...

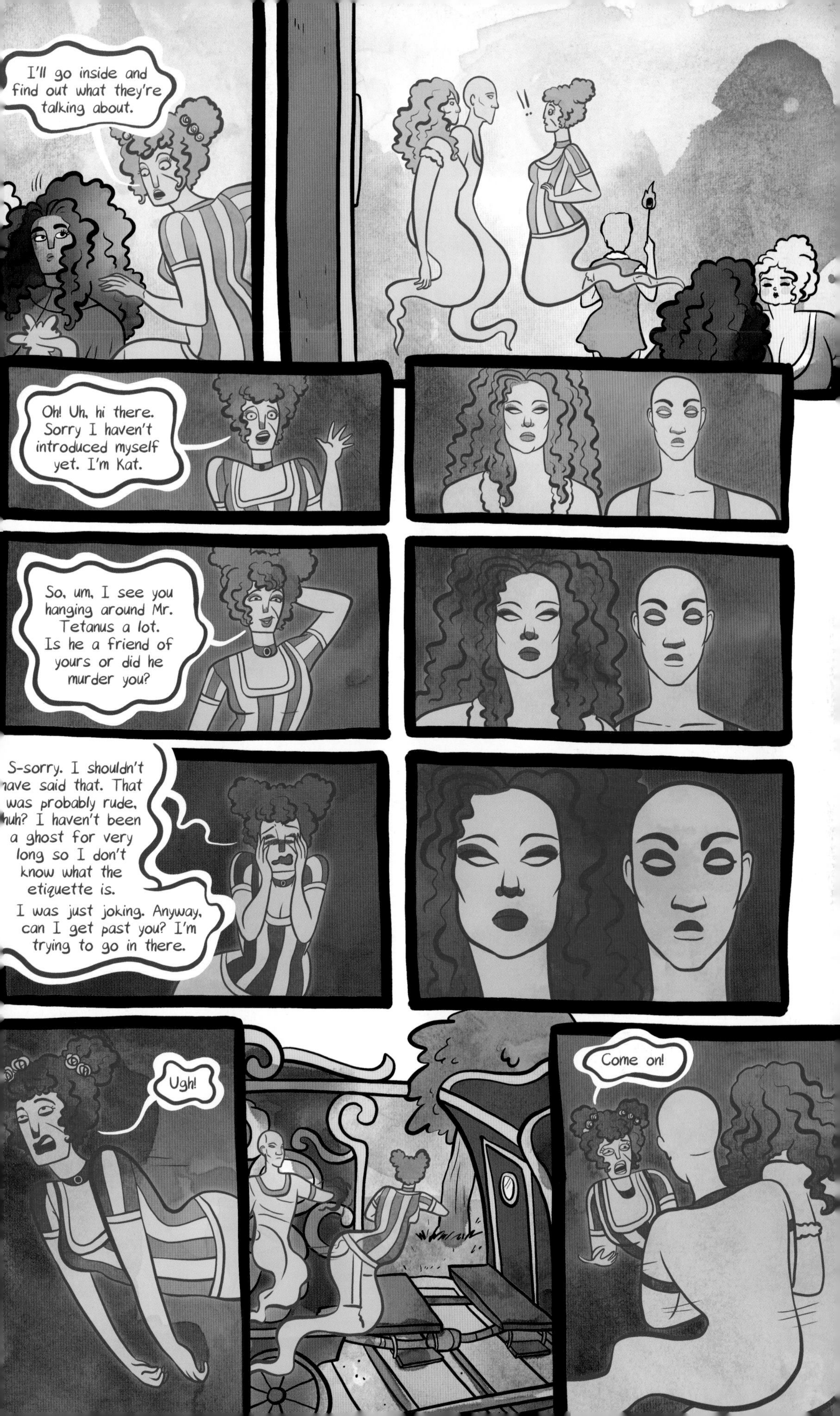
I'll go inside and find out what they're talking about.
!!
Oh! Uh, hi there. Sorry I haven't introduced myself yet. I'm Kat.
So, um, I see you hanging around Mr. Tetanus a lot. Is he a friend of yours or did he murder you?
S-sorry. I shouldn't have said that. That was probably rude, huh? I haven't been a ghost for very long so I don't know what the etiquette is.
I was just joking. Anyway, can I get past you? I'm trying to go in there.
Ugh!
Come on!

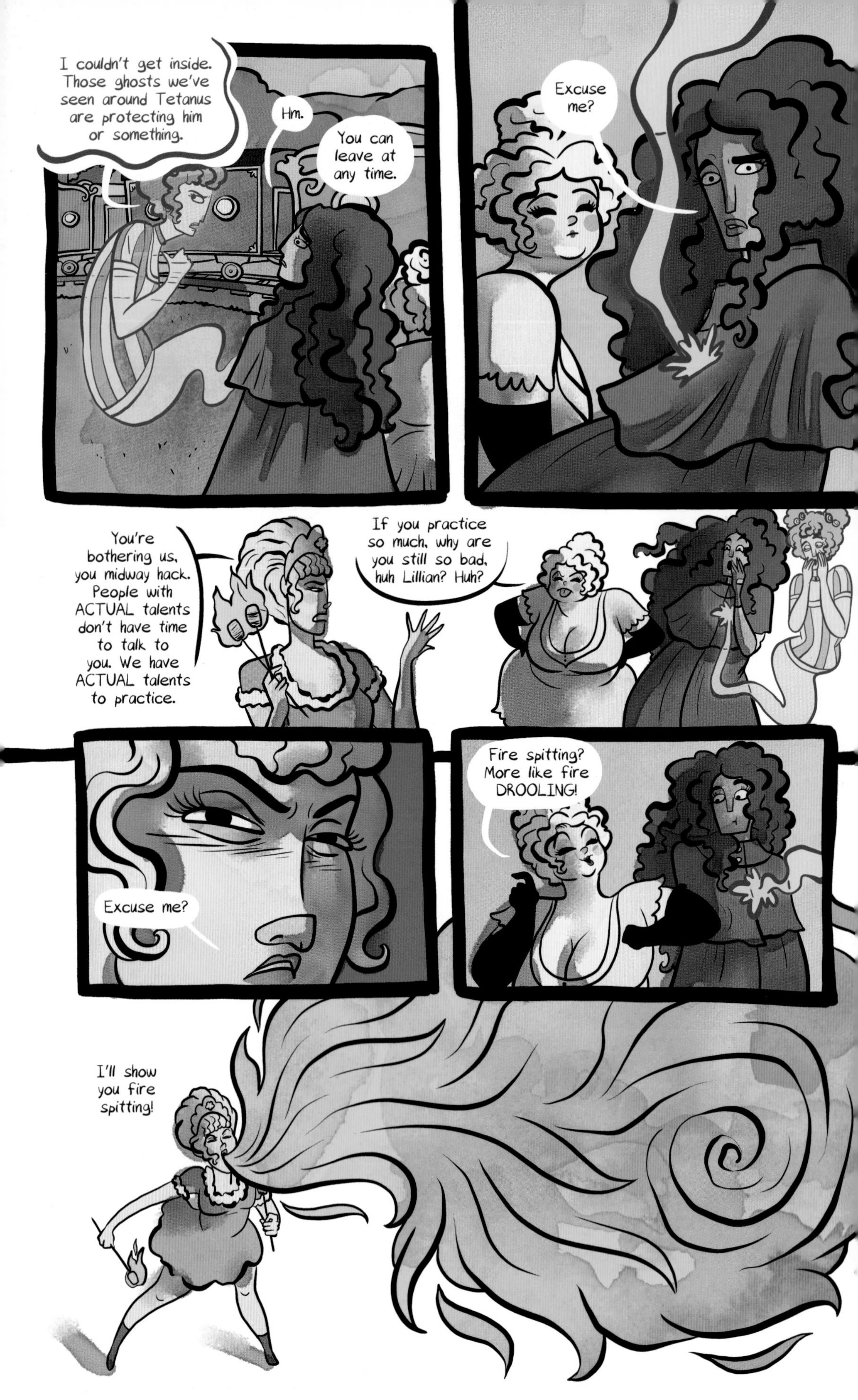

I couldn't get inside. Those ghosts we've seen around Tetanus are protecting him or something.
Hm.
You can leave at any time.
Excuse me?
You're bothering us, you midway hack. People with ACTUAL talents don't have time to talk to you. We have ACTUAL talents to practice.
If you practice so much, why are you still so bad, huh Lillian? Huh?
Excuse me?
Fire spitting? More like fire DROOLING!
I'll show you fire spitting!

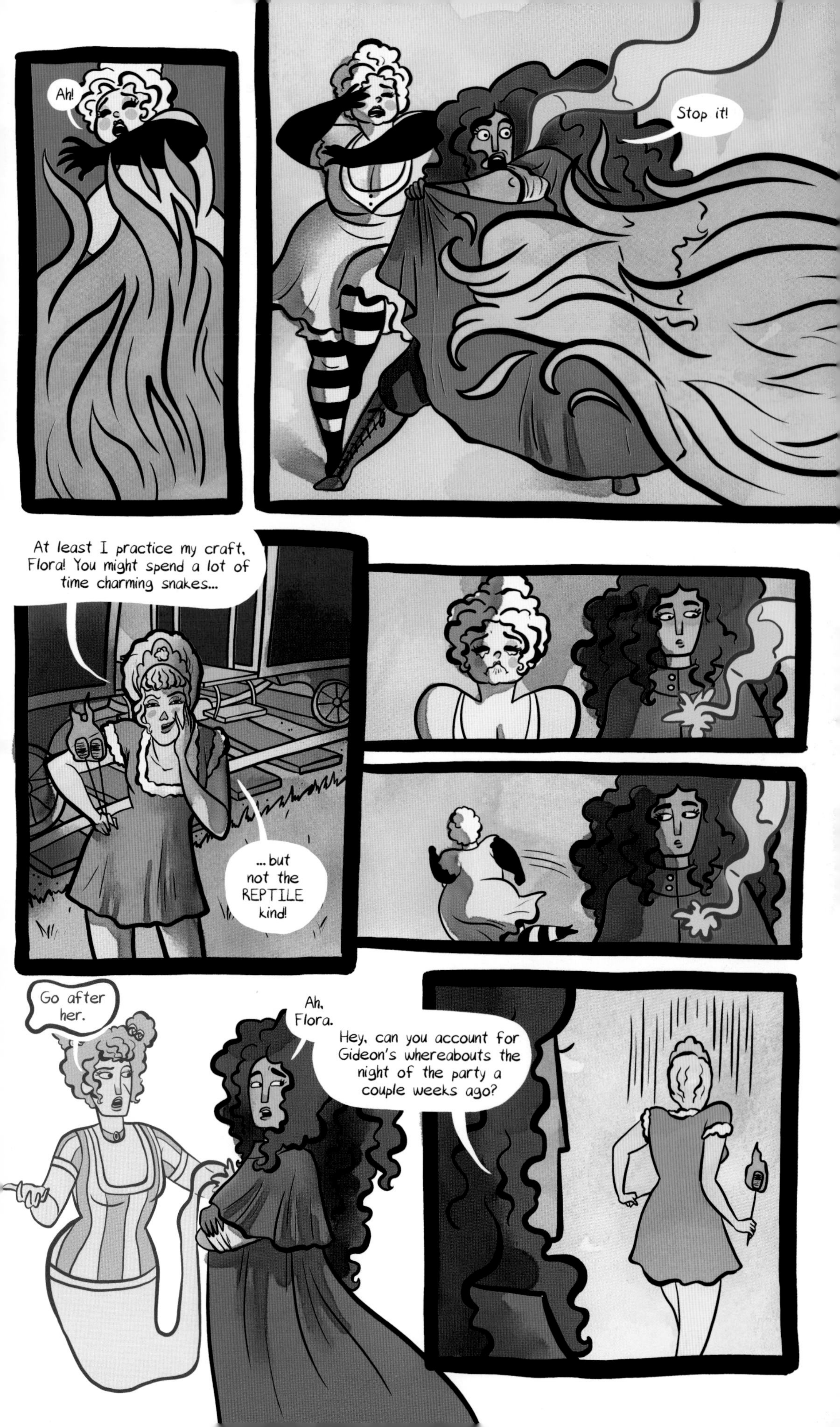
Ah!
Stop it!
At least I practice my craft, Flora! You might spend a lot of time charming snakes...
...but not the REPTILE kind!
Go after her.
Ah, Flora.
Hey, can you account for Gideon's whereabouts the night of the party a couple weeks ago?

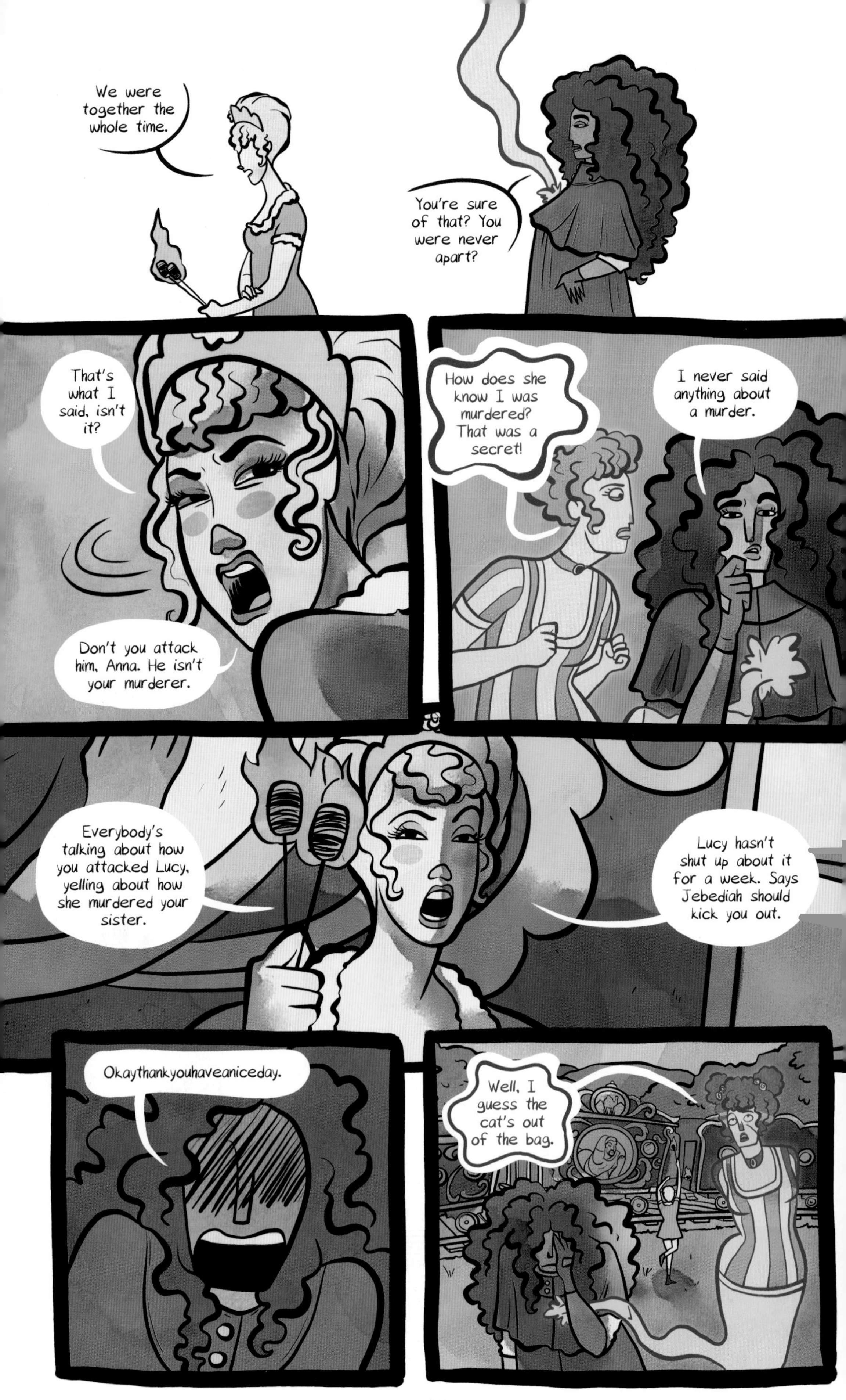
We were together the whole time.
You're sure of that? You were never apart?
That's what I said, isn't it?
Don't you attack him, Anna. He isn't your murderer.
How does she know I was murdered? That was a secret!
I never said anything about a murder.
Everybody's talking about how you attacked Lucy, yelling about how she murdered your sister.
Lucy hasn't shut up about it for a week. Says Jebediah should kick you out.
Okaythankyouhaveaniceday.
Well, I guess the cat's out of the bag.

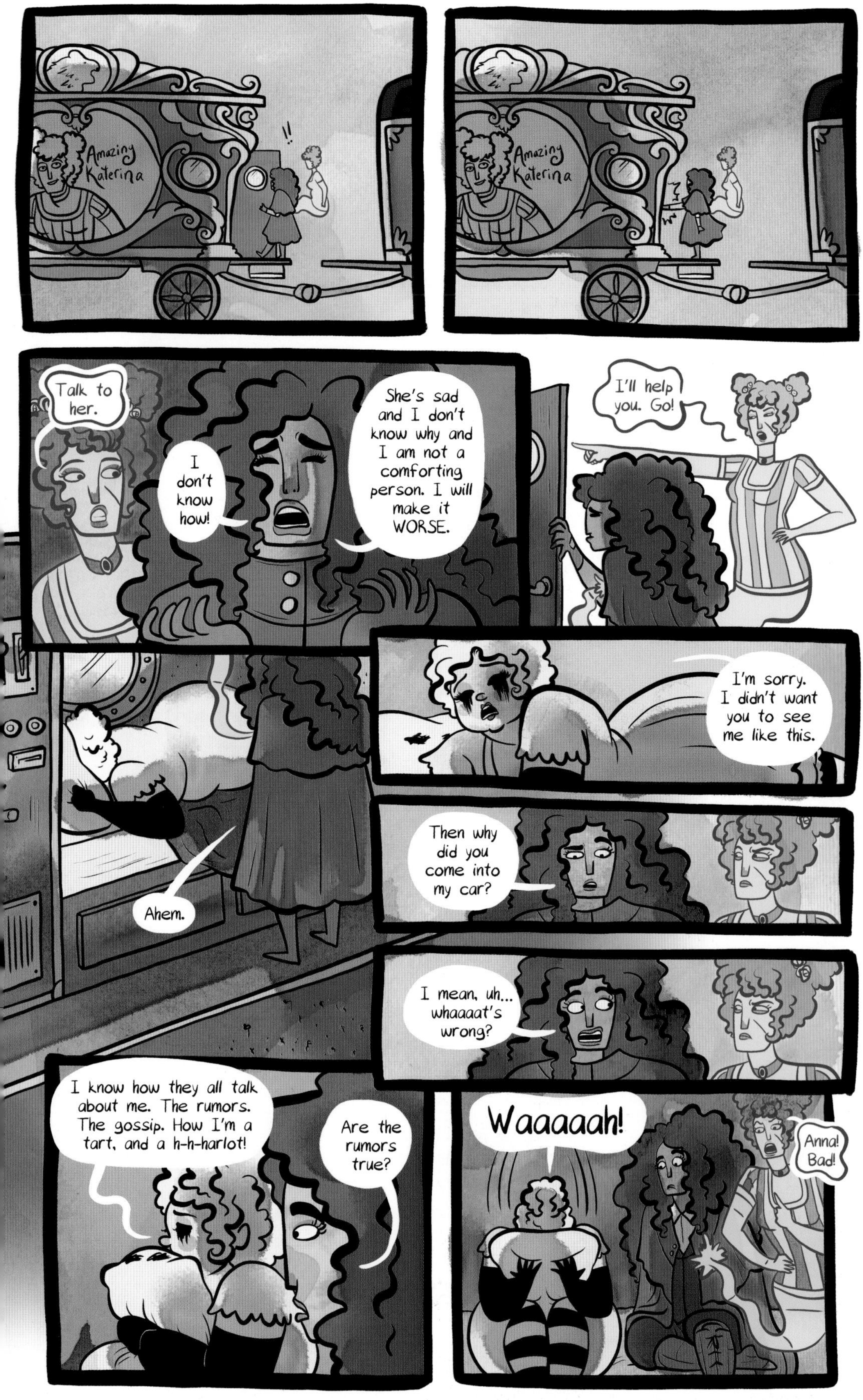
!!
Amazing Katerina
Talk to her.
I don't know how!
She's sad and I don't know why and I am not a comforting person. I will make it WORSE.
I'll help you. Go!
Ahem.
I'm sorry. I didn't want you to see me like this.
Then why did you come into my car?
I mean, uh... whaaaat's wrong?
I know how they all talk about me. The rumors. The gossip. How I'm a tart, and a h-h-harlot!
Are the rumors true?
Waaaaah!
Anna! Bad!

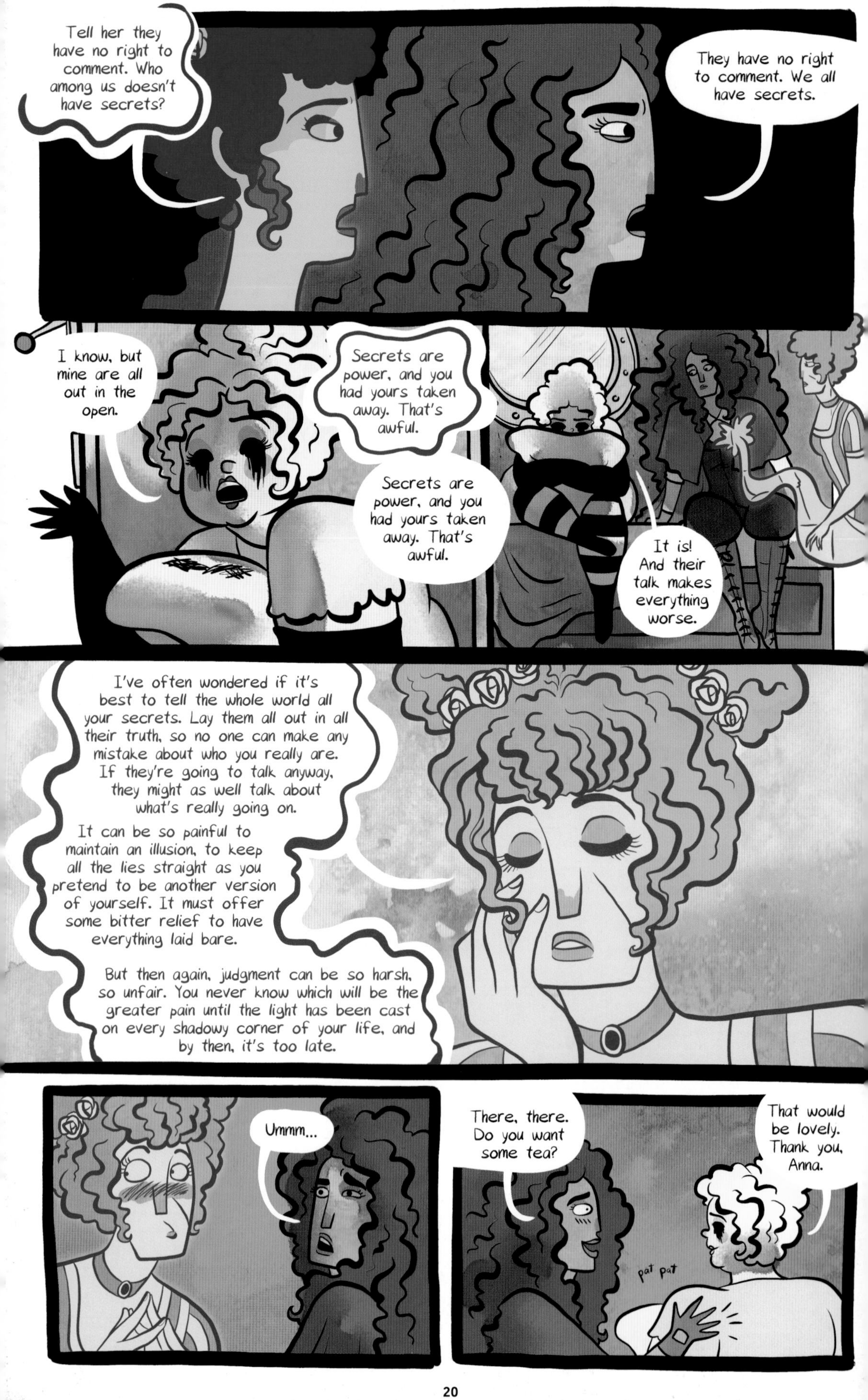
Tell her they have no right to comment. Who among us doesn't have secrets?
They have no right to comment. We all have secrets.
I know, but mine are all out in the open.
Secrets are power, and you had yours taken away. That's awful.
Secrets are power, and you had yours taken away. That's awful.
It is! And their talk makes everything worse.
I've often wondered if it's best to tell the whole world all your secrets. Lay them all out in all their truth, so no one can make any mistake about who you really are. If they're going to talk anyway, they might as well talk about what's really going on.
It can be so painful to maintain an illusion, to keep all the lies straight as you pretend to be another version of yourself. It must offer some bitter relief to have everything laid bare.
But then again, judgment can be so harsh, so unfair. You never know which will be the greater pain until the light has been cast on every shadowy corner of your life, and by then, it's too late.
Ummm...
There, there. Do you want some tea?
pat pat
That would be lovely. Thank you, Anna.

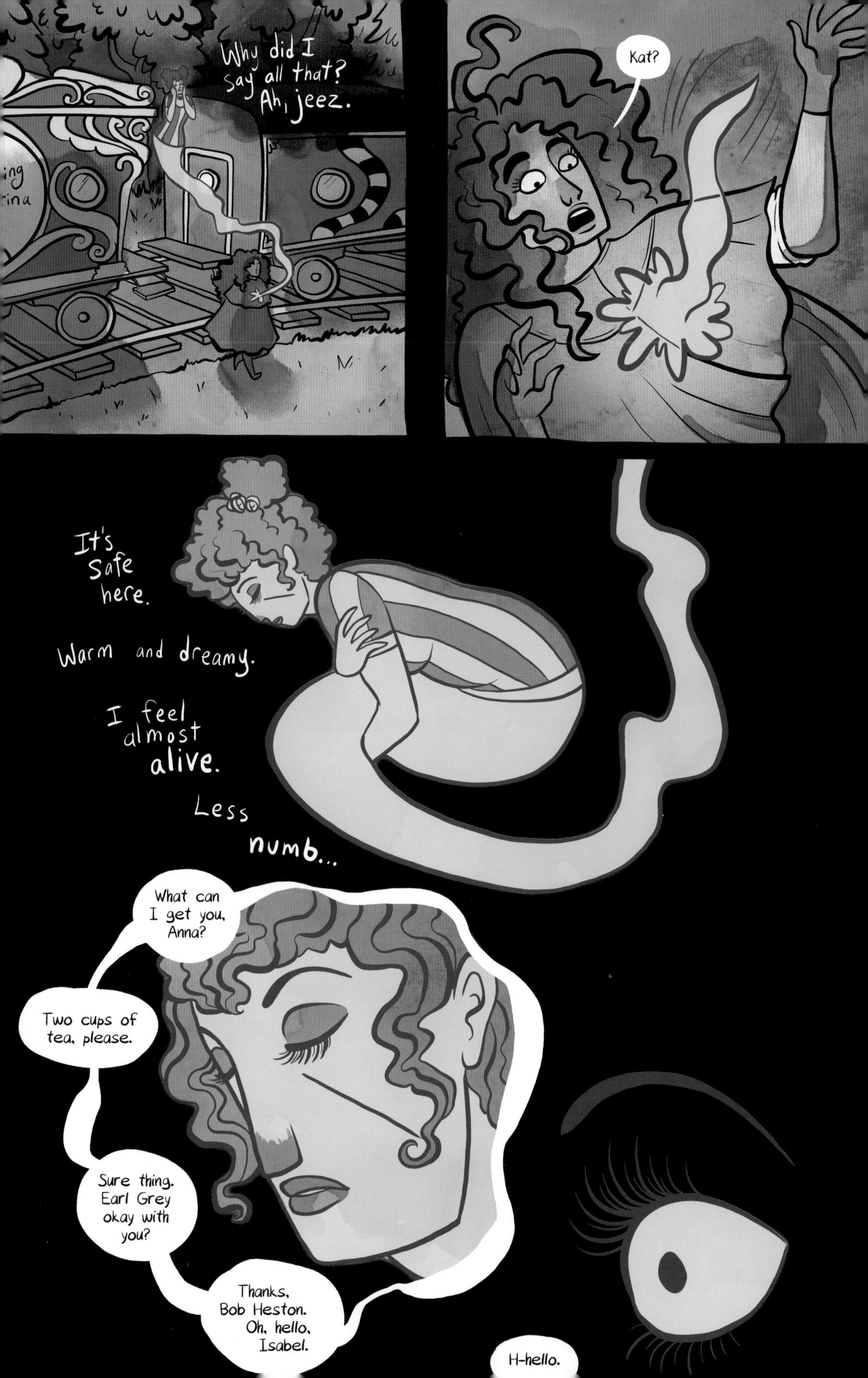
Why did I say all that? Ah, jeez.
Kat?
It's safe here.
Warm and dreamy.
I feel almost alive.
Less numb...
What can I get you, Anna?
Two cups of tea, please.
Sure thing. Earl Grey okay with you?
Thanks, Bob Heston. Oh, hello, Isabel.
H-hello.

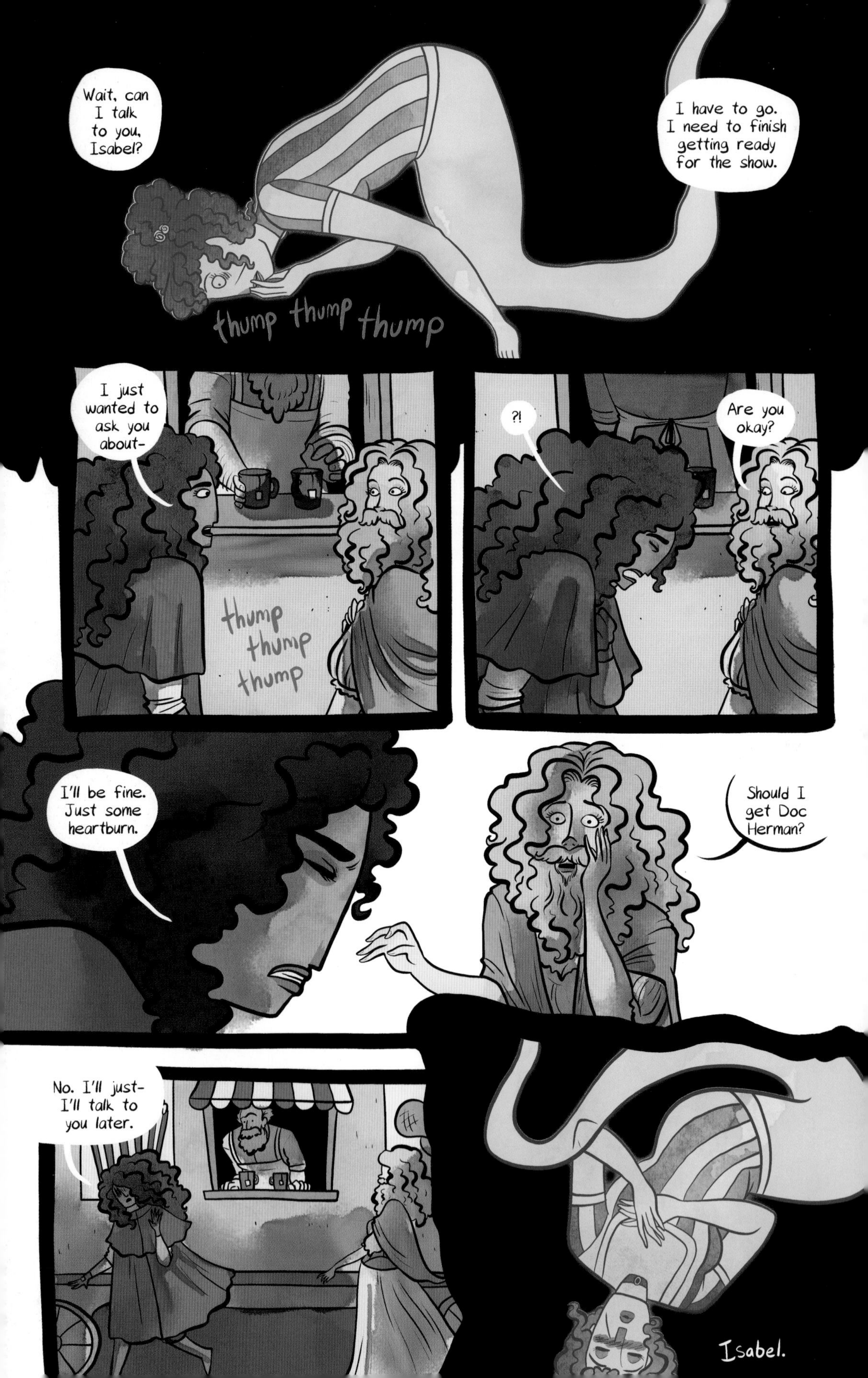
Wait, can I talk to you, Isabel?
I have to go. I need to finish getting ready for the show.
thump thump thump
I just wanted to ask you about-
thump thump thump
?!
Are you okay?
I'll be fine. Just some heartburn.
Should I get Doc Herman?
No. I'll just- I'll talk to you later.
Isabel.

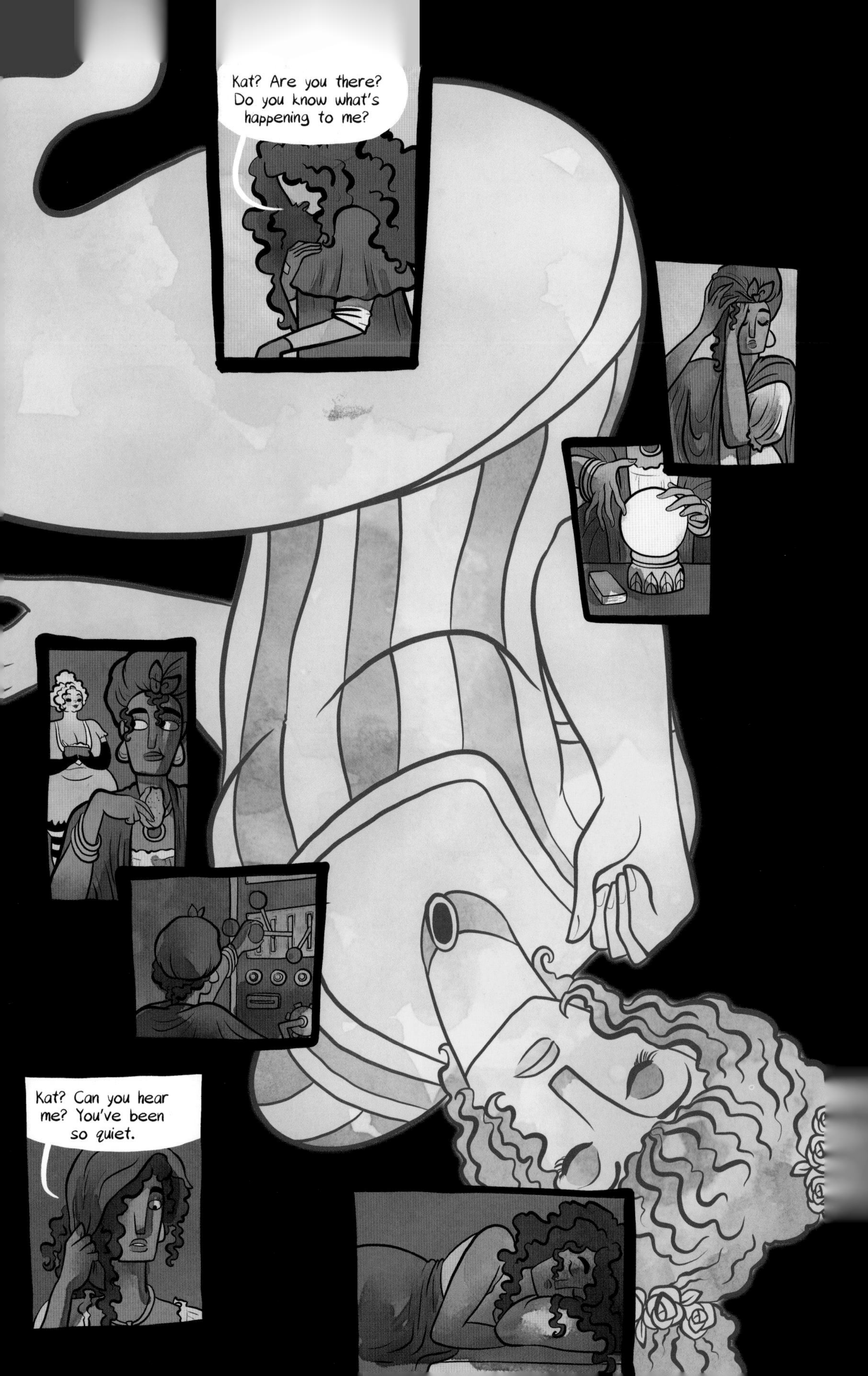
Kat? Are you there? Do you know what's happening to me?
Kat? Can you hear me? You've been so quiet.

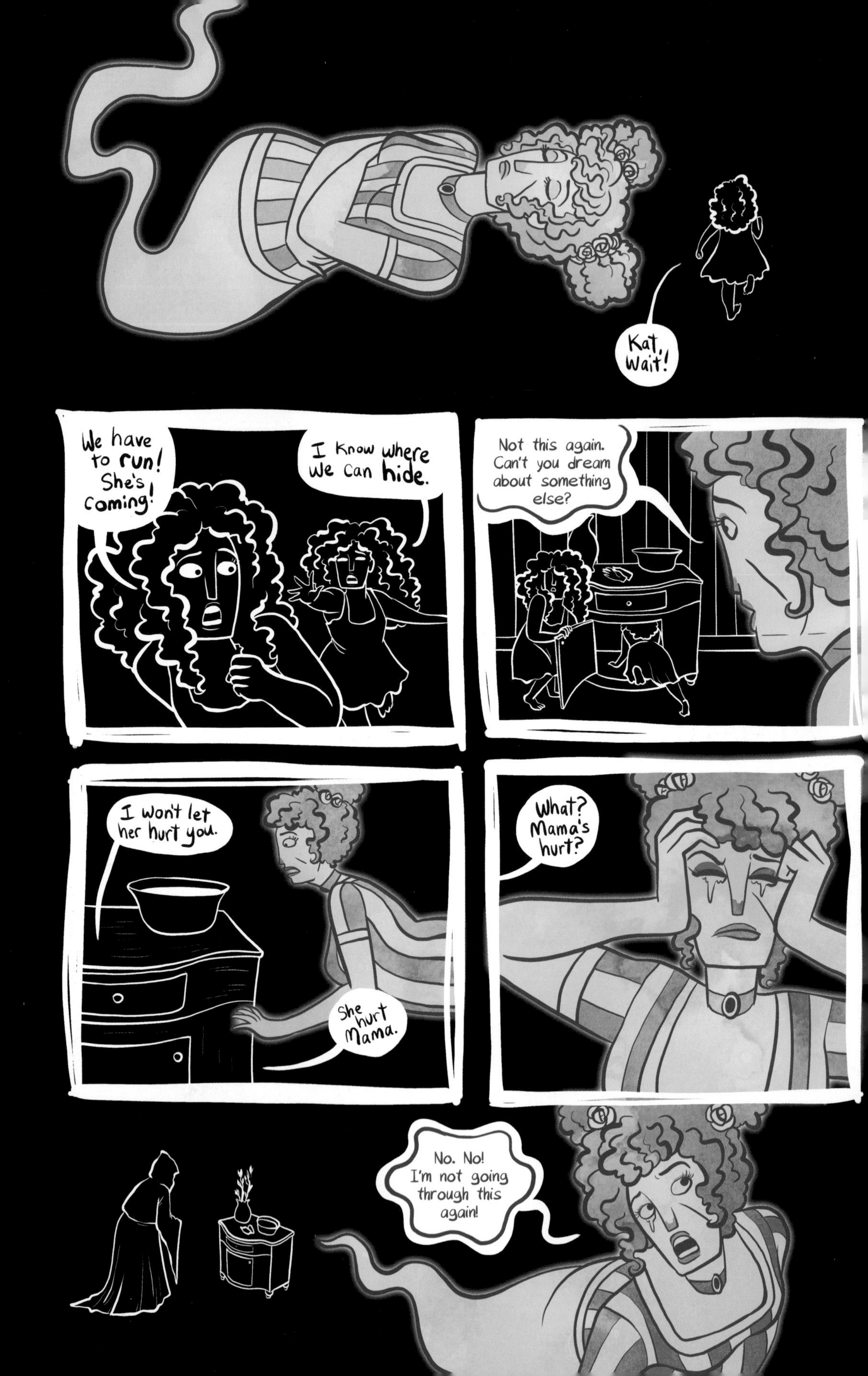

Kat, wait!
We have to run! She's coming!
I know where we can hide.
Not this again. Can't you dream about something else?
I won't let her hurt you.
She hurt Mama.
What? Mama's hurt?
No. No! I'm not going through this again!

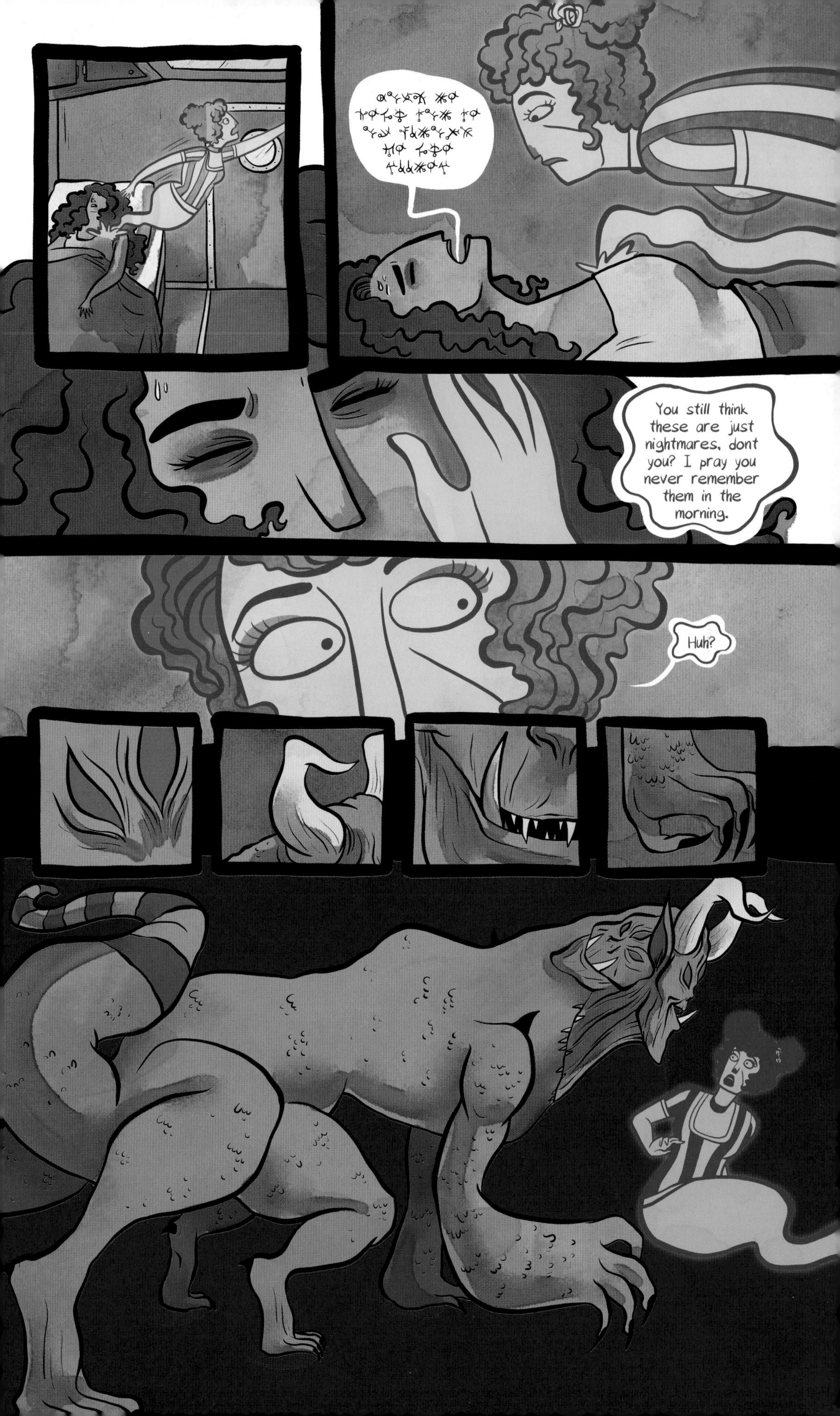
You still think these are just nightmares, dont you? I pray you never remember them in the morning.
Huh?

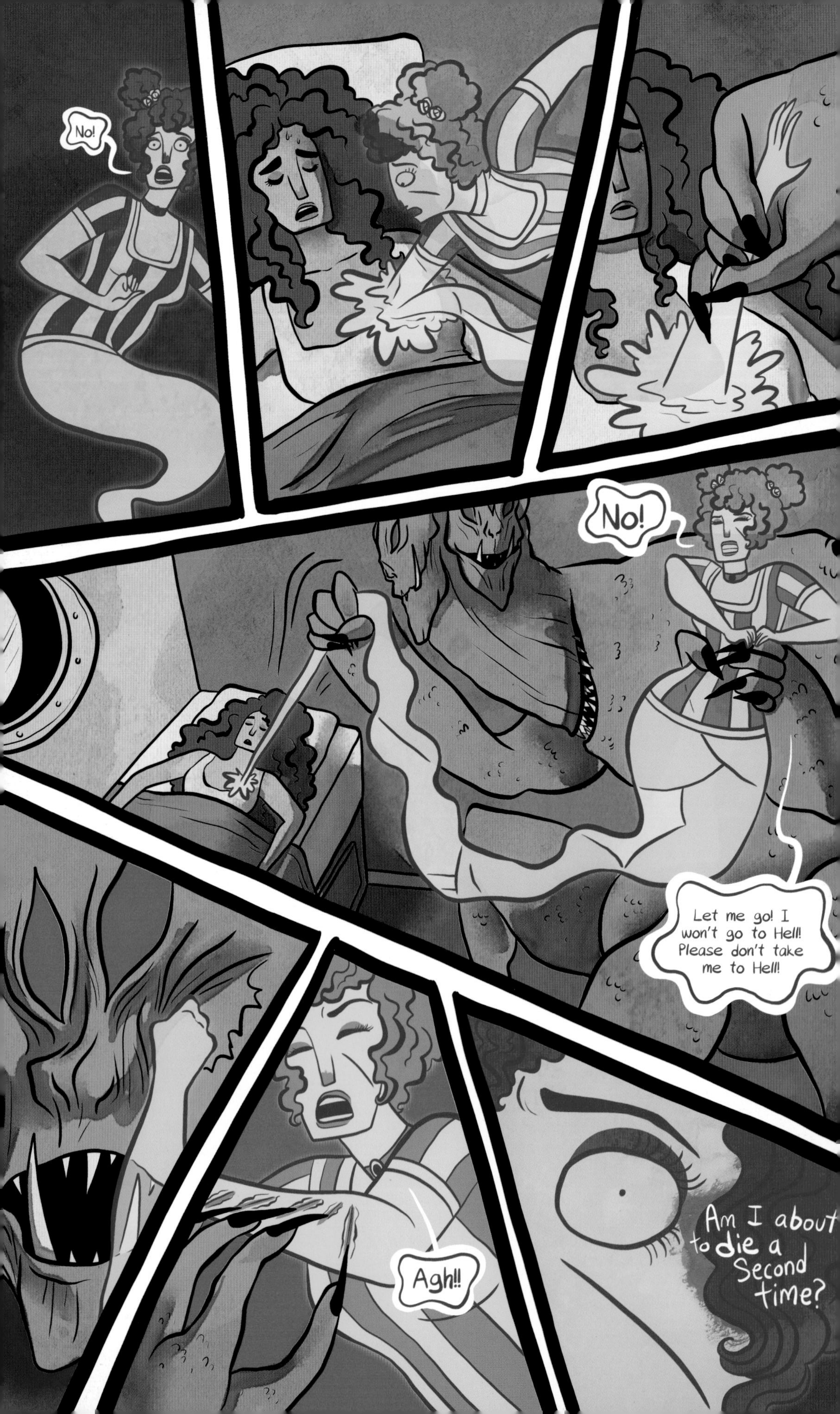
No!
No!
Let me go! I won't go to Hell! Please don't take me to Hell!
Agh!!
Am I about to die a second time?

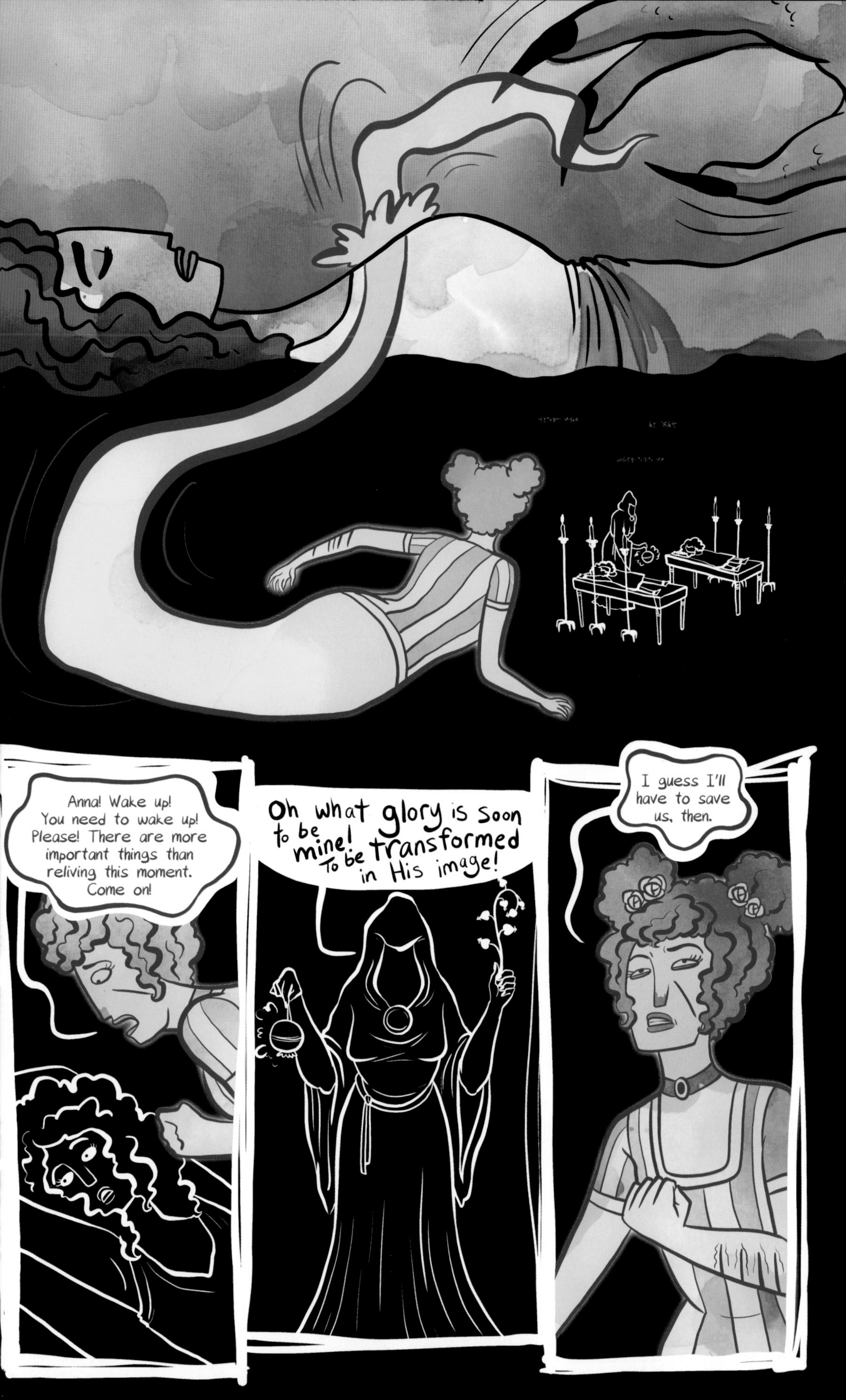
Anna! Wake up! You need to wake up! Please! There are more important things than reliving this moment. Come on!
Oh what glory is soon to be mine! To be transformed in His image!
I guess I'll have to save us, then.

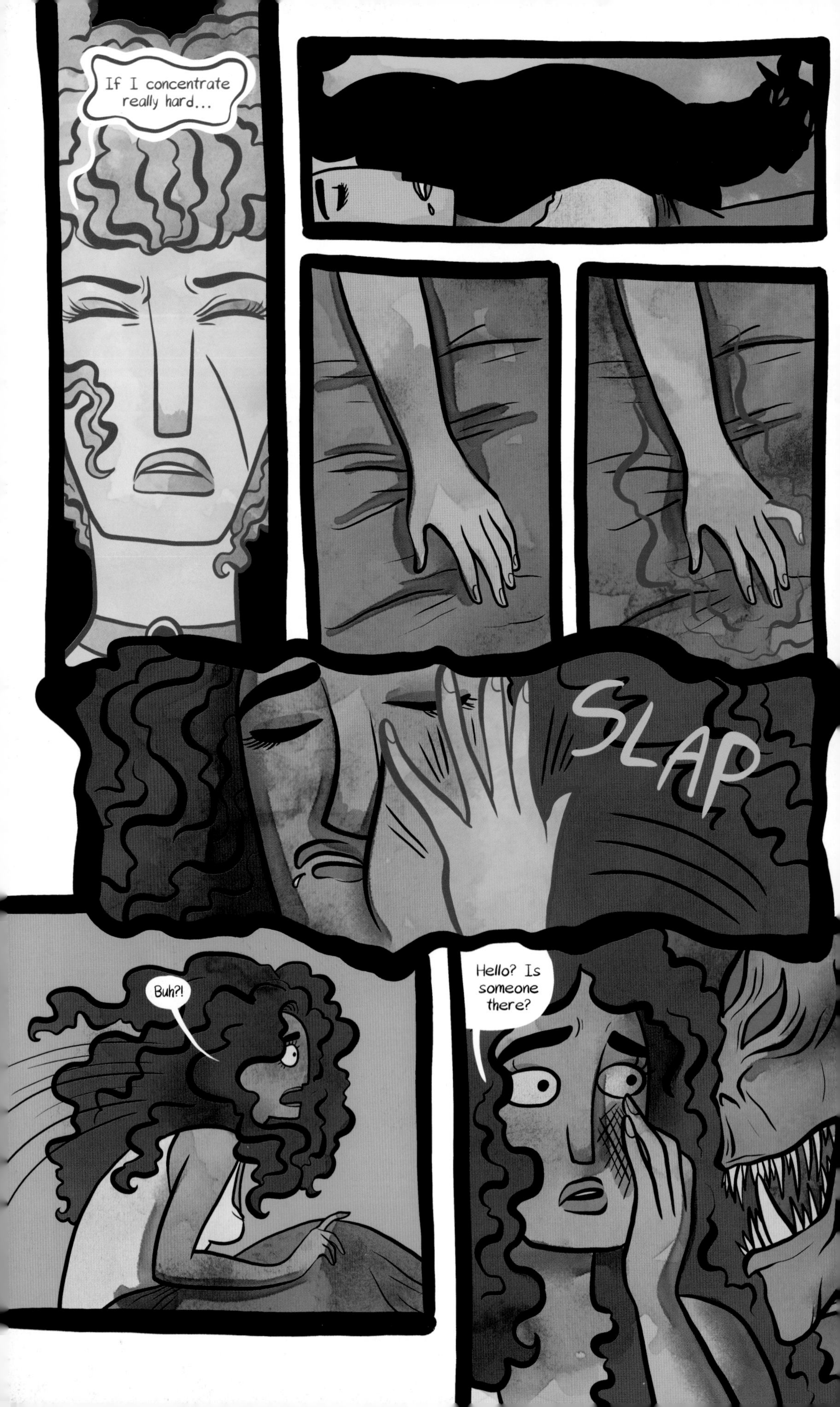
If I concentrate really hard...
SLAP
Buh?!
Hello? Is someone there?

Chapter Two

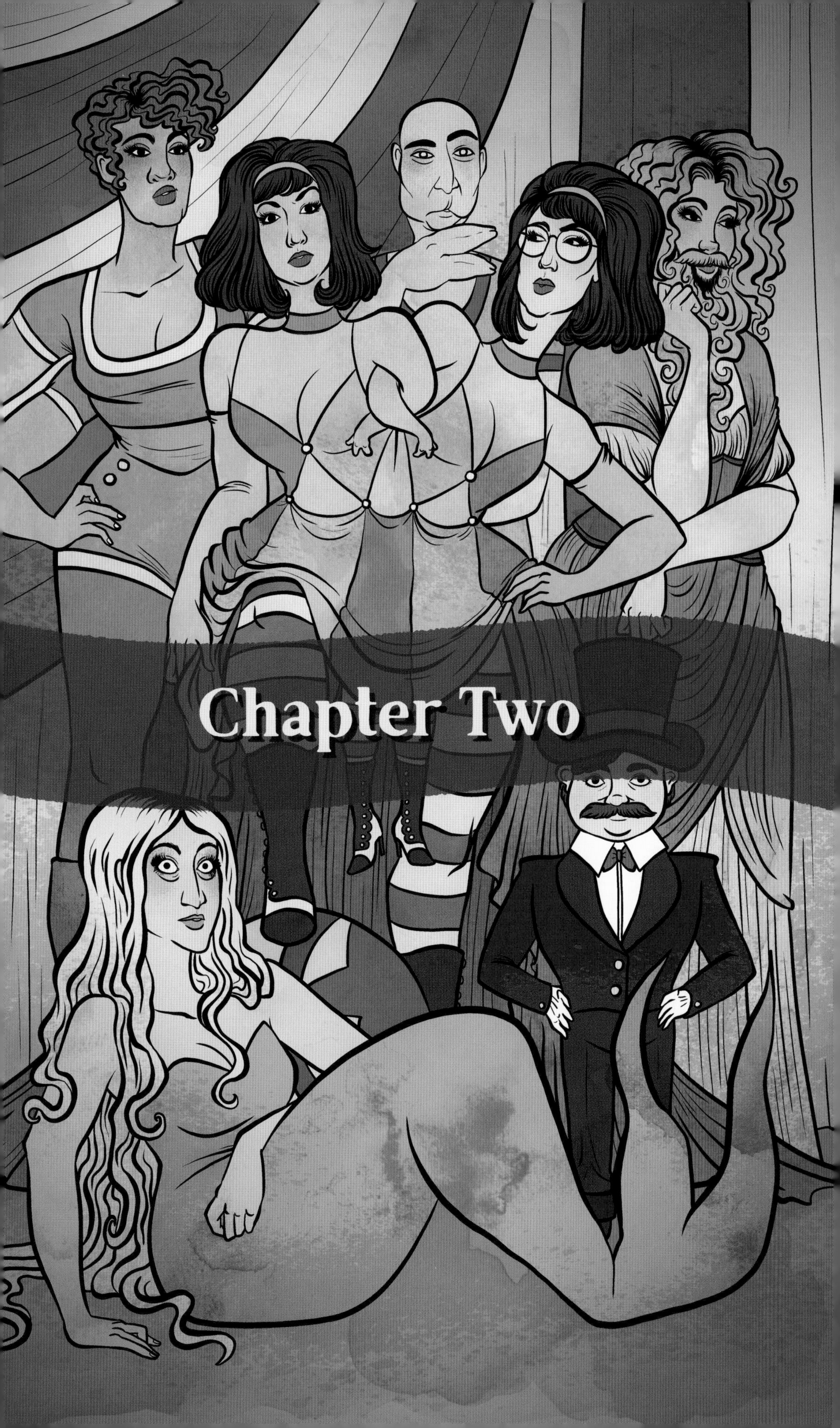

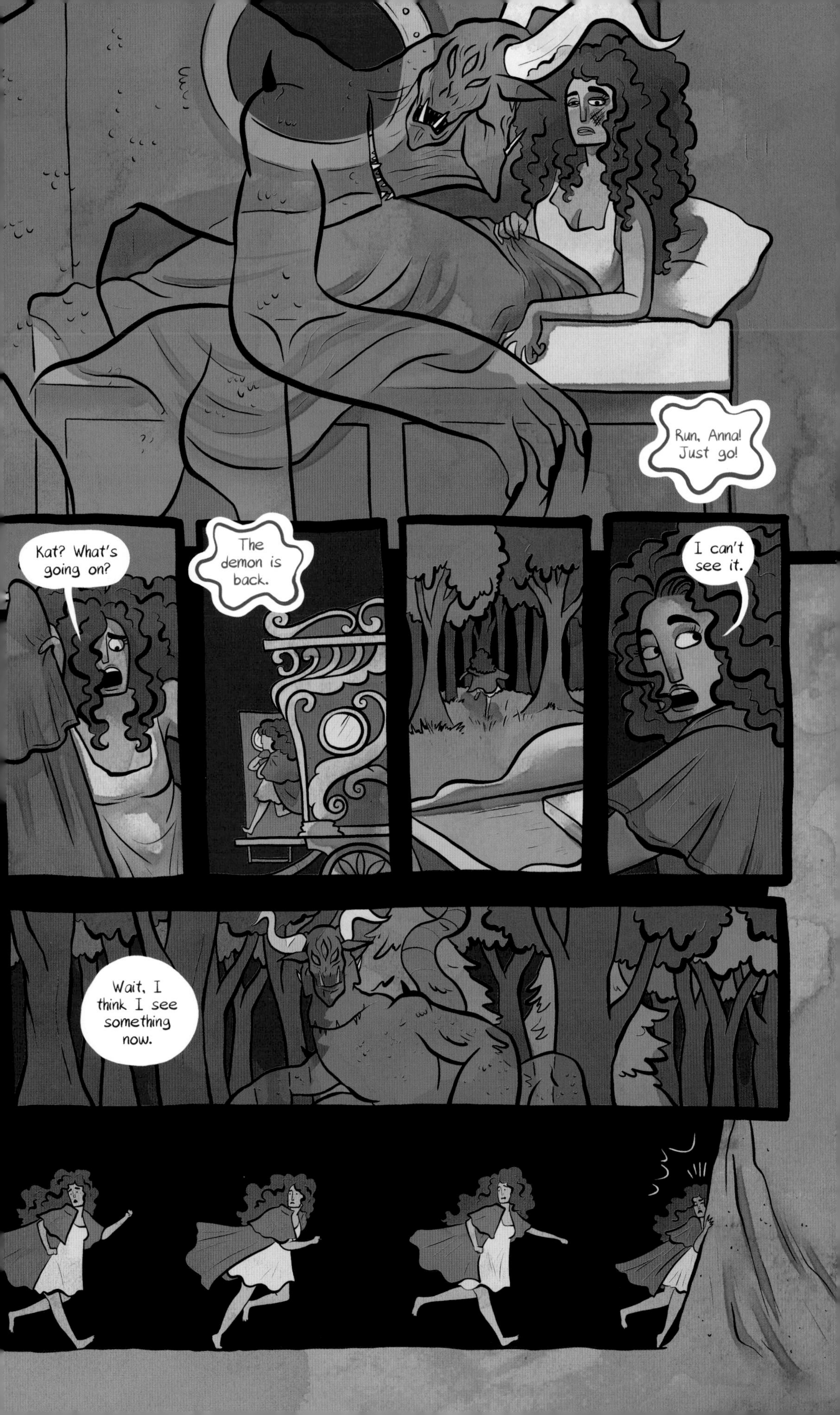
Run, Anna! Just go!
Kat? What's going on?
The demon is back.
I can't see it.
Wait, I think I see something now.

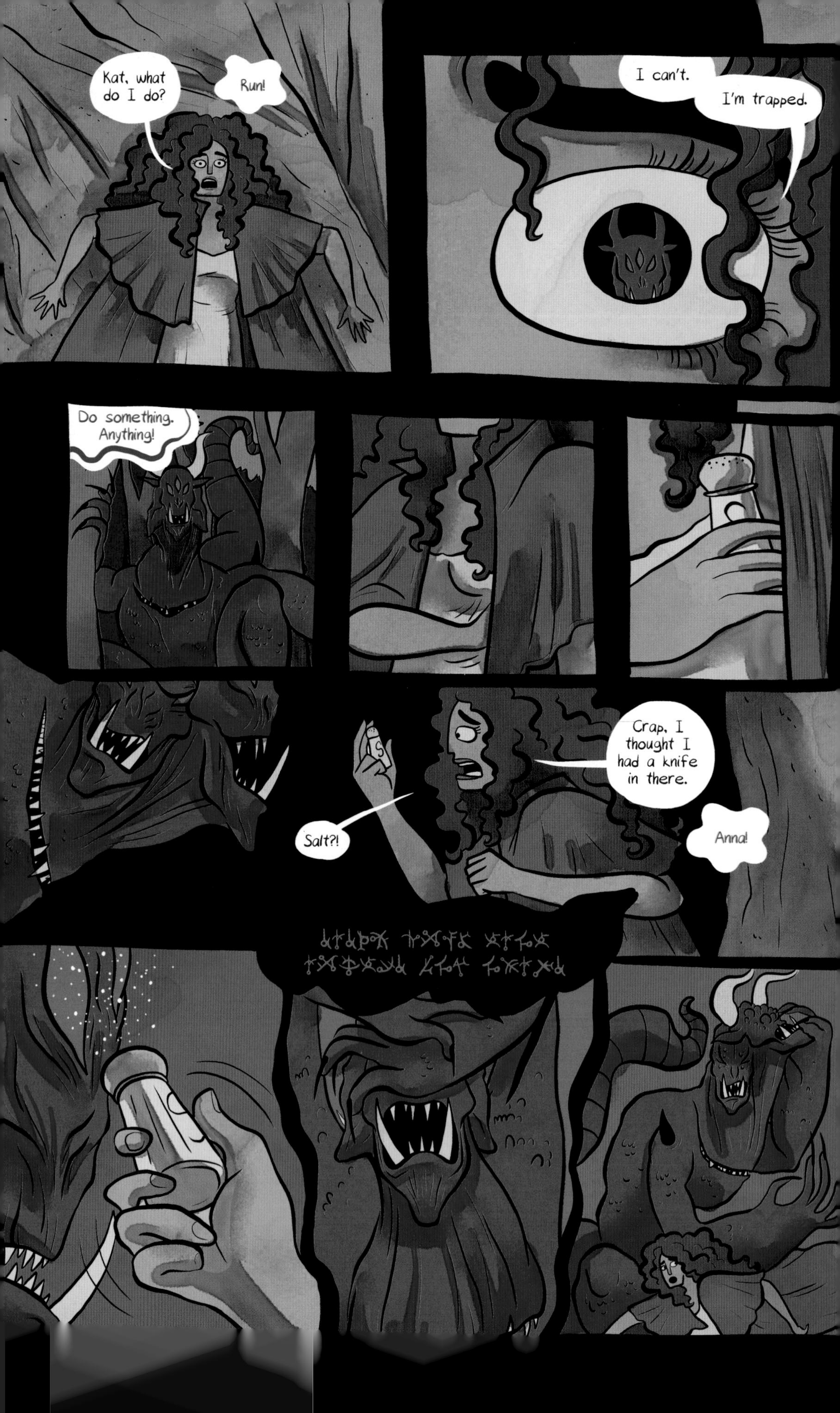
Kat, what do I do?
Run!
I can't.
I'm trapped.
Do something. Anything!
Salt?!
Crap, I thought I had a knife in there.
Anna!

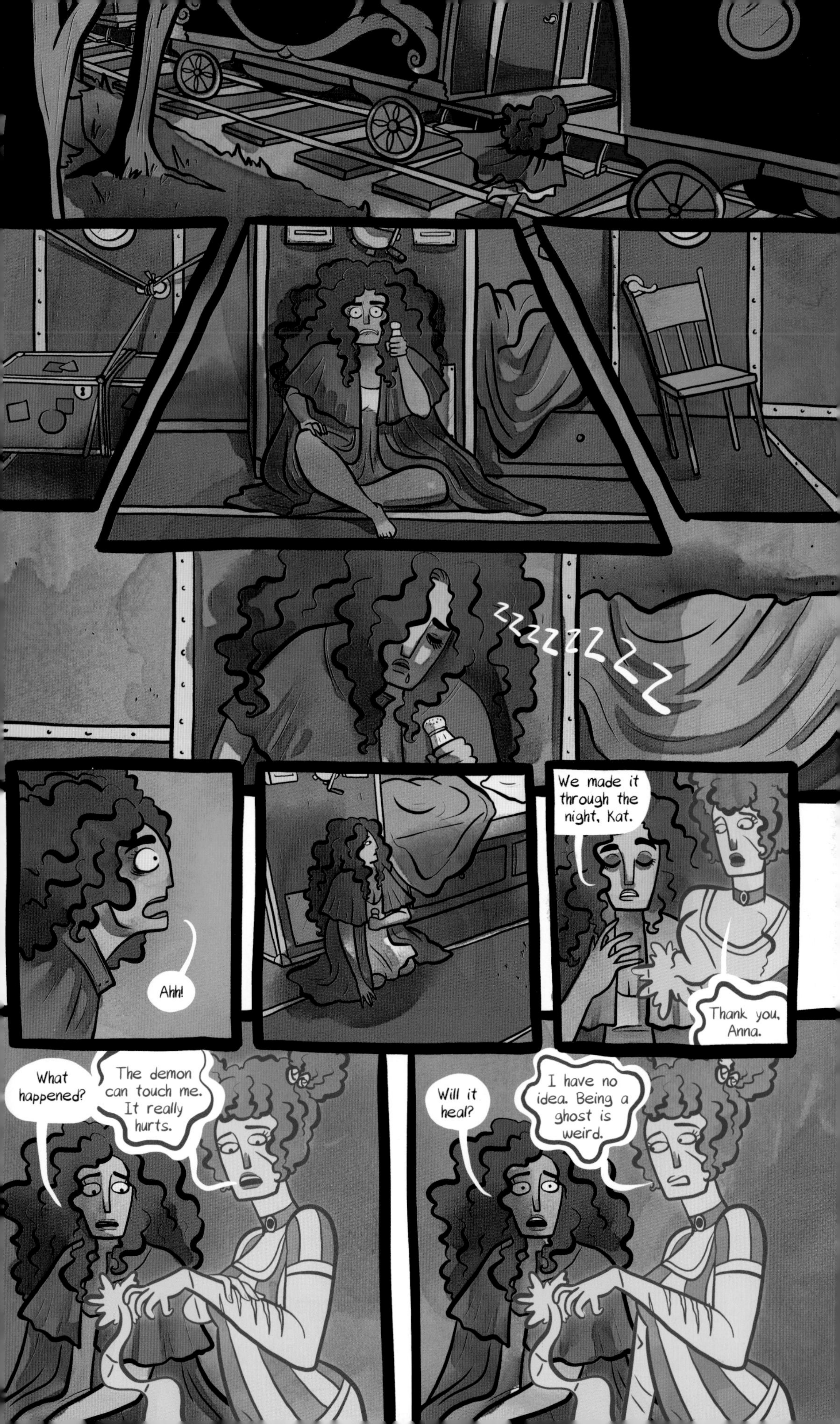
ZZZZZZZZ
Ahh!
We made it through the night, Kat.
Thank you, Anna.
What happened?
The demon can touch me. It really hurts.
Will it heal?
I have no idea. Being a ghost is weird.

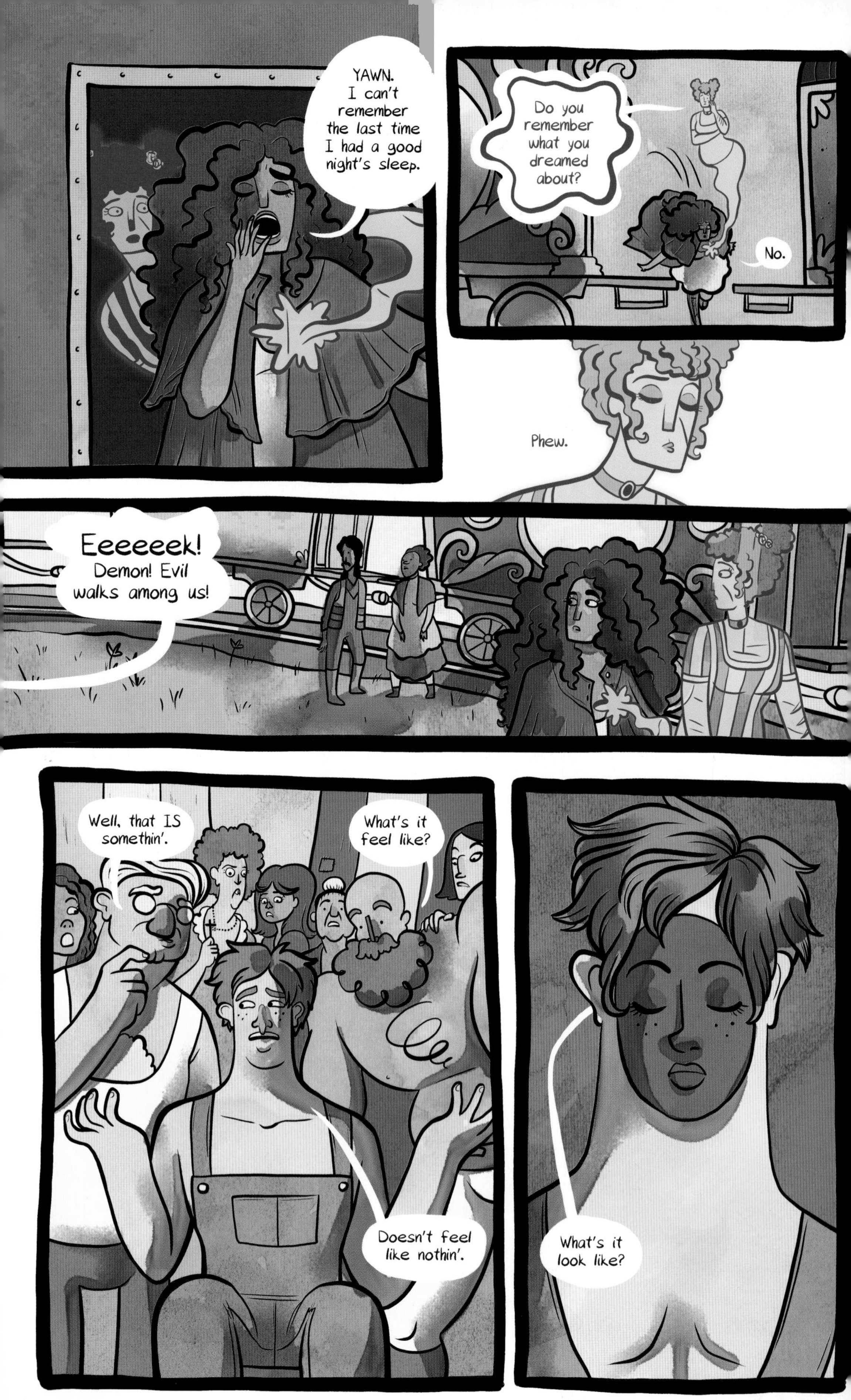
YAWN. I can't remember the last time I had a good night's sleep.
Do you remember what you dreamed about?
No.
Phew.
Eeeeeek! Demon! Evil walks among us!
Well, that IS somethin'.
What's it feel like?
Doesn't feel like nothin'.
What's it look like?

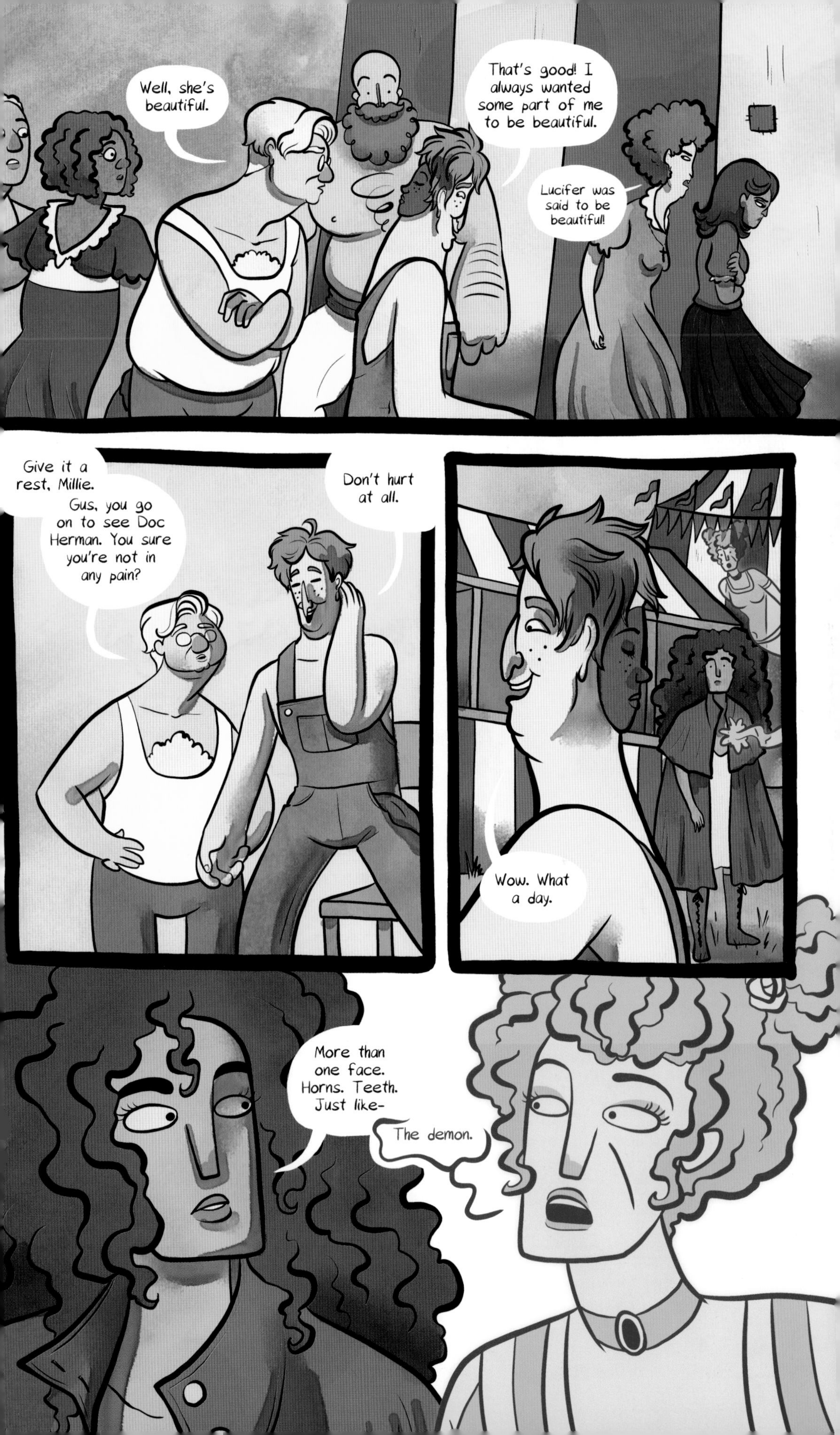
Well, she's beautiful.
That's good! I always wanted some part of me to be beautiful.
Lucifer was said to be beautiful!
Give it a rest, Millie.
Gus, you go on to see Doc Herman. You sure you're not in any pain?
Don't hurt at all.
Wow. What a day.
More than one face. Horns. Teeth. Just like-
The demon.

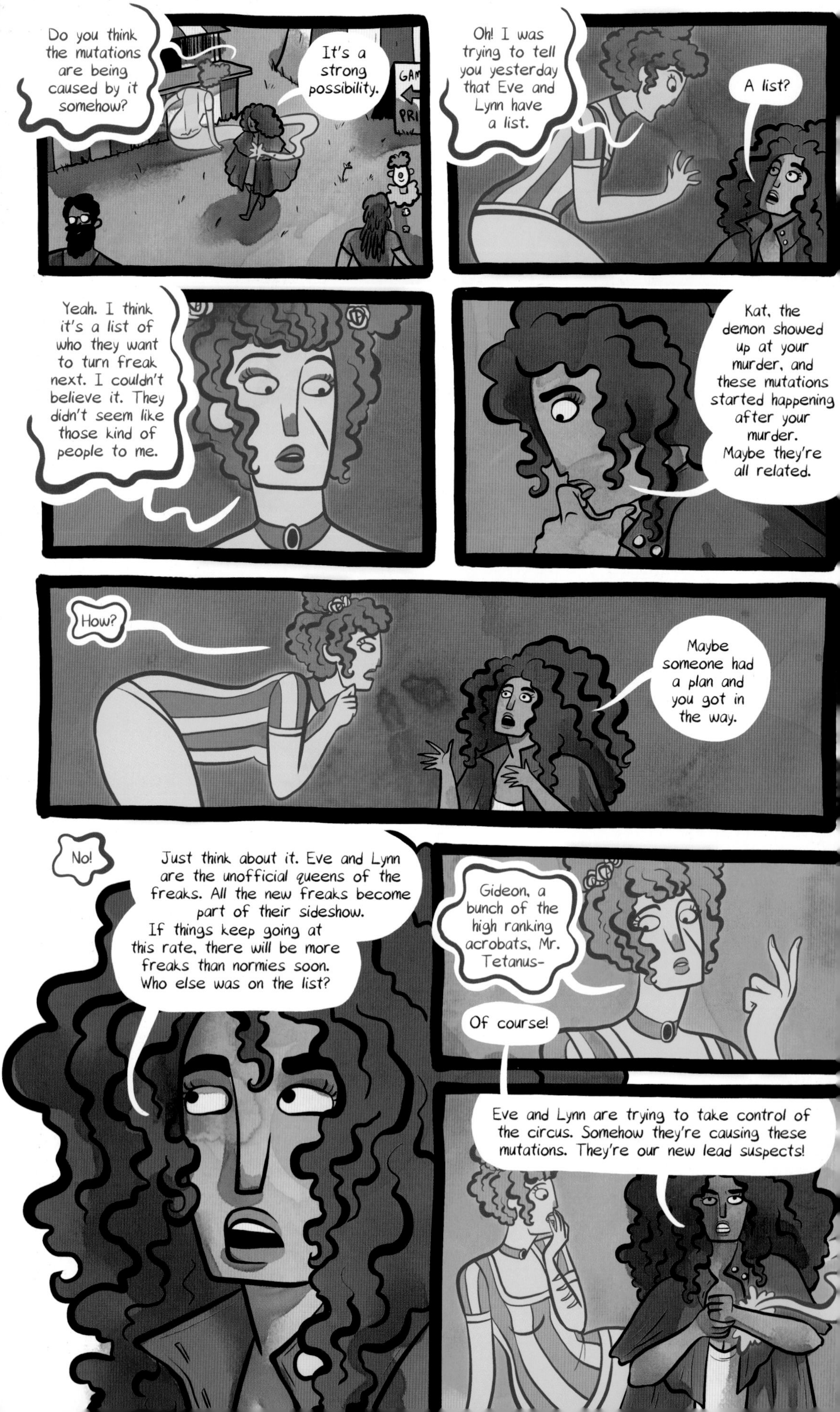
Do you think the mutations are being caused by it somehow?
It's a strong possibility.
Oh! I was trying to tell you yesterday that Eve and Lynn have a list.
A list?
Yeah. I think it's a list of who they want to turn freak next. I couldn't believe it. They didn't seem like those kind of people to me.
Kat, the demon showed up at your murder, and these mutations started happening after your murder. Maybe they're all related.
How?
Maybe someone had a plan and you got in the way.
No!
Just think about it. Eve and Lynn are the unofficial queens of the freaks. All the new freaks become part of their sideshow.
If things keep going at this rate, there will be more freaks than normies soon. Who else was on the list?
Gideon, a bunch of the high ranking acrobats, Mr. Tetanus-
Of course!
Eve and Lynn are trying to take control of the circus. Somehow they're causing these mutations. They're our new lead suspects!

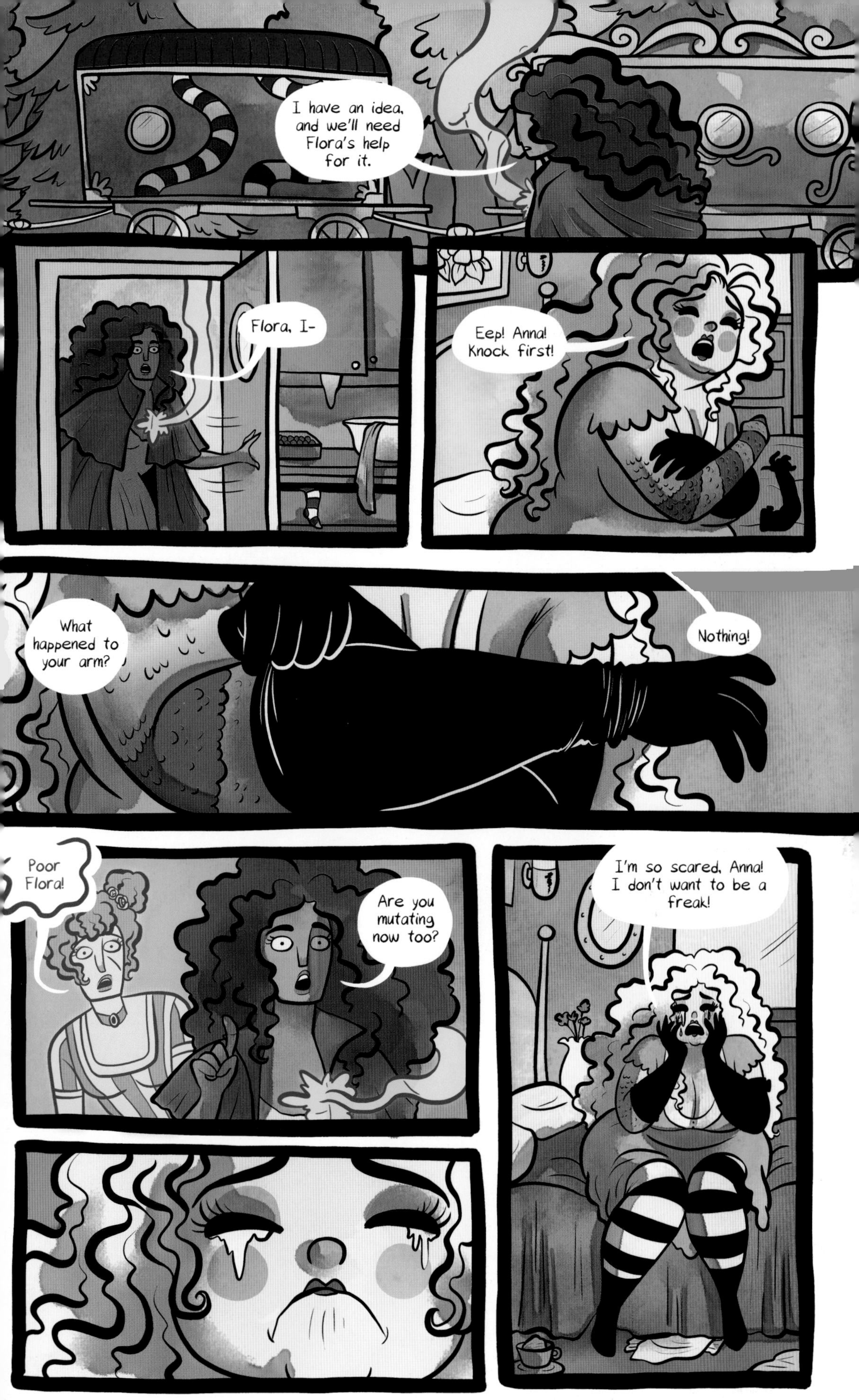
I have an idea, and we'll need Flora's help for it.
Flora, I-
Eep! Anna! Knock first!
What happened to your arm?
Nothing!
Poor Flora!
Are you mutating now too?
I'm so scared, Anna! I don't want to be a freak!

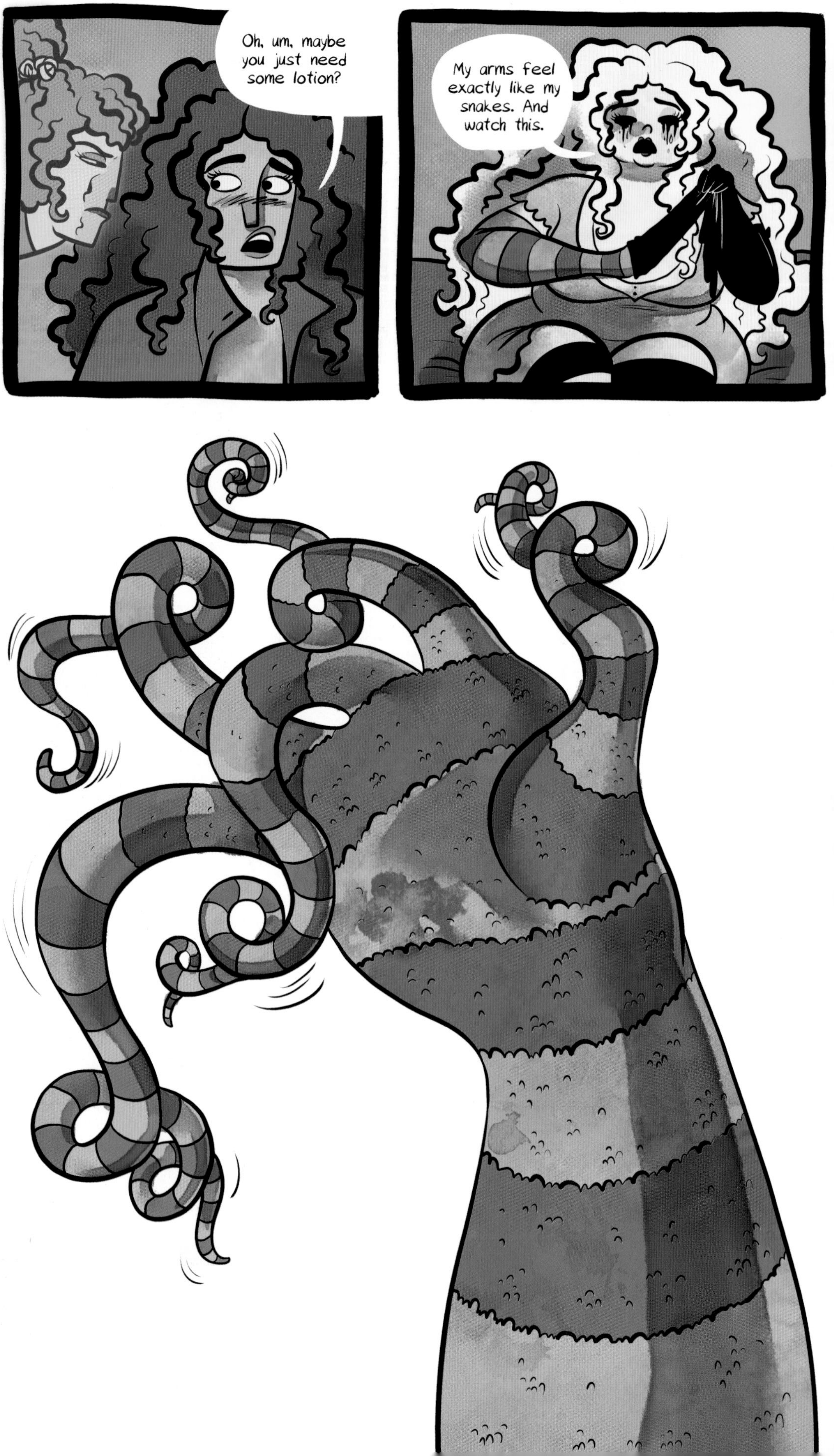
Oh, um, maybe you just need some lotion?
My arms feel exactly like my snakes. And watch this.

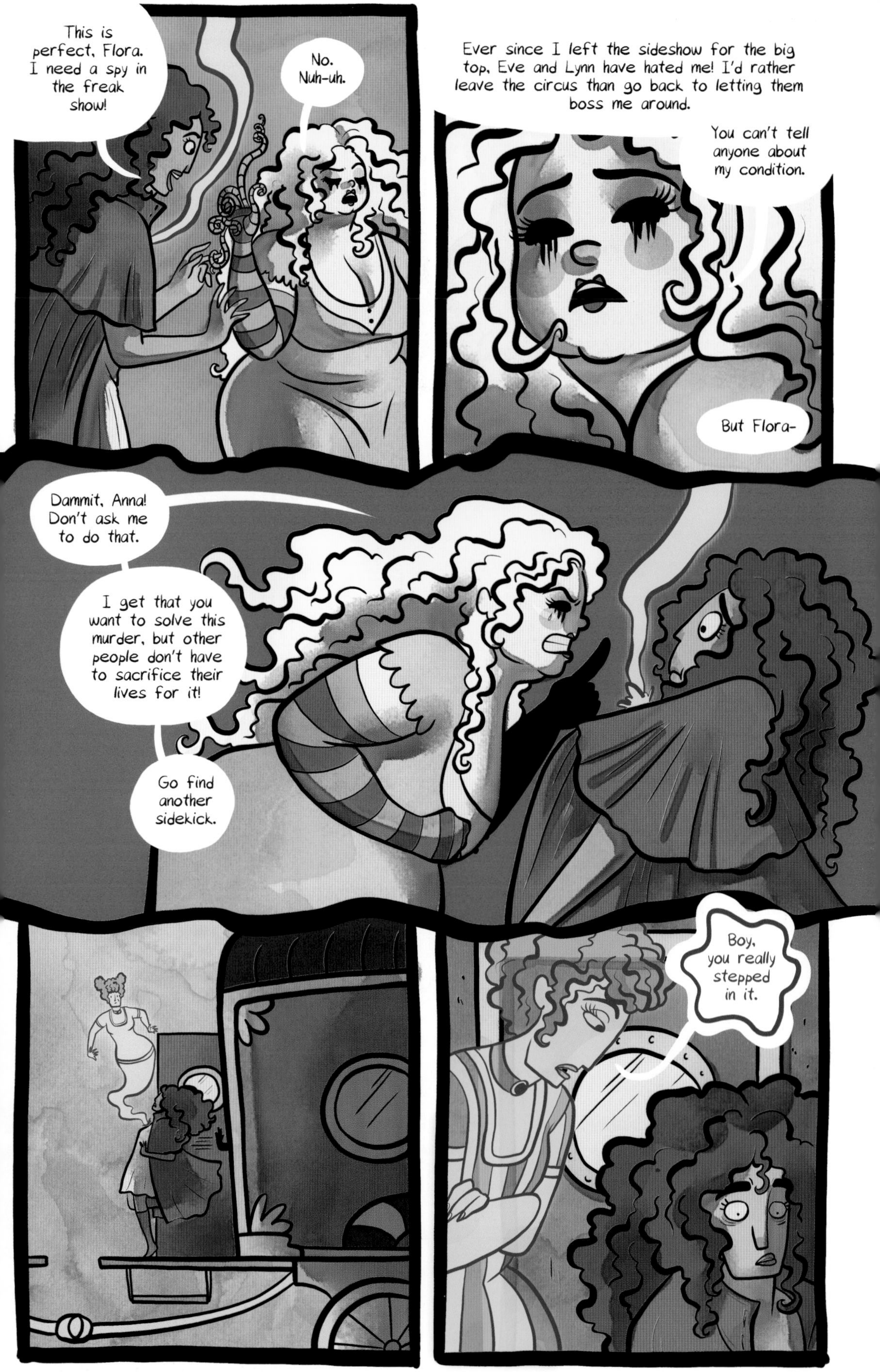
This is perfect, Flora. I need a spy in the freak show!
No. Nuh-uh.
Ever since I left the sideshow for the big top, Eve and Lynn have hated me! I'd rather leave the circus than go back to letting them boss me around.
You can't tell anyone about my condition.
But Flora-
Dammit, Anna! Don't ask me to do that.
I get that you want to solve this murder, but other people don't have to sacrifice their lives for it!
Go find another sidekick.
Boy, you really stepped in it.

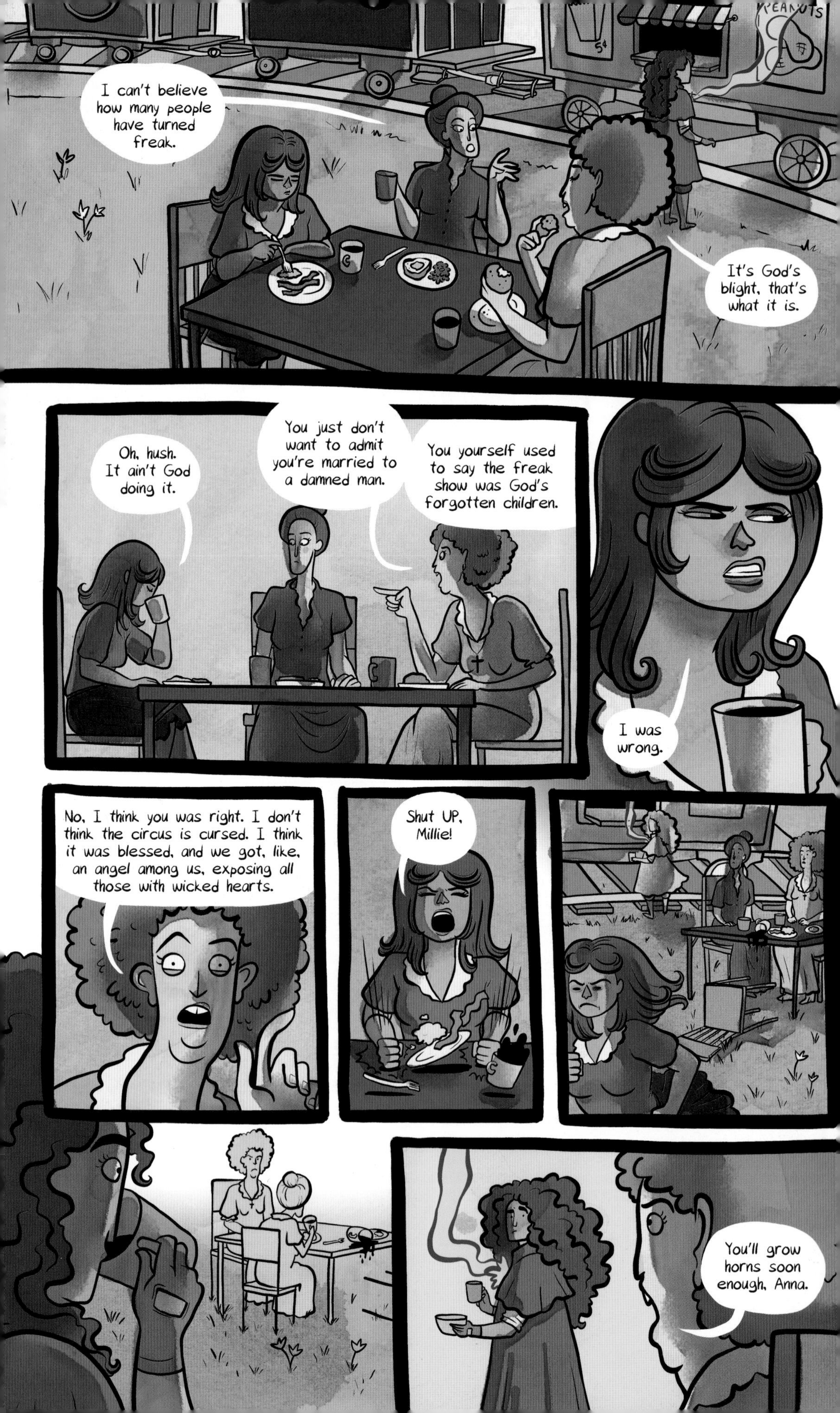
PEANUTS
5¢
I can't believe how many people have turned freak.
It's God's blight, that's what it is.
Oh, hush. It ain't God doing it.
You just don't want to admit you're married to a damned man.
You yourself used to say the freak show was God's forgotten children.
I was wrong.
No, I think you was right. I don't think the circus is cursed. I think it was blessed, and we got, like, an angel among us, exposing all those with wicked hearts.
Shut UP, Millie!
You'll grow horns soon enough, Anna.

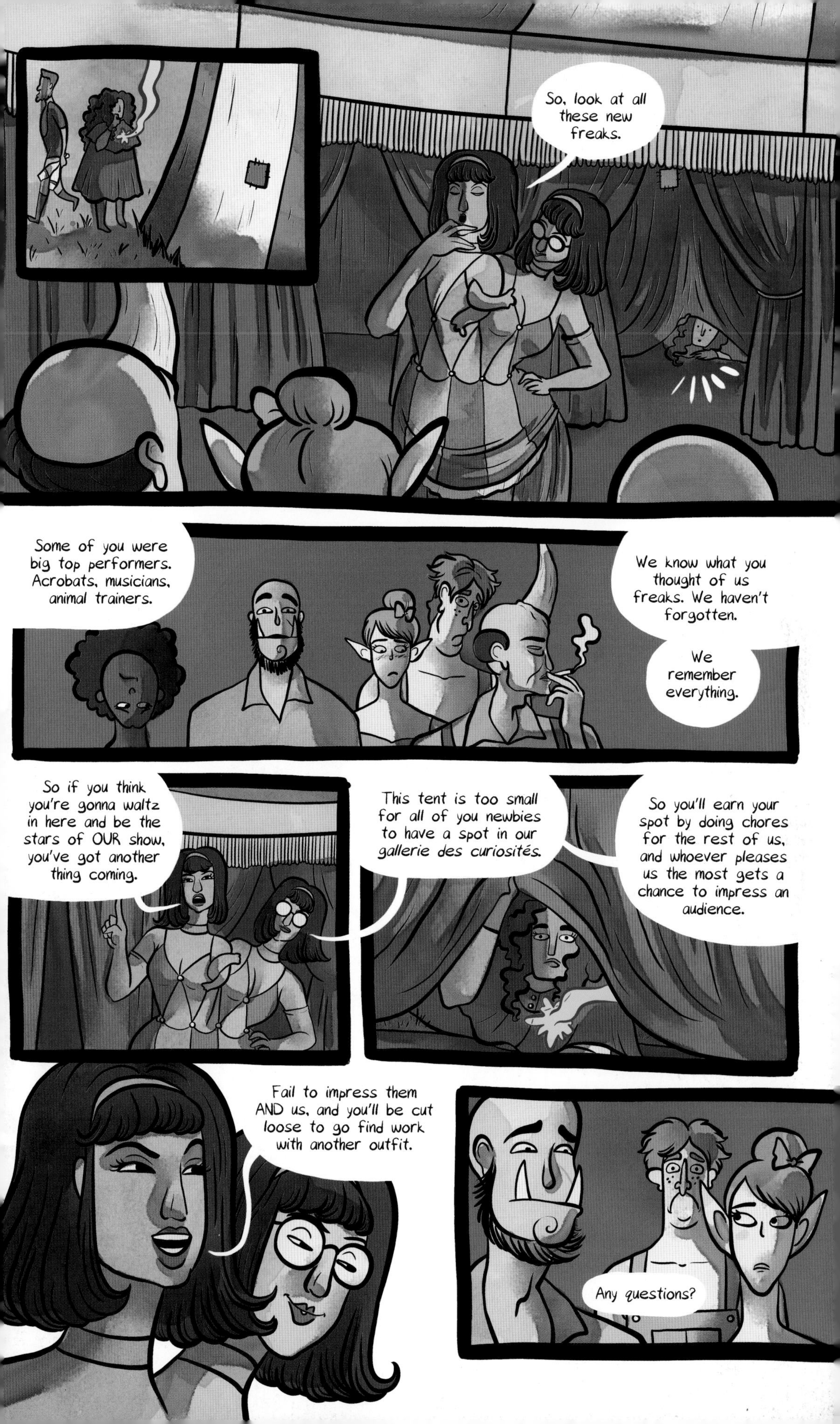
So, look at all these new freaks.
Some of you were big top performers. Acrobats, musicians, animal trainers.
We know what you thought of us freaks. We haven't forgotten.
We remember everything.
So if you think you're gonna waltz in here and be the stars of OUR show, you've got another thing coming.
This tent is too small for all of you newbies to have a spot in our gallerie des curiosités.
So you'll earn your spot by doing chores for the rest of us, and whoever pleases us the most gets a chance to impress an audience.
Fail to impress them AND us, and you'll be cut loose to go find work with another outfit.
Any questions?

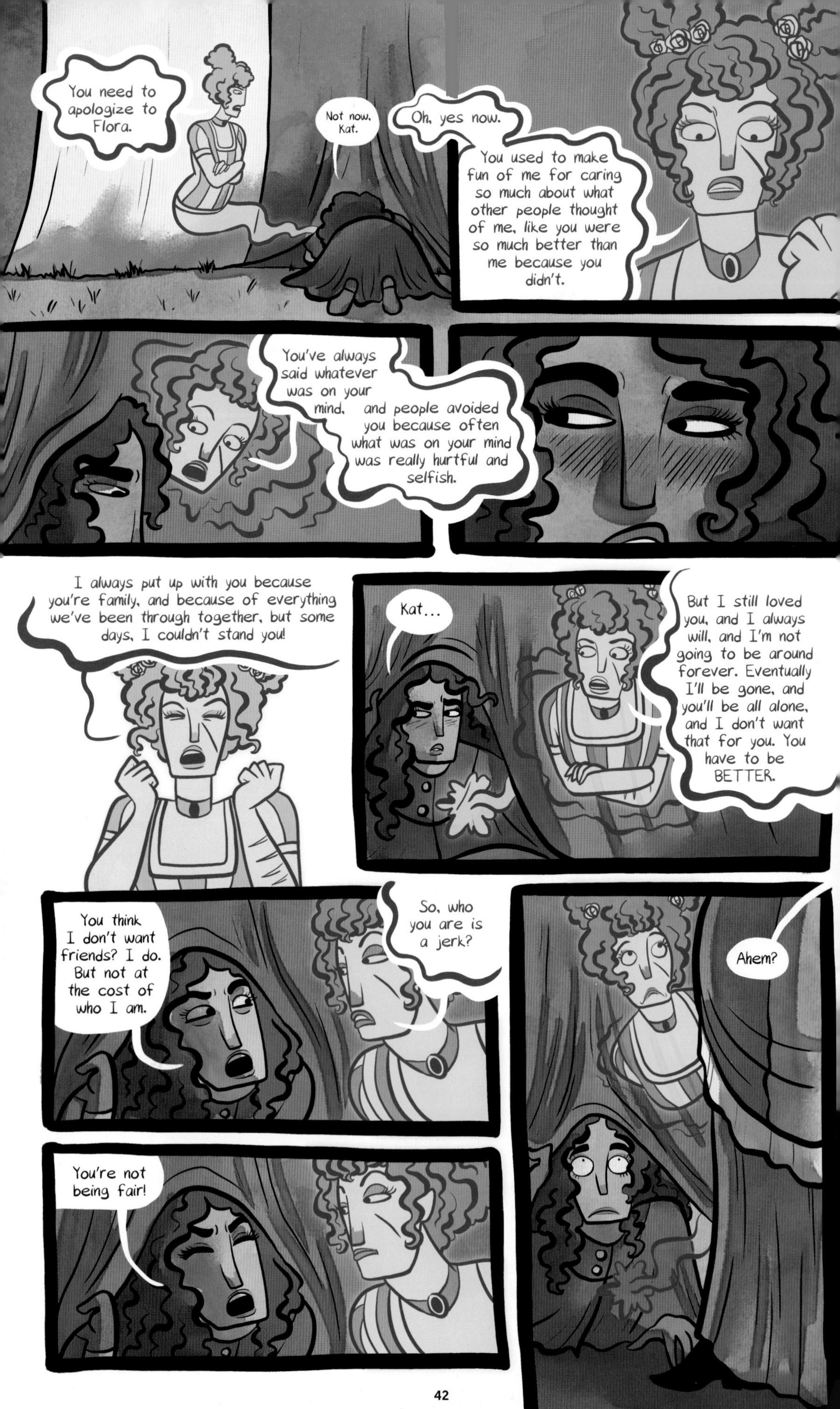

You need to apologize to Flora.
Not now, Kat.
Oh, yes now.
You used to make fun of me for caring so much about what other people thought of me, like you were so much better than me because you didn't.
You've always said whatever was on your mind,
and people avoided you because often what was on your mind was really hurtful and selfish.
I always put up with you because you're family, and because of everything we've been through together, but some days, I couldn't stand you!
Kat...
But I still loved you, and I always will, and I'm not going to be around forever. Eventually I'll be gone, and you'll be all alone, and I don't want that for you. You have to be BETTER.
You think I don't want friends? I do. But not at the cost of who I am.
So, who you are is a jerk?
You're not being fair!
Ahem?

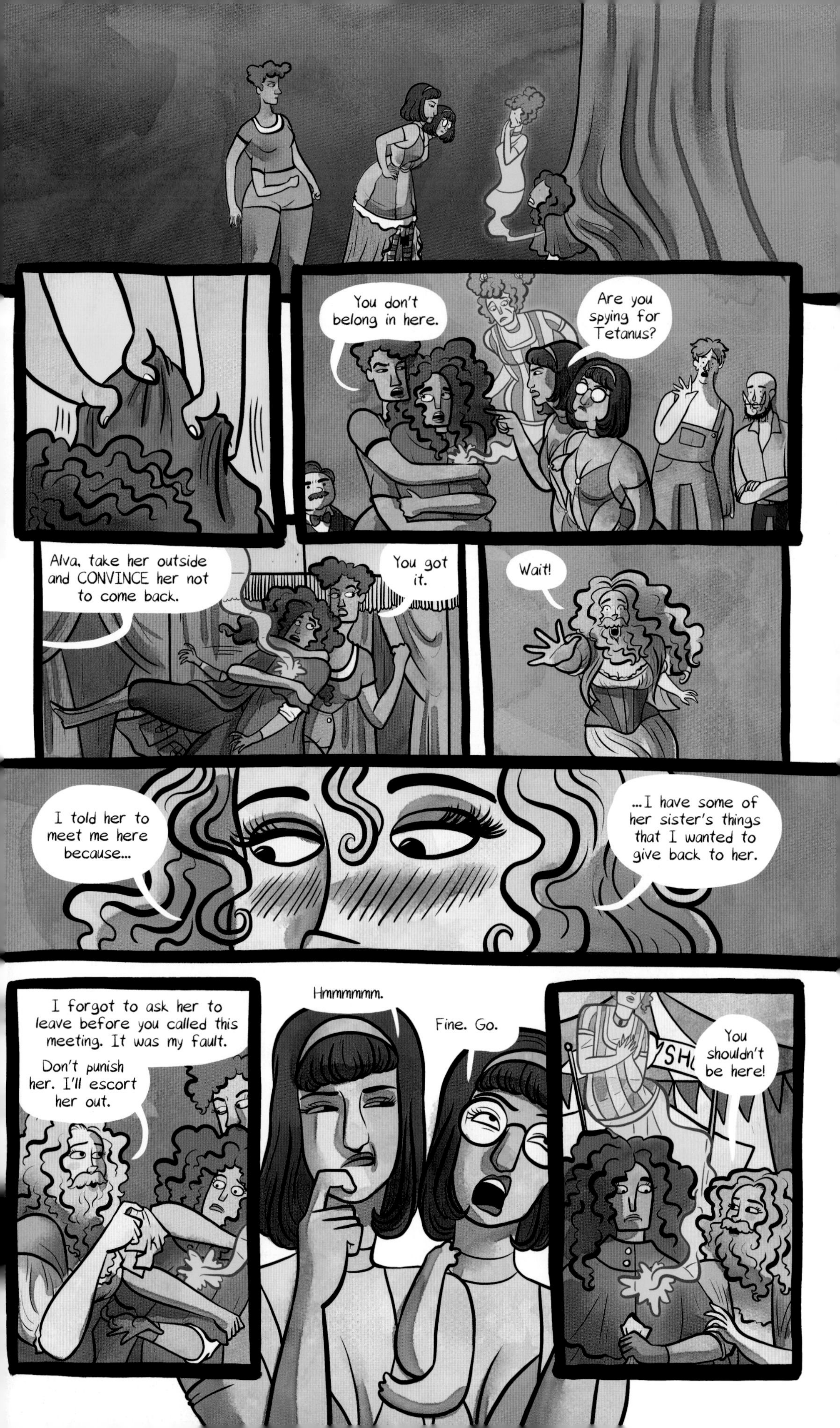
You don't belong in here.
Are you spying for Tetanus?
Alva, take her outside and CONVINCE her not to come back.
You got it.
Wait!
I told her to meet me here because...
...I have some of her sister's things that I wanted to give back to her.
I forgot to ask her to leave before you called this meeting. It was my fault.
Don't punish her. I'll escort her out.
Hmmmmmm.
Fine. Go.
You shouldn't be here!

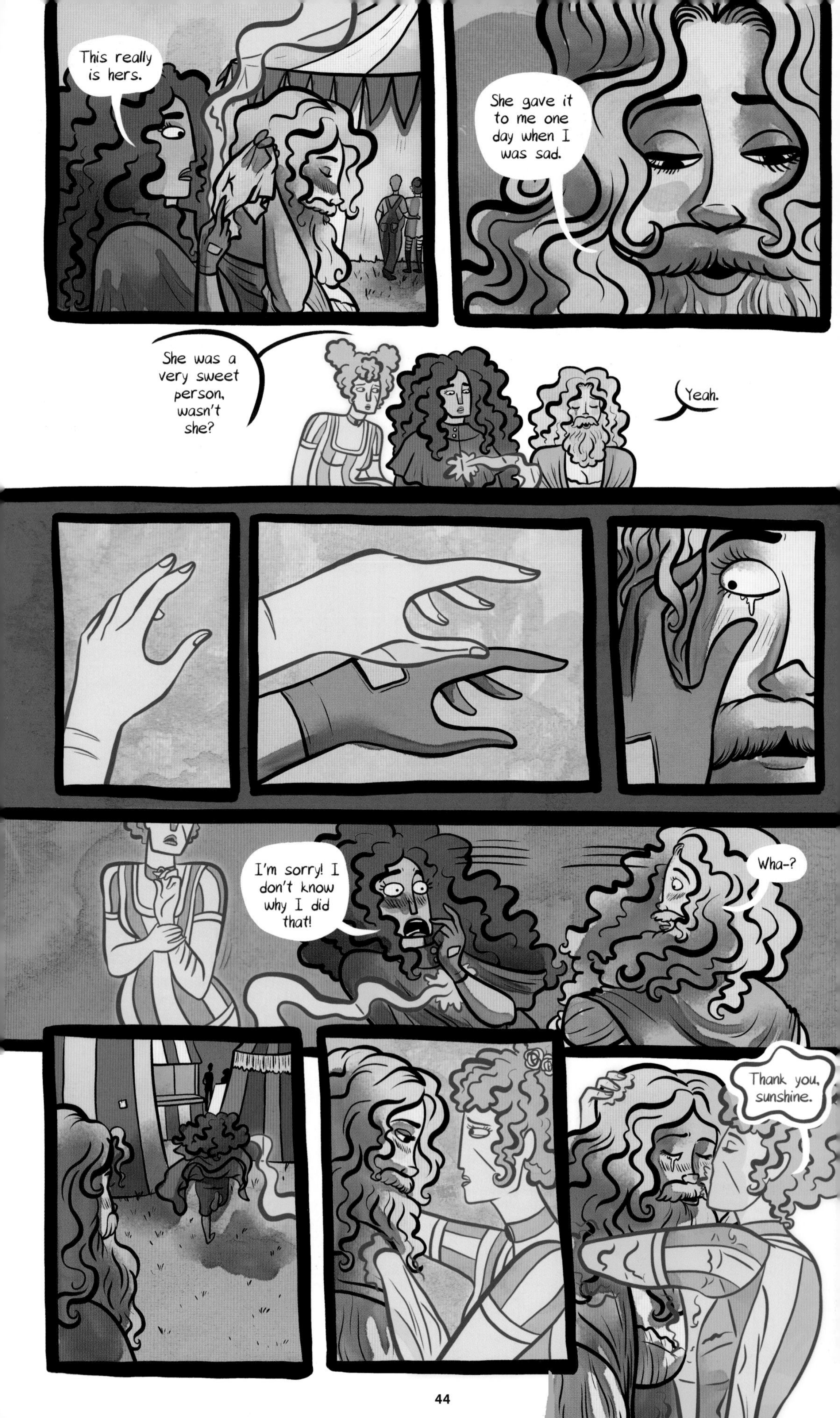
This really is hers.
She gave it to me one day when I was sad.
She was a very sweet person, wasn't she?
Yeah.
I'm sorry! I don't know why I did that!
Wha-?
Thank you, sunshine.

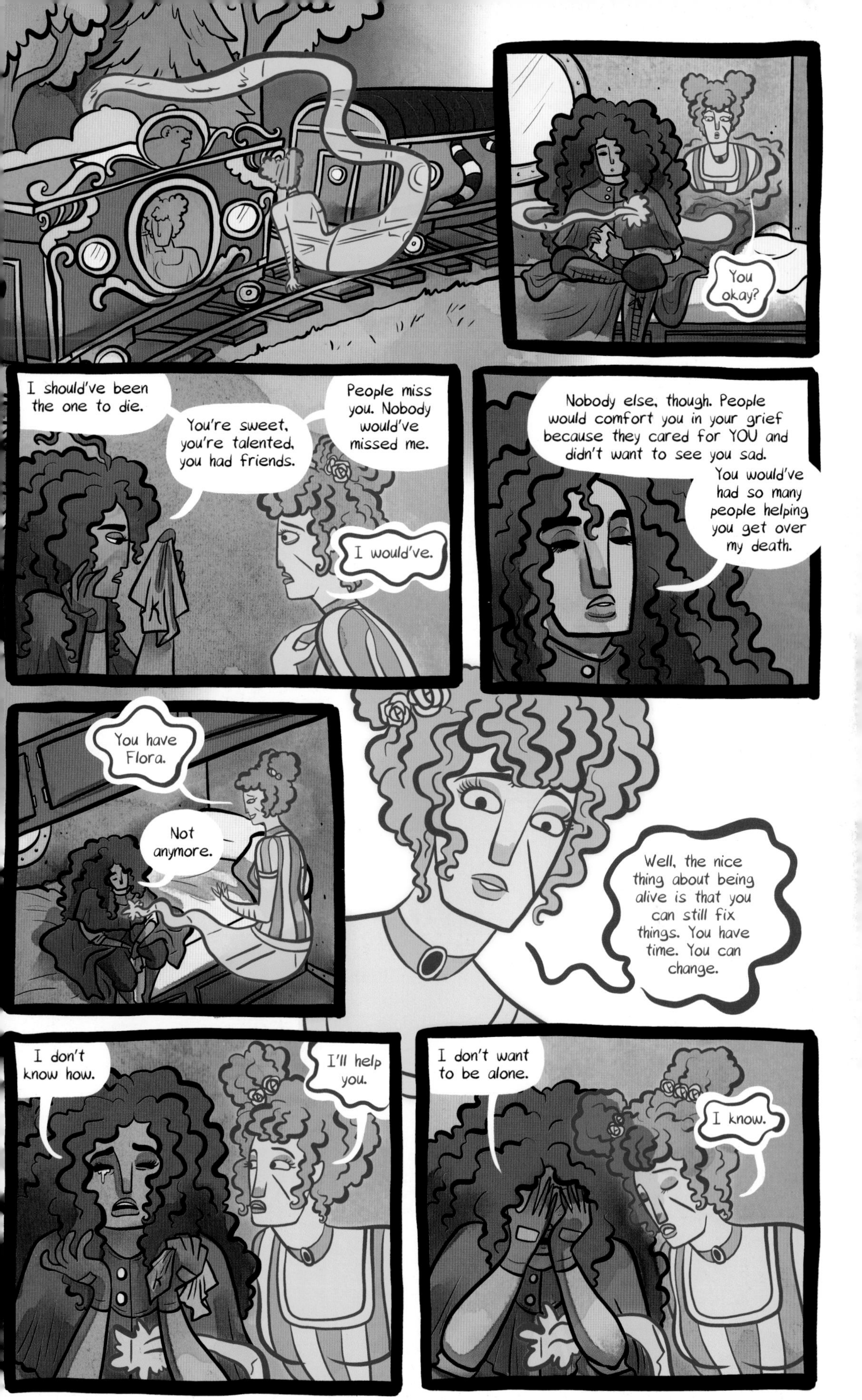

You okay?
I should've been the one to die.
You're sweet, you're talented, you had friends.
People miss you. Nobody would've missed me.
I would've.
Nobody else, though. People would comfort you in your grief because they cared for YOU and didn't want to see you sad.
You would've had so many people helping you get over my death.
You have Flora.
Not anymore.
Well, the nice thing about being alive is that you can still fix things. You have time. You can change.
I don't know how.
I'll help you.
I don't want to be alone.
I know.

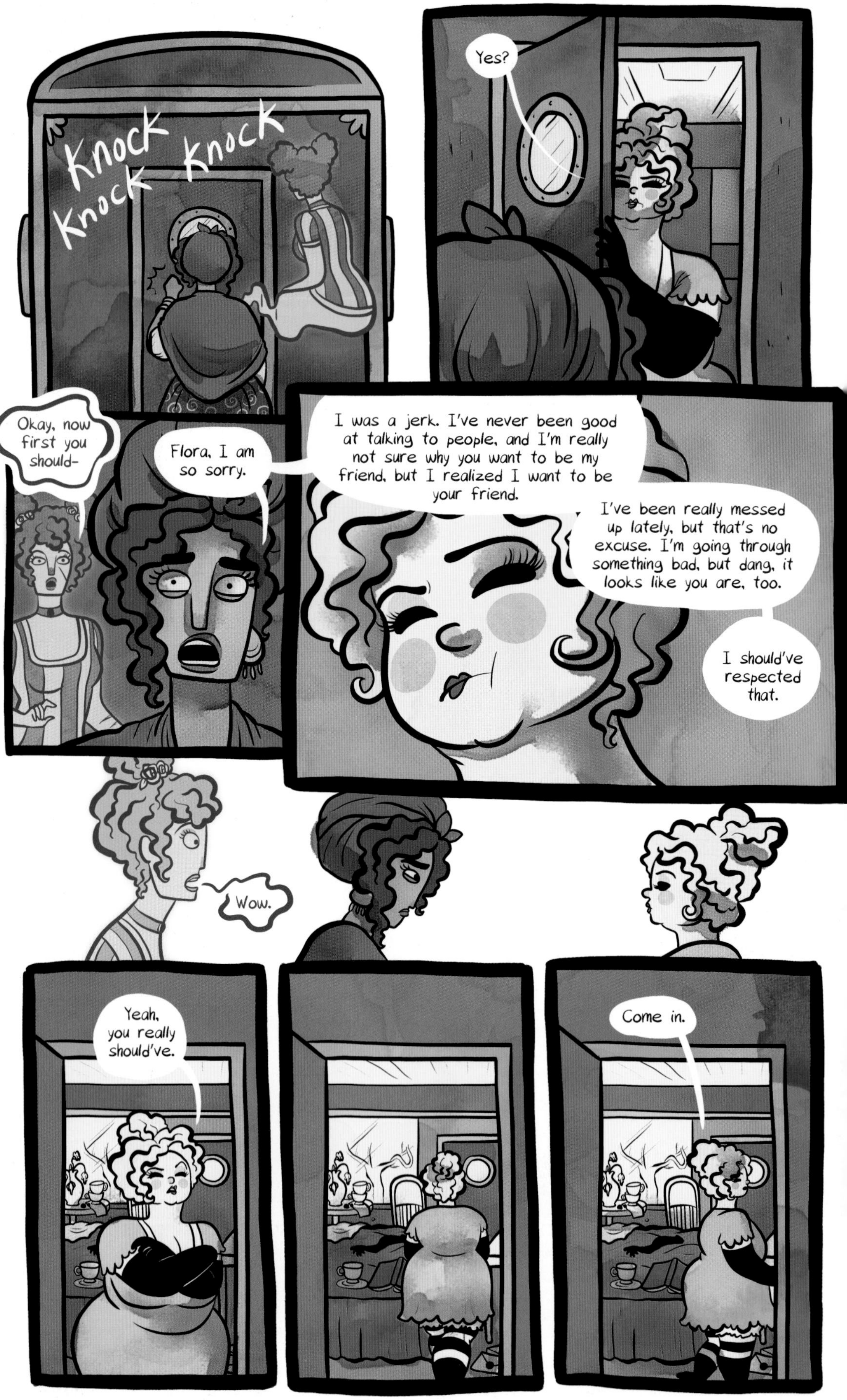
Knock Knock Knock
Yes?
Okay, now first you should-
Flora, I am so sorry.
I was a jerk. I've never been good at talking to people, and I'm really not sure why you want to be my friend, but I realized I want to be your friend.
I've been really messed up lately, but that's no excuse. I'm going through something bad, but dang, it looks like you are, too.
I should've respected that.
Wow.
Yeah, you really should've.
Come in.

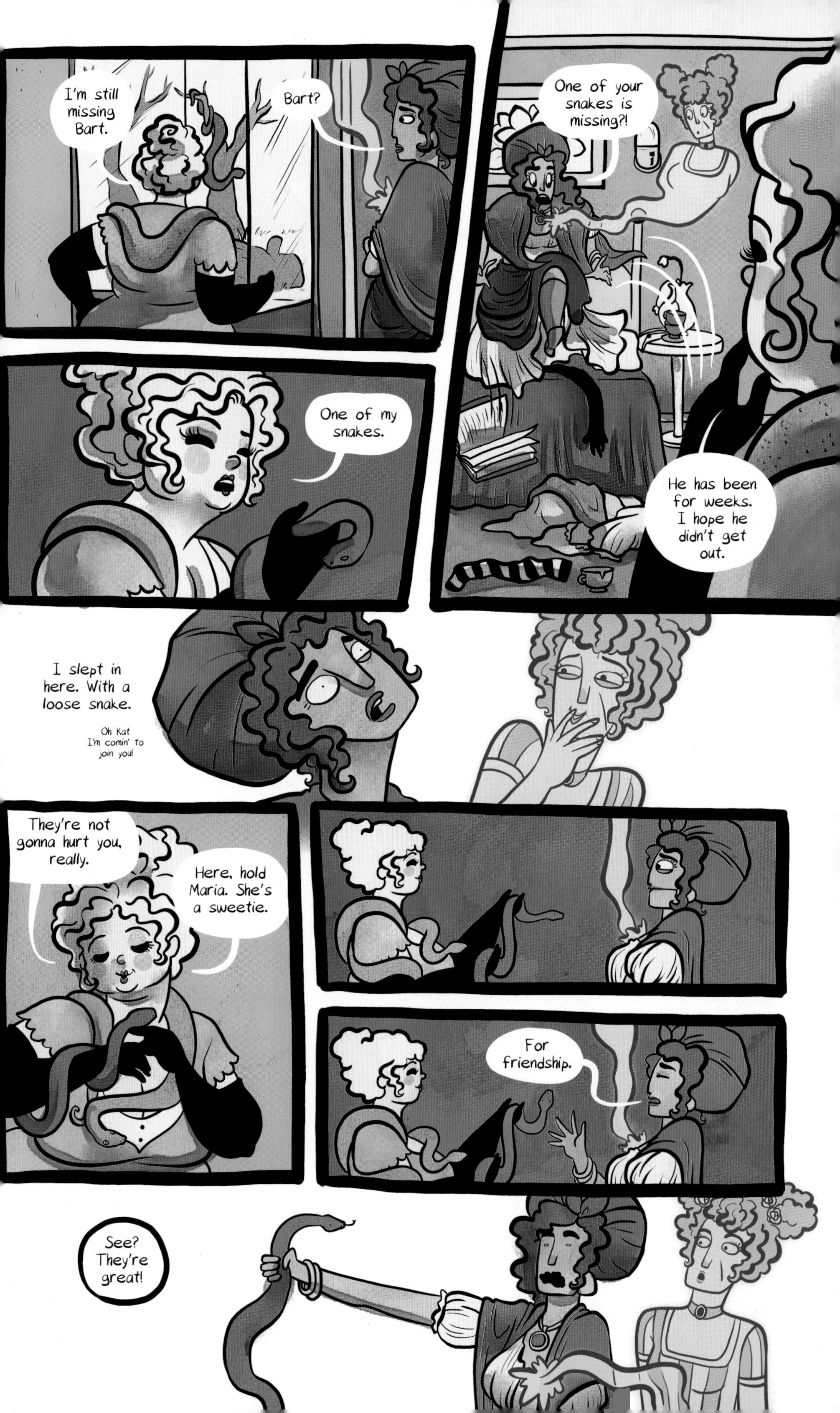
I'm still missing Bart.
Bart?
One of my snakes.
One of your snakes is missing?!
He has been for weeks. I hope he didn't get out.
I slept in here. With a loose snake.
Oh Kat I'm comin' to join you!
They're not gonna hurt you, really.
Here, hold Maria. She's a sweetie.
For friendship.
See? They're great!

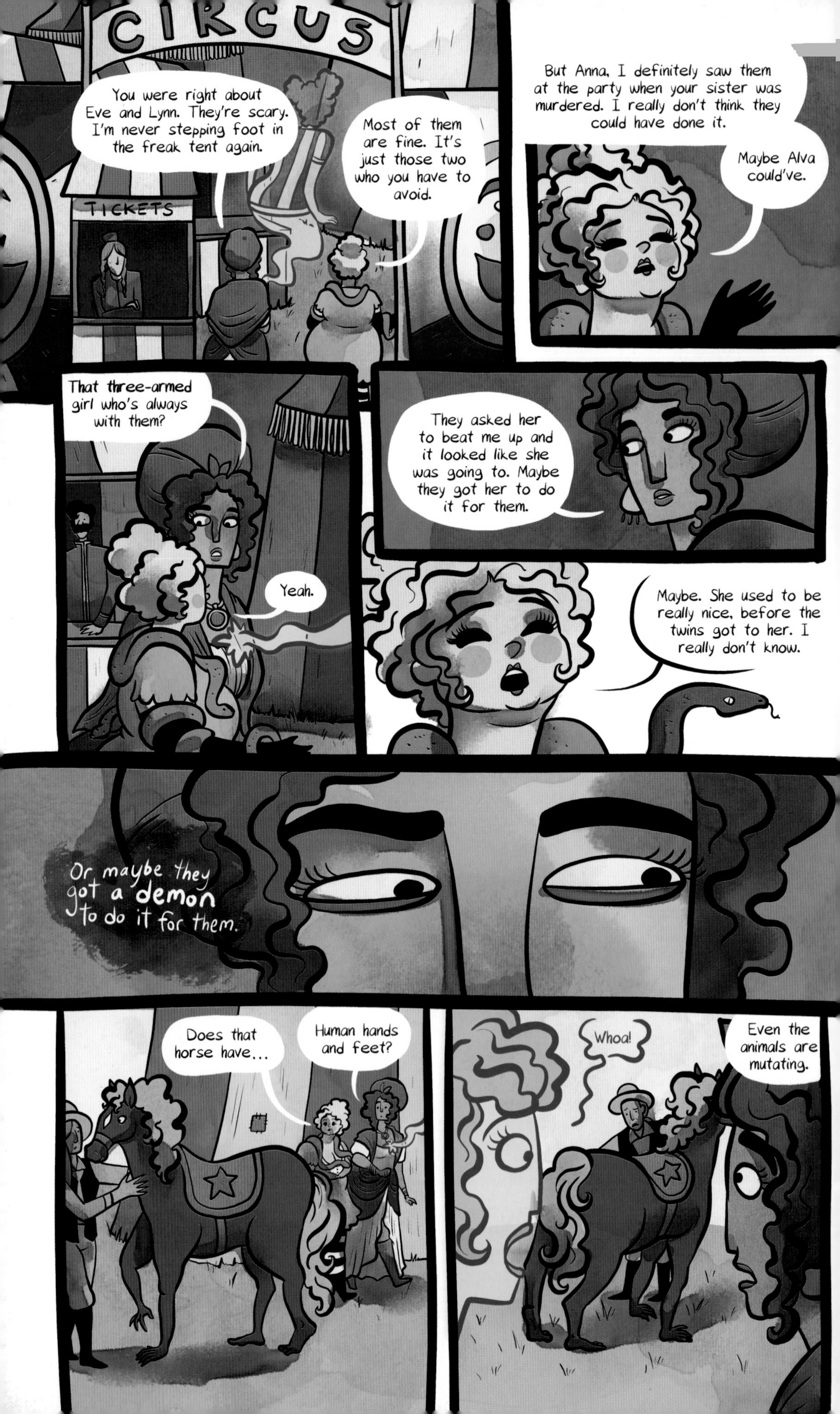

CIRCUS
TICKETS
You were right about Eve and Lynn. They're scary. I'm never stepping foot in the freak tent again.
Most of them are fine. It's just those two who you have to avoid.
But Anna, I definitely saw them at the party when your sister was murdered. I really don't think they could have done it.
Maybe Alva could've.
That three-armed girl who's always with them?
Yeah.
They asked her to beat me up and it looked like she was going to. Maybe they got her to do it for them.
Maybe. She used to be really nice, before the twins got to her. I really don't know.
Or maybe they got a demon to do it for them.
Does that horse have...
Human hands and feet?
Whoa!
Even the animals are mutating.

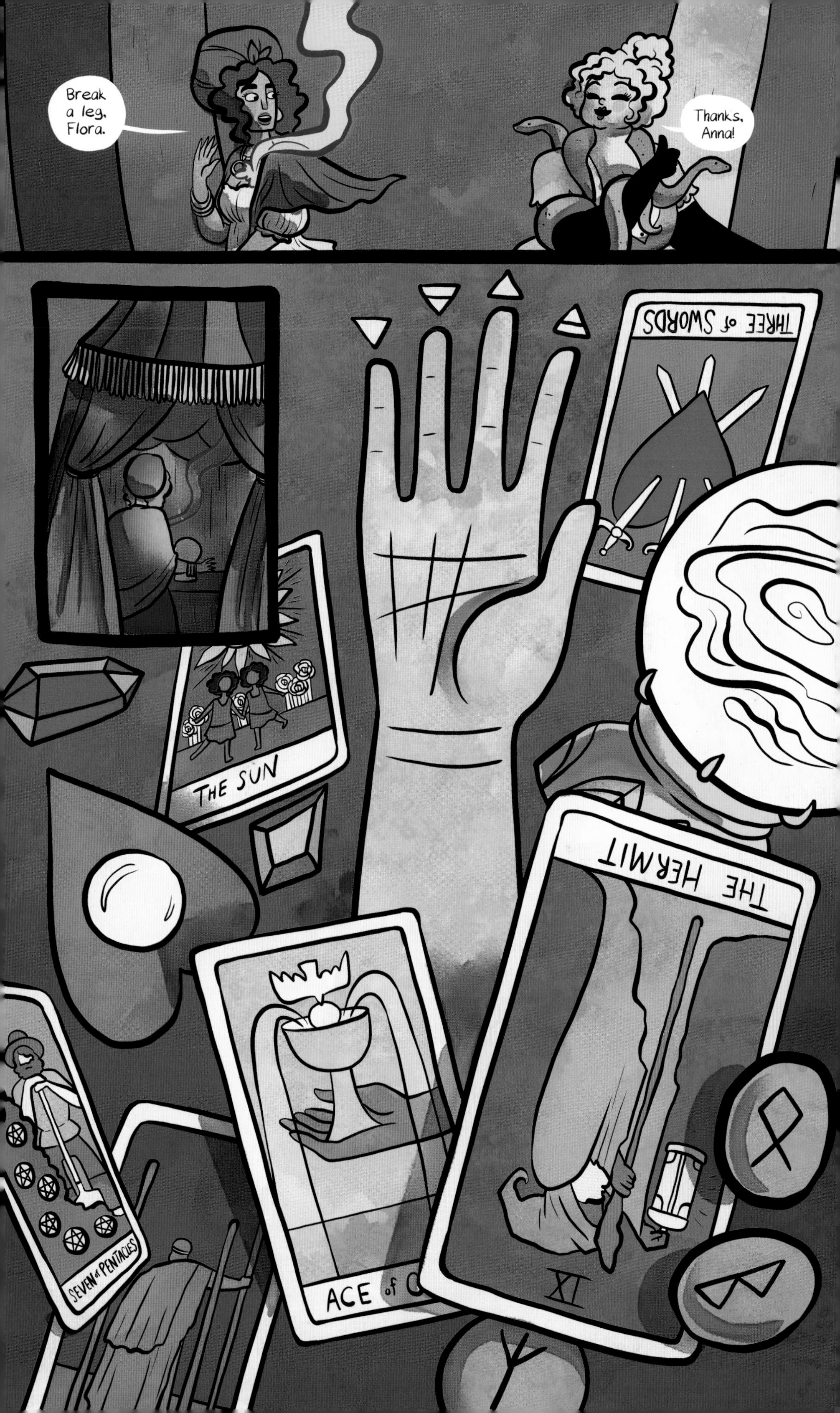
Break a leg, Flora.
Thanks, Anna!
THREE of SWORDS
THE SUN
THE HERMIT
SEVEN of PENTACLES
ACE of

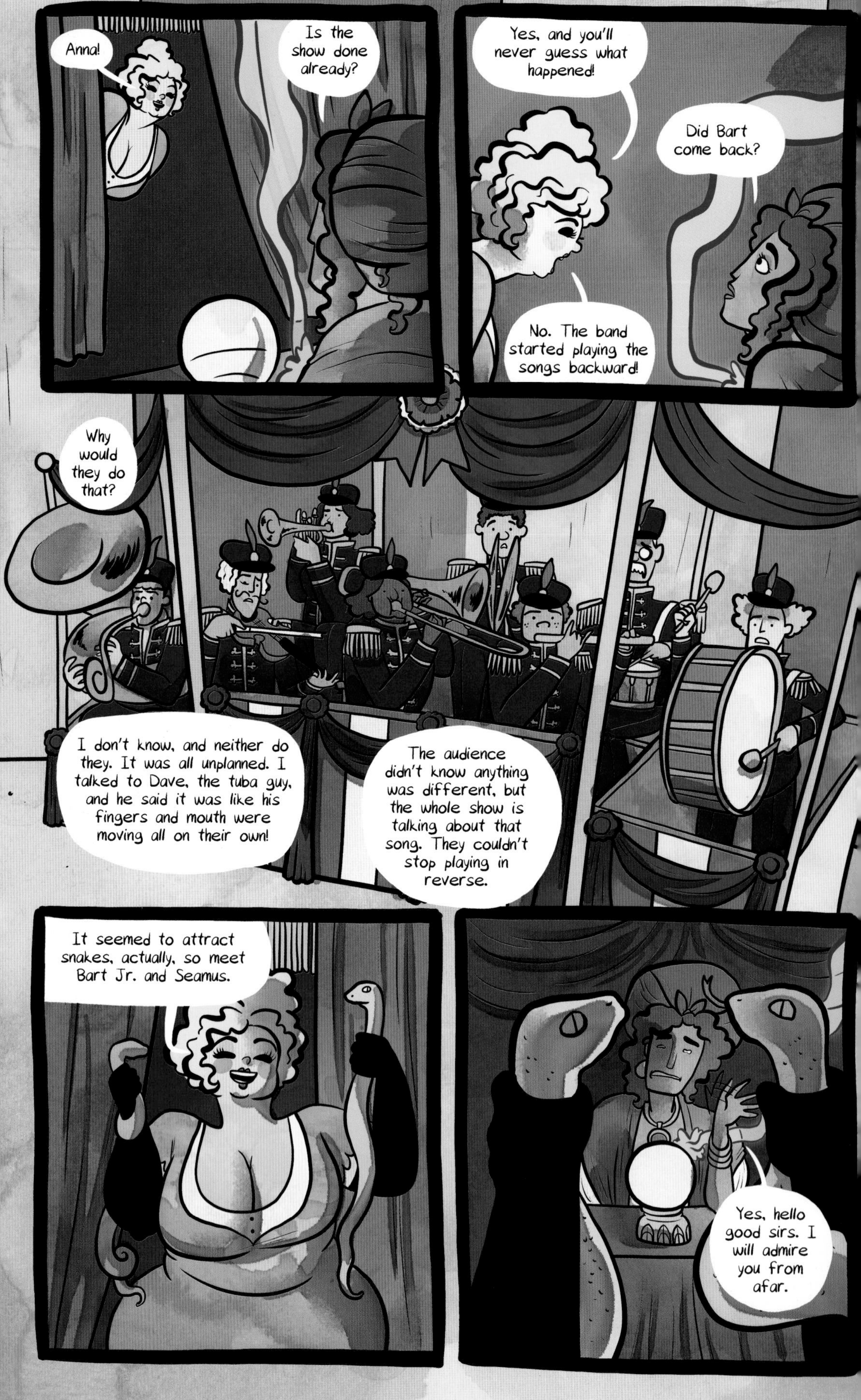
Anna!
Is the show done already?
Yes, and you'll never guess what happened!
Did Bart come back?
No. The band started playing the songs backward!
Why would they do that?
I don't know, and neither do they. It was all unplanned. I talked to Dave, the tuba guy, and he said it was like his fingers and mouth were moving all on their own!
The audience didn't know anything was different, but the whole show is talking about that song. They couldn't stop playing in reverse.
It seemed to attract snakes, actually, so meet Bart Jr. and Seamus.
Yes, hello good sirs. I will admire you from afar.

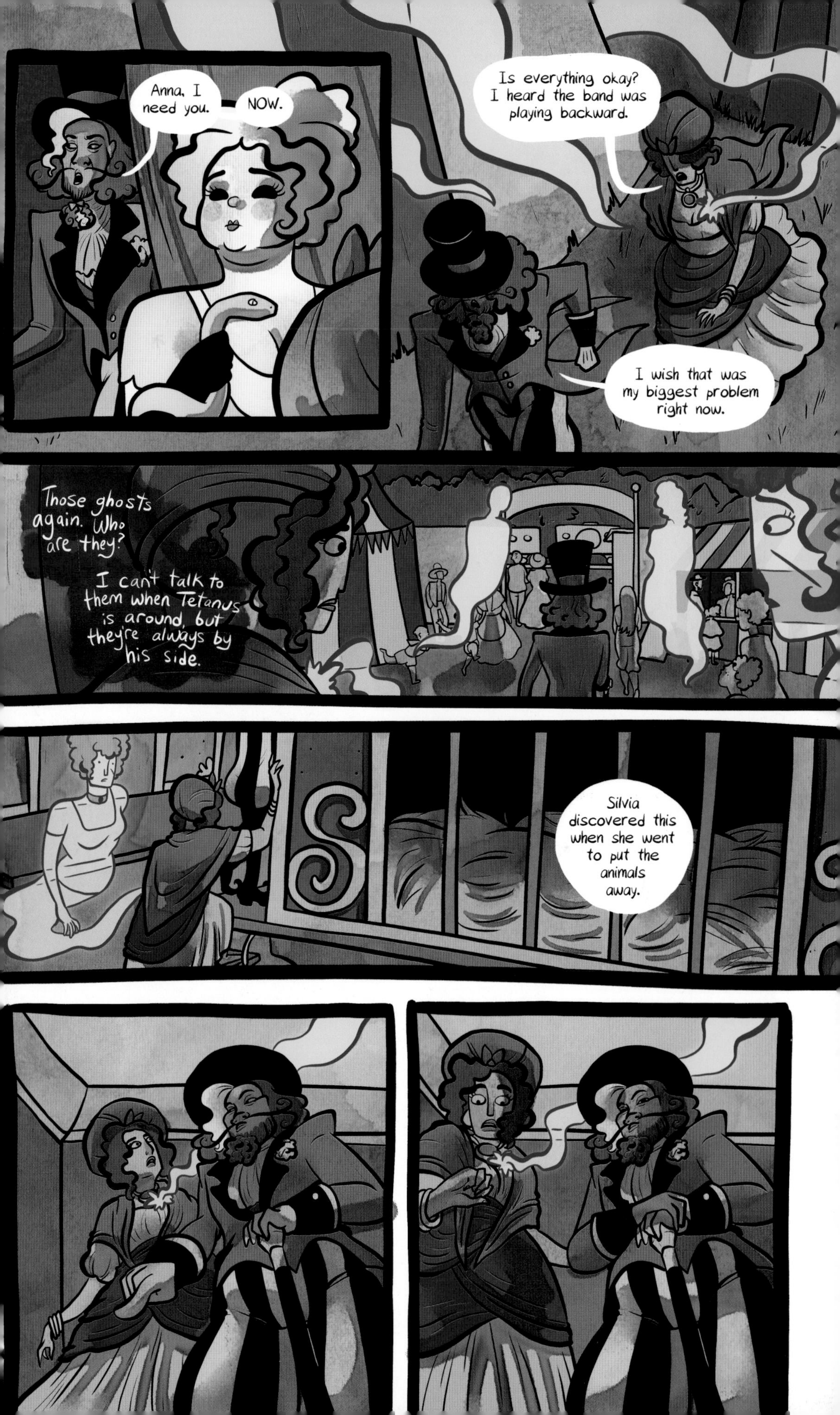
Anna, I need you.
NOW.
Is everything okay? I heard the band was playing backward.
I wish that was my biggest problem right now.
Those ghosts again. Who are they?
I can't talk to them when Tetanus is around, but they're always by his side.
Silvia discovered this when she went to put the animals away.

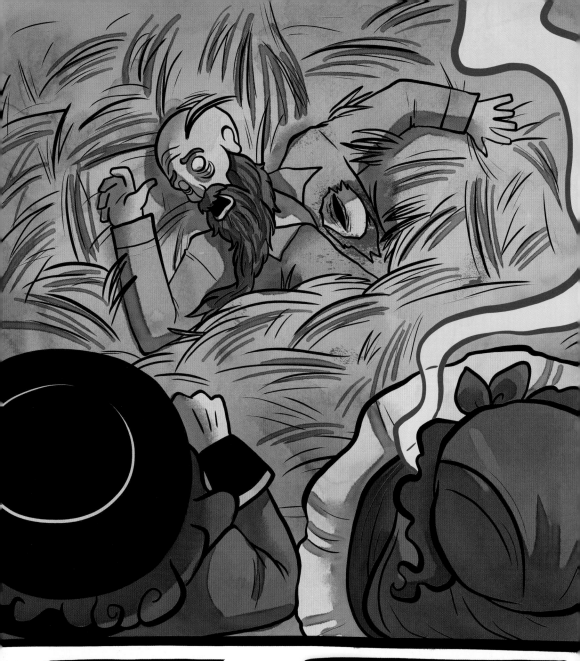

We have to bury him before anyone else finds out.

You've got five minutes to look for clues.

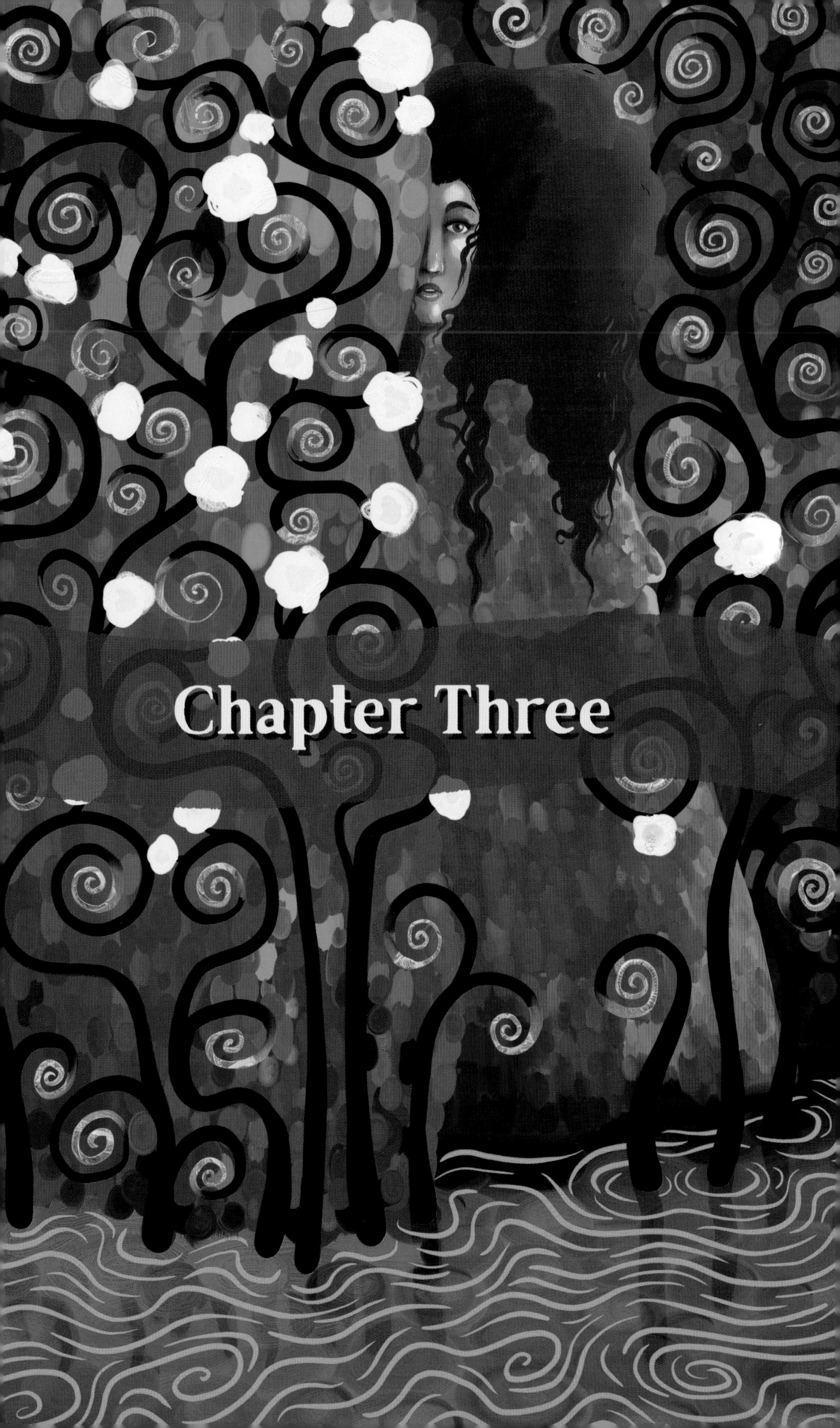

Chapter Three

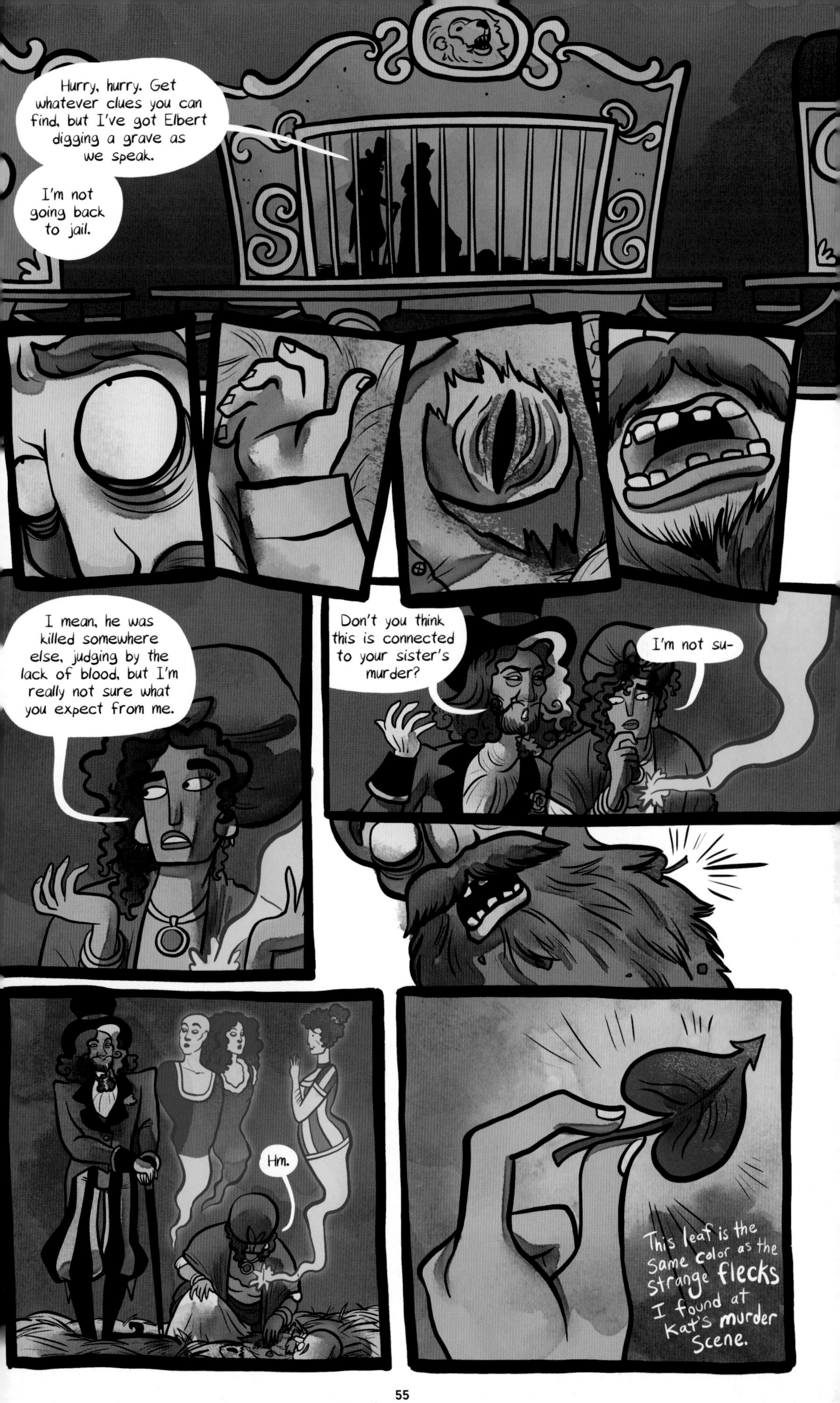
Hurry, hurry. Get whatever clues you can find, but I've got Elbert digging a grave as we speak.
I'm not going back to jail.
I mean, he was killed somewhere else, judging by the lack of blood, but I'm really not sure what you expect from me.
Don't you think this is connected to your sister's murder?
I'm not su-
Hm.
This leaf is the same color as the strange flecks I found at Kat's murder scene.

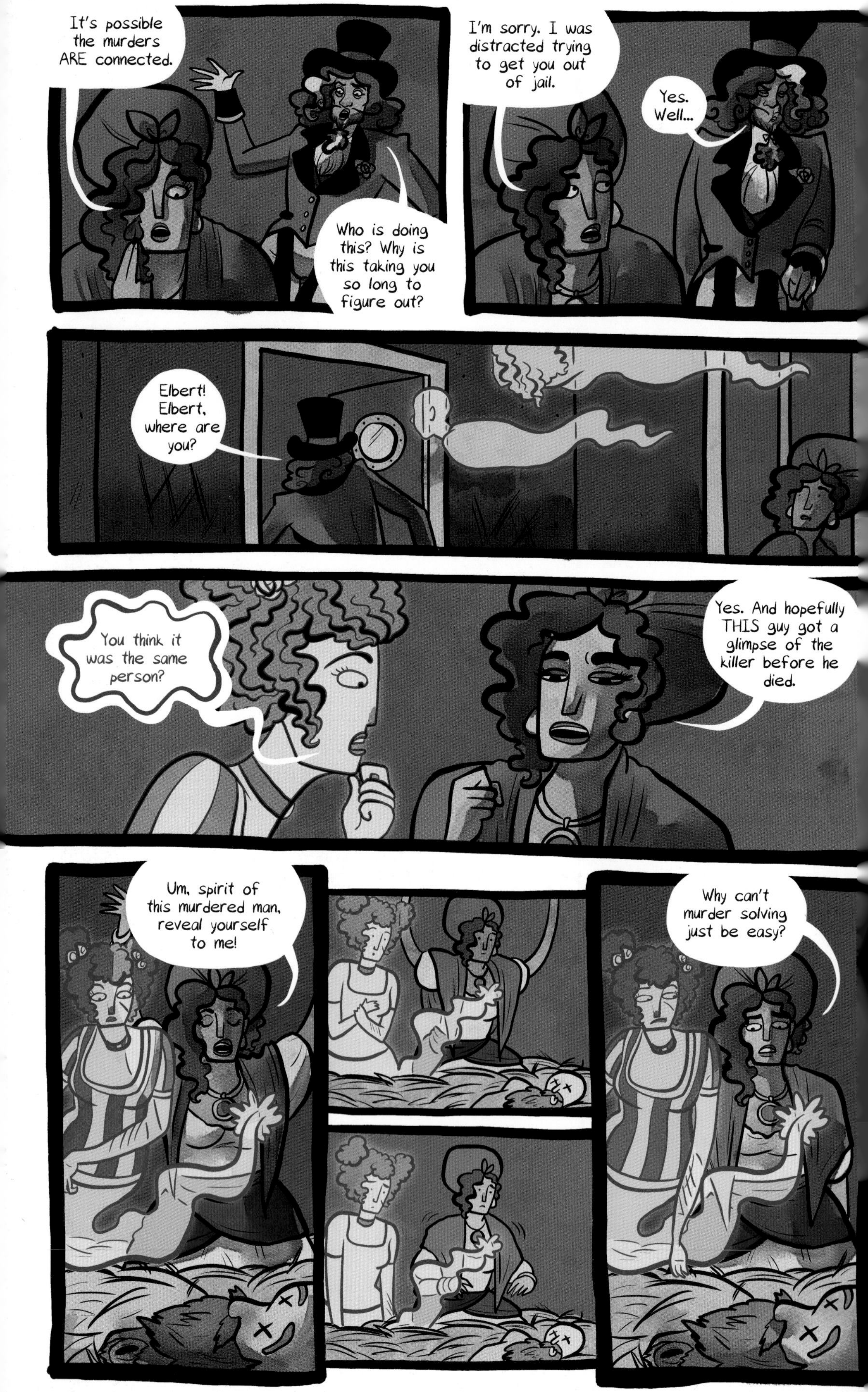
It's possible the murders ARE connected.
Who is doing this? Why is this taking you so long to figure out?
I'm sorry. I was distracted trying to get you out of jail.
Yes. Well...
Elbert! Elbert, where are you?
You think it was the same person?
Yes. And hopefully THIS guy got a glimpse of the killer before he died.
Um, spirit of this murdered man, reveal yourself to me!
Why can't murder solving just be easy?

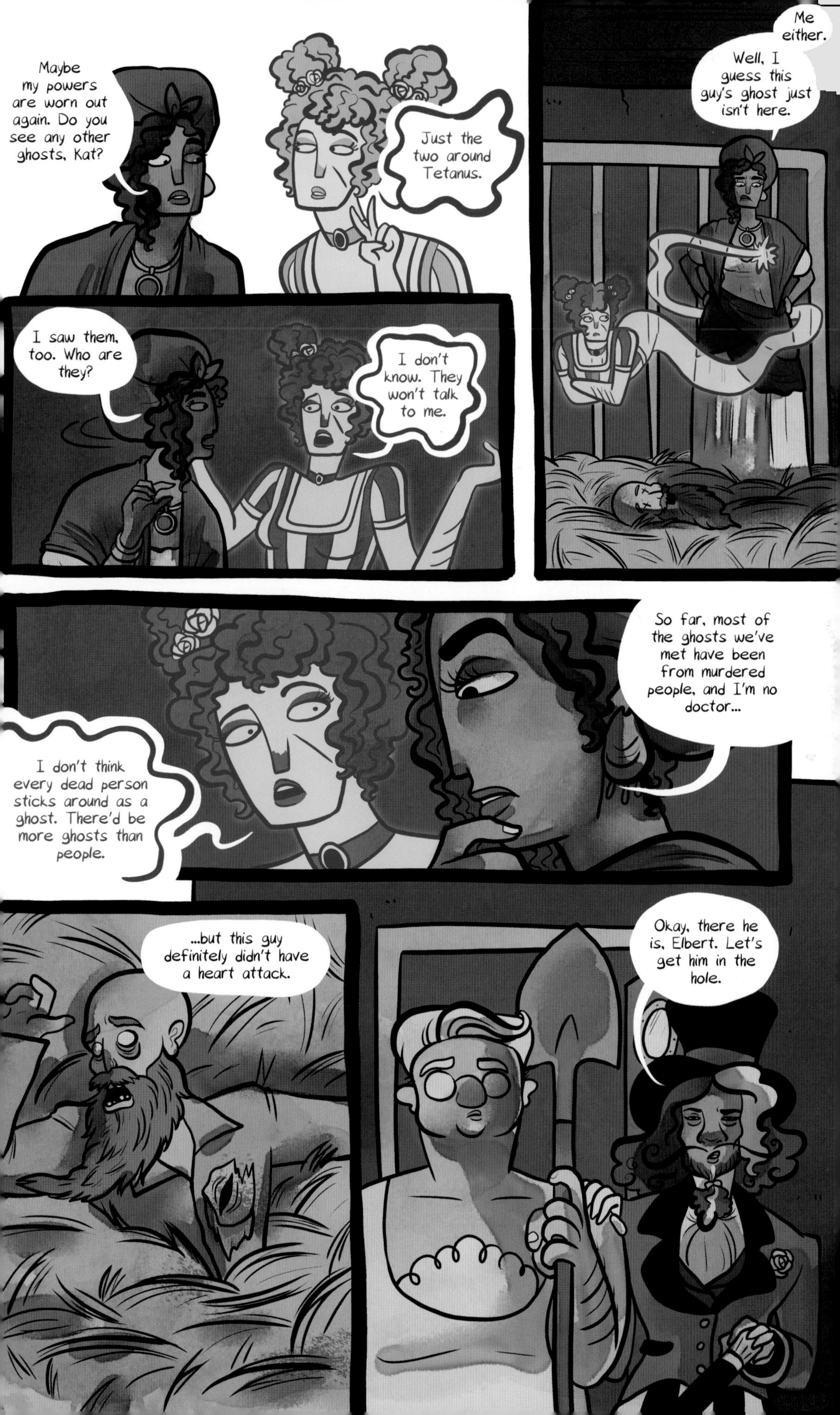

Maybe my powers are worn out again. Do you see any other ghosts, Kat?
Just the two around Tetanus.
Me either.
Well, I guess this guy's ghost just isn't here.
I saw them, too. Who are they?
I don't know. They won't talk to me.
So far, most of the ghosts we've met have been from murdered people, and I'm no doctor...
I don't think every dead person sticks around as a ghost. There'd be more ghosts than people.
...but this guy definitely didn't have a heart attack.
Okay, there he is, Elbert. Let's get him in the hole.

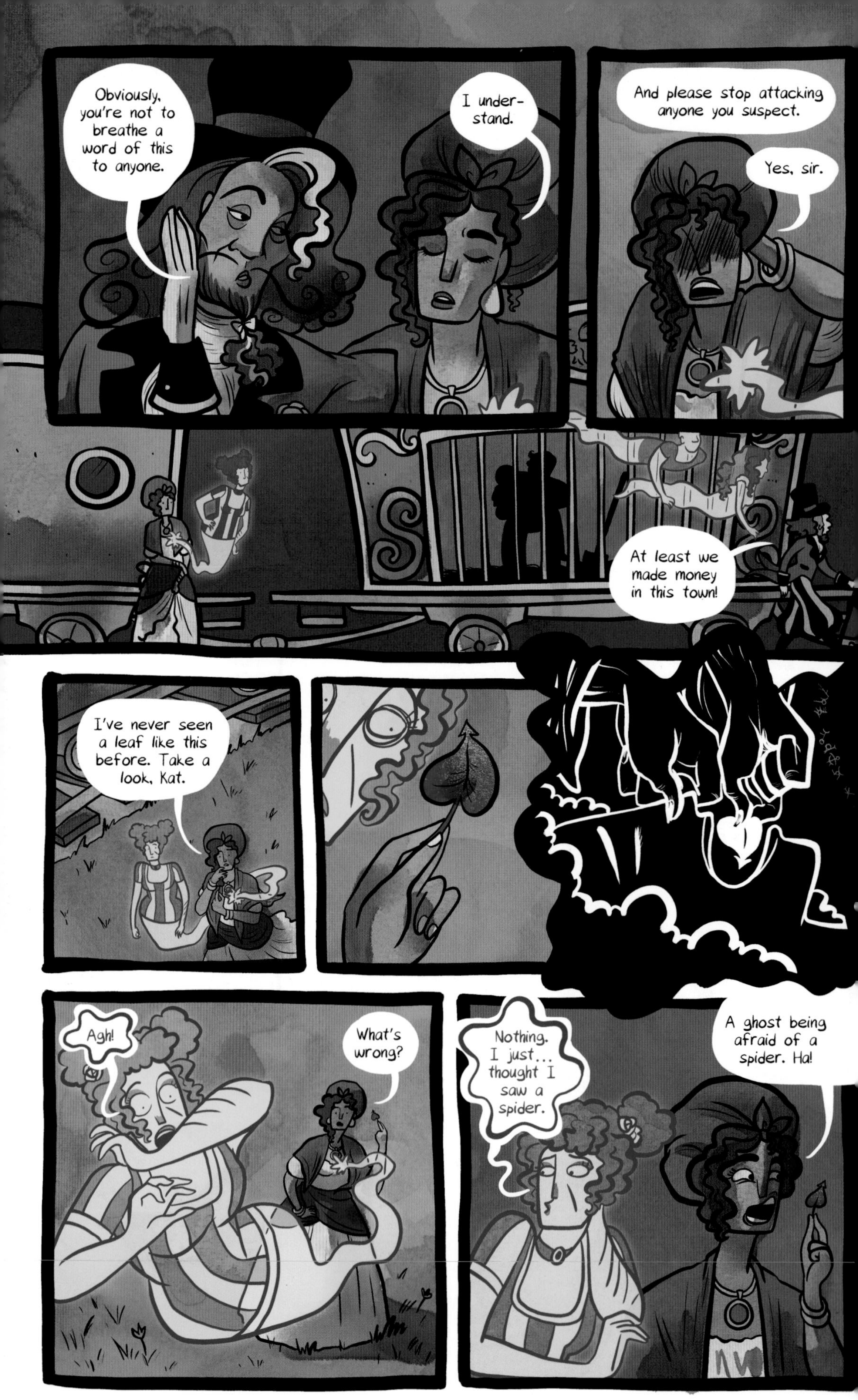
Obviously, you're not to breathe a word of this to anyone.
I under-stand.
And please stop attacking anyone you suspect.
Yes, sir.
At least we made money in this town!
I've never seen a leaf like this before. Take a look, Kat.
Agh!
What's wrong?
Nothing. I just... thought I saw a spider.
A ghost being afraid of a spider. Ha!

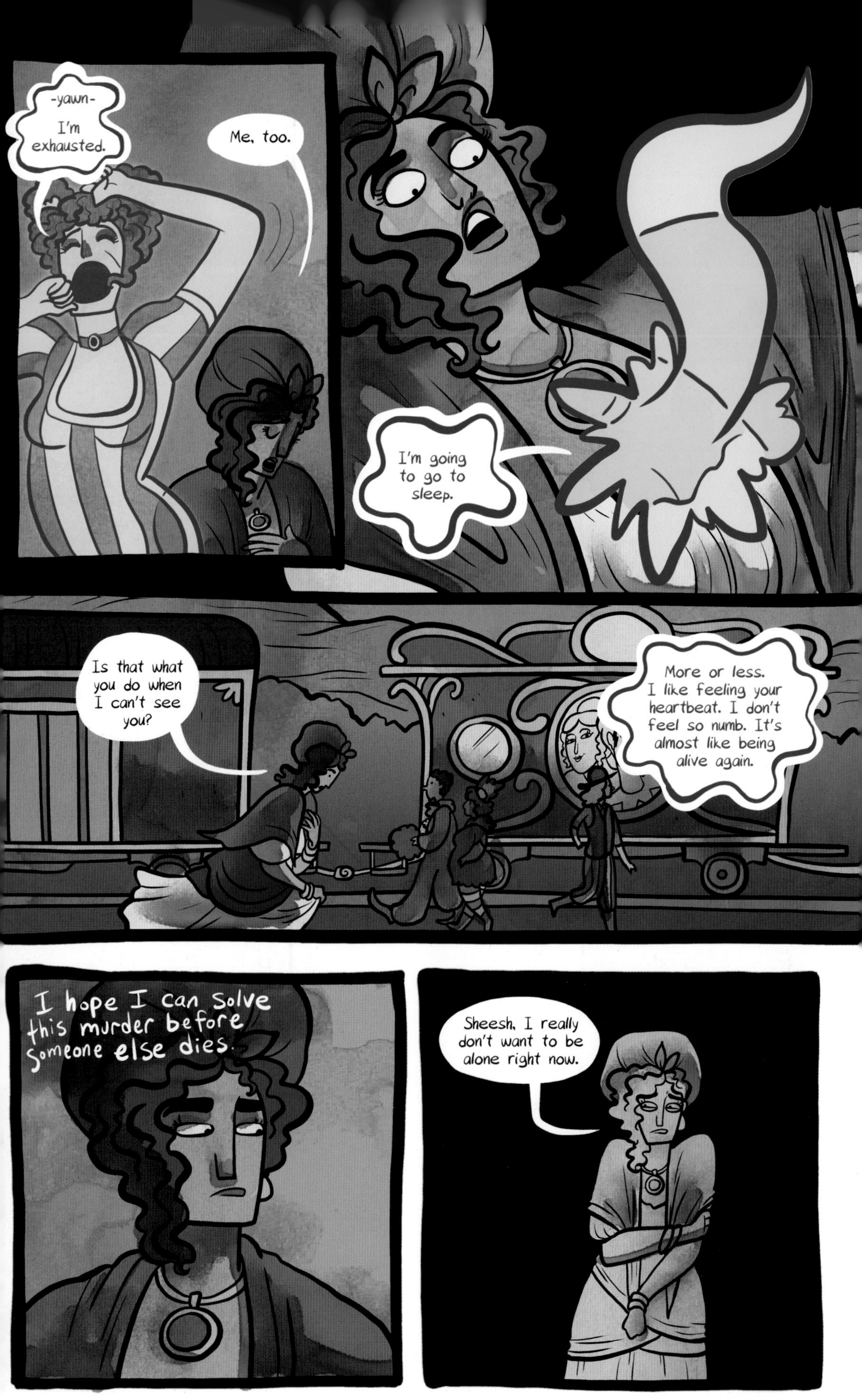

-yawn- I'm exhausted.
Me, too.
I'm going to go to sleep.
Is that what you do when I can't see you?
More or less. I like feeling your heartbeat. I don't feel so numb. It's almost like being alive again.
I hope I can solve this murder before someone else dies.
Sheesh, I really don't want to be alone right now.

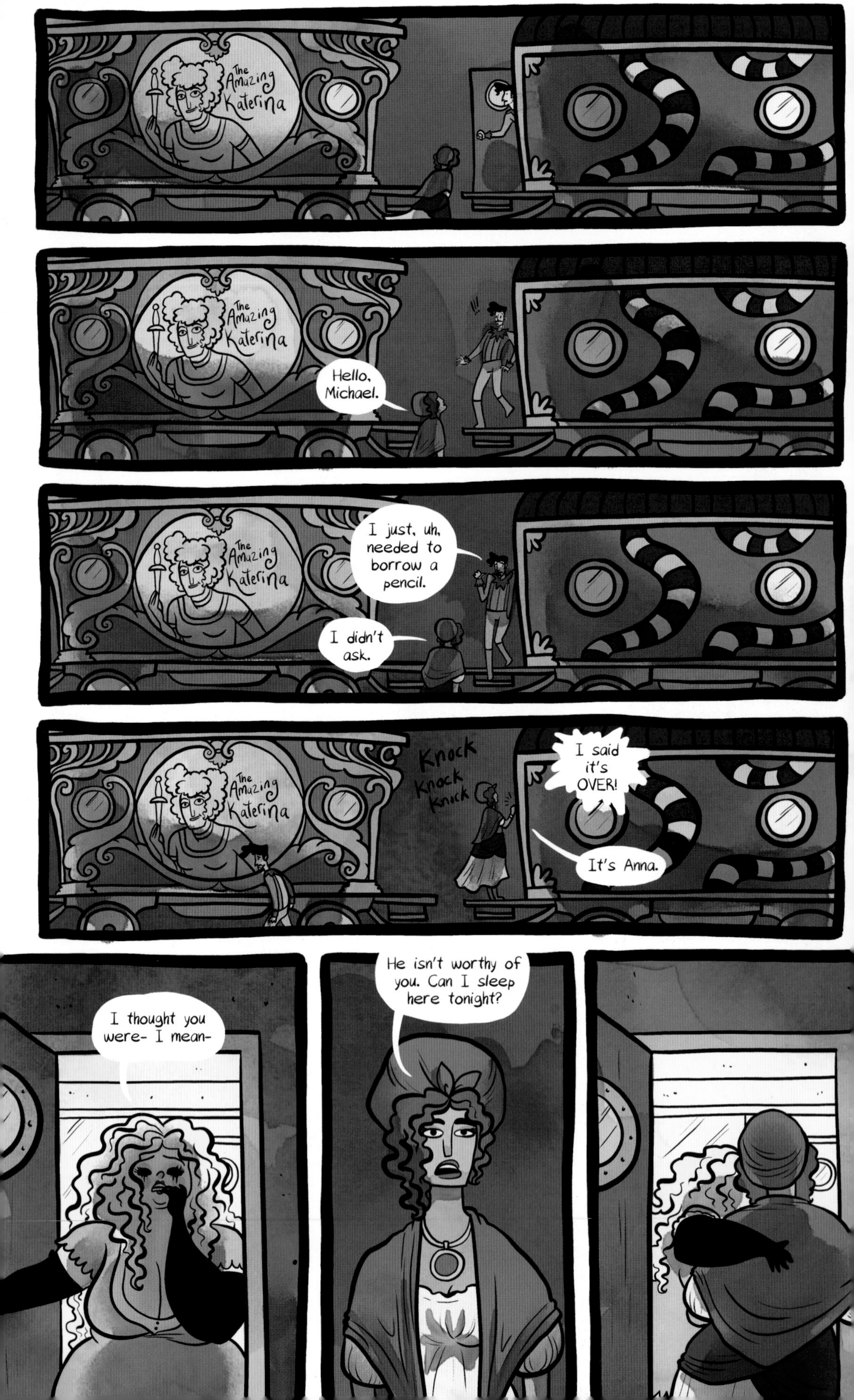

The Amazing Katerina
The Amazing Katerina
!!
Hello, Michael.
The Amazing Katerina
I just, uh, needed to borrow a pencil.
I didn't ask.
The Amazing Katerina
Knock Knock Knock
I said it's OVER!
It's Anna.
I thought you were- I mean-
He isn't worthy of you. Can I sleep here tonight?

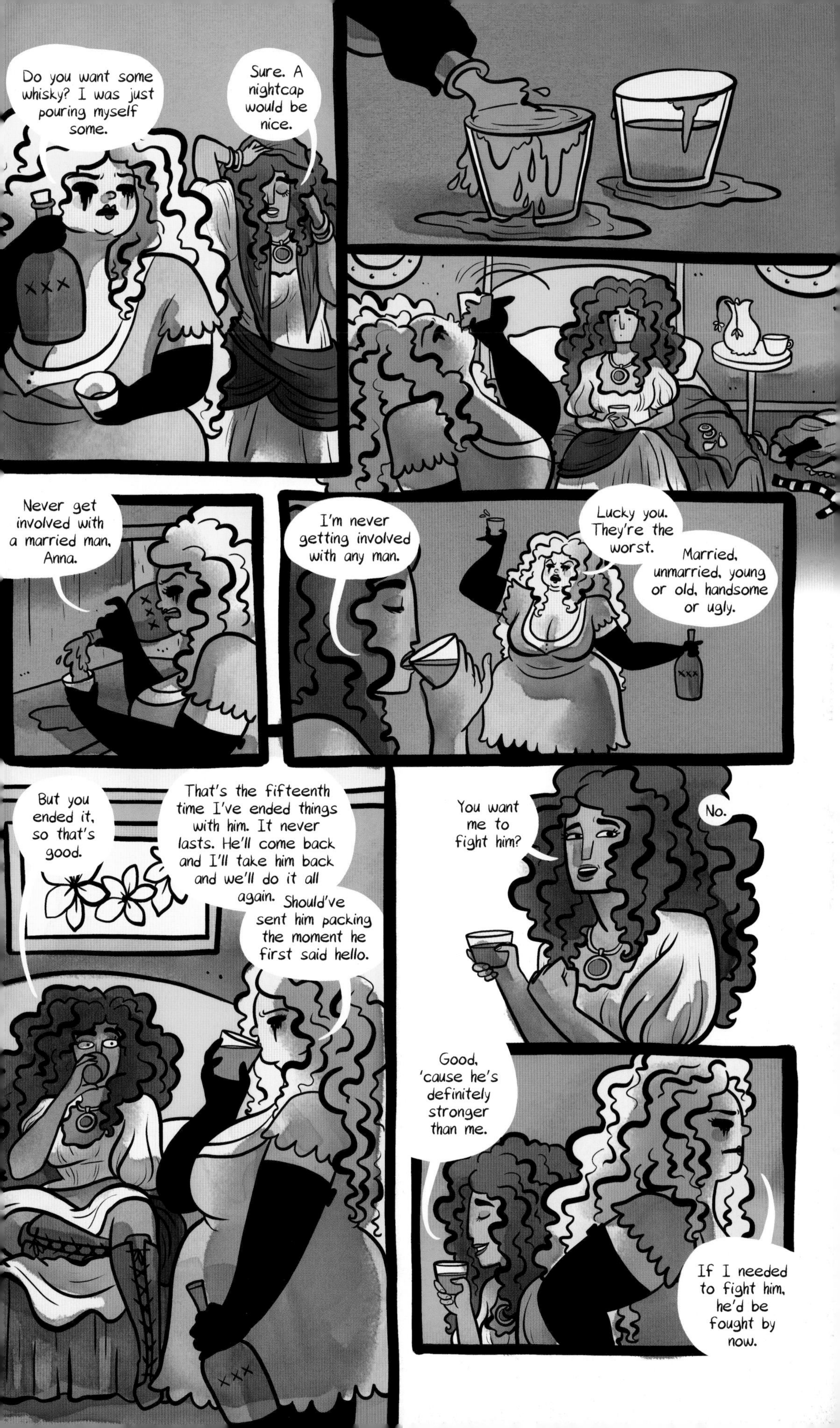
Do you want some whisky? I was just pouring myself some.
Sure. A nightcap would be nice.
Never get involved with a married man, Anna.
I'm never getting involved with any man.
Lucky you. They're the worst.
Married, unmarried, young or old, handsome or ugly.
But you ended it, so that's good.
That's the fifteenth time I've ended things with him. It never lasts. He'll come back and I'll take him back and we'll do it all again.
Should've sent him packing the moment he first said hello.
You want me to fight him?
No.
Good, 'cause he's definitely stronger than me.
If I needed to fight him, he'd be fought by now.

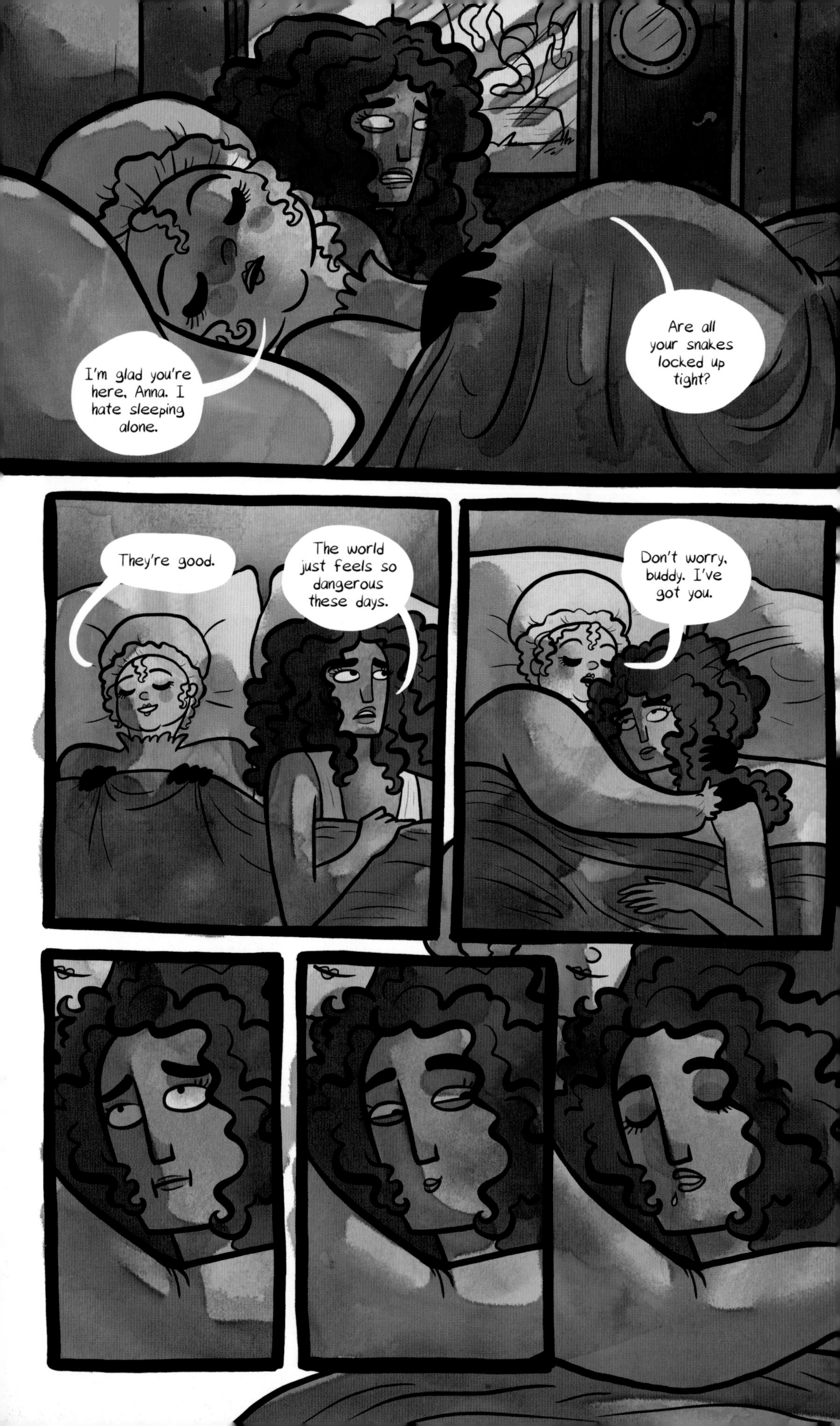
I'm glad you're here, Anna. I hate sleeping alone.
Are all your snakes locked up tight?
They're good.
The world just feels so dangerous these days.
Don't worry, buddy. I've got you.

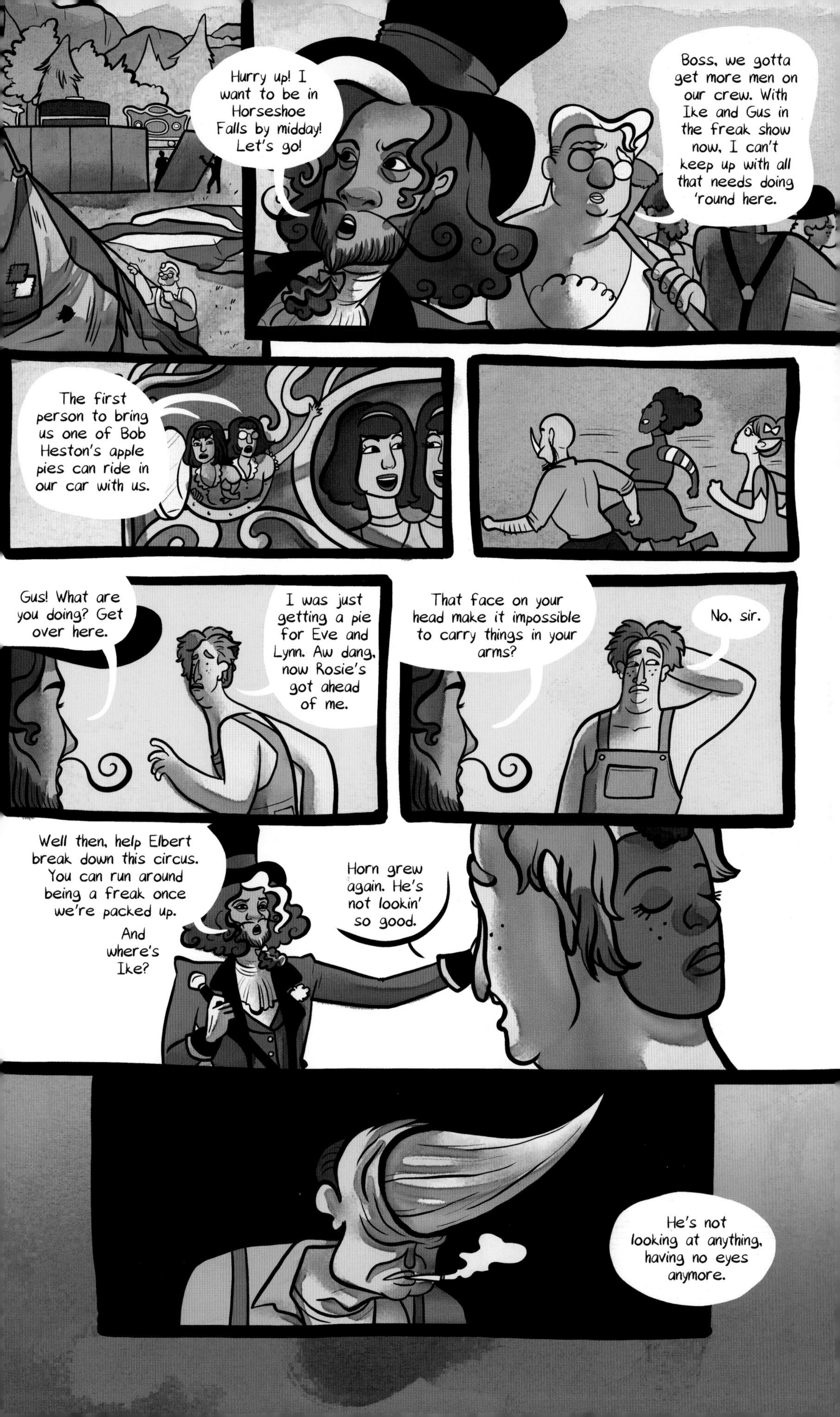
Hurry up! I want to be in Horseshoe Falls by midday! Let's go!
Boss, we gotta get more men on our crew. With Ike and Gus in the freak show now, I can't keep up with all that needs doing 'round here.
The first person to bring us one of Bob Heston's apple pies can ride in our car with us.
Gus! What are you doing? Get over here.
I was just getting a pie for Eve and Lynn. Aw dang, now Rosie's got ahead of me.
That face on your head make it impossible to carry things in your arms?
No, sir.
Well then, help Elbert break down this circus. You can run around being a freak once we're packed up.
And where's Ike?
Horn grew again. He's not lookin' so good.
He's not looking at anything, having no eyes anymore.

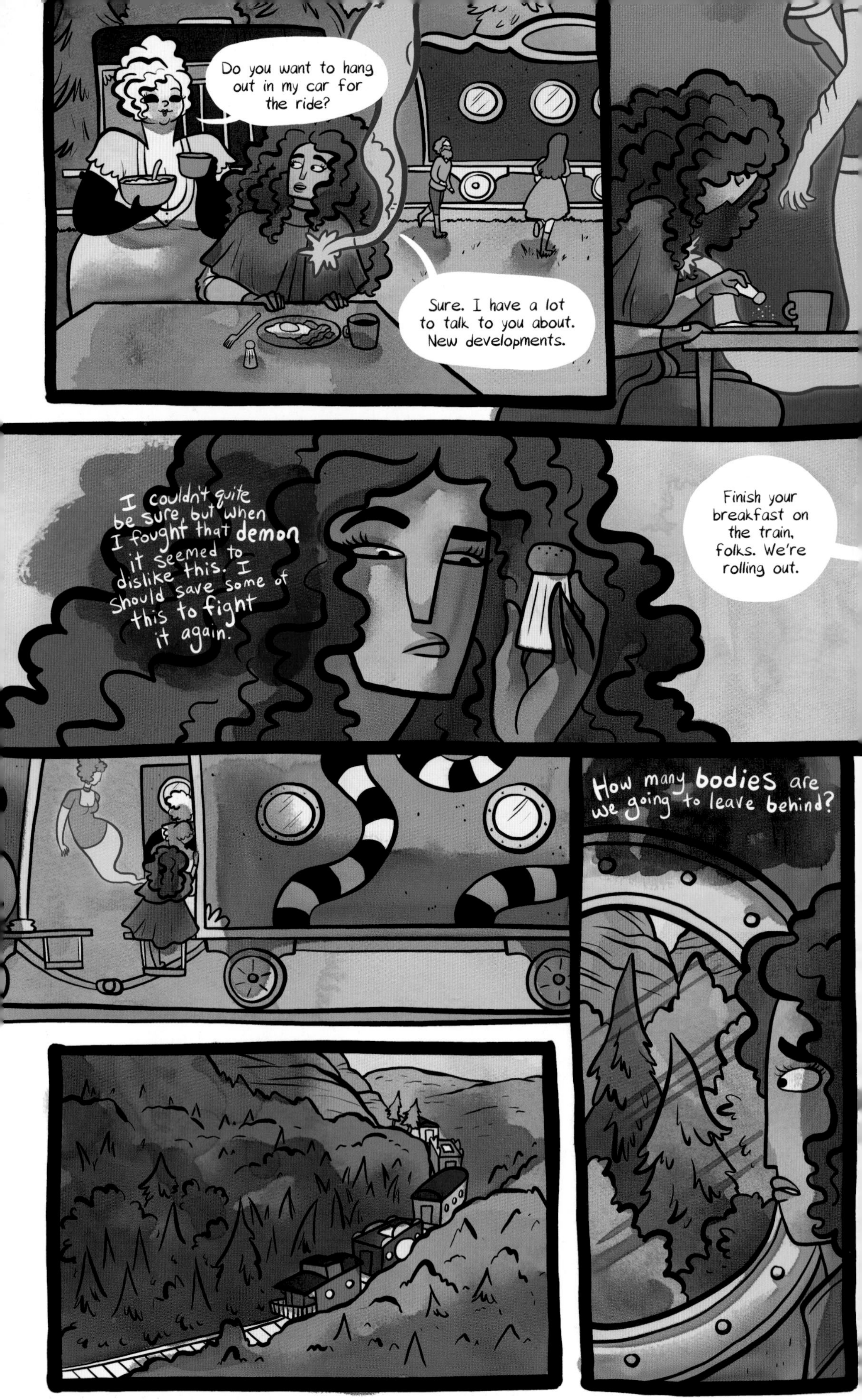

Do you want to hang out in my car for the ride?
Sure. I have a lot to talk to you about. New developments.
I couldn't quite be sure, but when I fought that **demon** it seemed to dislike this. I should save some of this to fight it again.
Finish your breakfast on the train, folks. We're rolling out.
How many **bodies** are we going to leave behind?

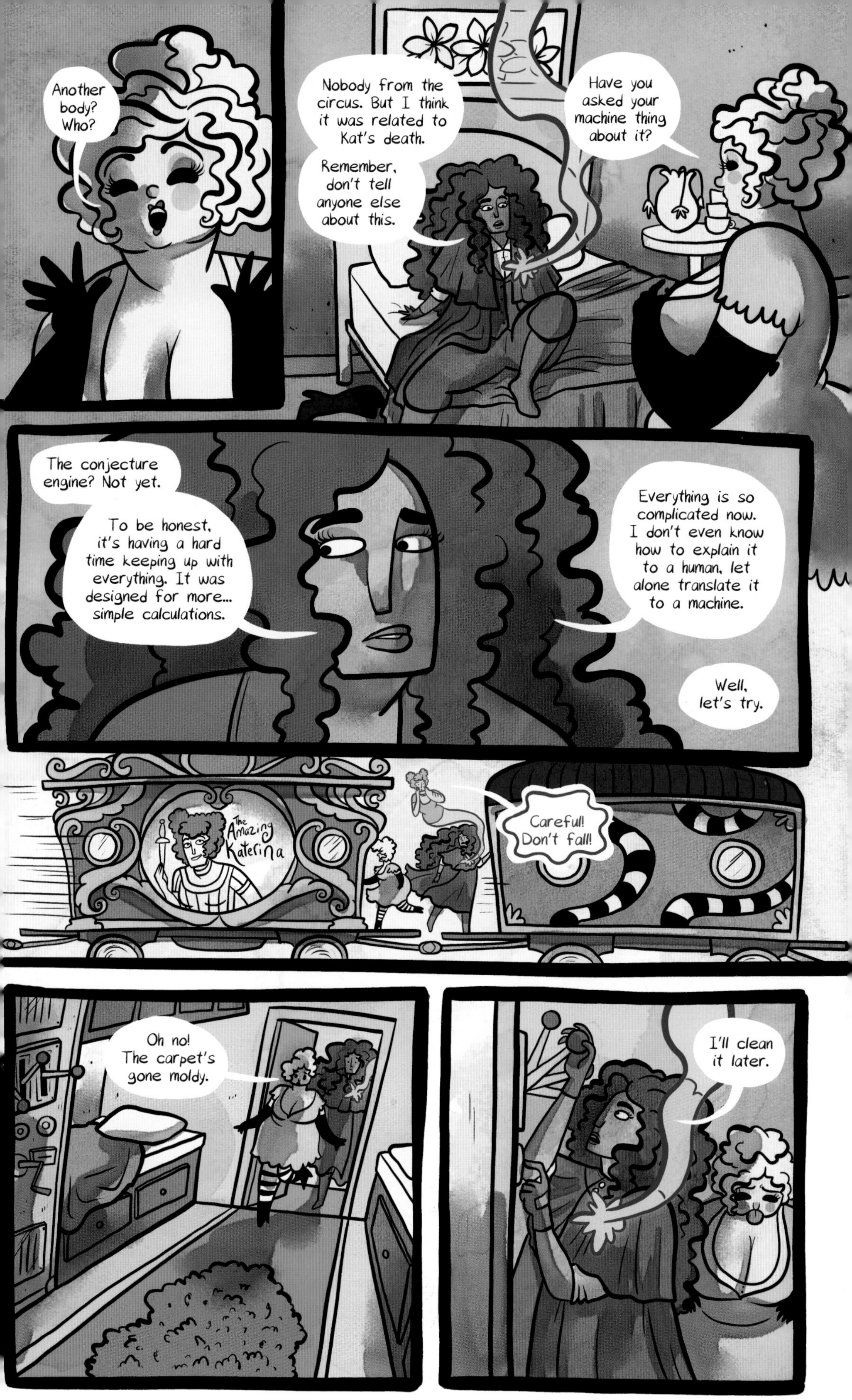
Another body? Who?
Nobody from the circus. But I think it was related to Kat's death.
Remember, don't tell anyone else about this.
Have you asked your machine thing about it?
The conjecture engine? Not yet.
To be honest, it's having a hard time keeping up with everything. It was designed for more... simple calculations.
Everything is so complicated now. I don't even know how to explain it to a human, let alone translate it to a machine.
Well, let's try.
The Amazing Katerina
Careful! Don't fall!
Oh no! The carpet's gone moldy.
I'll clean it later.

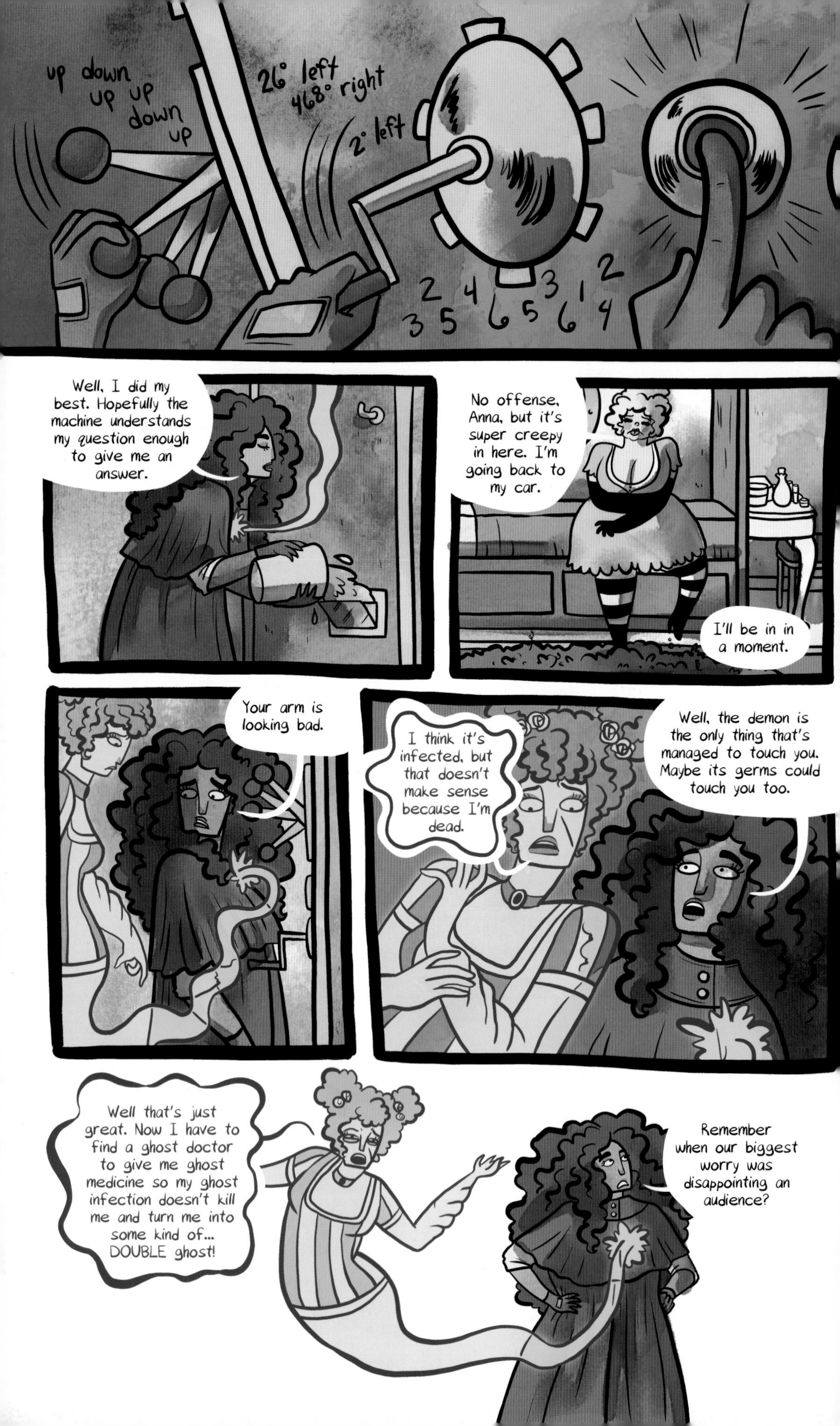
up down
up up
down
up
26° left
468° right
2° left
2 3 5 4 6 5 3 6 1 2 4
Well, I did my best. Hopefully the machine understands my question enough to give me an answer.
No offense, Anna, but it's super creepy in here. I'm going back to my car.
I'll be in in a moment.
Your arm is looking bad.
I think it's infected, but that doesn't make sense because I'm dead.
Well, the demon is the only thing that's managed to touch you. Maybe its germs could touch you too.
Well that's just great. Now I have to find a ghost doctor to give me ghost medicine so my ghost infection doesn't kill me and turn me into some kind of... DOUBLE ghost!
Remember when our biggest worry was disappointing an audience?

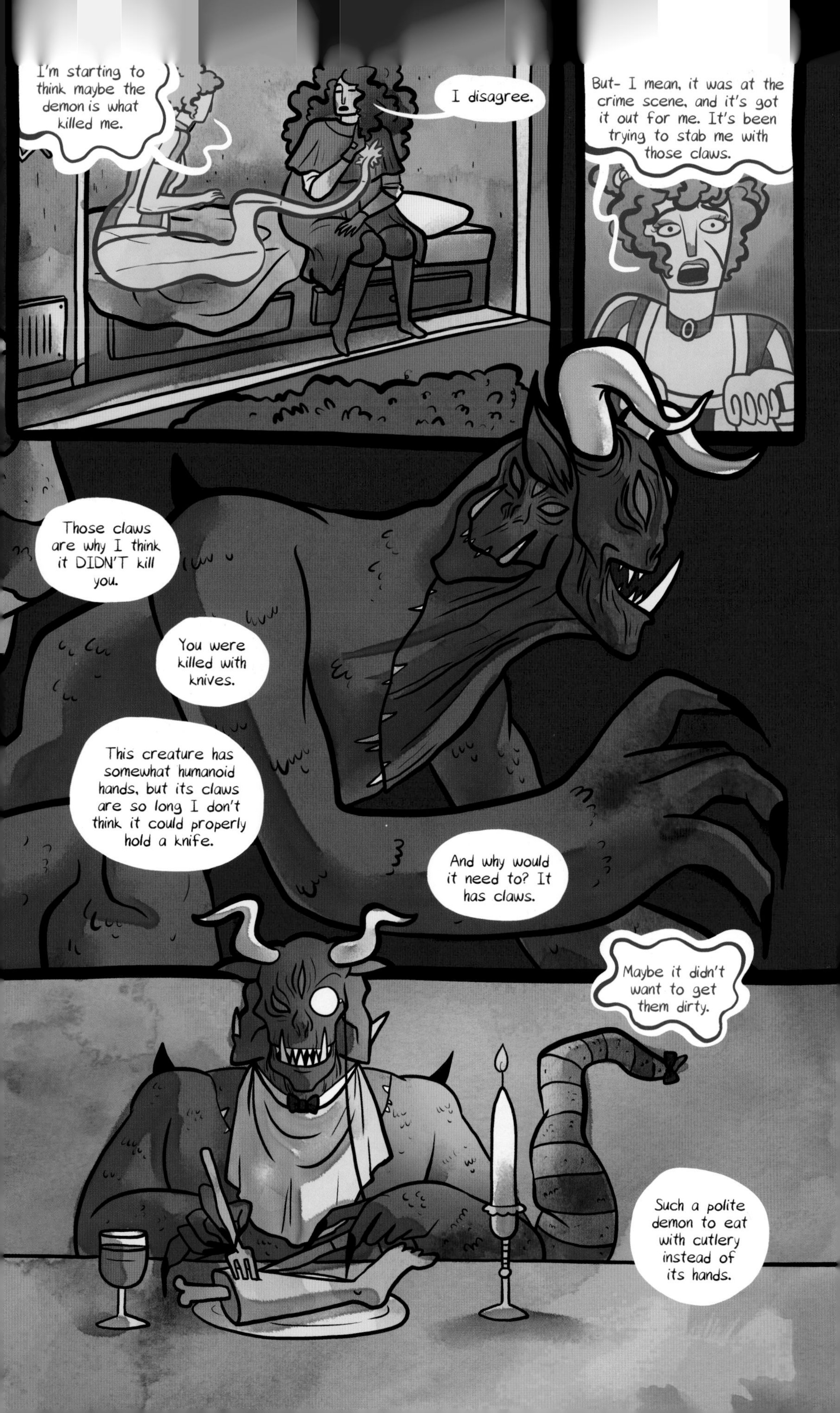

I'm starting to think maybe the demon is what killed me.
I disagree.
But- I mean, it was at the crime scene, and it's got it out for me. It's been trying to stab me with those claws.
Those claws are why I think it DIDN'T kill you.
You were killed with knives.
This creature has somewhat humanoid hands, but its claws are so long I don't think it could properly hold a knife.
And why would it need to? It has claws.
Maybe it didn't want to get them dirty.
Such a polite demon to eat with cutlery instead of its hands.

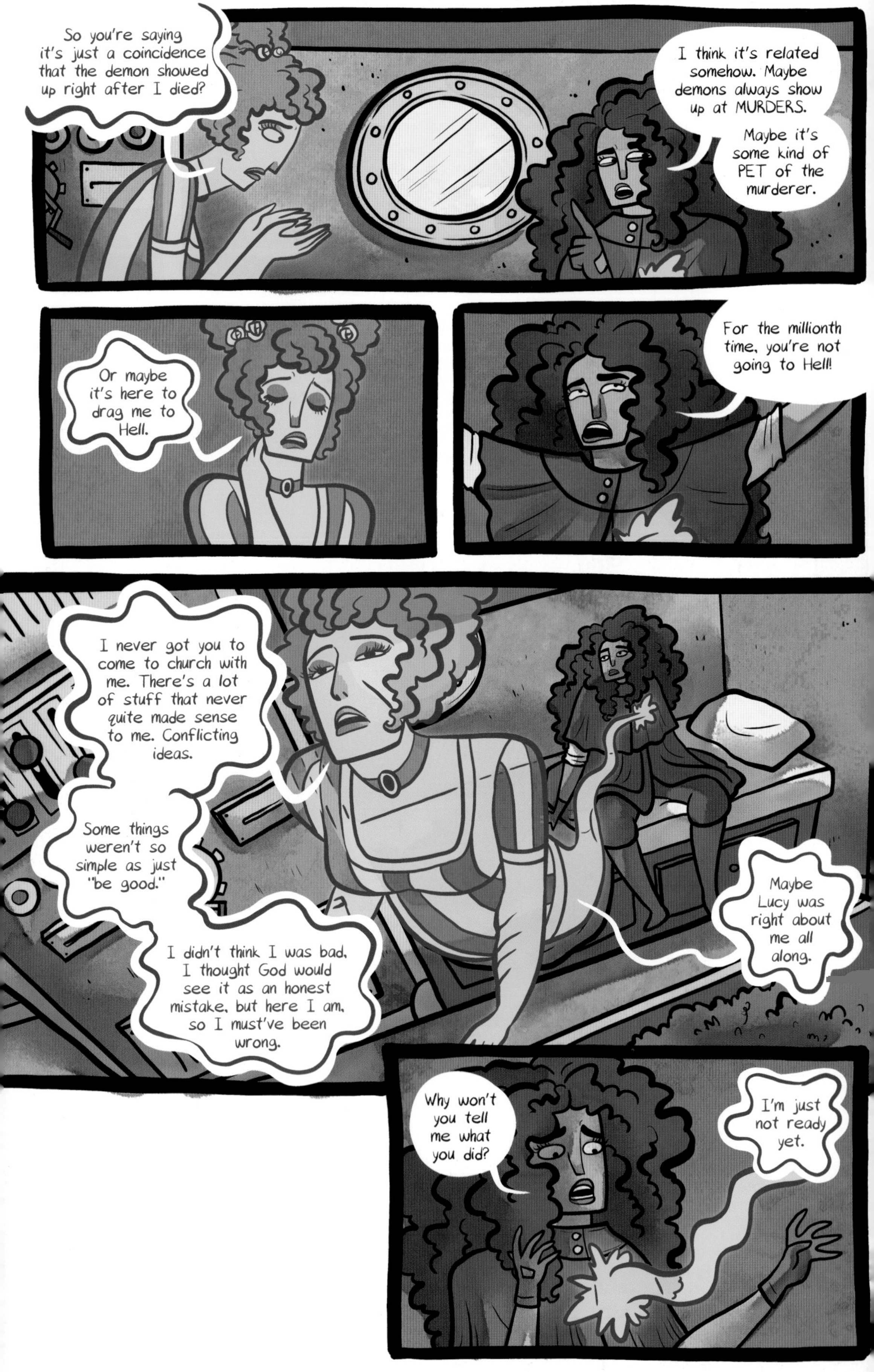
So you're saying it's just a coincidence that the demon showed up right after I died?
I think it's related somehow. Maybe demons always show up at MURDERS.
Maybe it's some kind of PET of the murderer.
Or maybe it's here to drag me to Hell.
For the millionth time, you're not going to Hell!
I never got you to come to church with me. There's a lot of stuff that never quite made sense to me. Conflicting ideas.
Some things weren't so simple as just "be good."
I didn't think I was bad. I thought God would see it as an honest mistake, but here I am, so I must've been wrong.
Maybe Lucy was right about me all along.
Why won't you tell me what you did?
I'm just not ready yet.

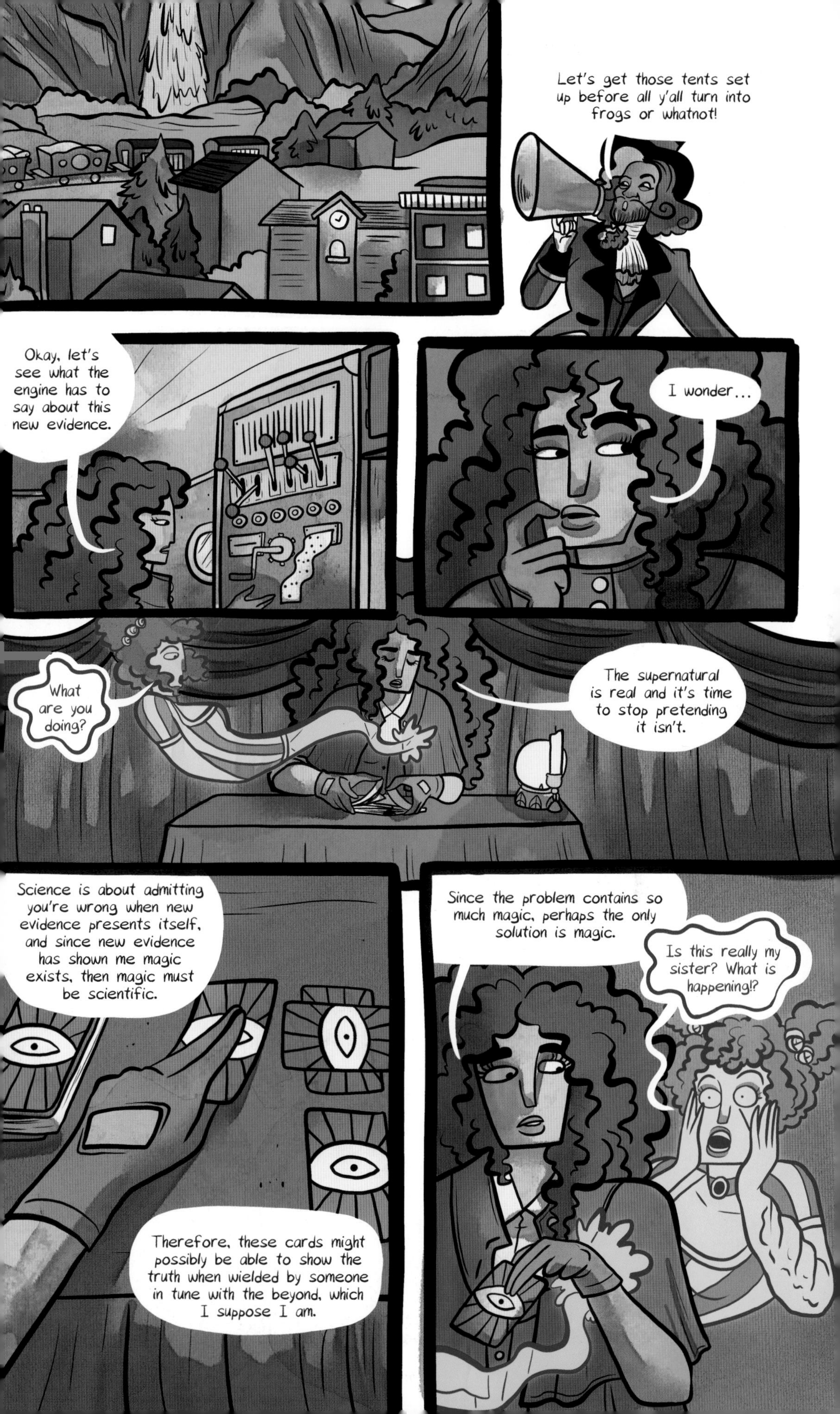
Let's get those tents set up before all y'all turn into frogs or whatnot!
Okay, let's see what the engine has to say about this new evidence.
I wonder...
What are you doing?
The supernatural is real and it's time to stop pretending it isn't.
Science is about admitting you're wrong when new evidence presents itself, and since new evidence has shown me magic exists, then magic must be scientific.
Therefore, these cards might possibly be able to show the truth when wielded by someone in tune with the beyond, which I suppose I am.
Since the problem contains so much magic, perhaps the only solution is magic.
Is this really my sister? What is happening!?

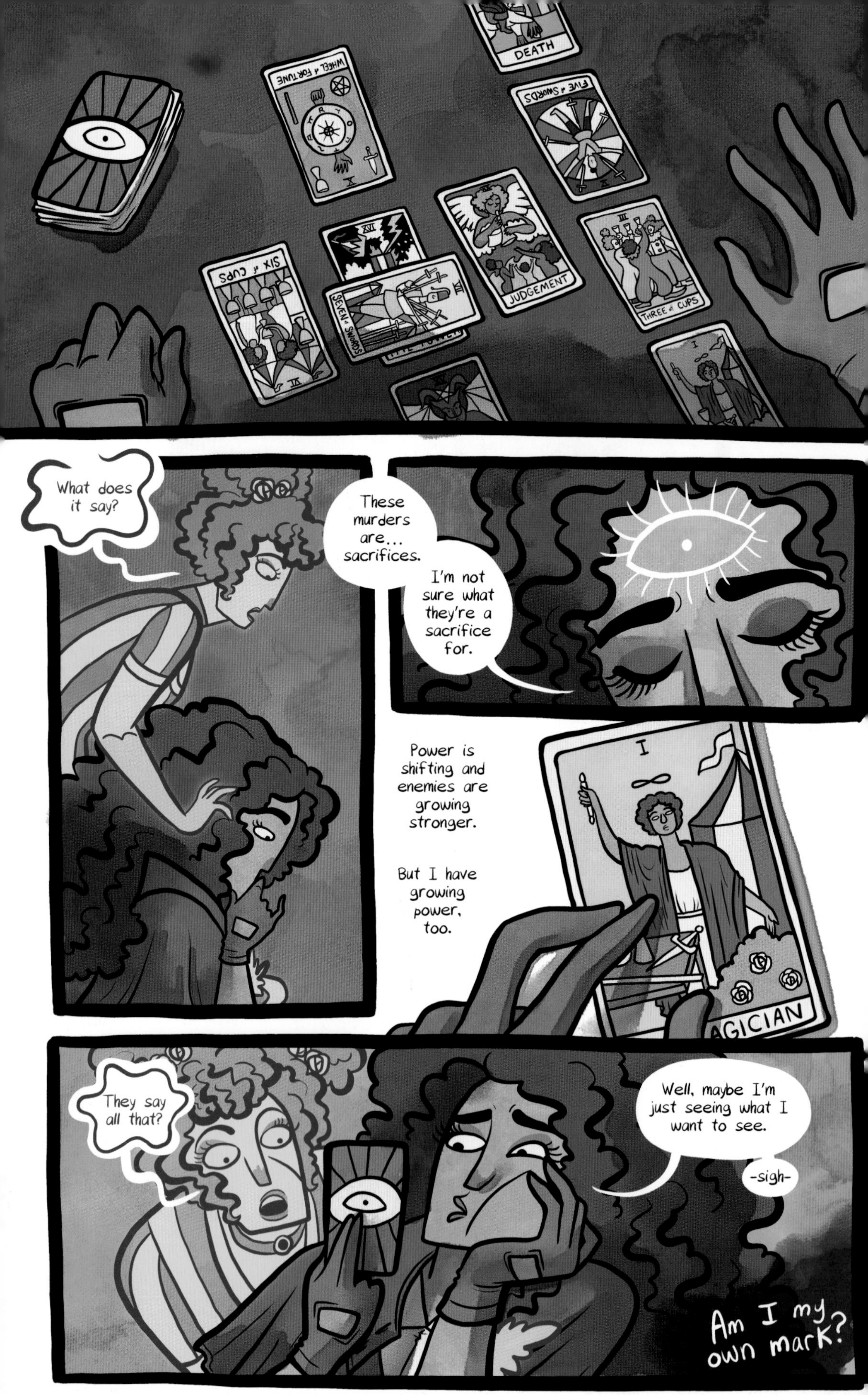
DEATH
WHEEL of FORTUNE
FIVE of SWORDS
SIX of CUPS
SEVEN of SWORDS
JUDGEMENT
THREE of CUPS
What does it say?
These murders are... sacrifices.
I'm not sure what they're a sacrifice for.
Power is shifting and enemies are growing stronger.
But I have growing power, too.
AGICIAN
They say all that?
Well, maybe I'm just seeing what I want to see.
-sigh-
Am I my own mark?

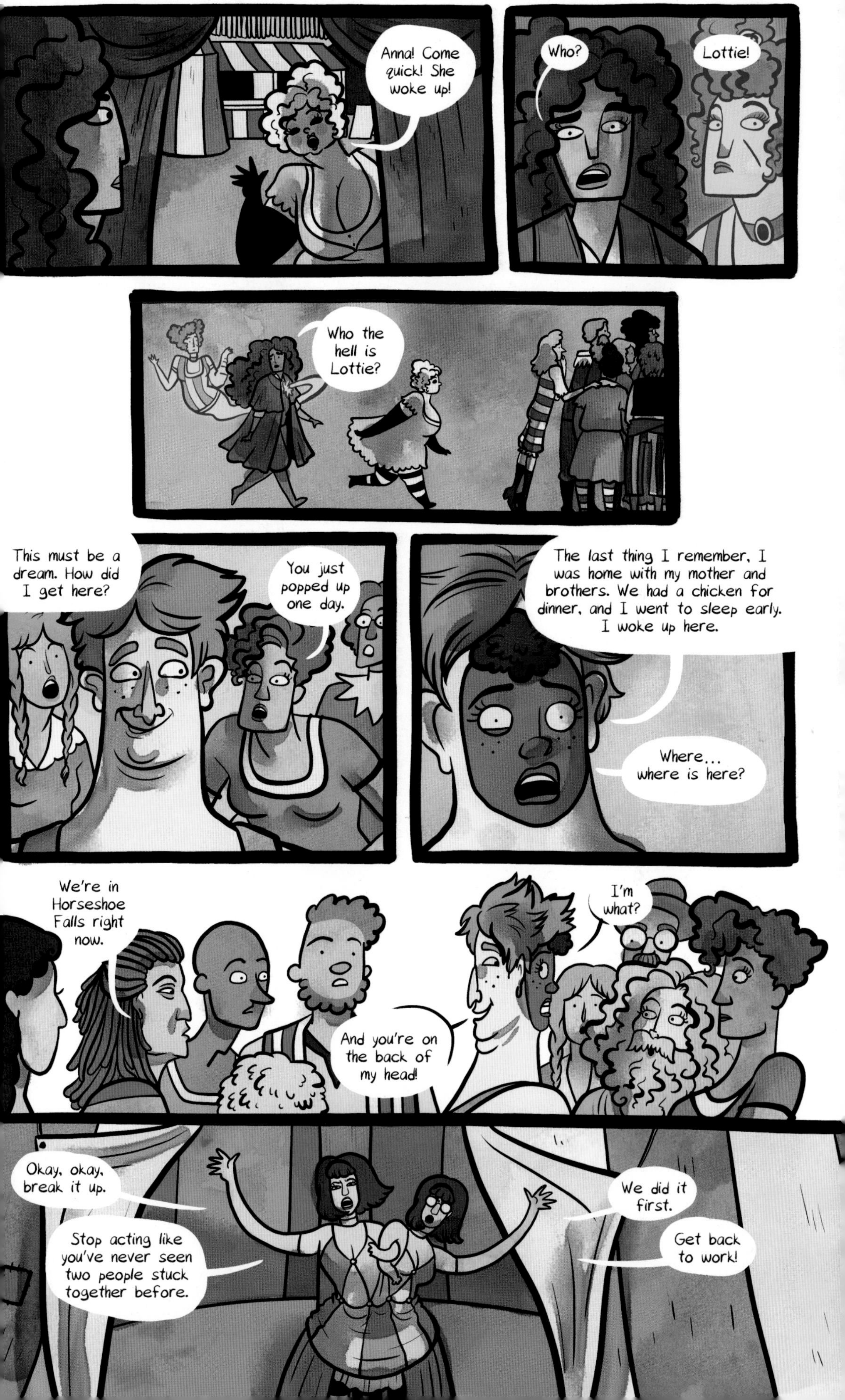
Anna! Come quick! She woke up!
Who?
Lottie!
Who the hell is Lottie?
This must be a dream. How did I get here?
You just popped up one day.
The last thing I remember, I was home with my mother and brothers. We had a chicken for dinner, and I went to sleep early. I woke up here.
Where... where is here?
We're in Horseshoe Falls right now.
I'm what?
And you're on the back of my head!
Okay, okay, break it up.
Stop acting like you've never seen two people stuck together before.
We did it first.
Get back to work!

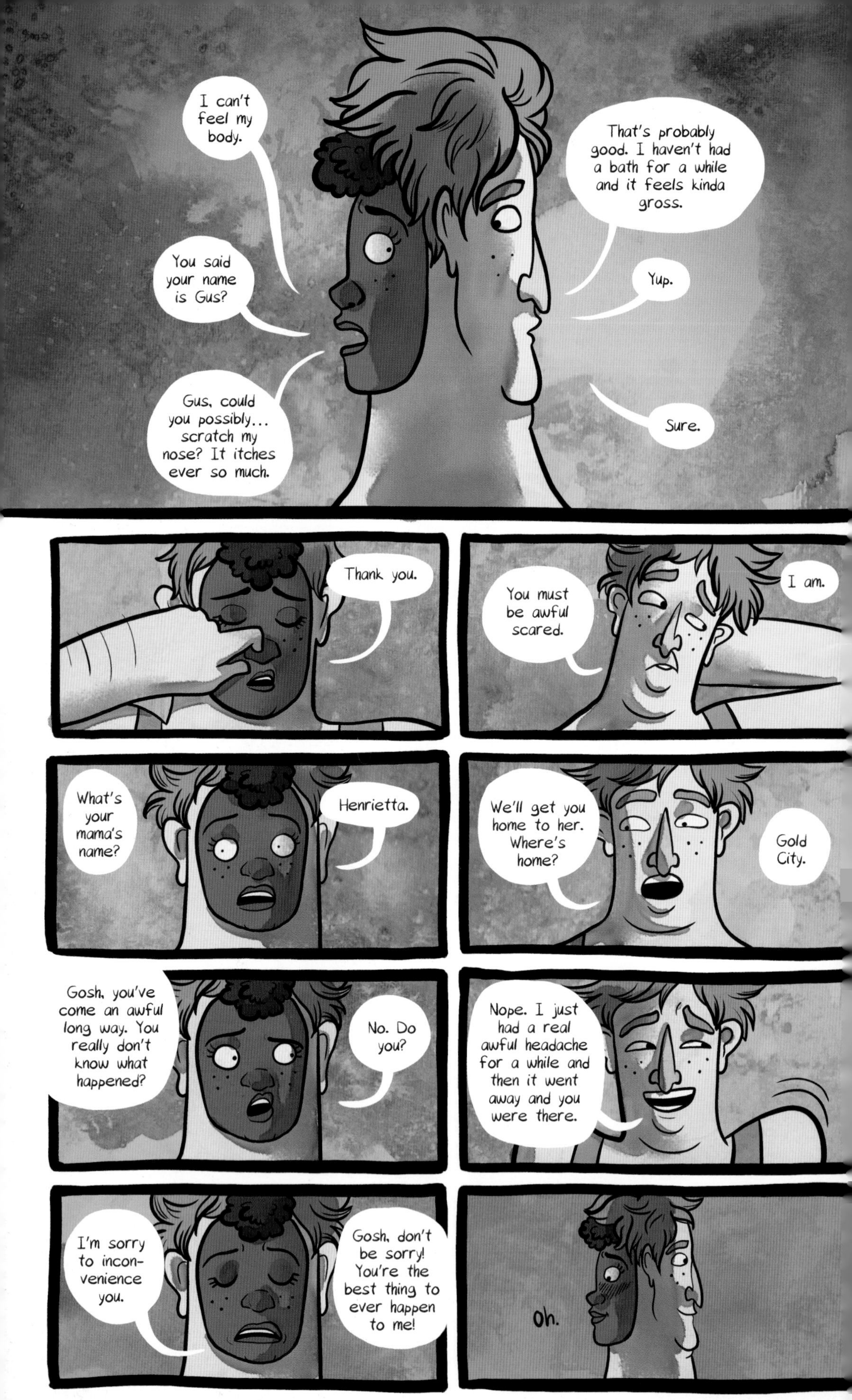
I can't feel my body.
That's probably good. I haven't had a bath for a while and it feels kinda gross.
You said your name is Gus?
Yup.
Gus, could you possibly... scratch my nose? It itches ever so much.
Sure.
Thank you.
You must be awful scared.
I am.
What's your mama's name?
Henrietta.
We'll get you home to her. Where's home?
Gold City.
Gosh, you've come an awful long way. You really don't know what happened?
No. Do you?
Nope. I just had a real awful headache for a while and then it went away and you were there.
I'm sorry to incon-venience you.
Gosh, don't be sorry! You're the best thing to ever happen to me!
Oh.

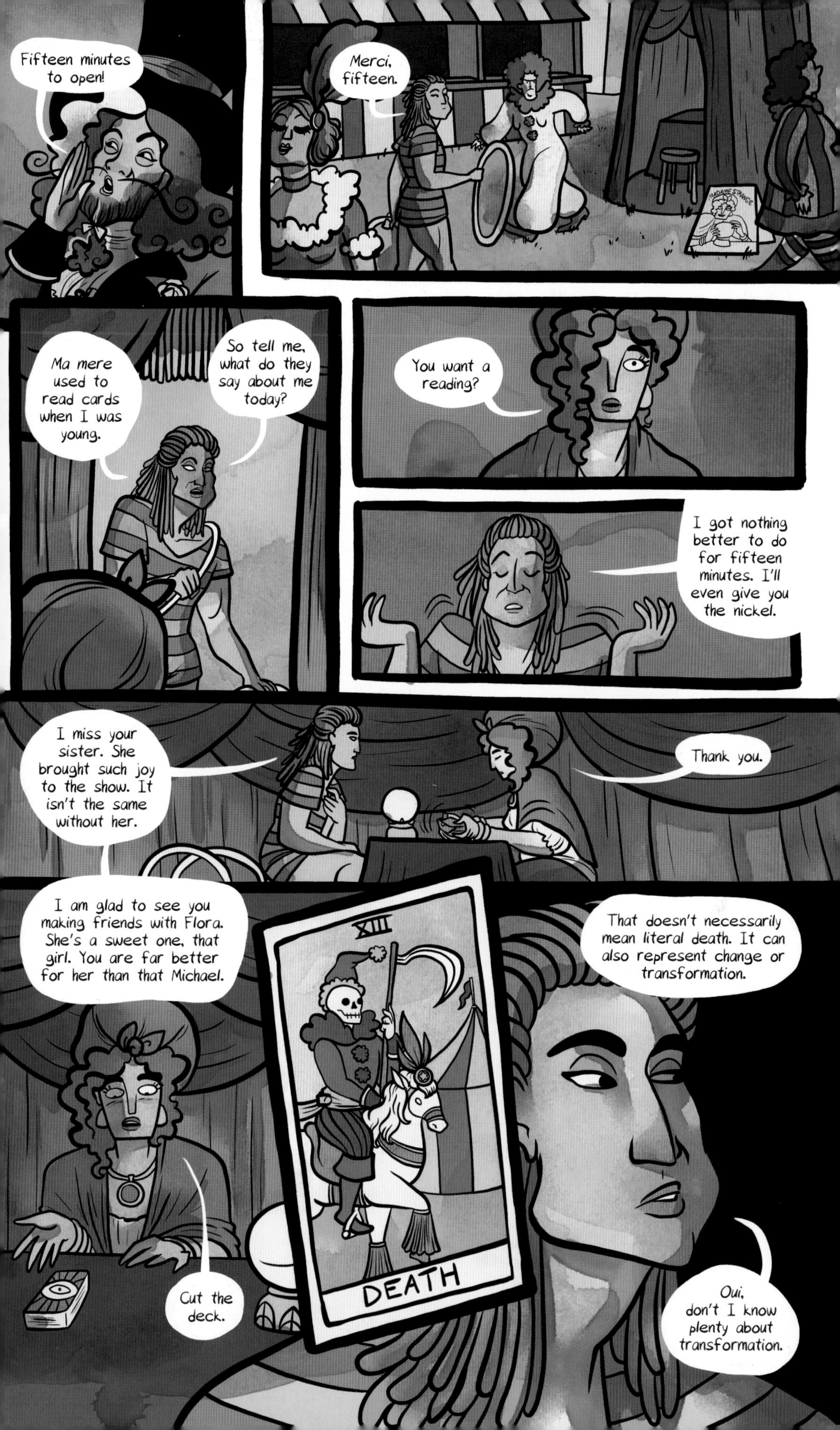

Fifteen minutes to open!
Merci, fifteen.
MADAME STRANGE
Ma mere used to read cards when I was young.
So tell me, what do they say about me today?
You want a reading?
I got nothing better to do for fifteen minutes. I'll even give you the nickel.
I miss your sister. She brought such joy to the show. It isn't the same without her.
Thank you.
I am glad to see you making friends with Flora. She's a sweet one, that girl. You are far better for her than that Michael.
Cut the deck.
XIII
DEATH
That doesn't necessarily mean literal death. It can also represent change or transformation.
Oui, don't I know plenty about transformation.

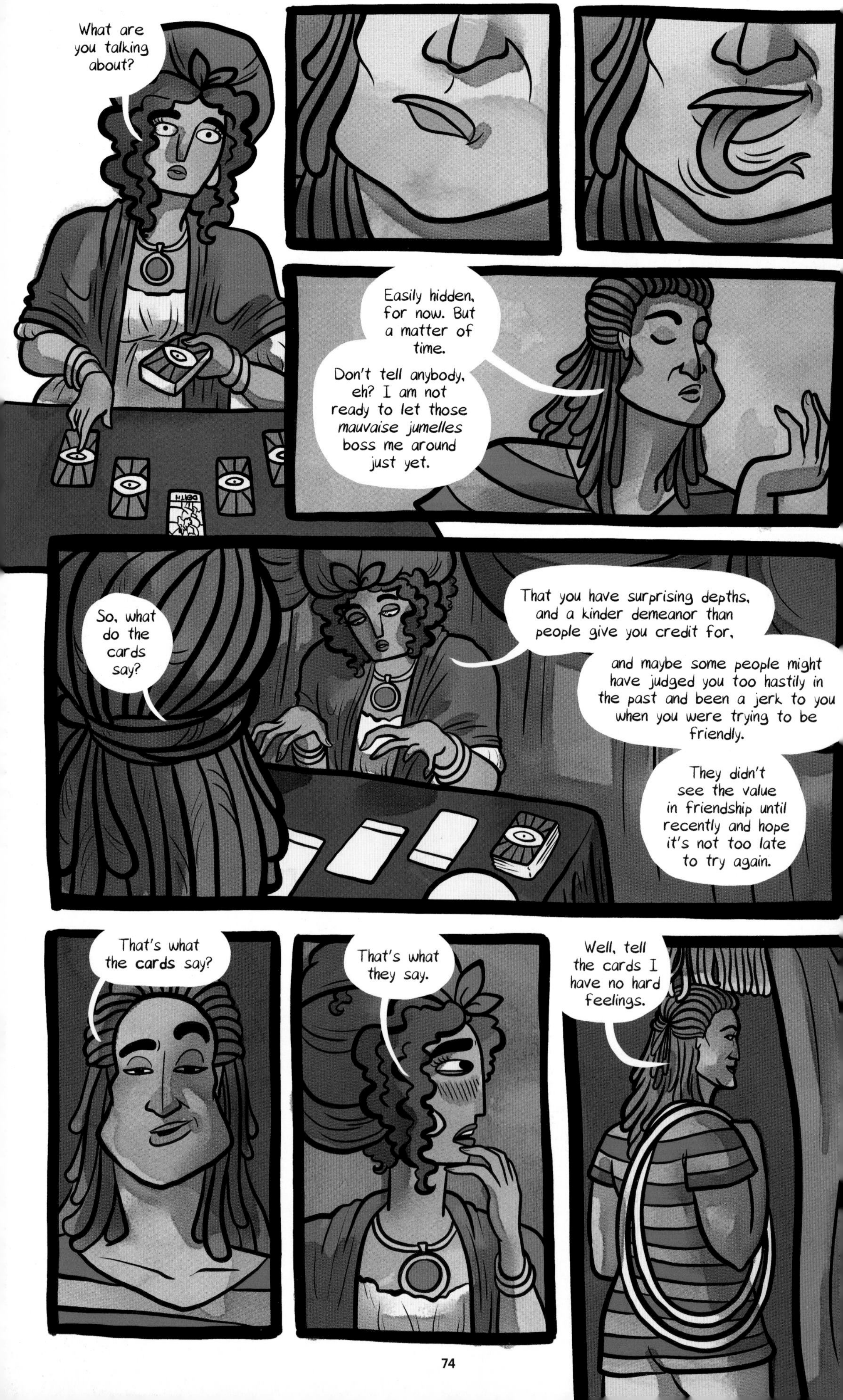
What are you talking about?
Easily hidden, for now. But a matter of time.
Don't tell anybody, eh? I am not ready to let those *mauvaise jumelles* boss me around just yet.
So, what do the cards say?
That you have surprising depths, and a kinder demeanor than people give you credit for,
and maybe some people might have judged you too hastily in the past and been a jerk to you when you were trying to be friendly.
They didn't see the value in friendship until recently and hope it's not too late to try again.
That's what the **cards** say?
That's what they say.
Well, tell the cards I have no hard feelings.

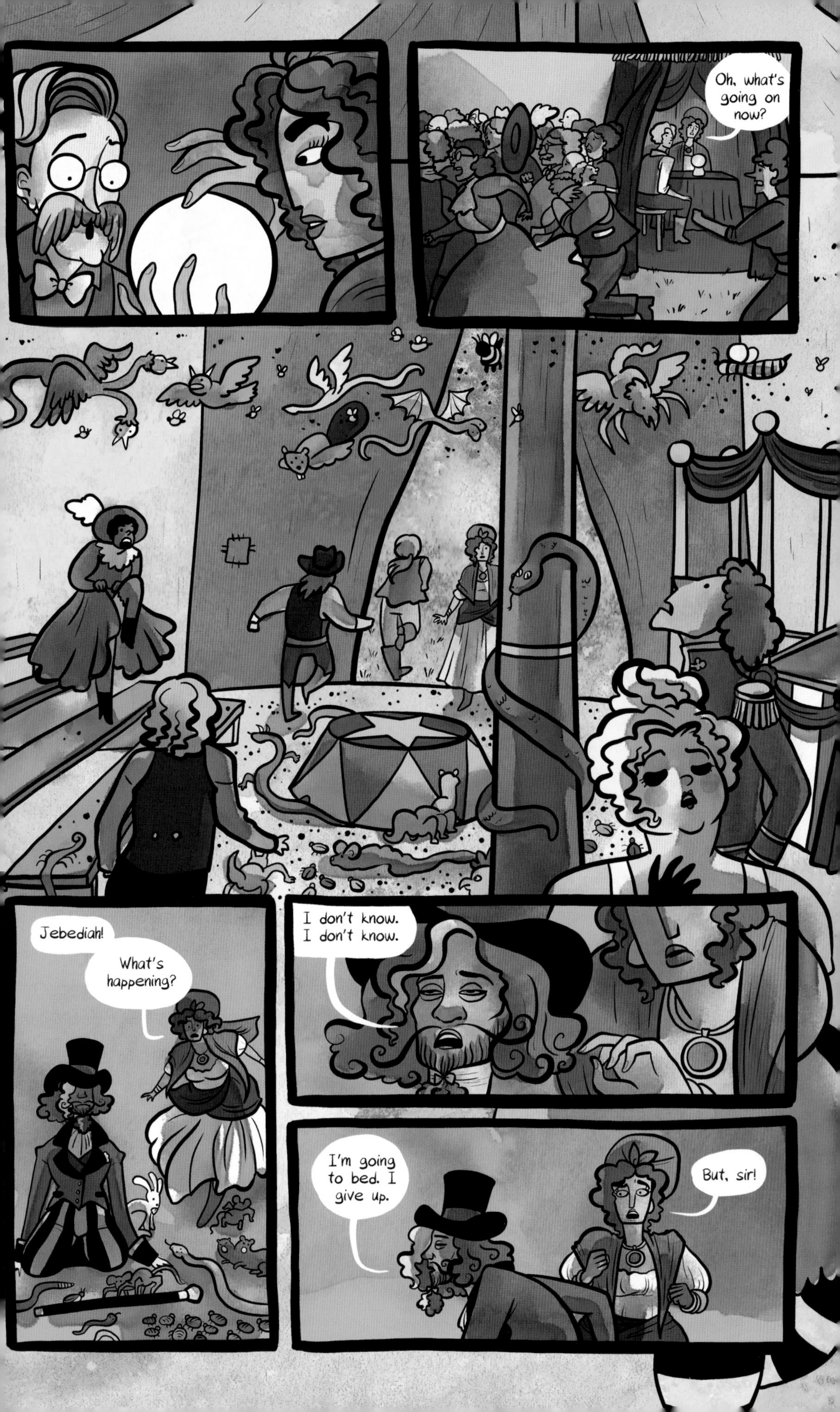

Oh, what's going on now?
Jebediah!
What's happening?
I don't know. I don't know.
I'm going to bed. I give up.
But, sir!

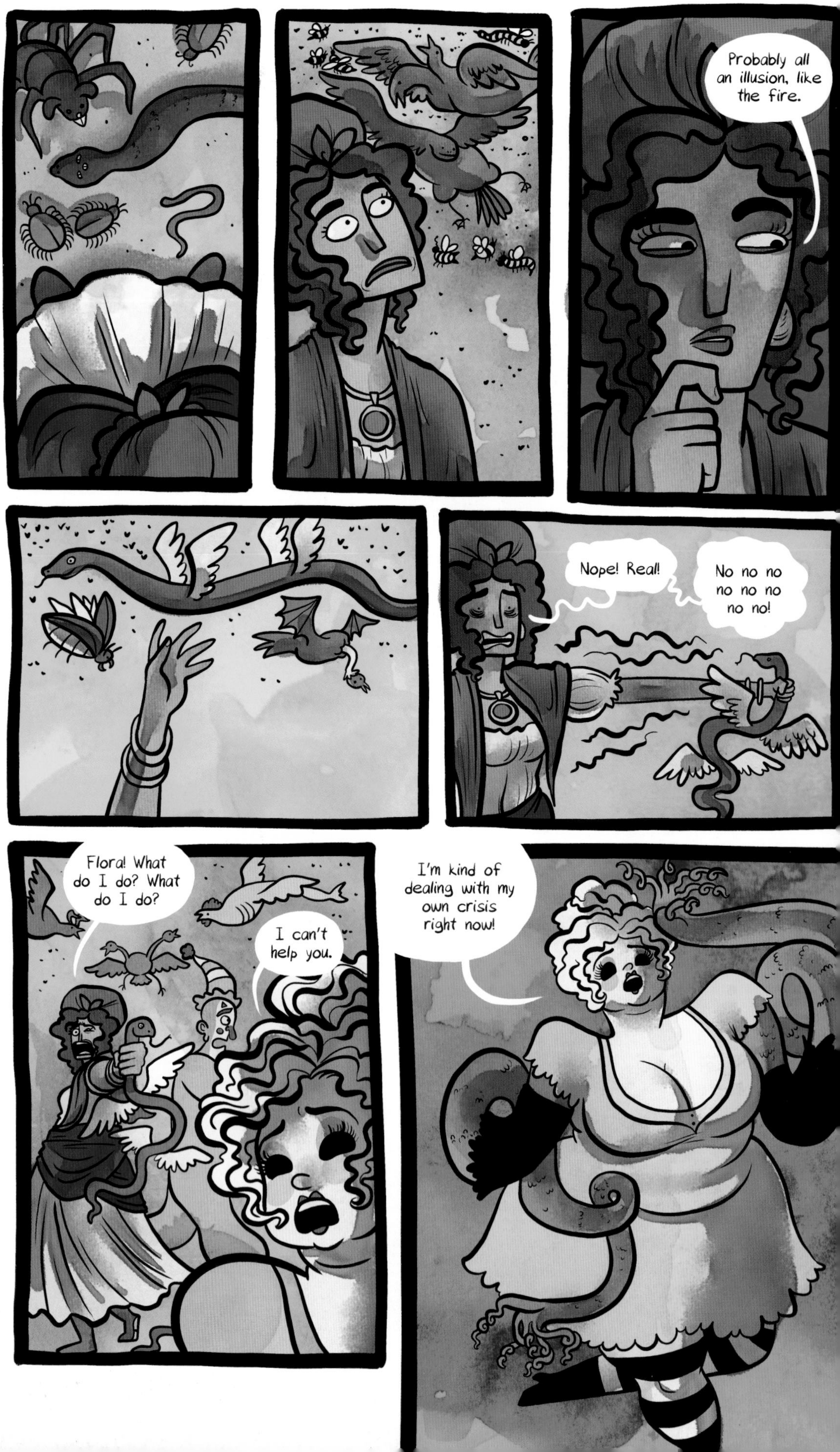
Probably all an illusion, like the fire.
Nope! Real!
No no no no no no no no!
Flora! What do I do? What do I do?
I can't help you.
I'm kind of dealing with my own crisis right now!

Chapter Four

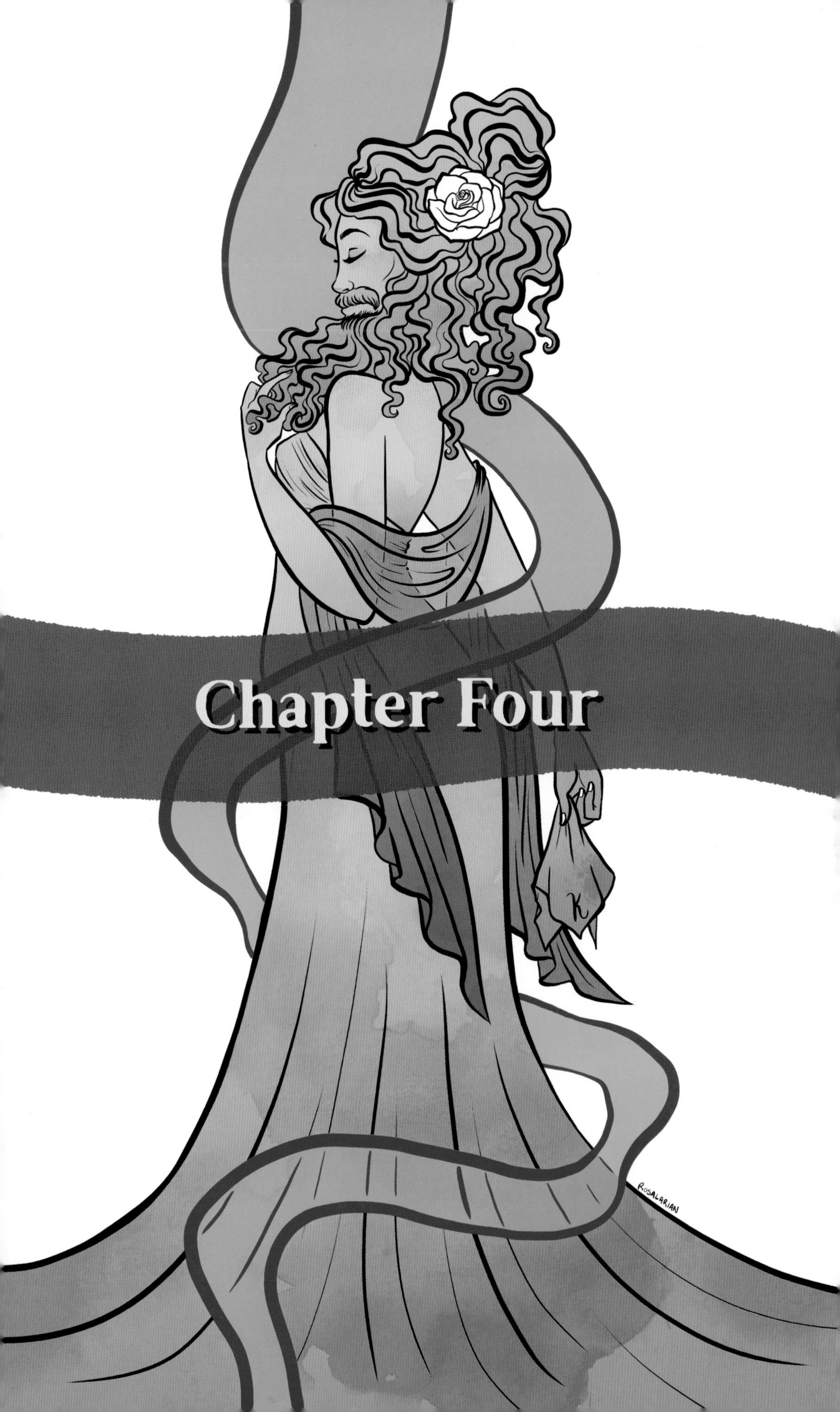
ROSALARIAN

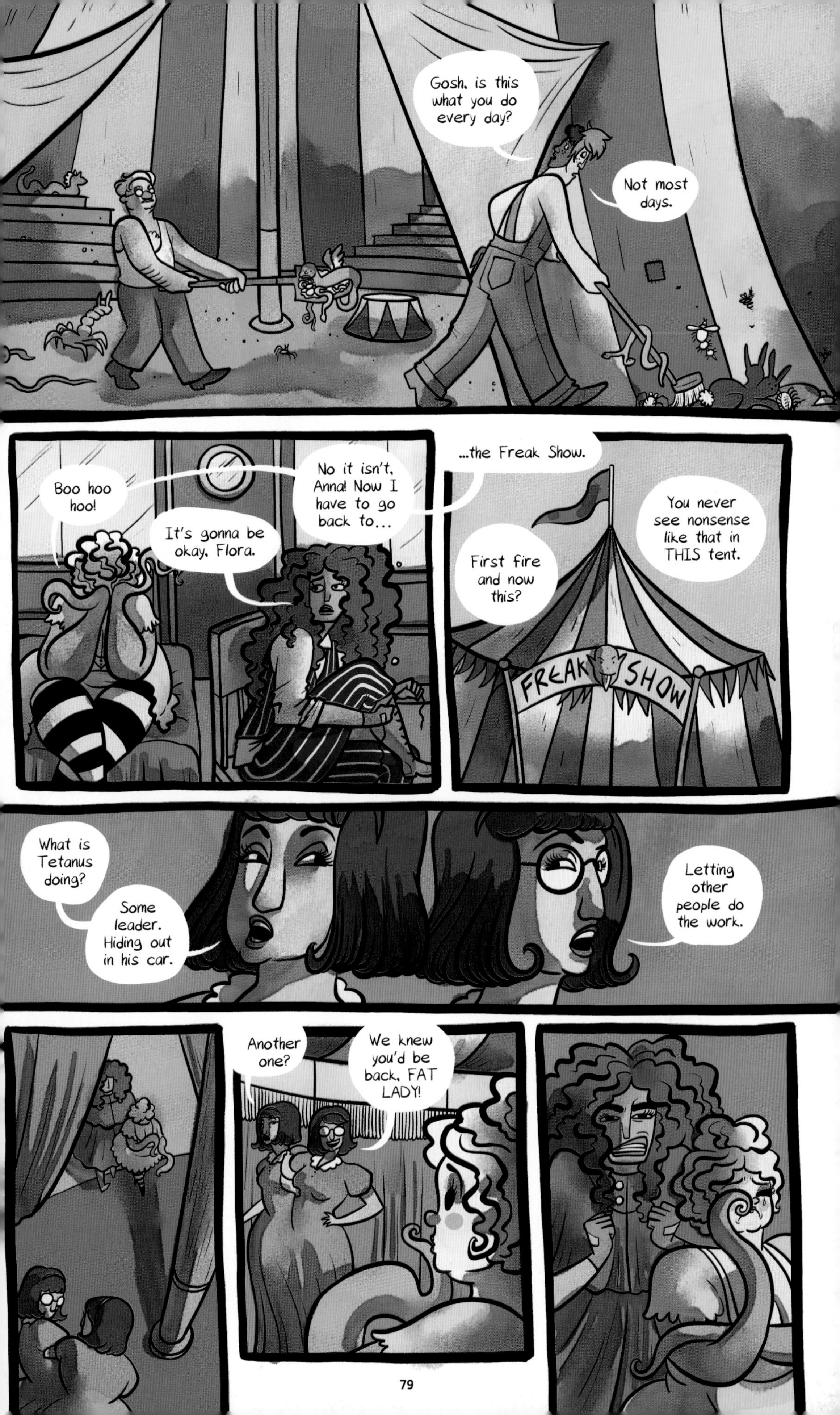
Gosh, is this what you do every day?
Not most days.
Boo hoo hoo!
No it isn't, Anna! Now I have to go back to...
It's gonna be okay, Flora.
...the Freak Show.
First fire and now this?
You never see nonsense like that in THIS tent.
FREAK SHOW
What is Tetanus doing?
Some leader. Hiding out in his car.
Letting other people do the work.
Another one?
We knew you'd be back, FAT LADY!

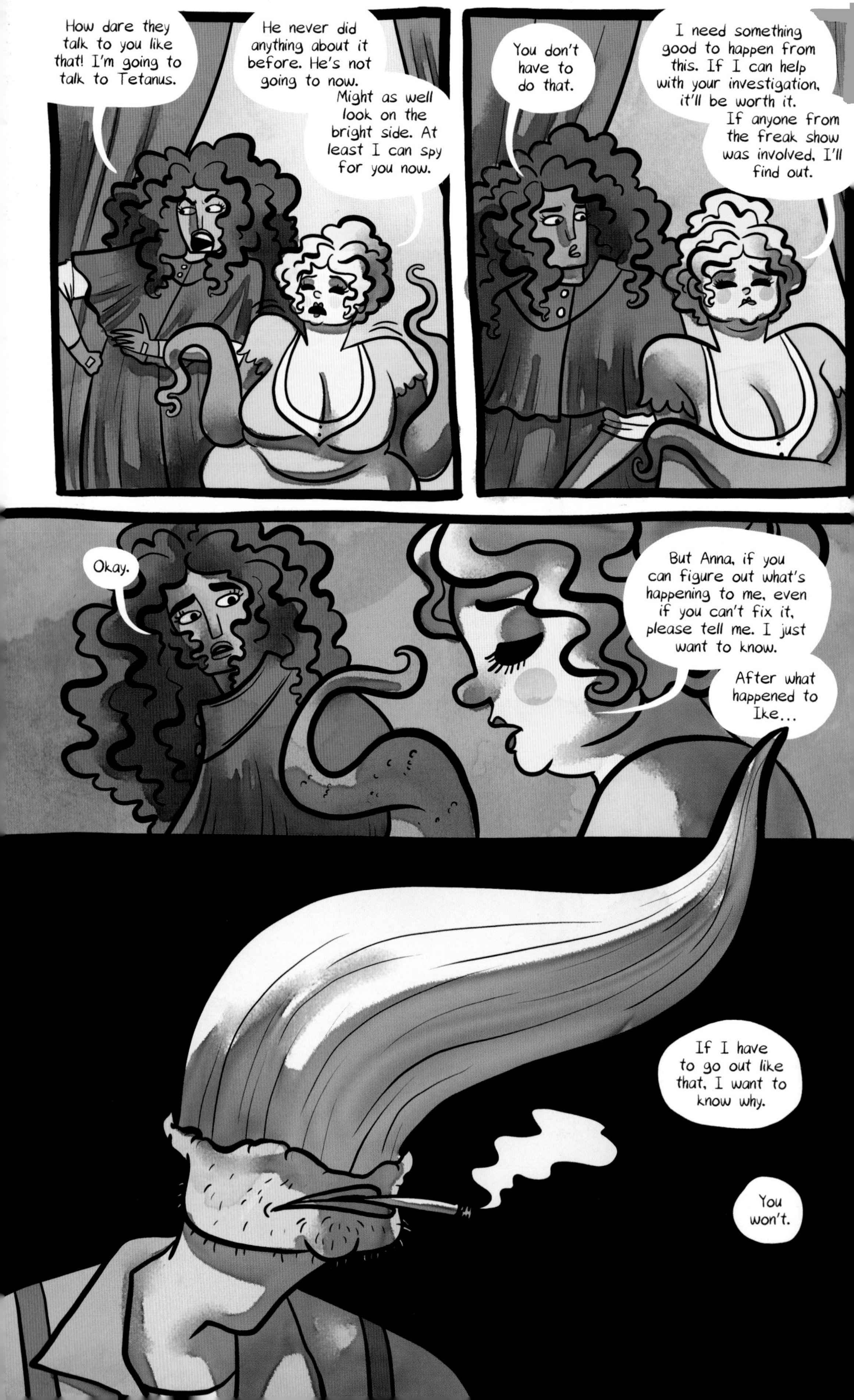
How dare they talk to you like that! I'm going to talk to Tetanus.
He never did anything about it before. He's not going to now.
Might as well look on the bright side. At least I can spy for you now.
You don't have to do that.
I need something good to happen from this. If I can help with your investigation, it'll be worth it.
If anyone from the freak show was involved, I'll find out.
Okay.
But Anna, if you can figure out what's happening to me, even if you can't fix it, please tell me. I just want to know.
After what happened to Ike...
If I have to go out like that, I want to know why.
You won't.

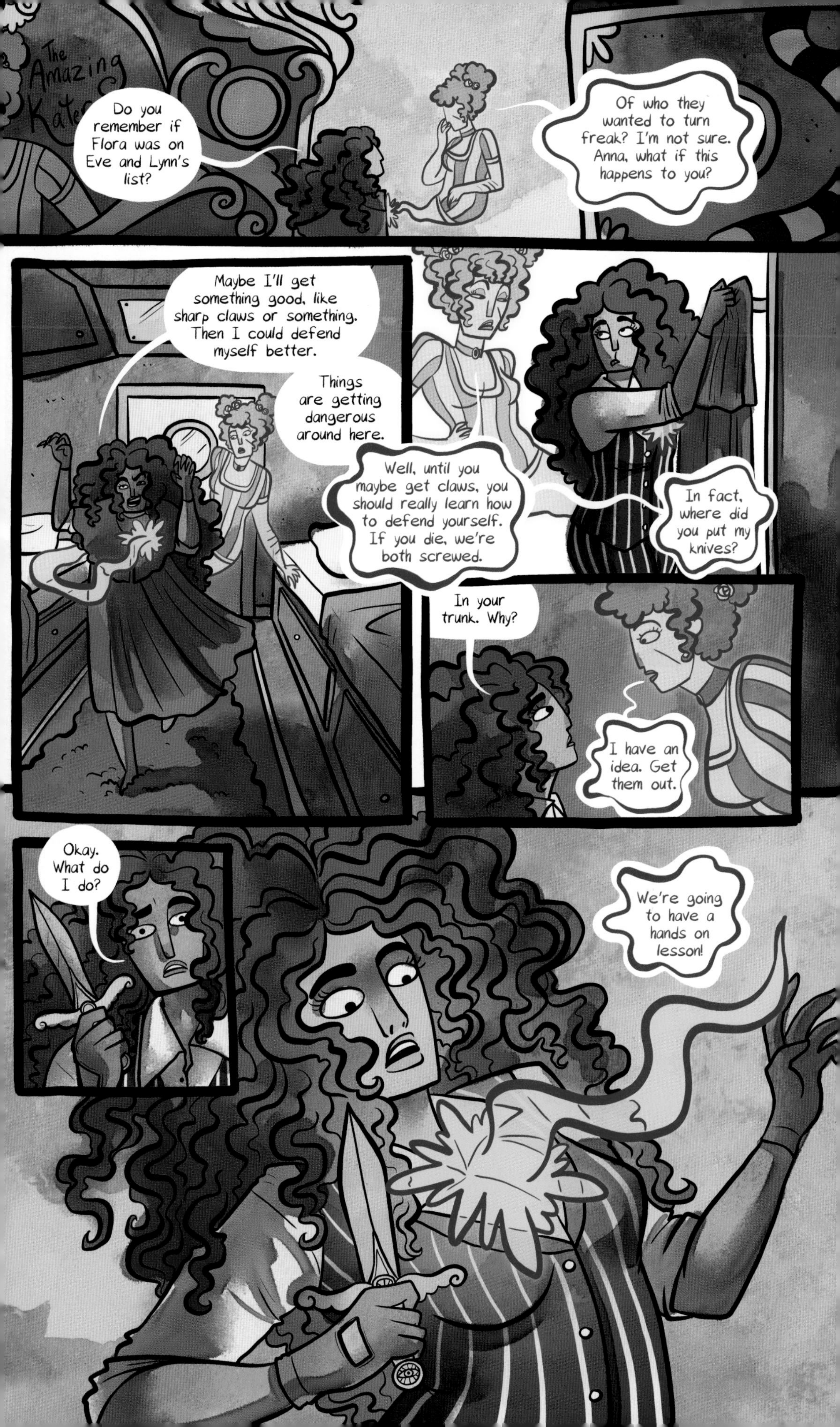
The Amazing Kate
Do you remember if Flora was on Eve and Lynn's list?
Of who they wanted to turn freak? I'm not sure. Anna, what if this happens to you?
Maybe I'll get something good, like sharp claws or something. Then I could defend myself better.
Things are getting dangerous around here.
Well, until you maybe get claws, you should really learn how to defend yourself. If you die, we're both screwed.
In fact, where did you put my knives?
In your trunk. Why?
I have an idea. Get them out.
Okay. What do I do?
We're going to have a hands on lesson!

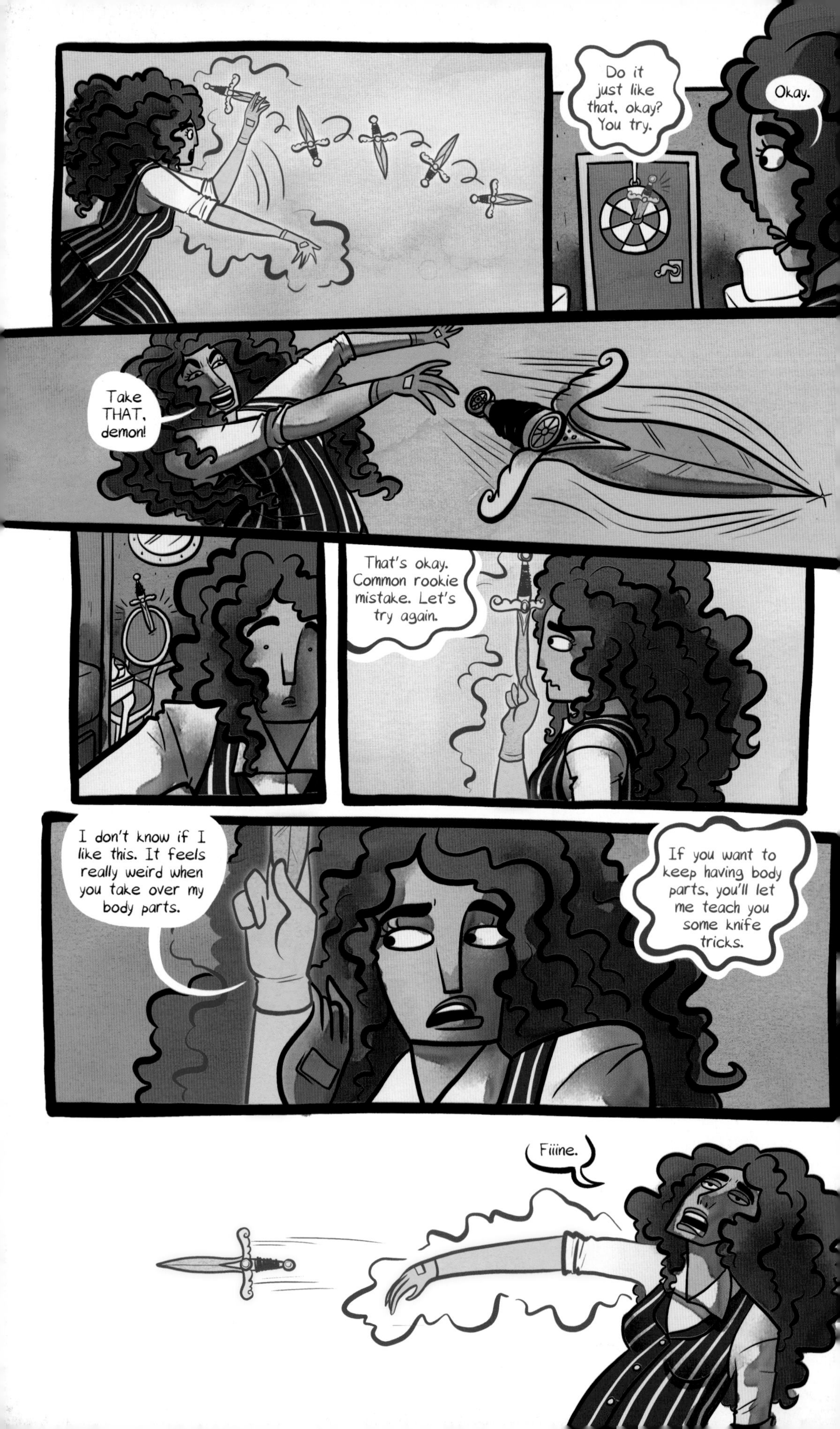
Do it just like that, okay? You try.
Okay.
Take THAT, demon!
That's okay. Common rookie mistake. Let's try again.
I don't know if I like this. It feels really weird when you take over my body parts.
If you want to keep having body parts, you'll let me teach you some knife tricks.
Fiiine.

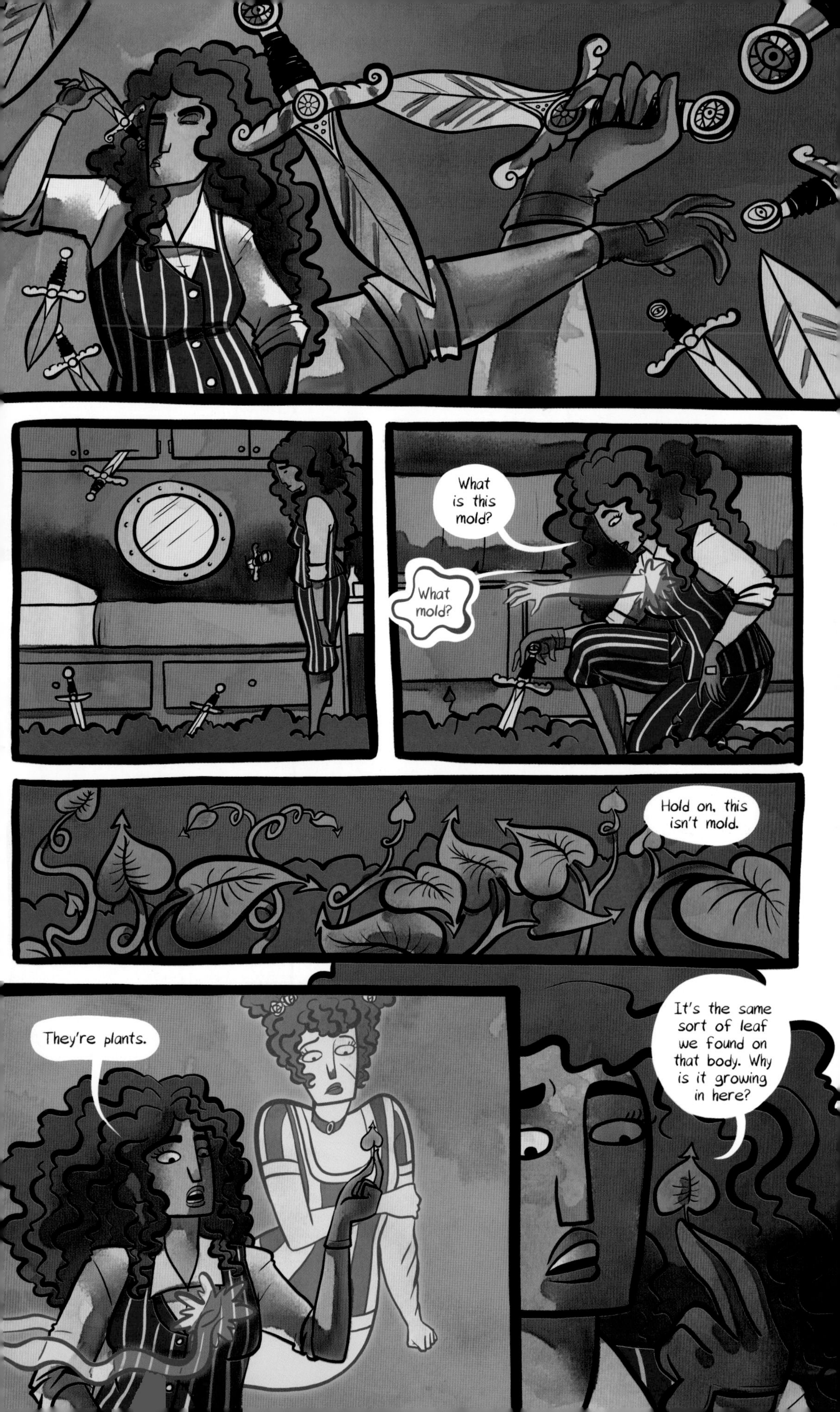
What is this mold?
What mold?
Hold on, this isn't mold.
They're plants.
It's the same sort of leaf we found on that body. Why is it growing in here?

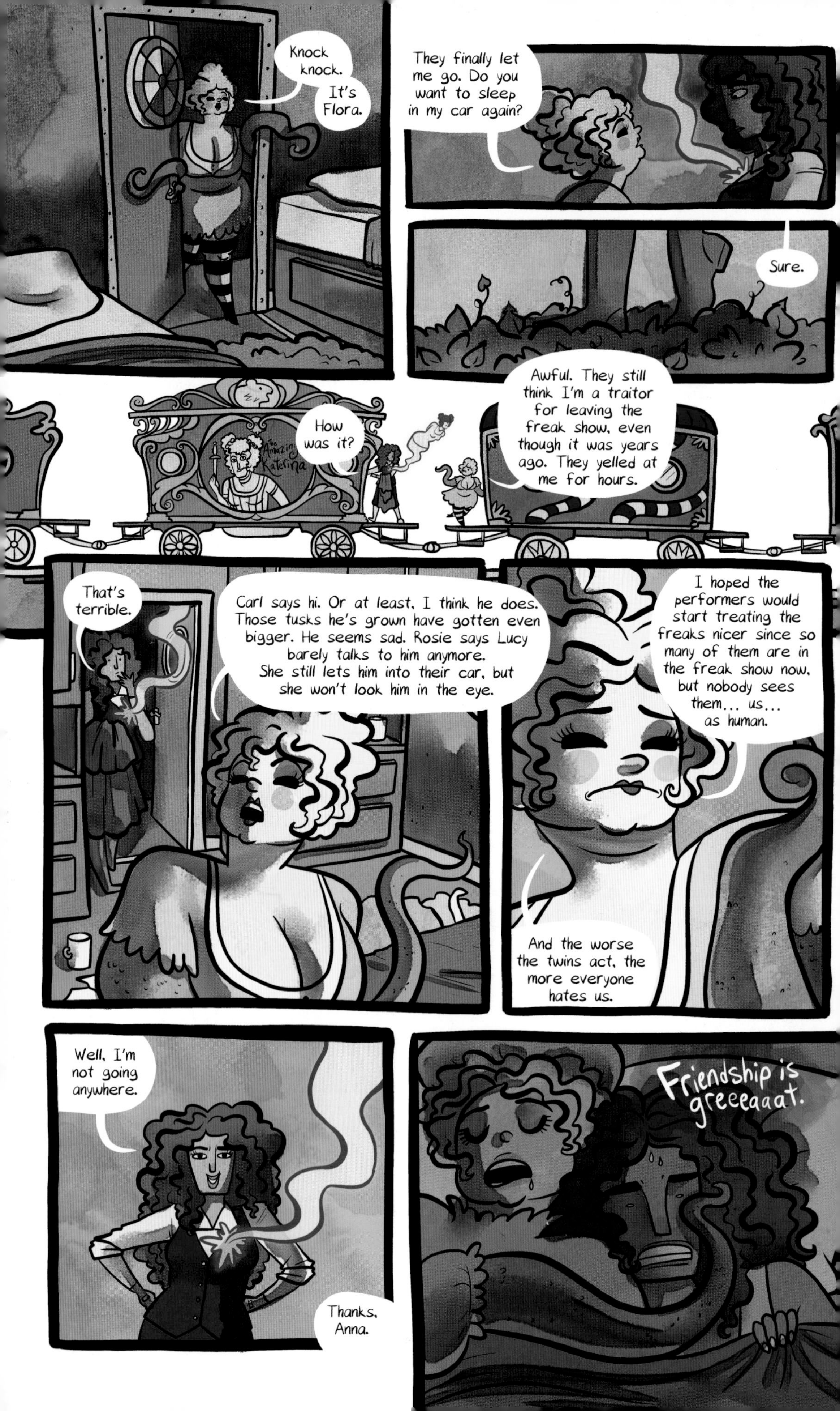
Knock knock.
It's Flora.
They finally let me go. Do you want to sleep in my car again?
Sure.
How was it?
Awful. They still think I'm a traitor for leaving the freak show, even though it was years ago. They yelled at me for hours.
The Amazing Katerina
That's terrible.
Carl says hi. Or at least, I think he does. Those tusks he's grown have gotten even bigger. He seems sad. Rosie says Lucy barely talks to him anymore. She still lets him into their car, but she won't look him in the eye.
I hoped the performers would start treating the freaks nicer since so many of them are in the freak show now, but nobody sees them... us... as human.
And the worse the twins act, the more everyone hates us.
Well, I'm not going anywhere.
Thanks, Anna.
Friendship is greeeaaat.

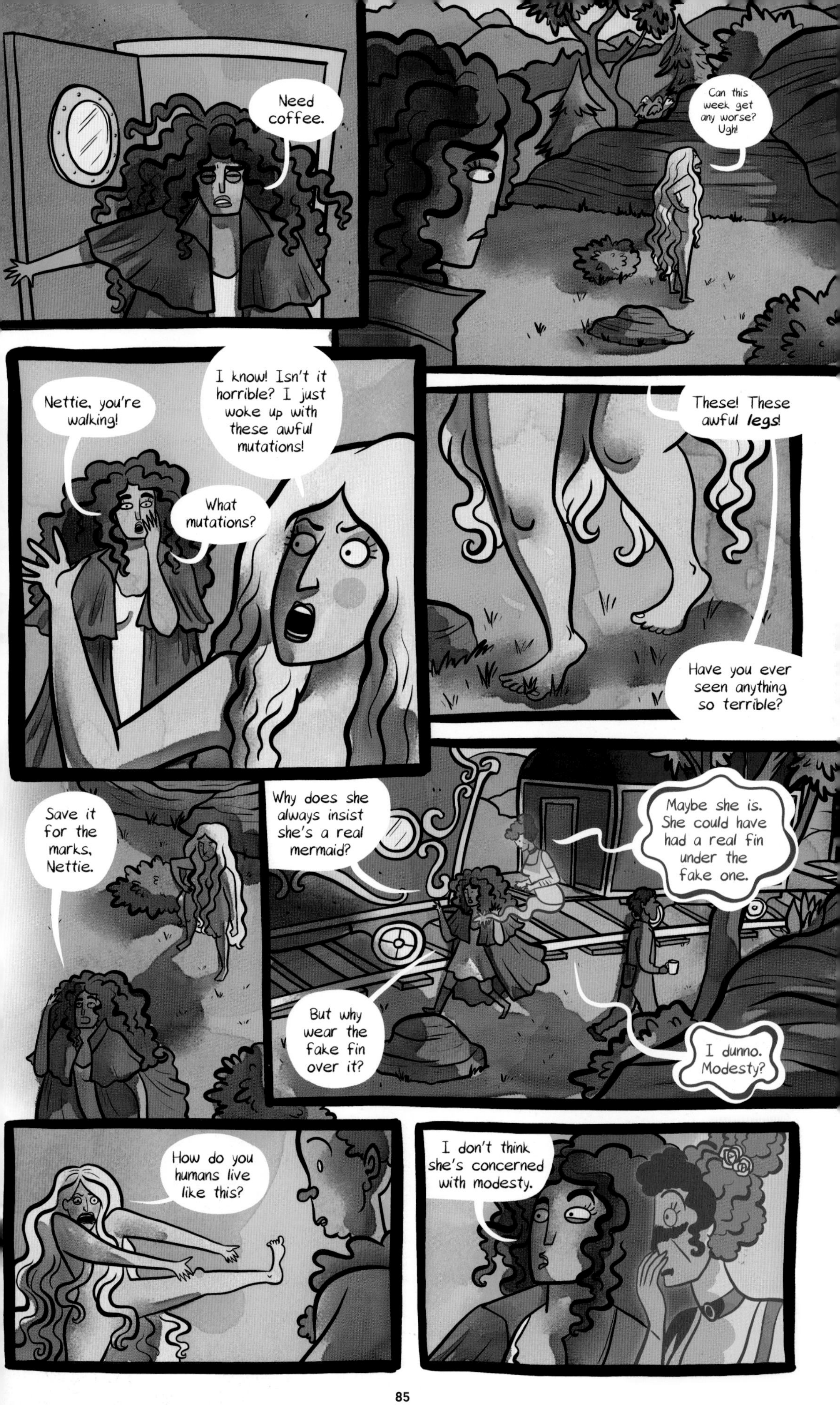
Need coffee.
Can this week get any worse? Ugh!
Nettie, you're walking!
I know! Isn't it horrible? I just woke up with these awful mutations!
What mutations?
These! These awful ***legs***!
Have you ever seen anything so terrible?
Save it for the marks, Nettie.
Why does she always insist she's a real mermaid?
Maybe she is. She could have had a real fin under the fake one.
But why wear the fake fin over it?
I dunno. Modesty?
How do you humans live like this?
I don't think she's concerned with modesty.

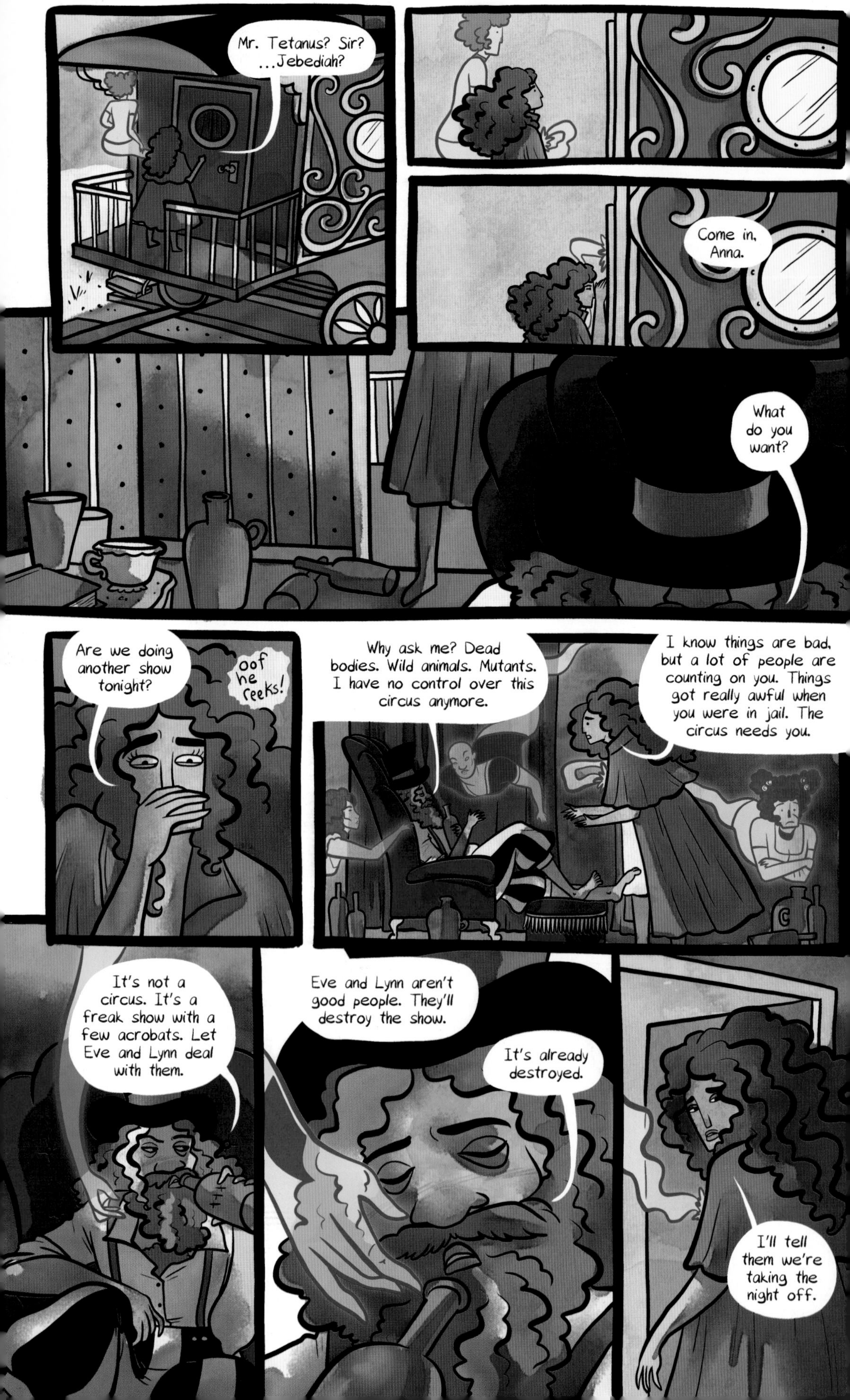
Mr. Tetanus? Sir? ...Jebediah?
Come in, Anna.
What do you want?
Are we doing another show tonight?
oof he reeks!
Why ask me? Dead bodies. Wild animals. Mutants. I have no control over this circus anymore.
I know things are bad, but a lot of people are counting on you. Things got really awful when you were in jail. The circus needs you.
It's not a circus. It's a freak show with a few acrobats. Let Eve and Lynn deal with them.
Eve and Lynn aren't good people. They'll destroy the show.
It's already destroyed.
I'll tell them we're taking the night off.

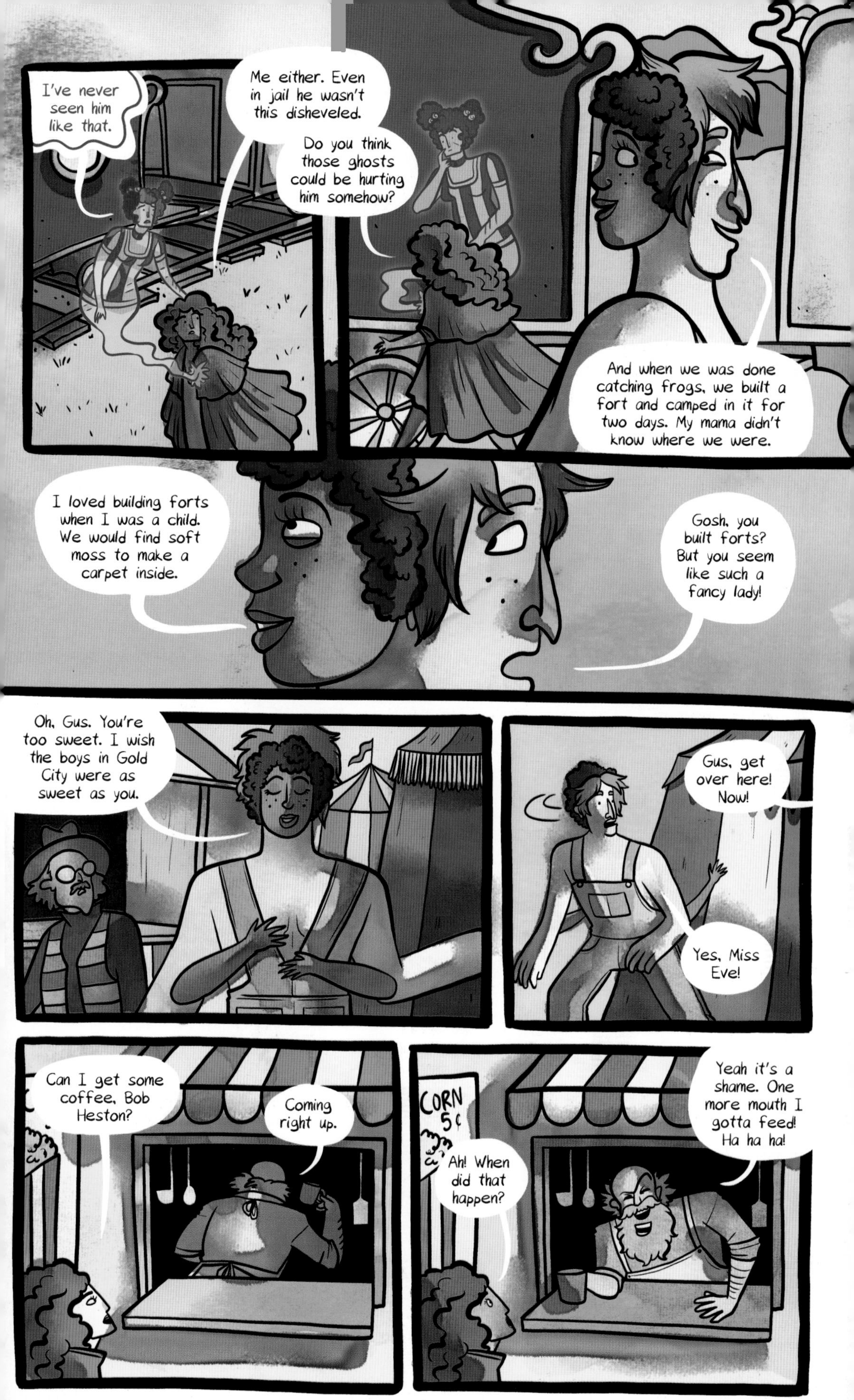
I've never seen him like that.
Me either. Even in jail he wasn't this disheveled.
Do you think those ghosts could be hurting him somehow?
And when we was done catching frogs, we built a fort and camped in it for two days. My mama didn't know where we were.
I loved building forts when I was a child. We would find soft moss to make a carpet inside.
Gosh, you built forts? But you seem like such a fancy lady!
Oh, Gus. You're too sweet. I wish the boys in Gold City were as sweet as you.
Gus, get over here! Now!
Yes, Miss Eve!
Can I get some coffee, Bob Heston?
Coming right up.
CORN 5¢
Ah! When did that happen?
Yeah it's a shame. One more mouth I gotta feed! Ha ha ha!

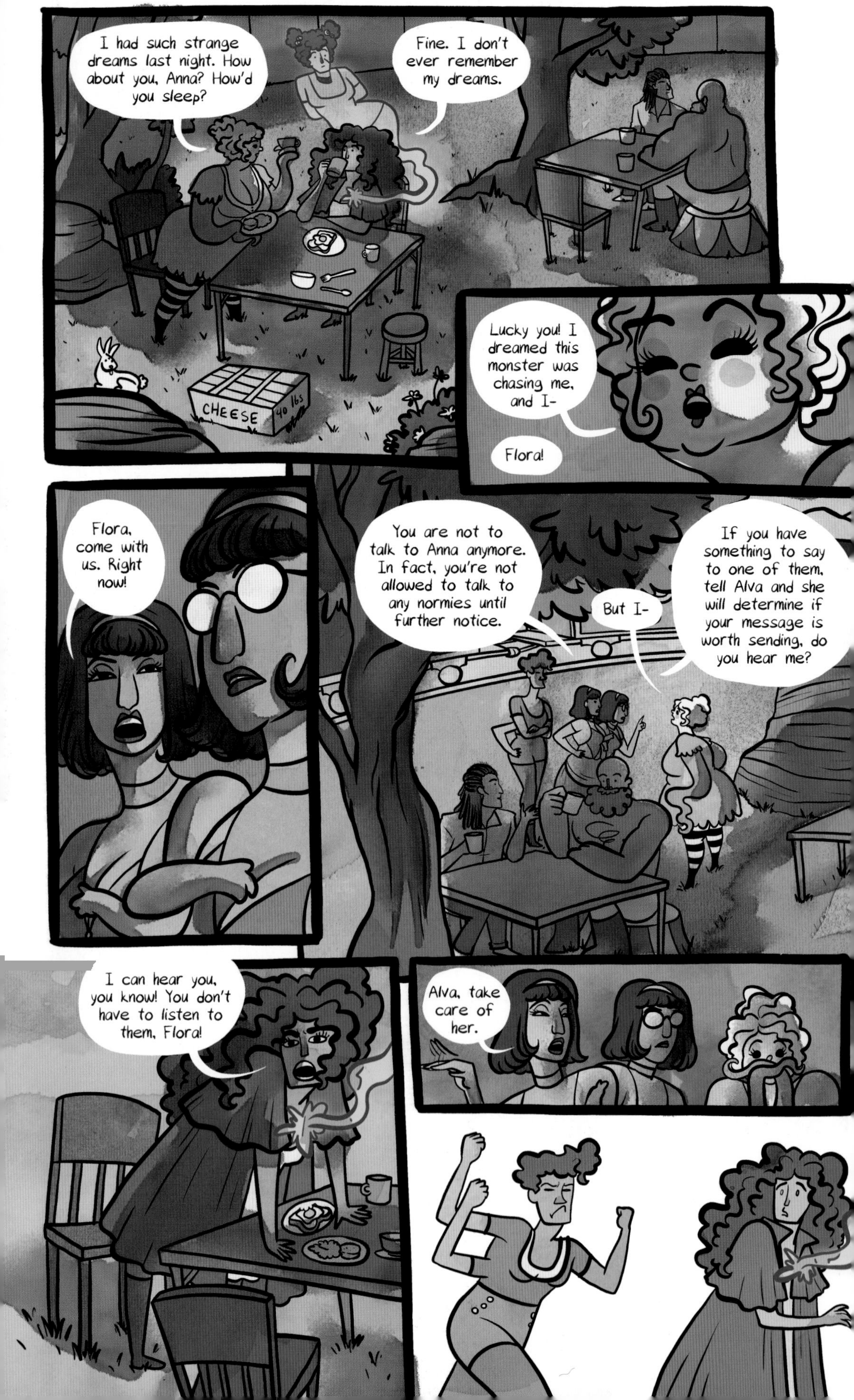
I had such strange dreams last night. How about you, Anna? How'd you sleep?
Fine. I don't ever remember my dreams.
CHEESE 40 lbs
Lucky you! I dreamed this monster was chasing me, and I-
Flora!
Flora, come with us. Right now!
You are not to talk to Anna anymore. In fact, you're not allowed to talk to any normies until further notice.
But I-
If you have something to say to one of them, tell Alva and she will determine if your message is worth sending, do you hear me?
I can hear you, you know! You don't have to listen to them, Flora!
Alva, take care of her.

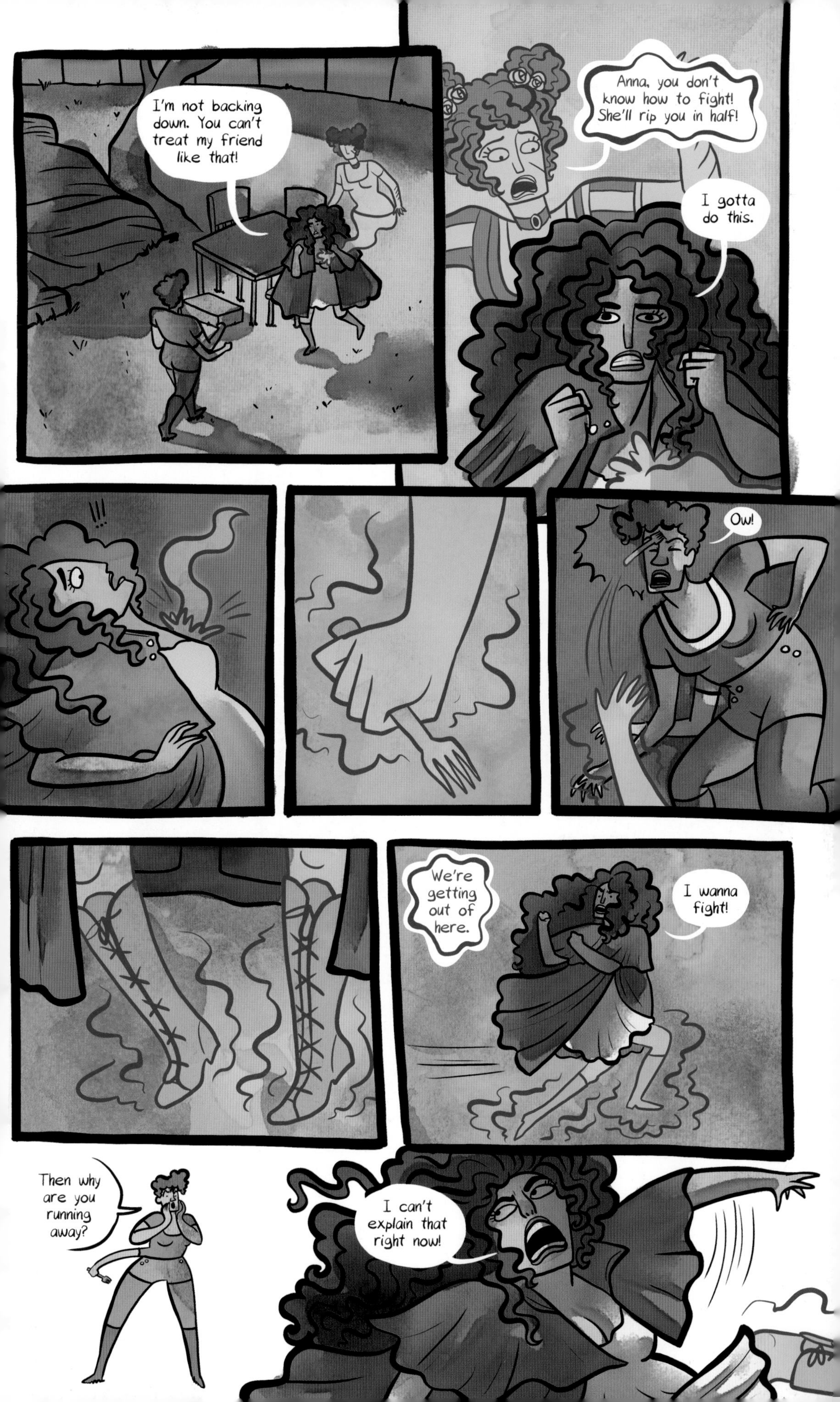
I'm not backing down. You can't treat my friend like that!
Anna, you don't know how to fight! She'll rip you in half!
I gotta do this.
!!!
Ow!
We're getting out of here.
I wanna fight!
Then why are you running away?
I can't explain that right now!

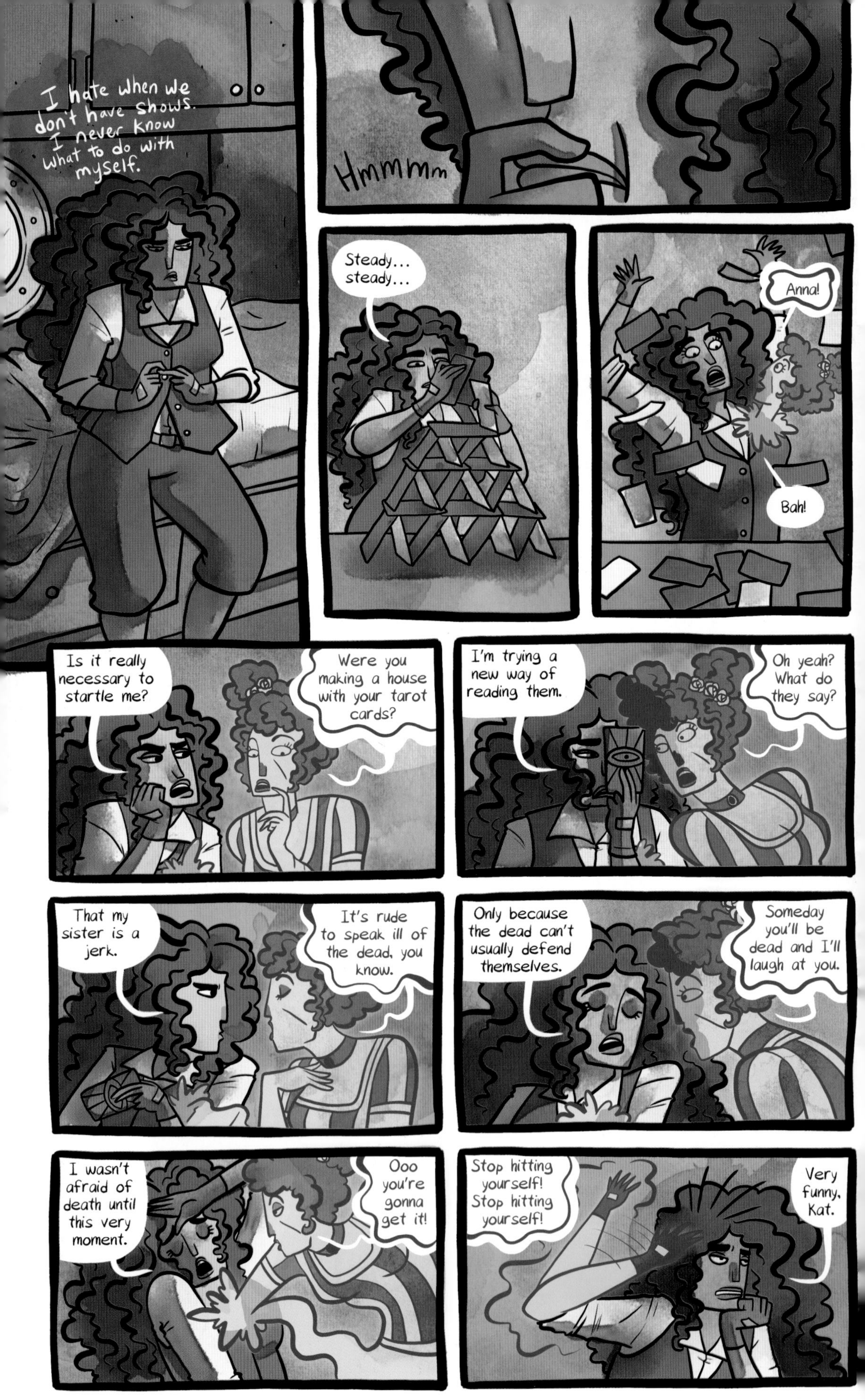
I hate when we don't have shows. I never know what to do with myself.
Hmmmm
Steady... steady...
Anna!
Bah!
Is it really necessary to startle me?
Were you making a house with your tarot cards?
I'm trying a new way of reading them.
Oh yeah? What do they say?
That my sister is a jerk.
It's rude to speak ill of the dead, you know.
Only because the dead can't usually defend themselves.
Someday you'll be dead and I'll laugh at you.
I wasn't afraid of death until this very moment.
Ooo you're gonna get it!
Stop hitting yourself! Stop hitting yourself!
Very funny, Kat.

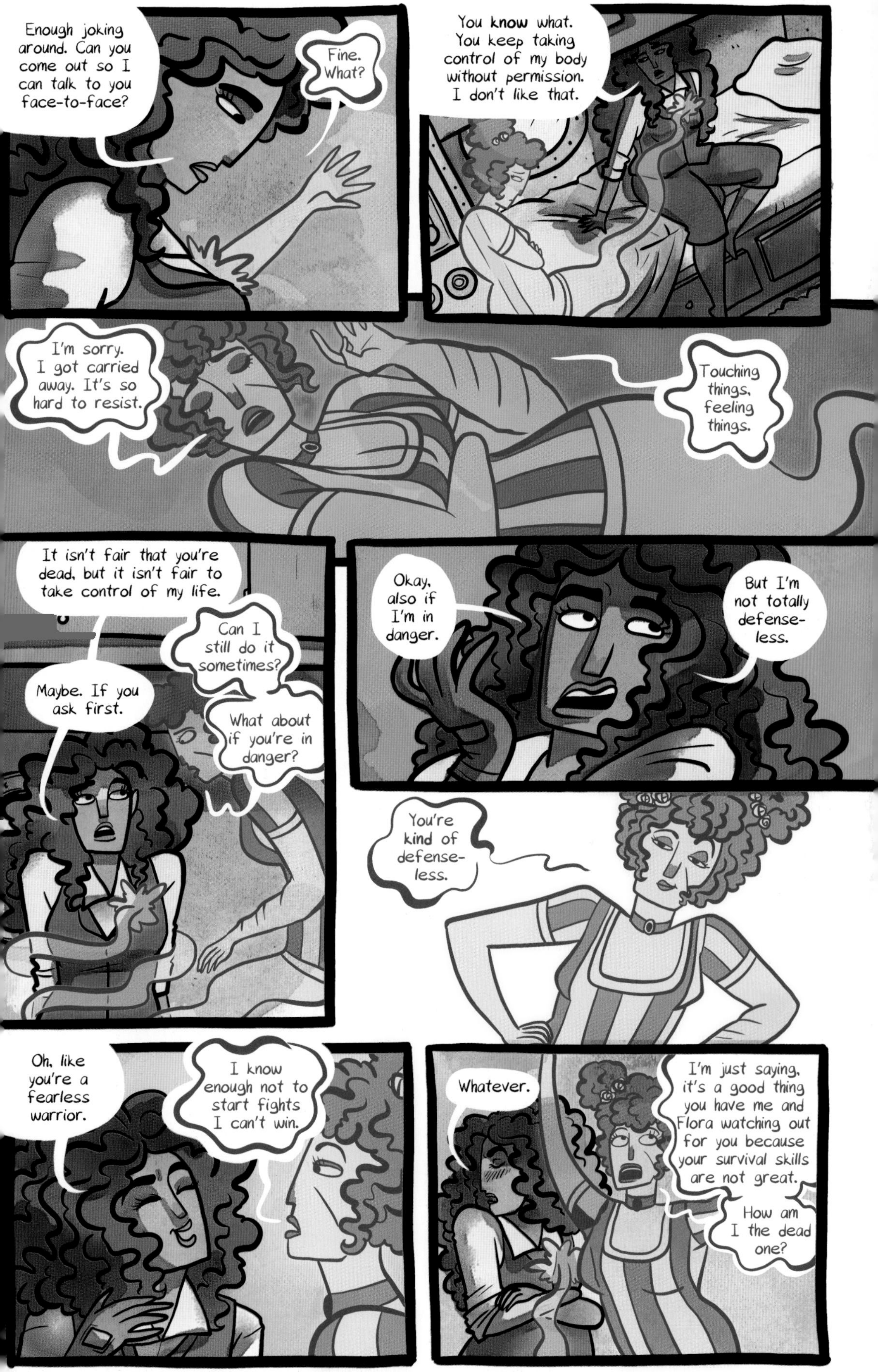
Enough joking around. Can you come out so I can talk to you face-to-face?
Fine. What?
You **know** what. You keep taking control of my body without permission. I don't like that.
I'm sorry. I got carried away. It's so hard to resist.
Touching things, feeling things.
It isn't fair that you're dead, but it isn't fair to take control of my life.
Can I still do it sometimes?
Maybe. If you ask first.
What about if you're in danger?
Okay, also if I'm in danger.
But I'm not totally defense-less.
You're **kind** of defense-less.
Oh, like you're a fearless warrior.
I know enough not to start fights I can't win.
Whatever.
I'm just saying, it's a good thing you have me and Flora watching out for you because your survival skills are not great.
How am I the dead one?

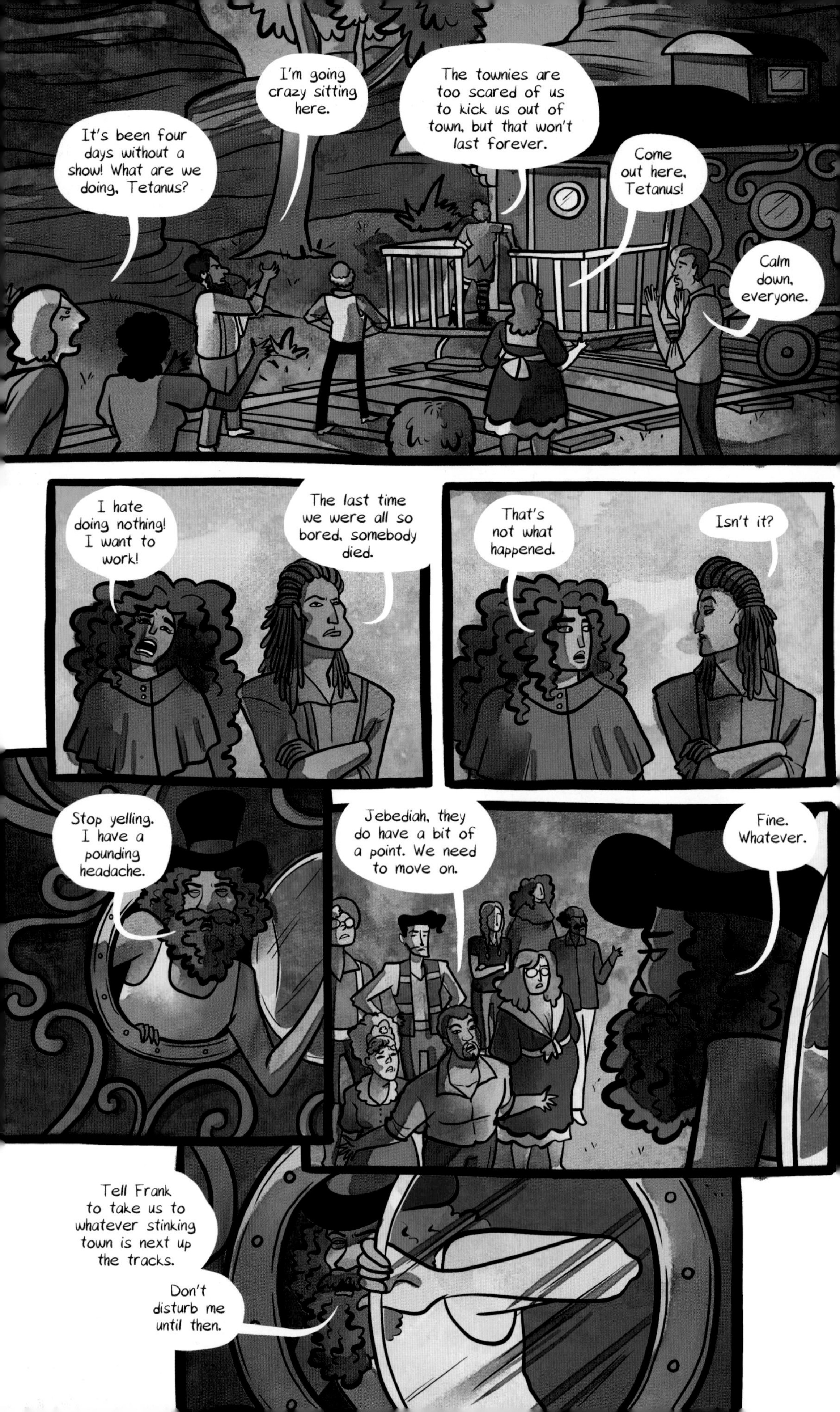
It's been four days without a show! What are we doing, Tetanus?
I'm going crazy sitting here.
The townies are too scared of us to kick us out of town, but that won't last forever.
Come out here, Tetanus!
Calm down, everyone.
I hate doing nothing! I want to work!
The last time we were all so bored, somebody died.
That's not what happened.
Isn't it?
Stop yelling. I have a pounding headache.
Jebediah, they do have a bit of a point. We need to move on.
Fine. Whatever.
Tell Frank to take us to whatever stinking town is next up the tracks.
Don't disturb me until then.

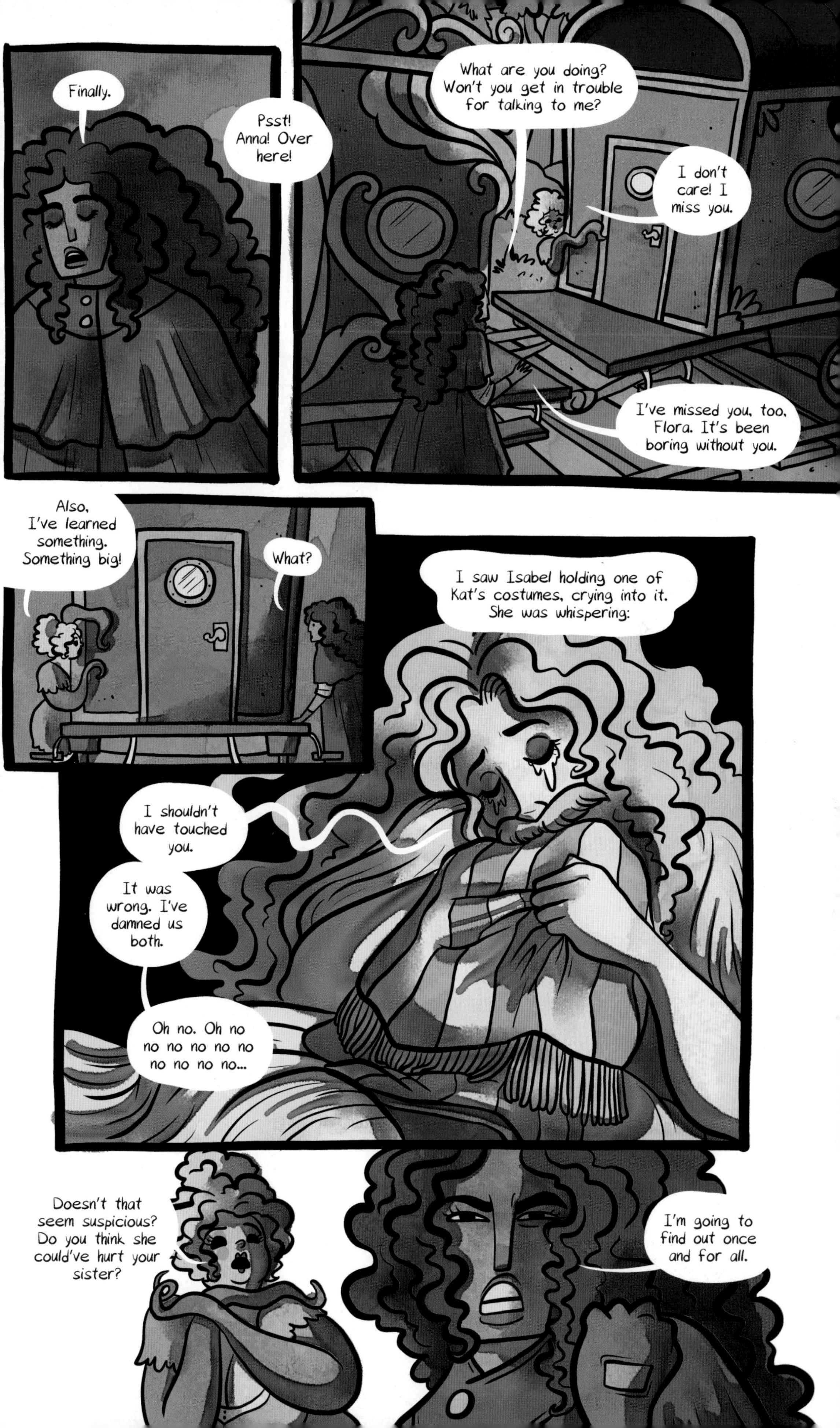
Finally.
Psst! Anna! Over here!
What are you doing? Won't you get in trouble for talking to me?
I don't care! I miss you.
I've missed you, too, Flora. It's been boring without you.
Also, I've learned something. Something big!
What?
I saw Isabel holding one of Kat's costumes, crying into it. She was whispering:
I shouldn't have touched you.
It was wrong. I've damned us both.
Oh no. Oh no no no no no no no no no no...
Doesn't that seem suspicious? Do you think she could've hurt your sister?
I'm going to find out once and for all.

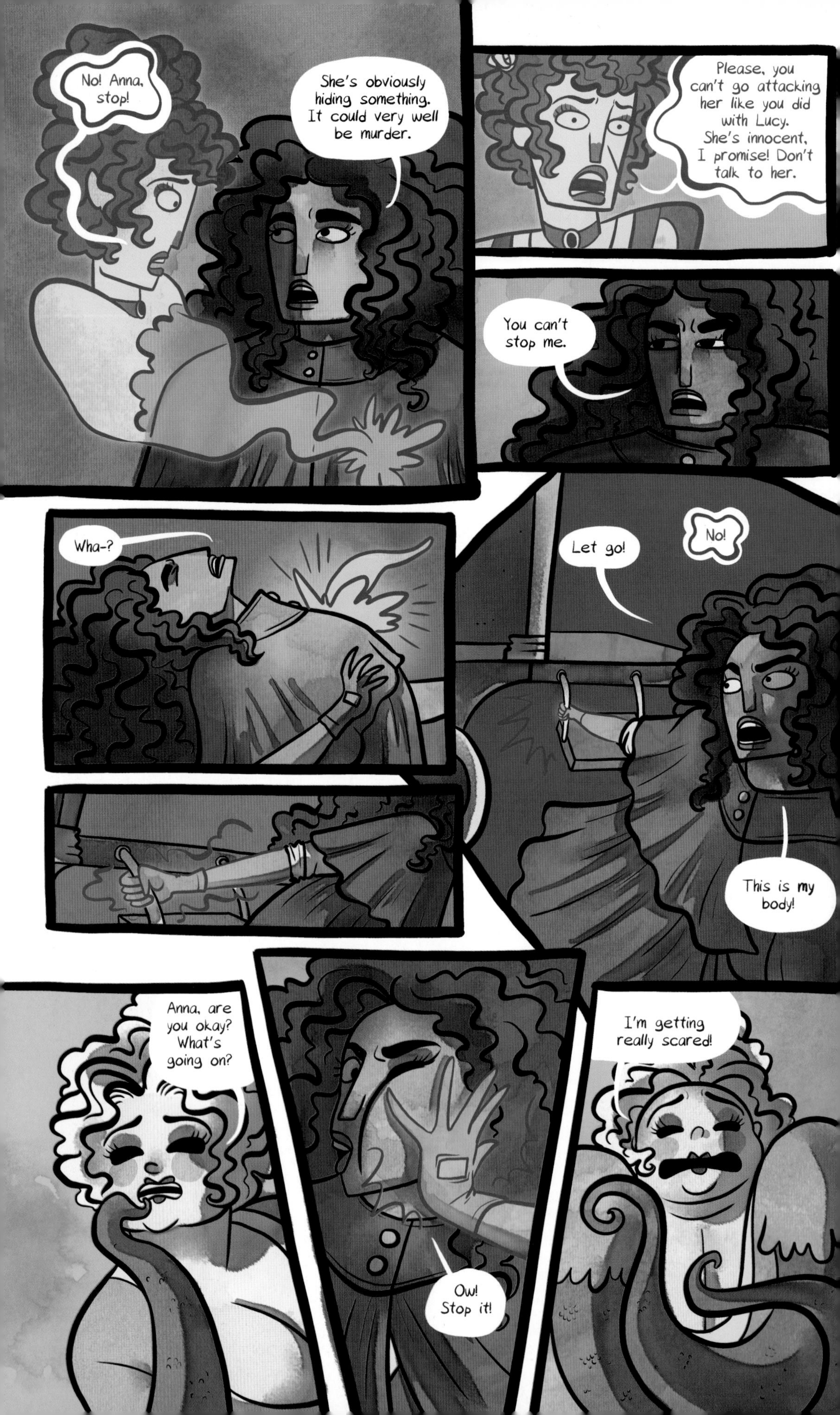

No! Anna, stop!
She's obviously hiding something. It could very well be murder.
Please, you can't go attacking her like you did with Lucy. She's innocent, I promise! Don't talk to her.
You can't stop me.
Wha-?
Let go!
No!
This is my body!
Anna, are you okay? What's going on?
Ow! Stop it!
I'm getting really scared!

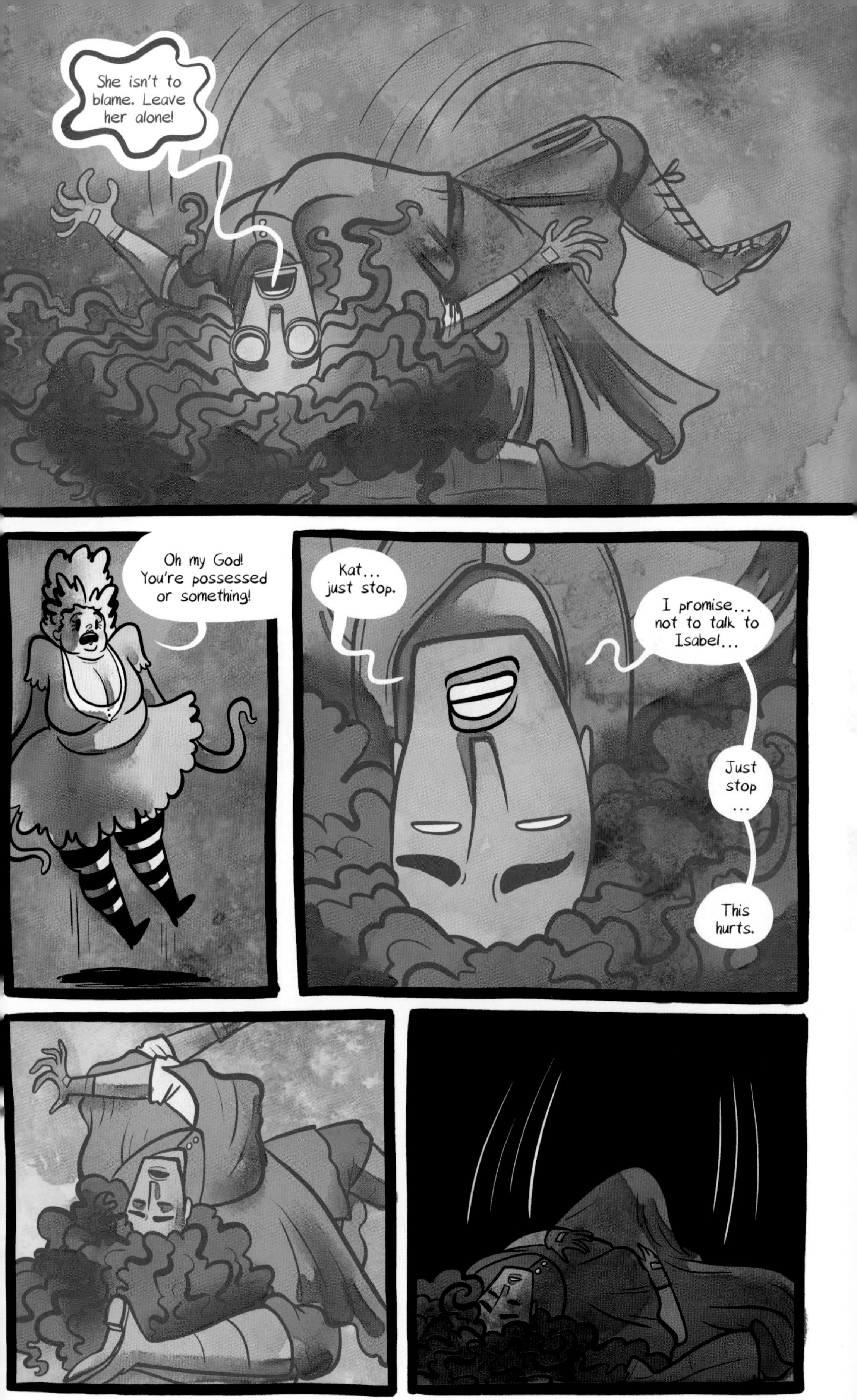
She isn't to blame. Leave her alone!
Oh my God! You're possessed or something!
Kat... just stop.
I promise... not to talk to Isabel...
Just stop ...
This hurts.

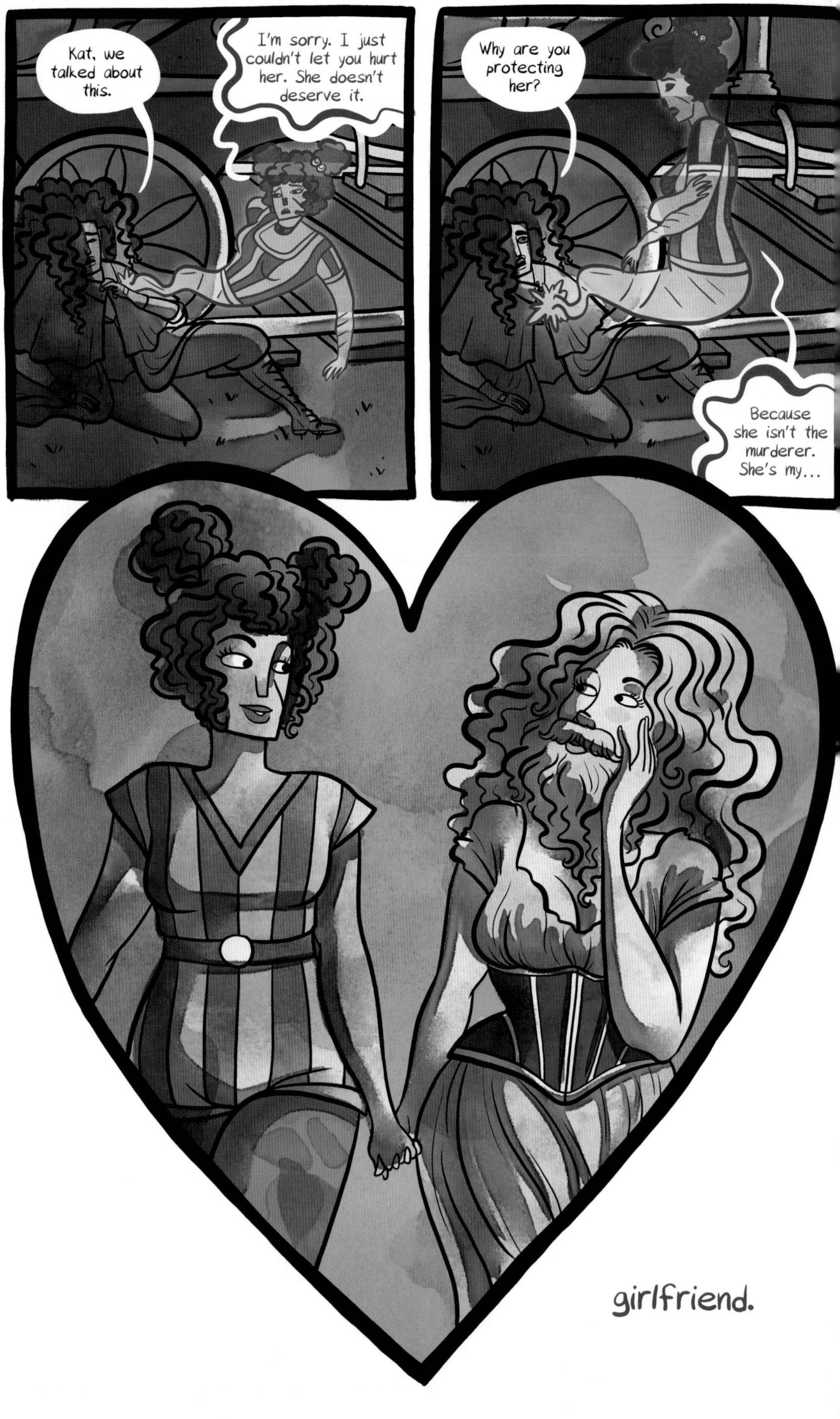
Kat, we talked about this.
I'm sorry. I just couldn't let you hurt her. She doesn't deserve it.
Why are you protecting her?
Because she isn't the murderer. She's my...
girlfriend.

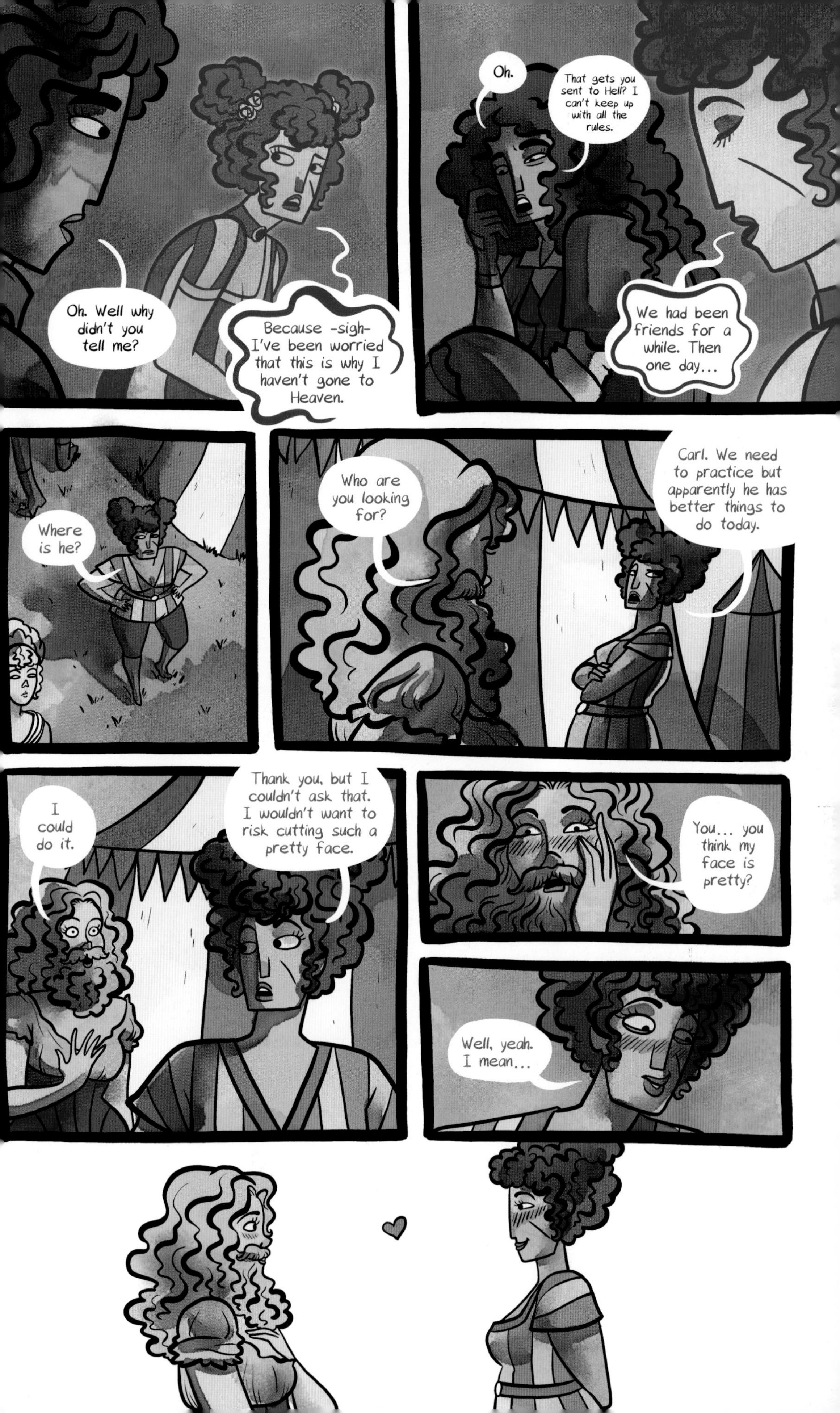

Oh. Well why didn't you tell me?
Because -sigh- I've been worried that this is why I haven't gone to Heaven.
Oh.
That gets you sent to Hell? I can't keep up with all the rules.
We had been friends for a while. Then one day...
Where is he?
Who are you looking for?
Carl. We need to practice but apparently he has better things to do today.
I could do it.
Thank you, but I couldn't ask that. I wouldn't want to risk cutting such a pretty face.
You... you think my face is pretty?
Well, yeah. I mean...

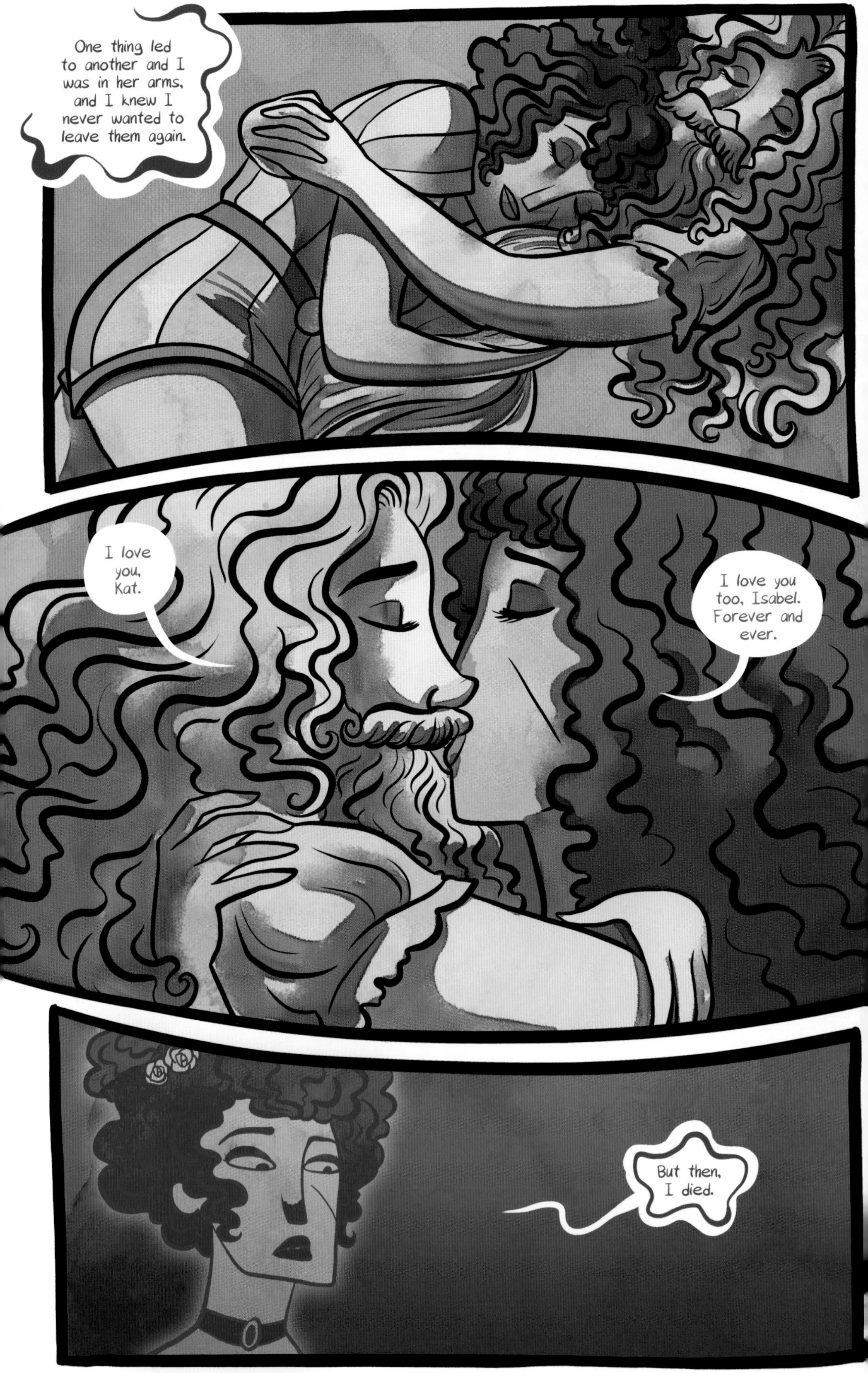

One thing led to another and I was in her arms, and I knew I never wanted to leave them again.
I love you, Kat.
I love you too, Isabel. Forever and ever.
But then, I died.

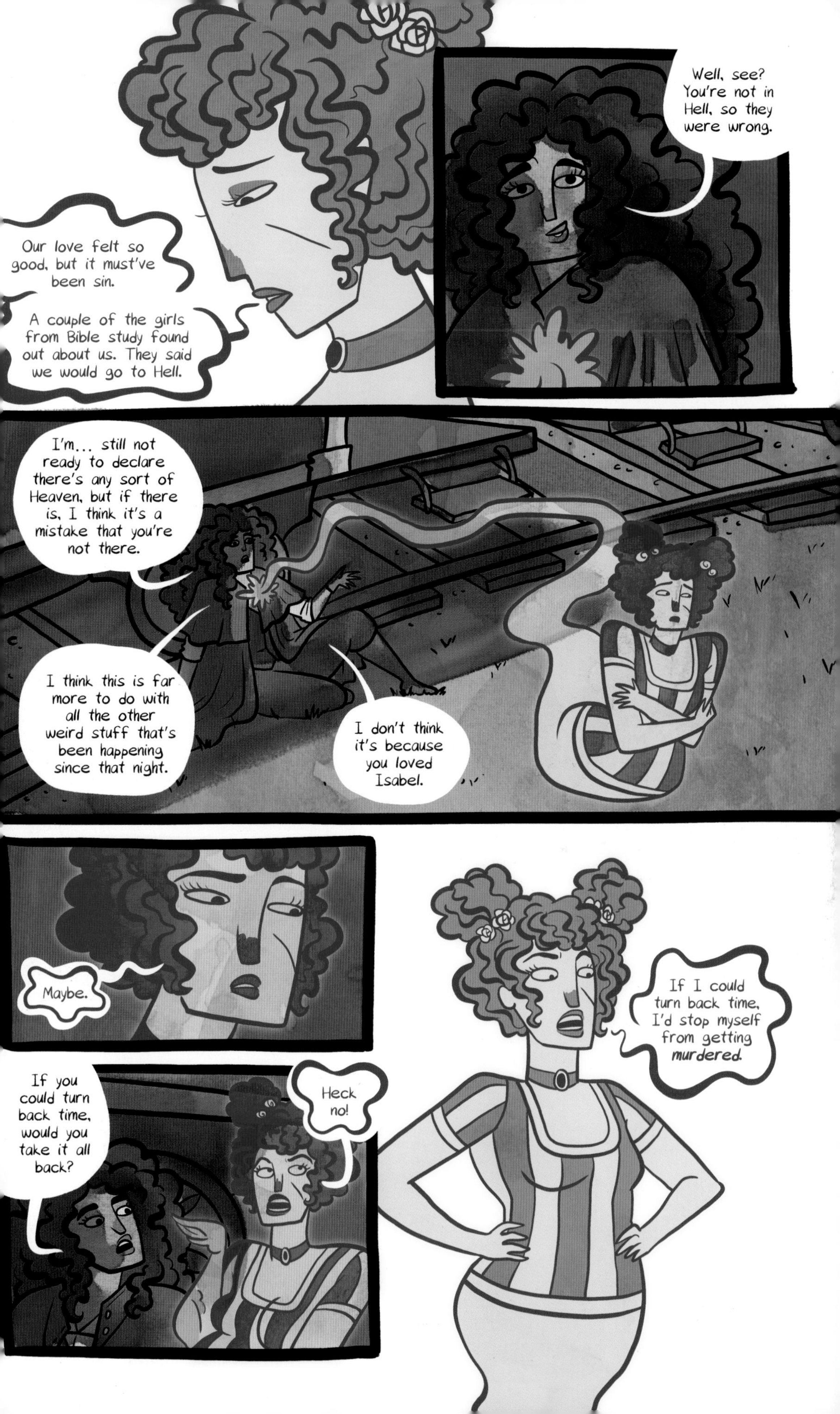
Our love felt so good, but it must've been sin.
A couple of the girls from Bible study found out about us. They said we would go to Hell.
Well, see? You're not in Hell, so they were wrong.
I'm... still not ready to declare there's any sort of Heaven, but if there is, I think it's a mistake that you're not there.
I think this is far more to do with all the other weird stuff that's been happening since that night.
I don't think it's because you loved Isabel.
Maybe.
If I could turn back time, I'd stop myself from getting *murdered*.
If you could turn back time, would you take it all back?
Heck no!

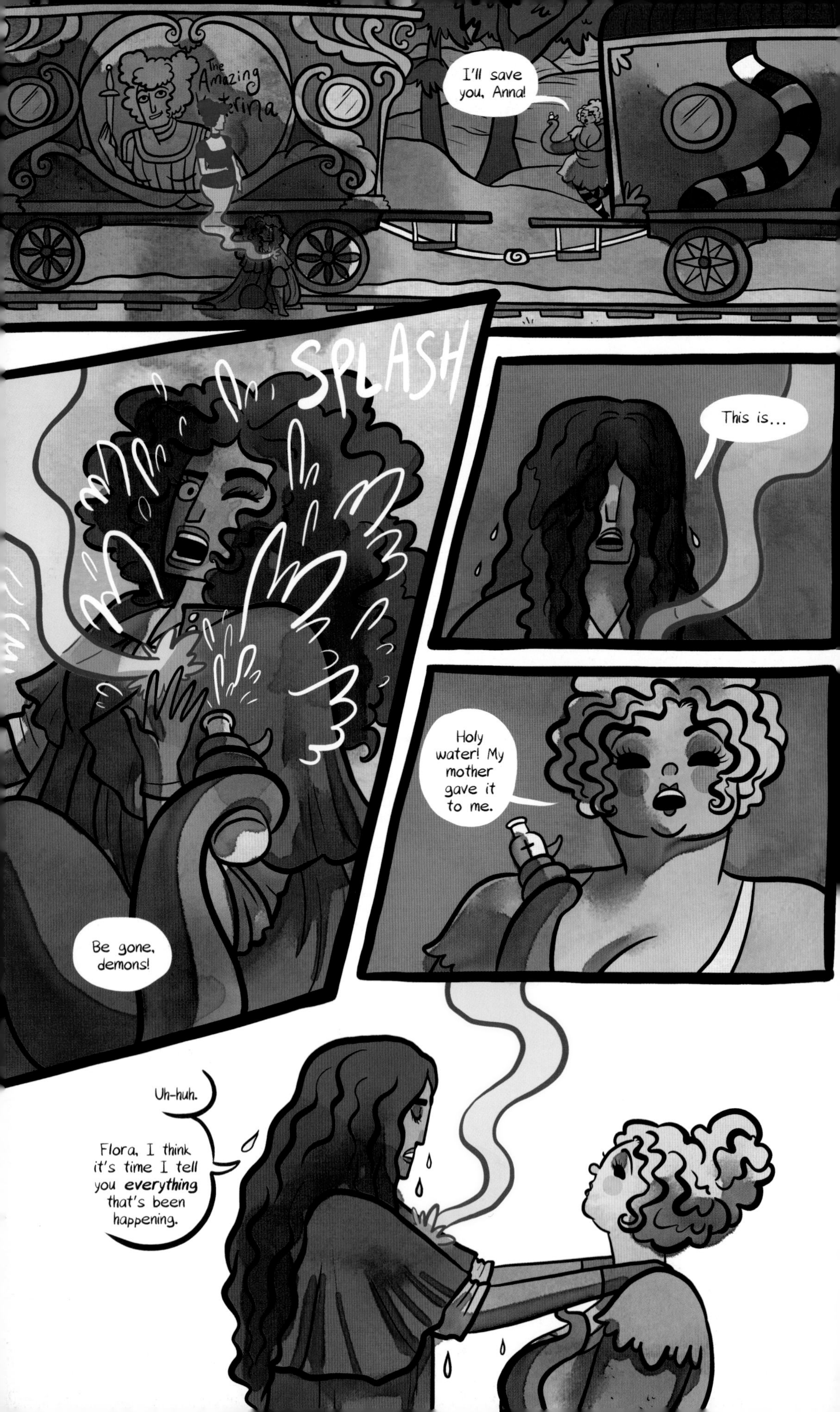
The Amazing
I'll save you, Anna!
SPLASH
Be gone, demons!
This is...
Holy water! My mother gave it to me.
Uh-huh.
Flora, I think it's time I tell you *everything* that's been happening.

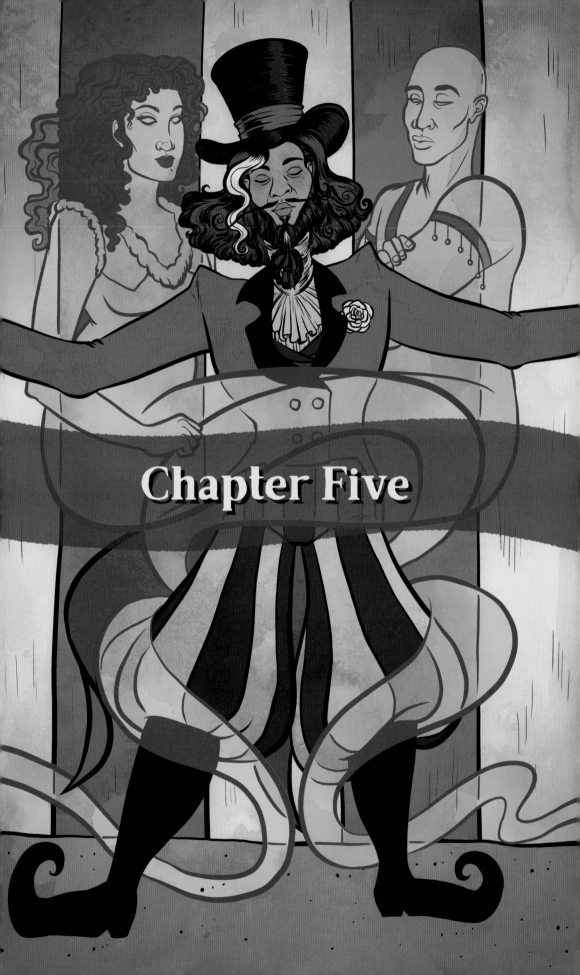

Chapter Five

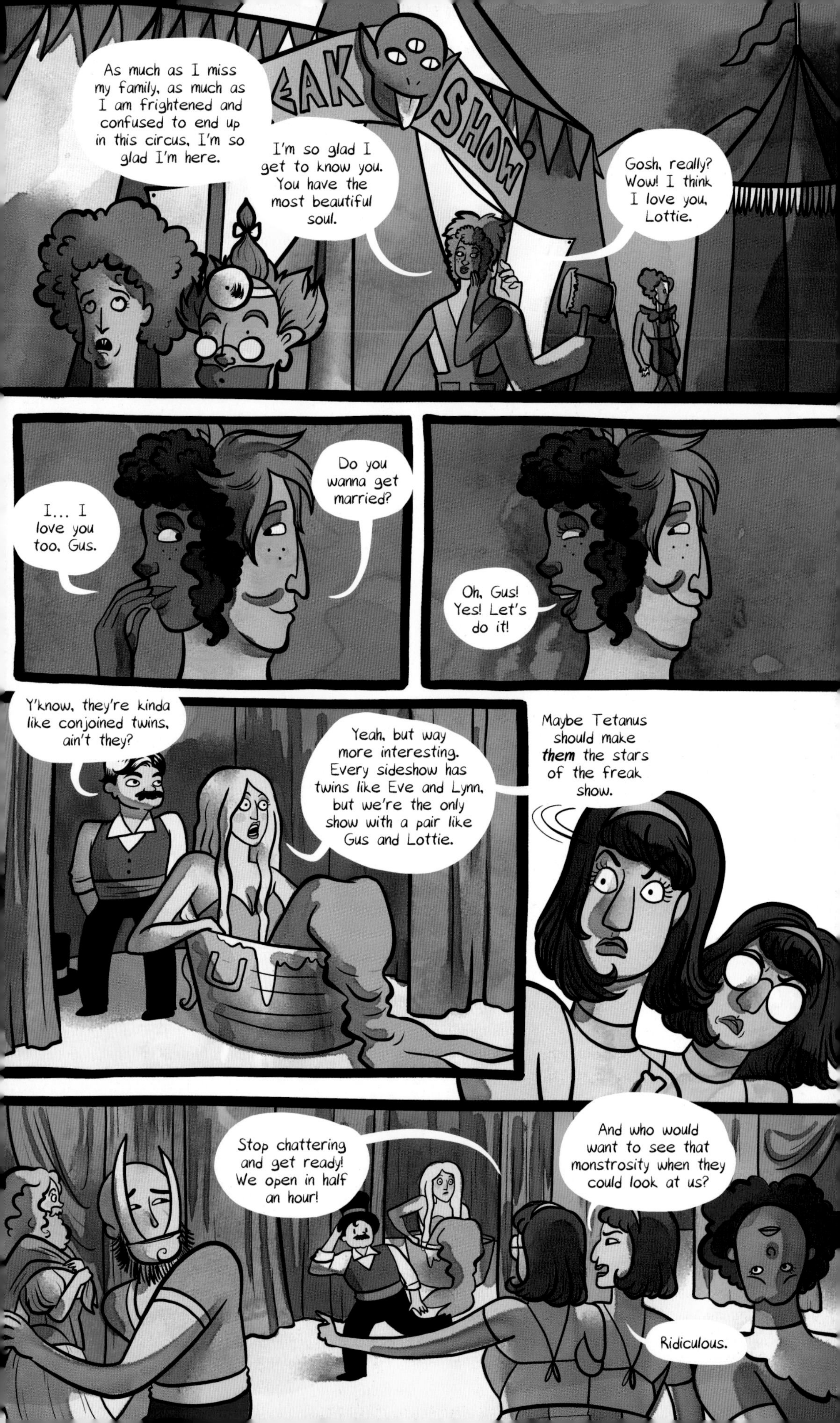

EAK SHOW
As much as I miss my family, as much as I am frightened and confused to end up in this circus, I'm so glad I'm here.
I'm so glad I get to know you. You have the most beautiful soul.
Gosh, really? Wow! I think I love you, Lottie.
I... I love you too, Gus.
Do you wanna get married?
Oh, Gus! Yes! Let's do it!
Y'know, they're kinda like conjoined twins, ain't they?
Yeah, but way more interesting. Every sideshow has twins like Eve and Lynn, but we're the only show with a pair like Gus and Lottie.
Maybe Tetanus should make *them* the stars of the freak show.
Stop chattering and get ready! We open in half an hour!
And who would want to see that monstrosity when they could look at us?
Ridiculous.

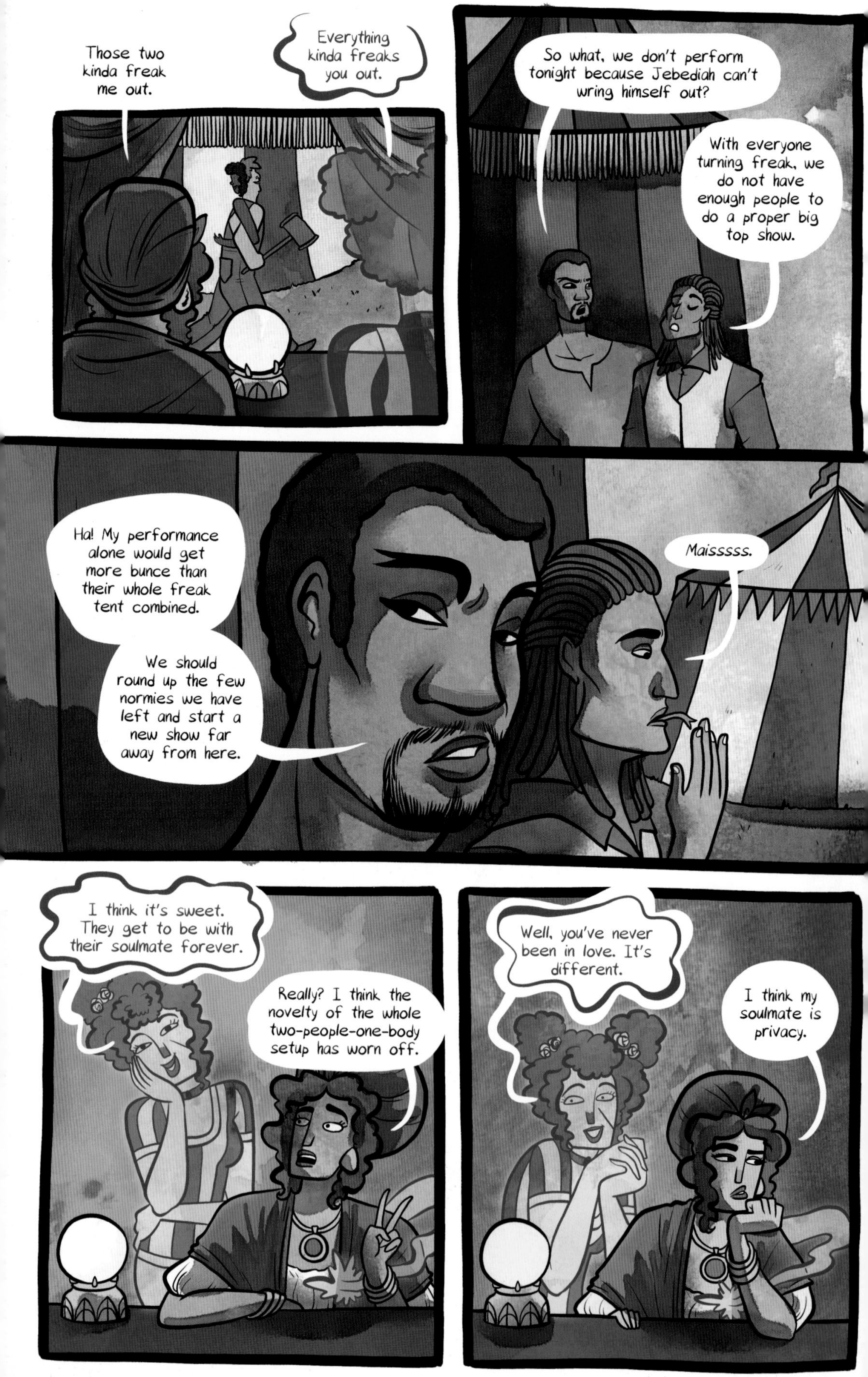

Those two kinda freak me out.
Everything kinda freaks you out.
So what, we don't perform tonight because Jebediah can't wring himself out?
With everyone turning freak, we do not have enough people to do a proper big top show.
Ha! My performance alone would get more bunce than their whole freak tent combined.
We should round up the few normies we have left and start a new show far away from here.
Maisssss.
I think it's sweet. They get to be with their soulmate forever.
Really? I think the novelty of the whole two-people-one-body setup has worn off.
Well, you've never been in love. It's different.
I think my soulmate is privacy.

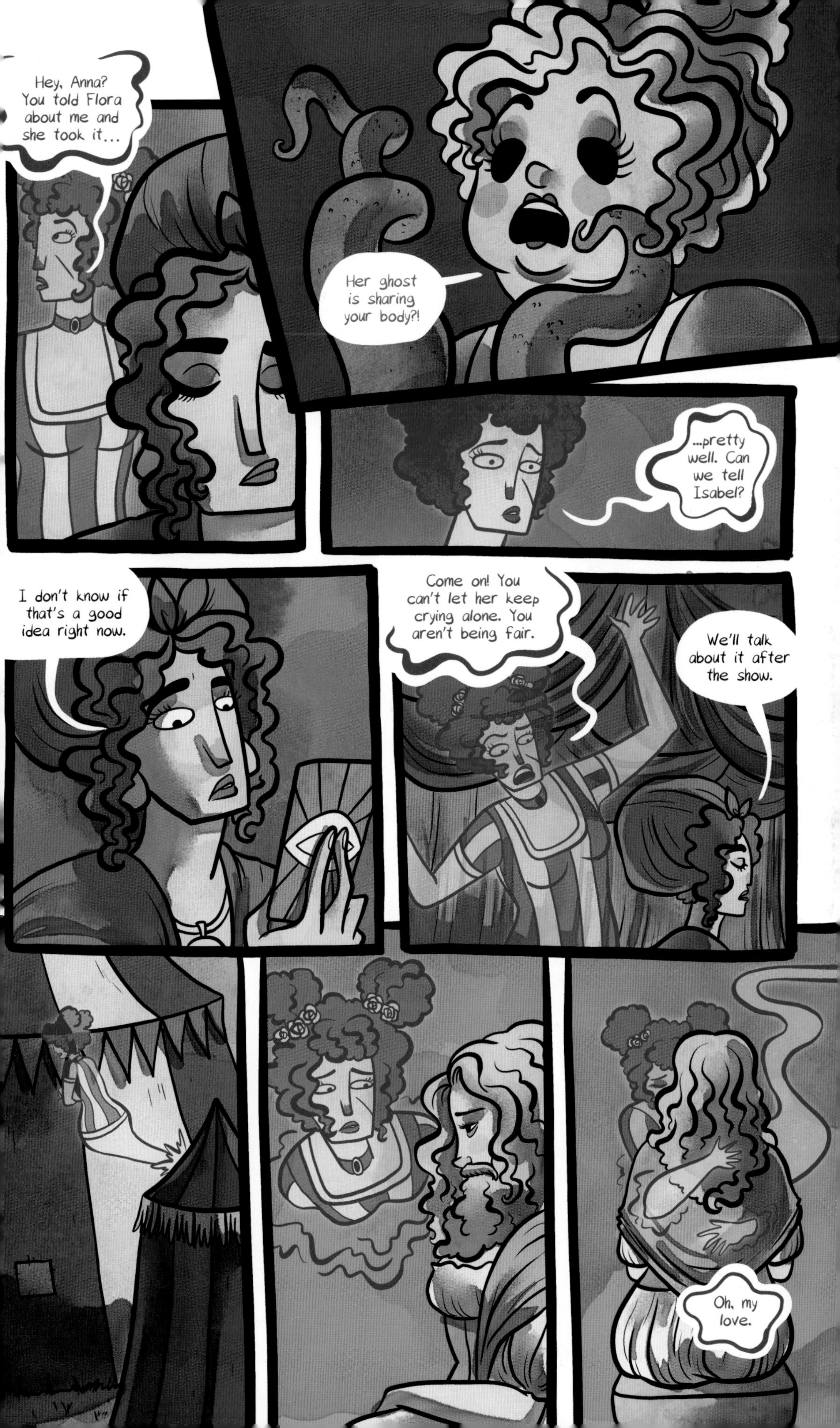
Hey, Anna? You told Flora about me and she took it...
Her ghost is sharing your body?!
...pretty well. Can we tell Isabel?
I don't know if that's a good idea right now.
Come on! You can't let her keep crying alone. You aren't being fair.
We'll talk about it after the show.
Oh, my love.

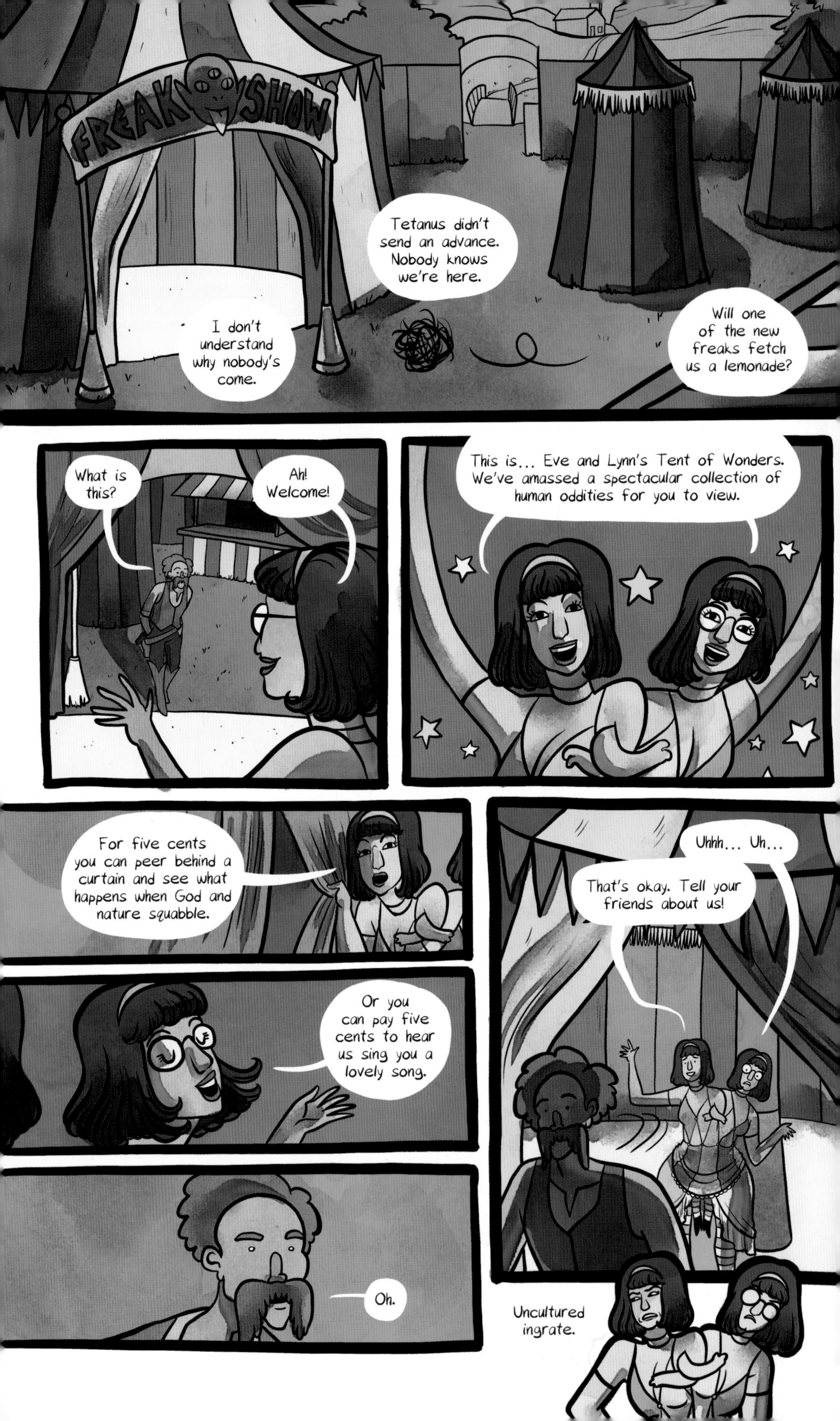
FREAK SHOW
Tetanus didn't send an advance. Nobody knows we're here.
I don't understand why nobody's come.
Will one of the new freaks fetch us a lemonade?
What is this?
Ah! Welcome!
This is... Eve and Lynn's Tent of Wonders. We've amassed a spectacular collection of human oddities for you to view.
For five cents you can peer behind a curtain and see what happens when God and nature squabble.
Or you can pay five cents to hear us sing you a lovely song.
Oh.
Uhhh... Uh...
That's okay. Tell your friends about us!
Uncultured ingrate.

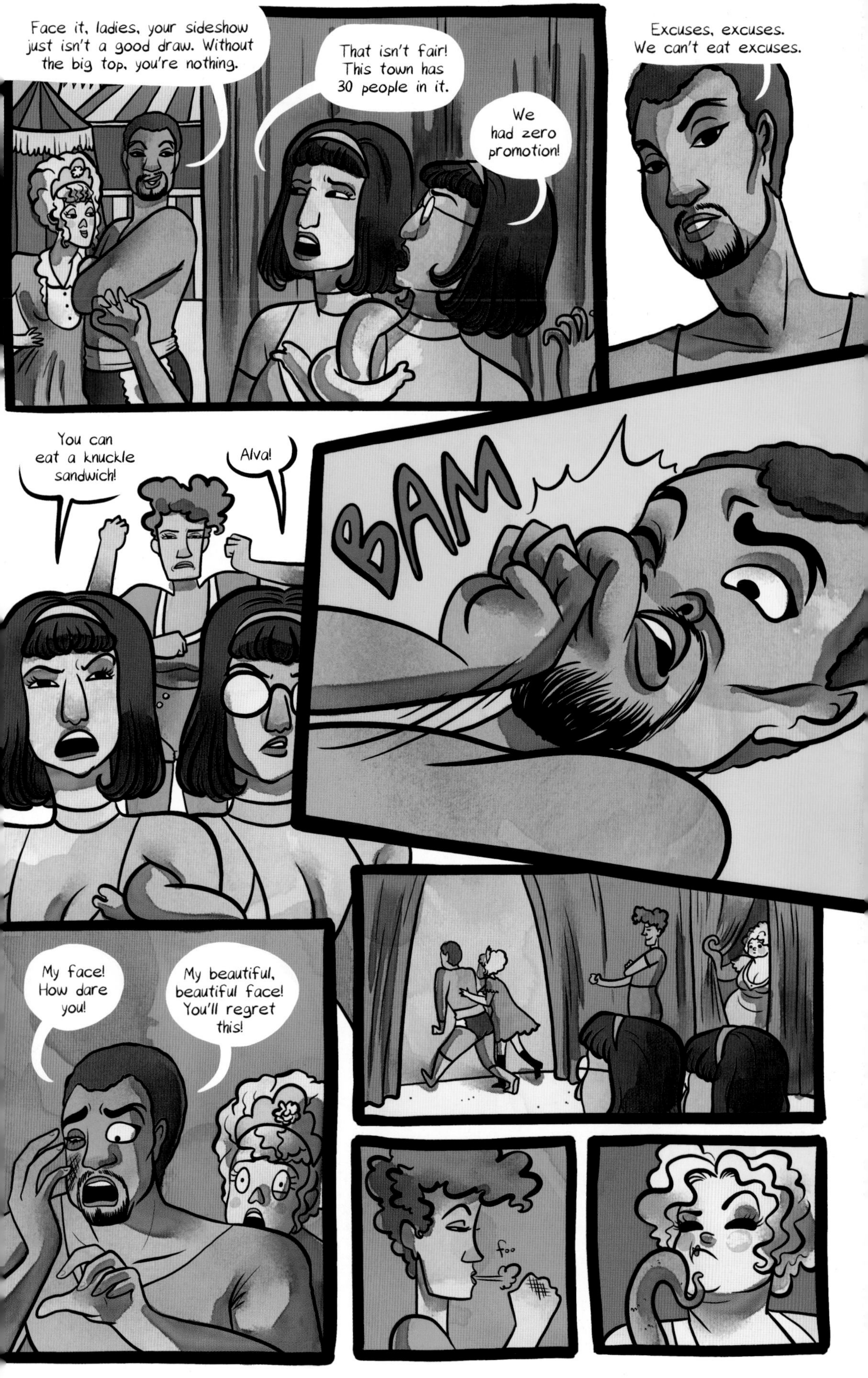
Face it, ladies, your sideshow just isn't a good draw. Without the big top, you're nothing.
That isn't fair! This town has 30 people in it.
We had zero promotion!
Excuses, excuses. We can't eat excuses.
You can eat a knuckle sandwich!
Alva!
BAM
My face! How dare you!
My beautiful, beautiful face! You'll regret this!
foo

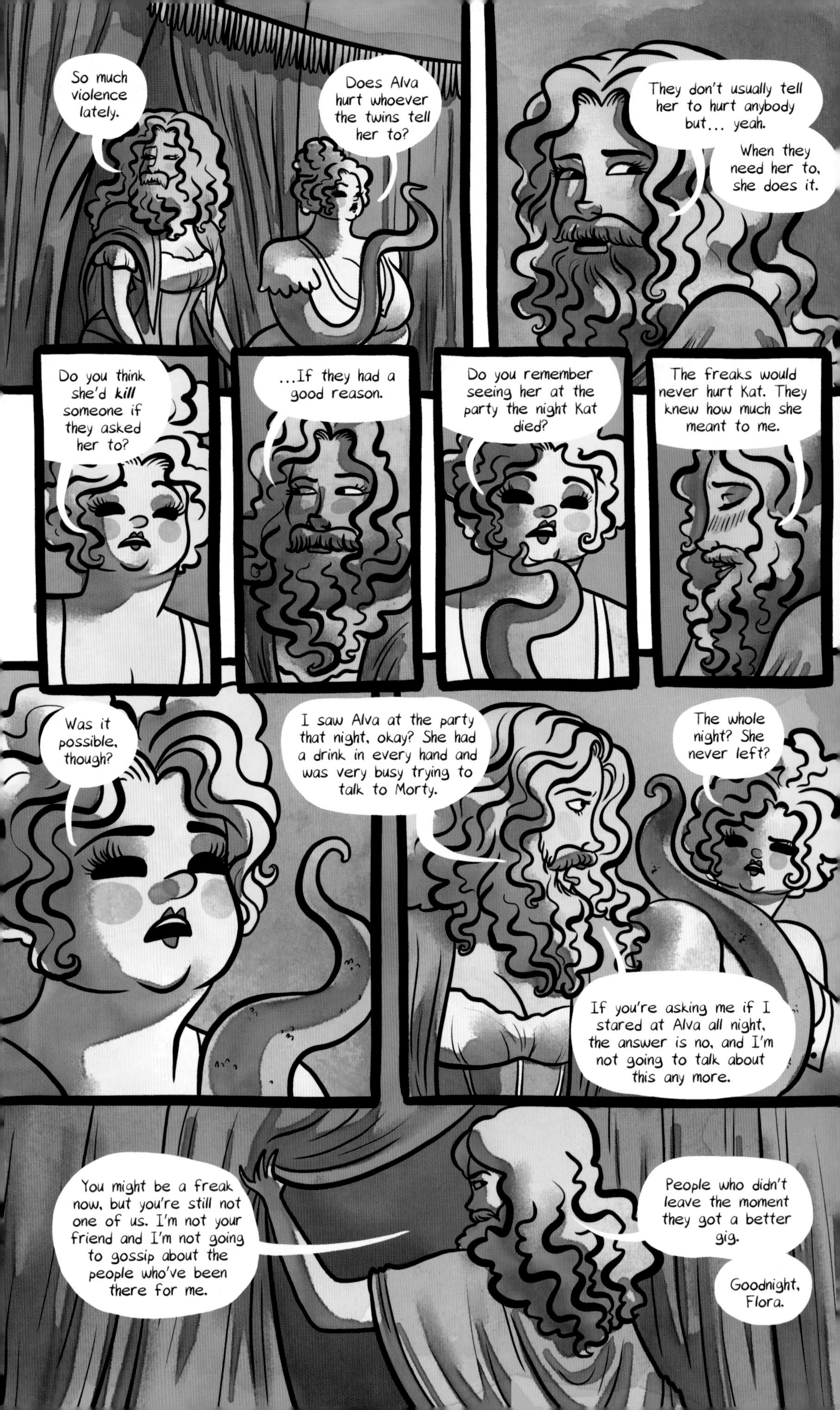
So much violence lately.
Does Alva hurt whoever the twins tell her to?
They don't usually tell her to hurt anybody but... yeah.
When they need her to, she does it.
Do you think she'd **kill** someone if they asked her to?
...If they had a good reason.
Do you remember seeing her at the party the night Kat died?
The freaks would never hurt Kat. They knew how much she meant to me.
Was it possible, though?
I saw Alva at the party that night, okay? She had a drink in every hand and was very busy trying to talk to Morty.
The whole night? She never left?
If you're asking me if I stared at Alva all night, the answer is no, and I'm not going to talk about this any more.
You might be a freak now, but you're still not one of us. I'm not your friend and I'm not going to gossip about the people who've been there for me.
People who didn't leave the moment they got a better gig.
Goodnight, Flora.

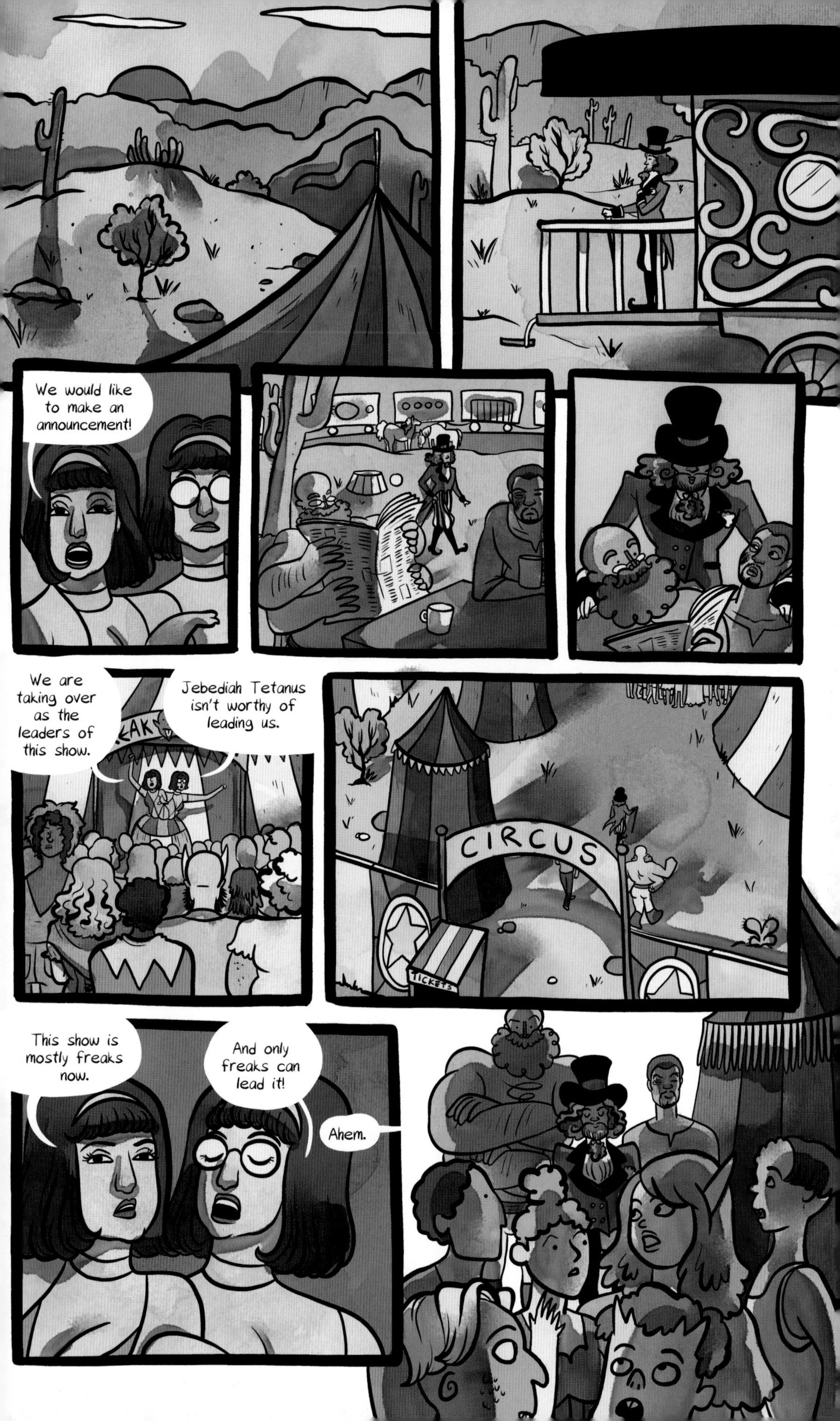
We would like to make an announcement!
We are taking over as the leaders of this show.
Jebediah Tetanus isn't worthy of leading us.
CIRCUS
TICKETS
This show is mostly freaks now.
And only freaks can lead it!
Ahem.

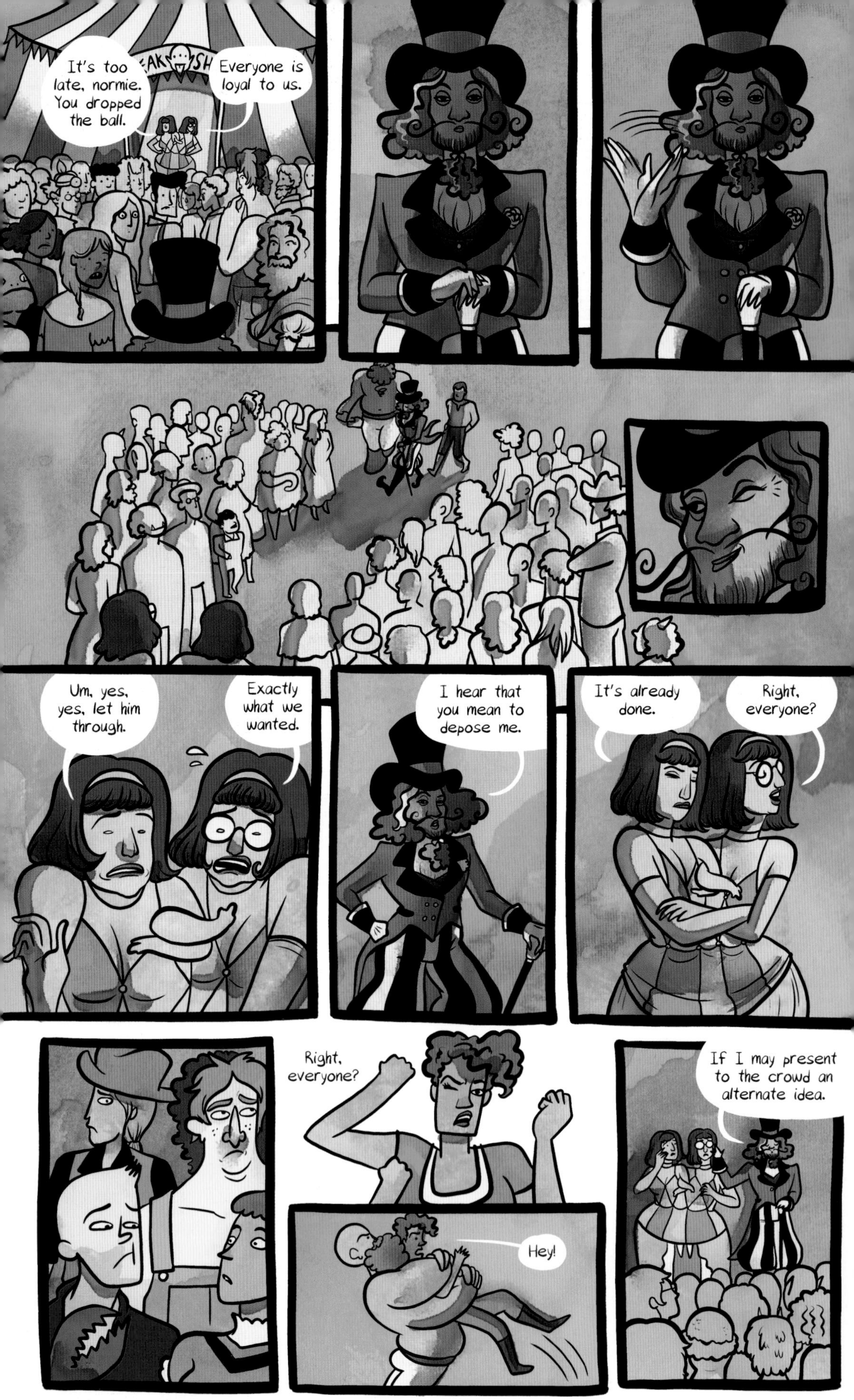

It's too late, normie. You dropped the ball.
Everyone is loyal to us.
Um, yes, yes, let him through.
Exactly what we wanted.
I hear that you mean to depose me.
It's already done.
Right, everyone?
Right, everyone?
Hey!
If I may present to the crowd an alternate idea.

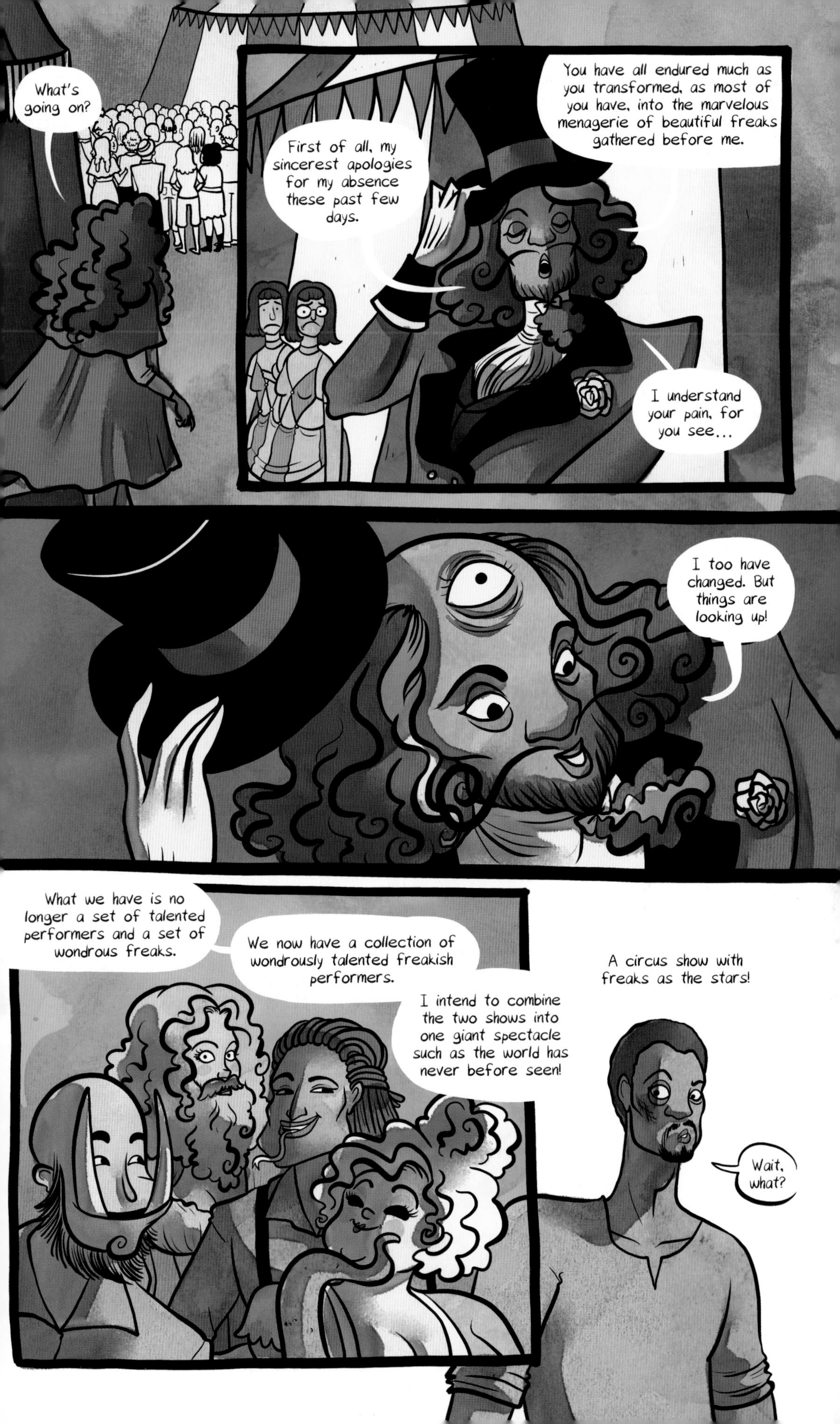
What's going on?
First of all, my sincerest apologies for my absence these past few days.
You have all endured much as you transformed, as most of you have, into the marvelous menagerie of beautiful freaks gathered before me.
I understand your pain, for you see...
I too have changed. But things are looking up!
What we have is no longer a set of talented performers and a set of wondrous freaks.
We now have a collection of wondrously talented freakish performers.
I intend to combine the two shows into one giant spectacle such as the world has never before seen!
A circus show with freaks as the stars!
Wait, what?

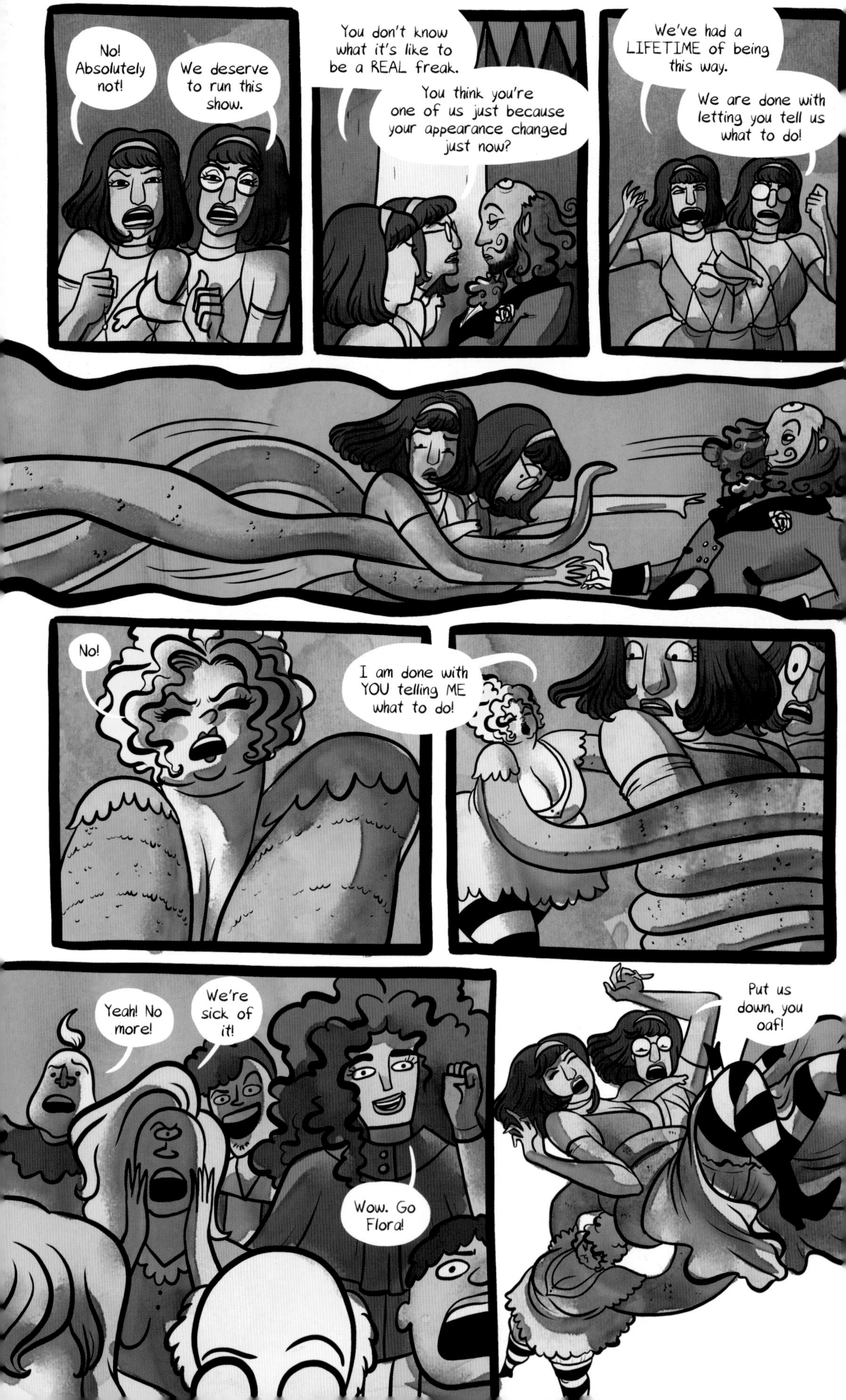
No! Absolutely not!
We deserve to run this show.
You don't know what it's like to be a REAL freak.
You think you're one of us just because your appearance changed just now?
We've had a LIFETIME of being this way.
We are done with letting you tell us what to do!
No!
I am done with YOU telling ME what to do!
Yeah! No more!
We're sick of it!
Wow. Go Flora!
Put us down, you oaf!

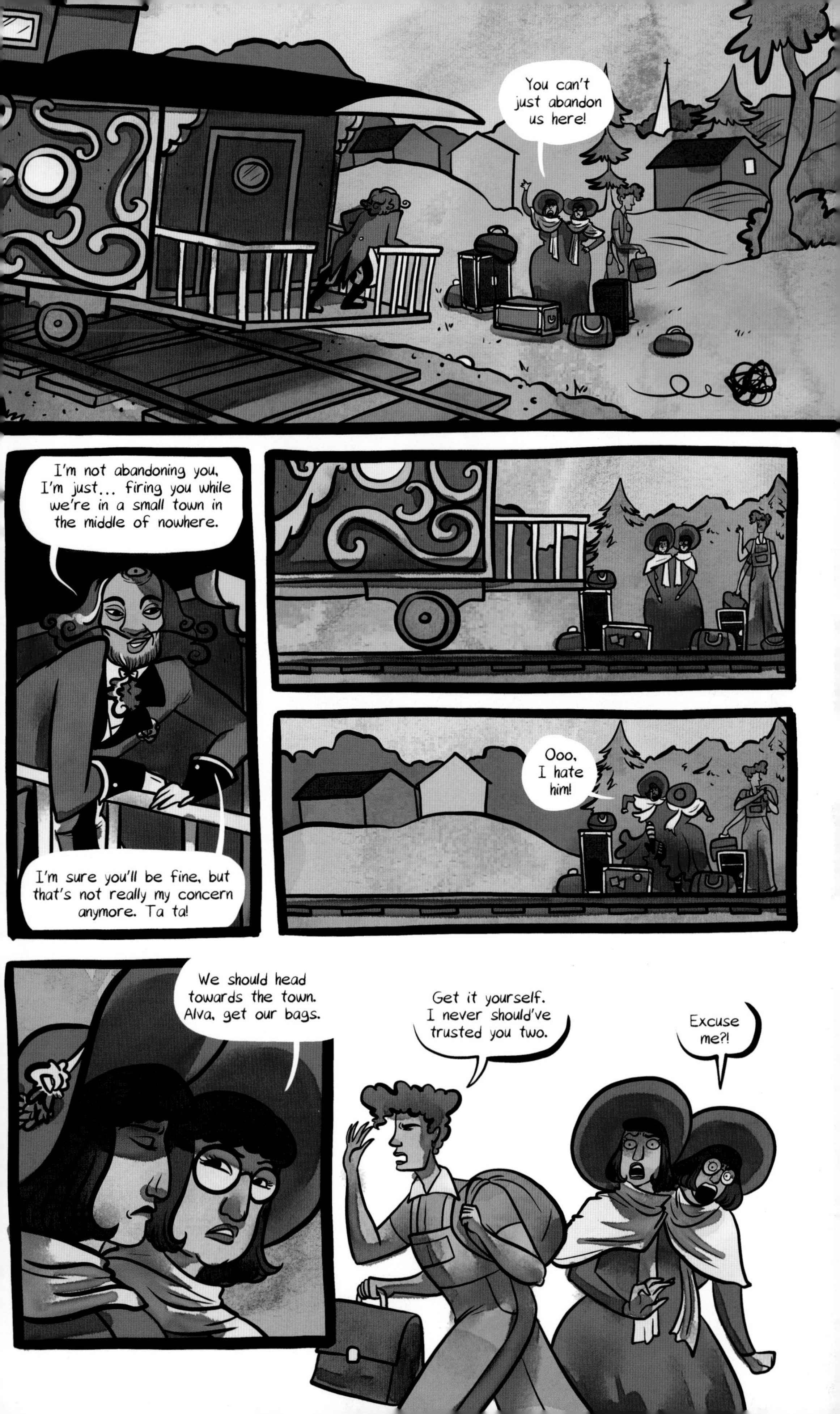
You can't just abandon us here!
I'm not abandoning you, I'm just... firing you while we're in a small town in the middle of nowhere.
I'm sure you'll be fine, but that's not really my concern anymore. Ta ta!
Ooo, I hate him!
We should head towards the town. Alva, get our bags.
Get it yourself. I never should've trusted you two.
Excuse me?!

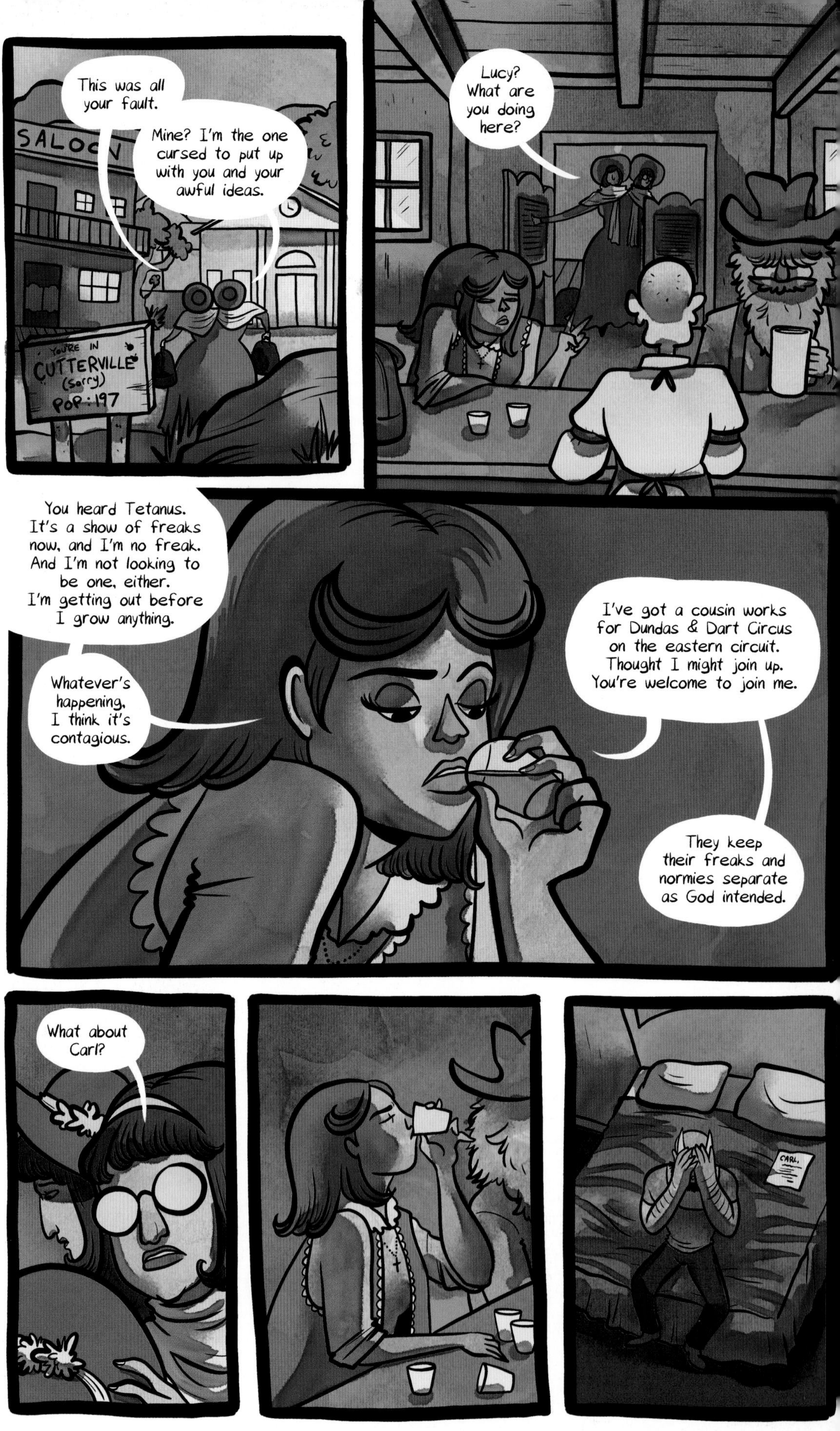

SALOON
YOU'RE IN CUTTERVILLE (sorry) POP: 197
This was all your fault.
Mine? I'm the one cursed to put up with you and your awful ideas.
Lucy? What are you doing here?
You heard Tetanus. It's a show of freaks now, and I'm no freak. And I'm not looking to be one, either. I'm getting out before I grow anything.
Whatever's happening, I think it's contagious.
I've got a cousin works for Dundas & Dart Circus on the eastern circuit. Thought I might join up. You're welcome to join me.
They keep their freaks and normies separate as God intended.
What about Carl?
CARL

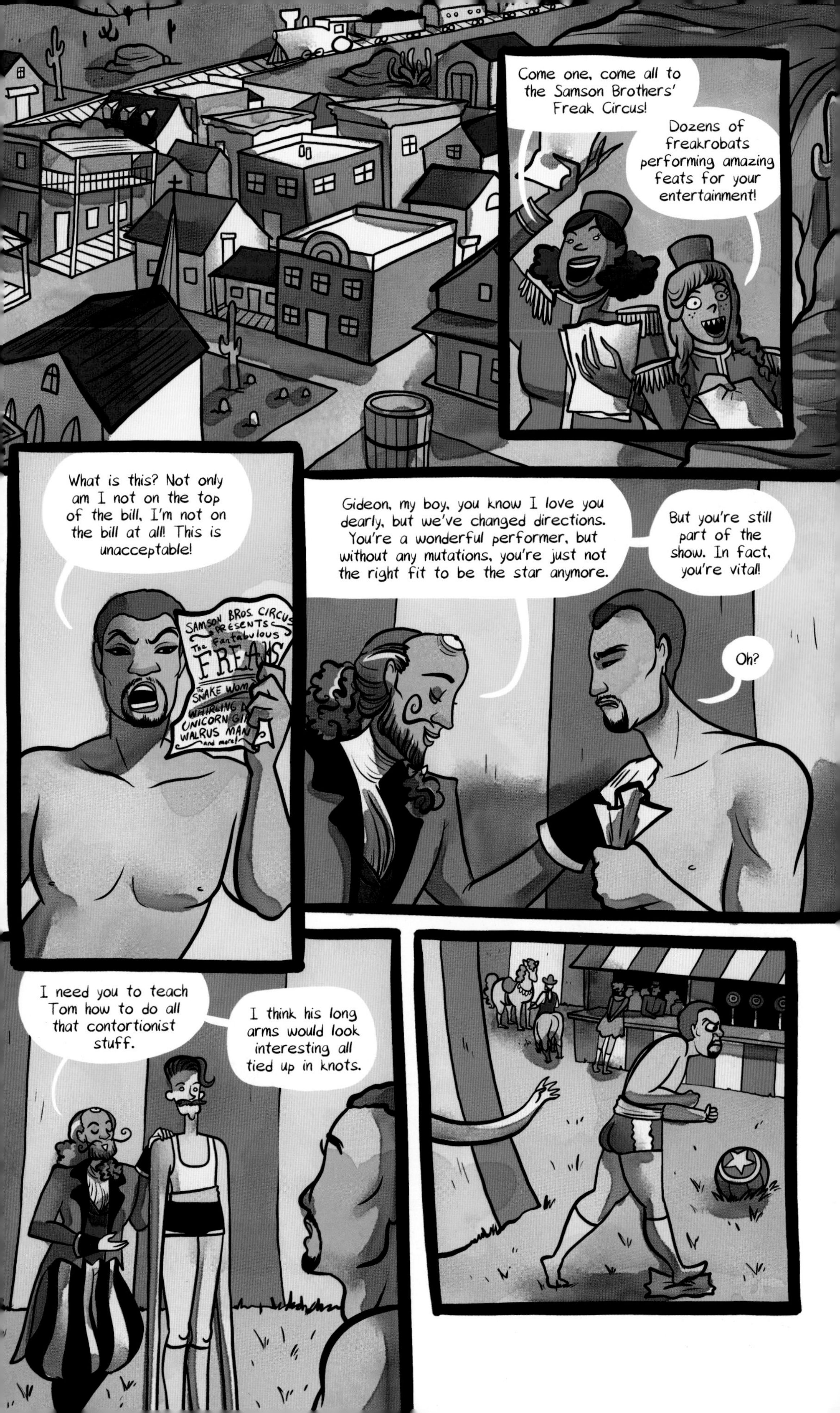

Come one, come all to the Samson Brothers' Freak Circus!
Dozens of freakrobats performing amazing feats for your entertainment!
What is this? Not only am I not on the top of the bill, I'm not on the bill at all! This is unacceptable!
SAMSON BROS. CIRCUS PRESENTS The Fantabulous
WALRUS MAN
and more!
Gideon, my boy, you know I love you dearly, but we've changed directions. You're a wonderful performer, but without any mutations, you're just not the right fit to be the star anymore.
But you're still part of the show. In fact, you're vital!
Oh?
I need you to teach Tom how to do all that contortionist stuff.
I think his long arms would look interesting all tied up in knots.

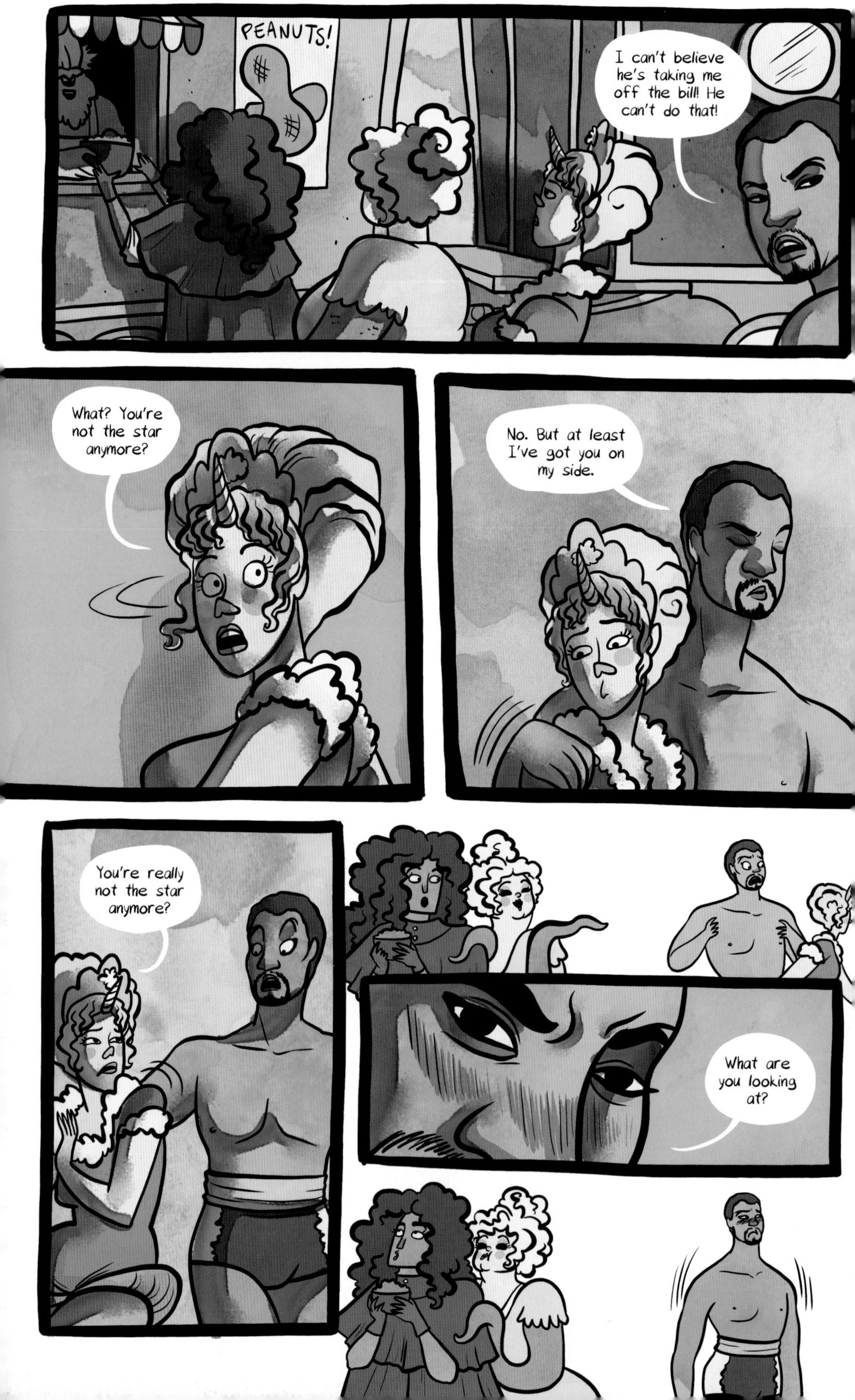
PEANUTS!
I can't believe he's taking me off the bill! He can't do that!
What? You're not the star anymore?
No. But at least I've got you on my side.
You're really not the star anymore?
What are you looking at?

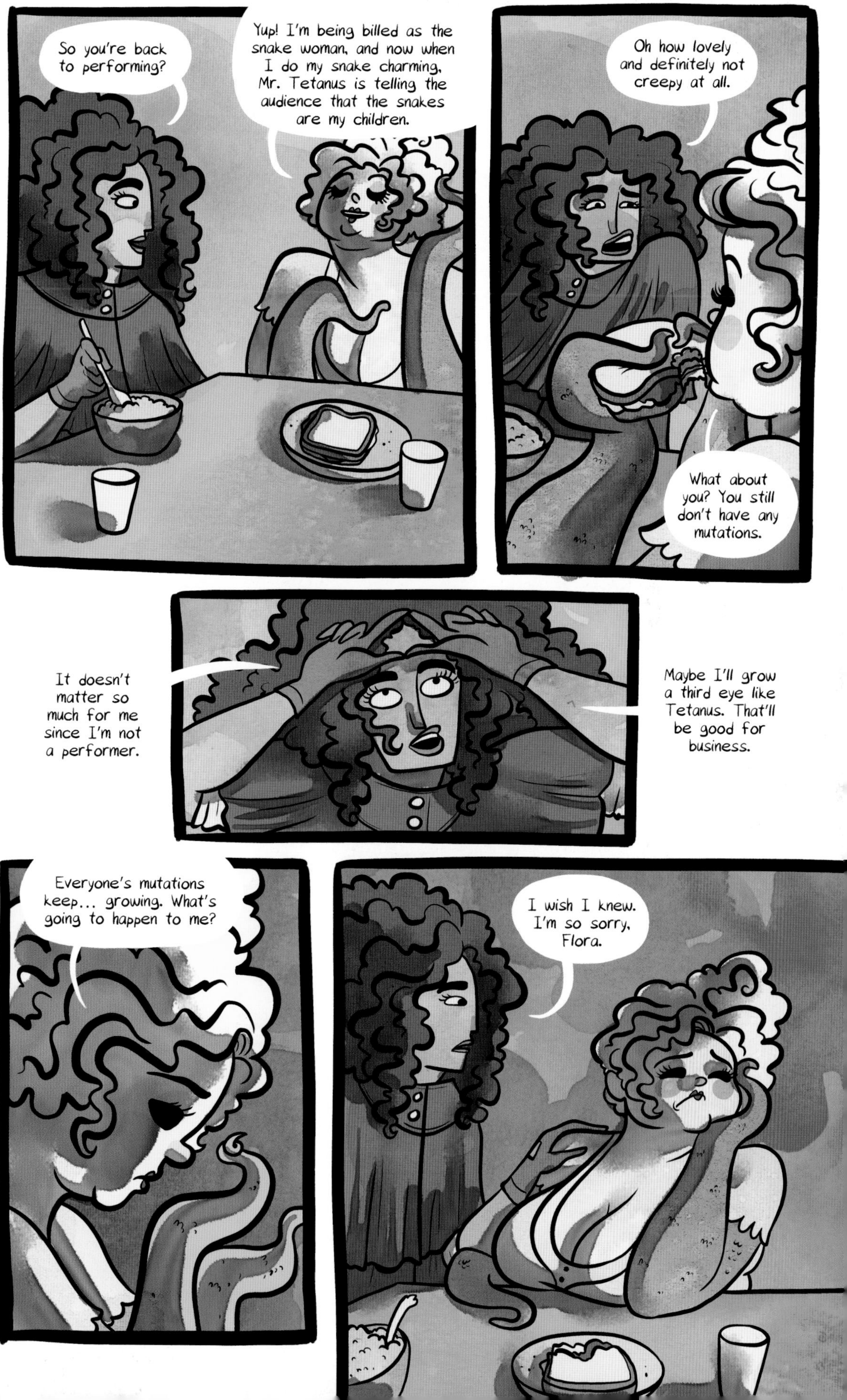

So you're back to performing?
Yup! I'm being billed as the snake woman, and now when I do my snake charming, Mr. Tetanus is telling the audience that the snakes are my children.
Oh how lovely and definitely not creepy at all.
What about you? You still don't have any mutations.
It doesn't matter so much for me since I'm not a performer.
Maybe I'll grow a third eye like Tetanus. That'll be good for business.
Everyone's mutations keep... growing. What's going to happen to me?
I wish I knew. I'm so sorry, Flora.

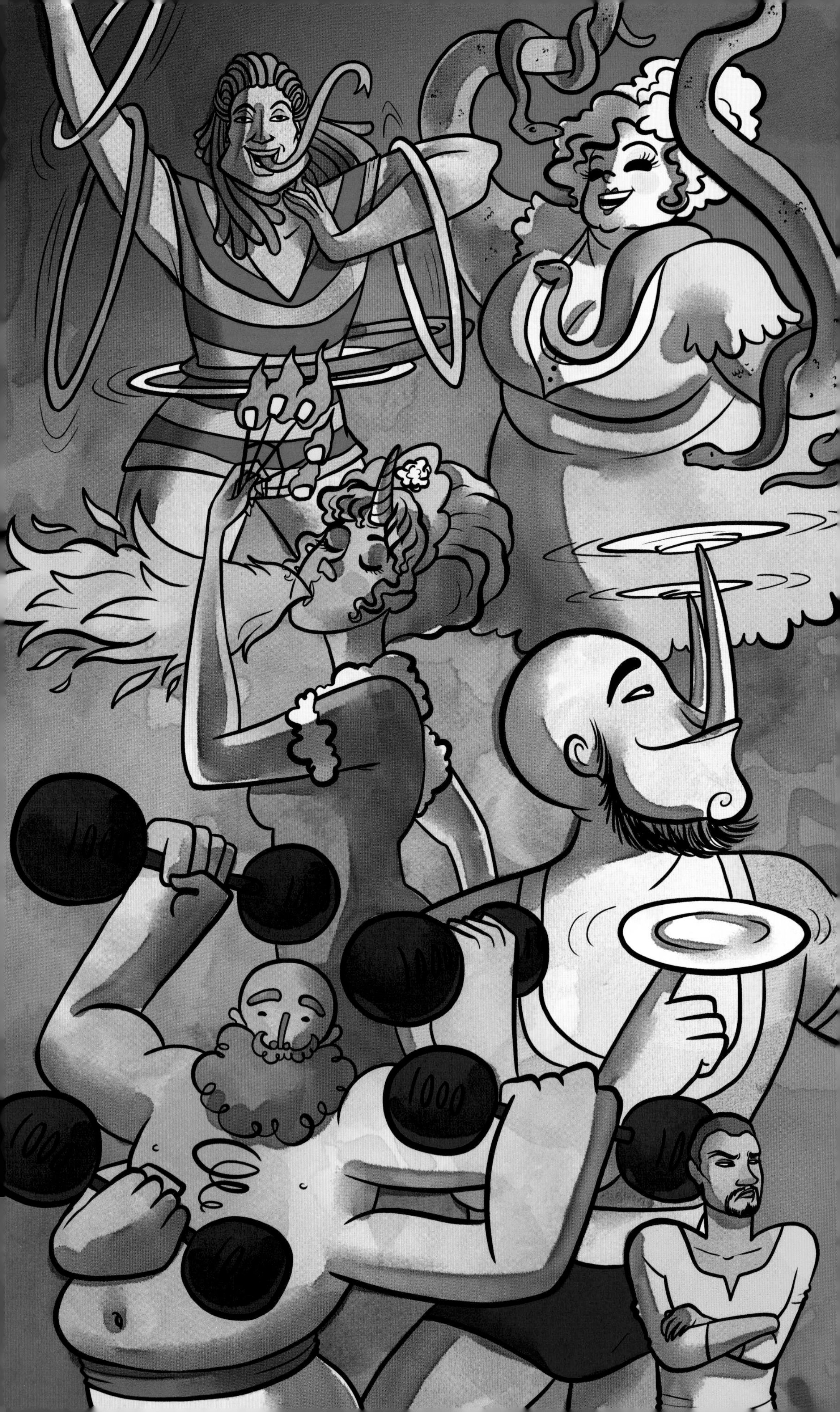
1000

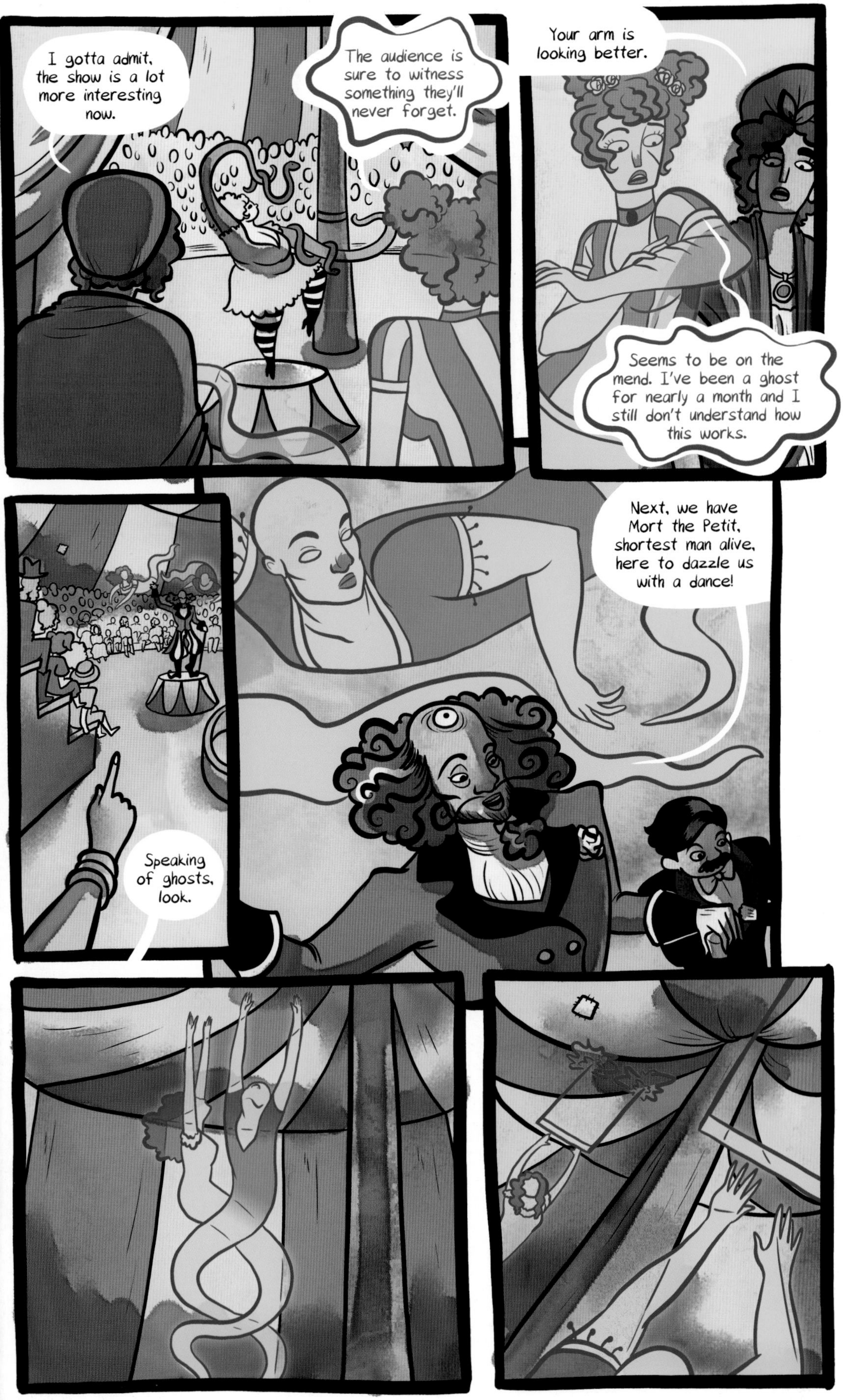
I gotta admit, the show is a lot more interesting now.
The audience is sure to witness something they'll never forget.
Your arm is looking better.
Seems to be on the mend. I've been a ghost for nearly a month and I still don't understand how this works.
Speaking of ghosts, look.
Next, we have Mort the Petit, shortest man alive, here to dazzle us with a dance!

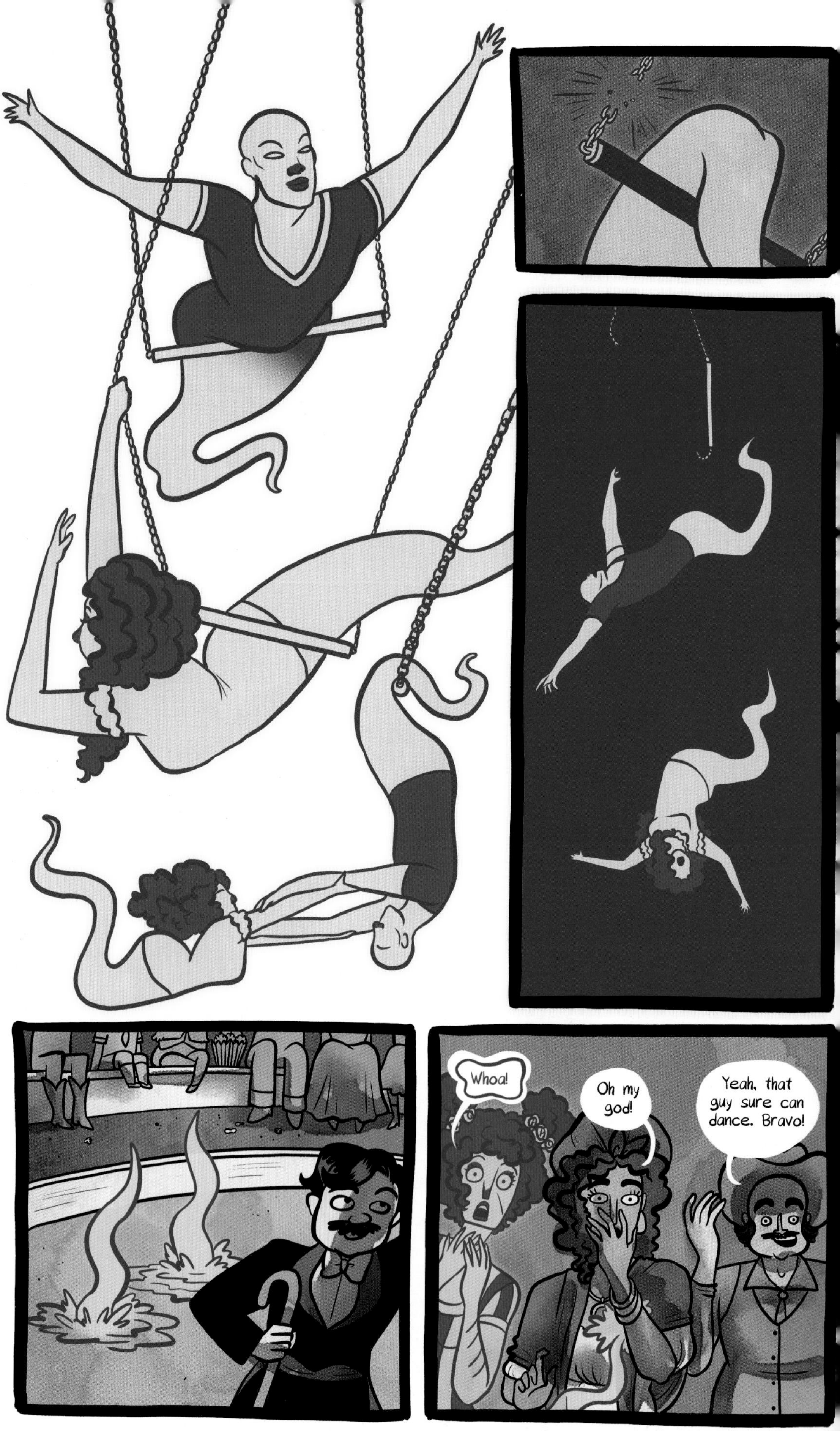
Whoa!
Oh my god!
Yeah, that guy sure can dance. Bravo!

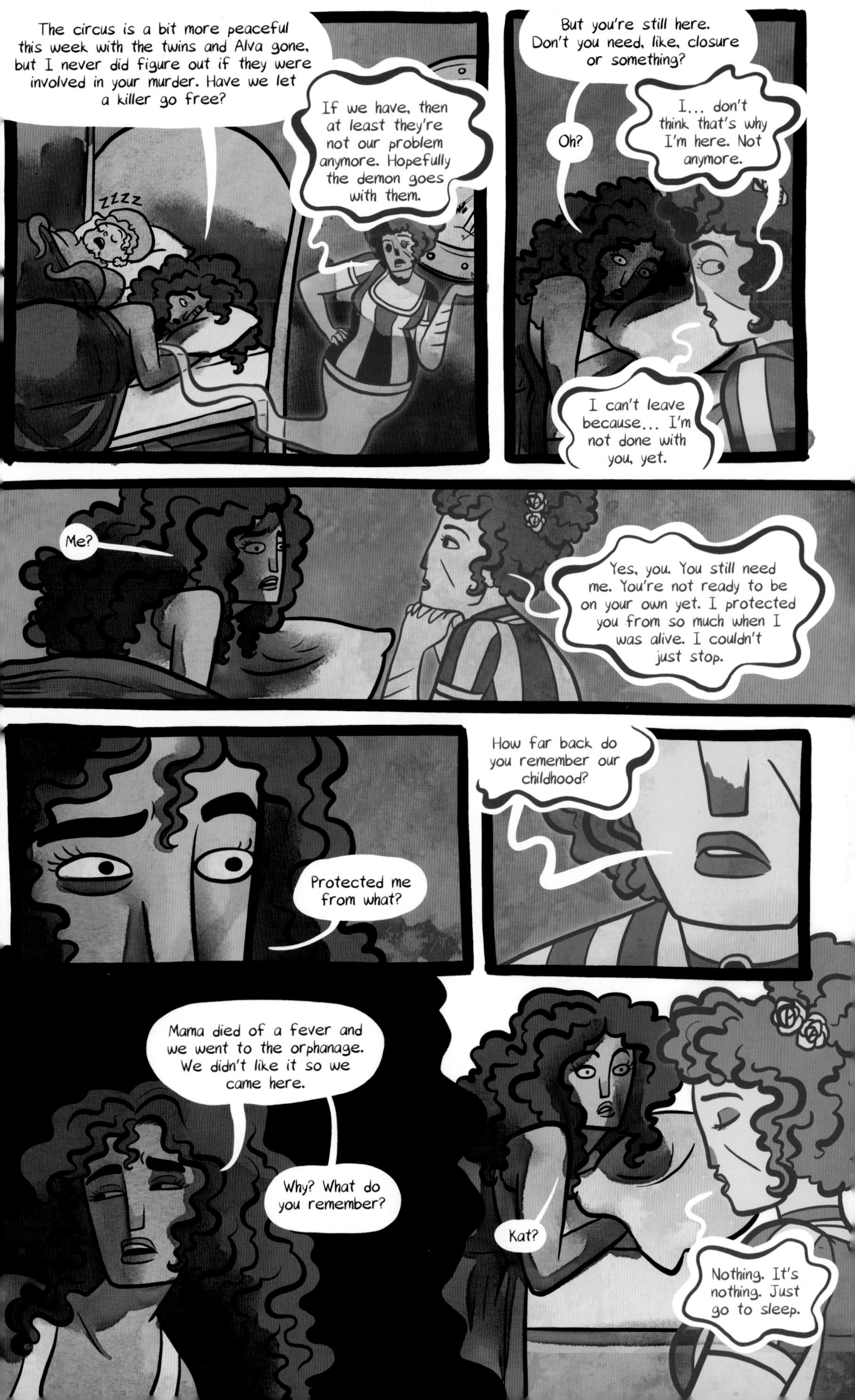
The circus is a bit more peaceful this week with the twins and Alva gone, but I never did figure out if they were involved in your murder. Have we let a killer go free?
ZZZZ
If we have, then at least they're not our problem anymore. Hopefully the demon goes with them.
But you're still here. Don't you need, like, closure or something?
Oh?
I... don't think that's why I'm here. Not anymore.
I can't leave because... I'm not done with you, yet.
Me?
Yes, you. You still need me. You're not ready to be on your own yet. I protected you from so much when I was alive. I couldn't just stop.
Protected me from what?
How far back do you remember our childhood?
Mama died of a fever and we went to the orphanage. We didn't like it so we came here.
Why? What do you remember?
Kat?
Nothing. It's nothing. Just go to sleep.

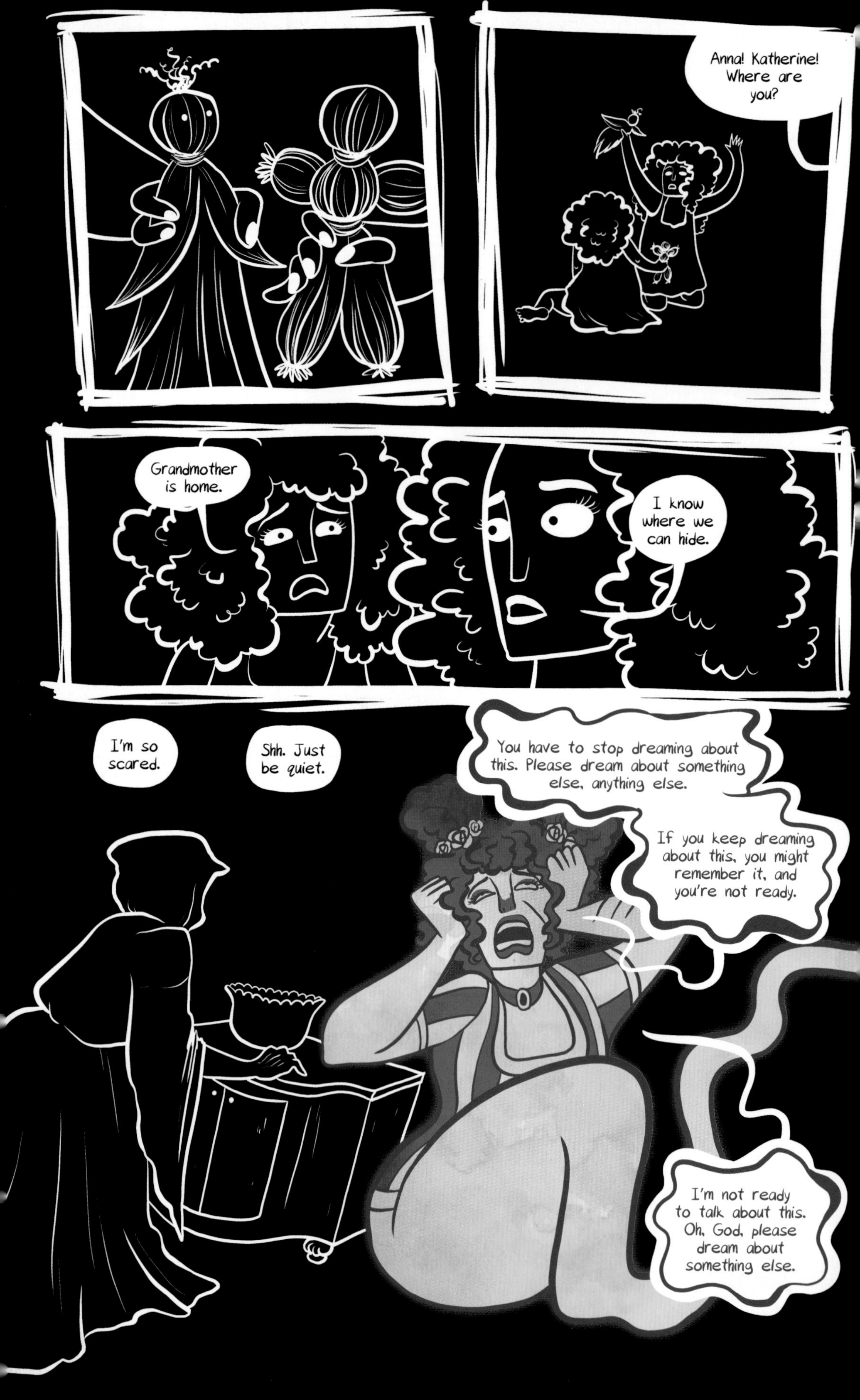

Anna! Katherine! Where are you?
Grandmother is home.
I know where we can hide.
I'm so scared.
Shh. Just be quiet.
You have to stop dreaming about this. Please dream about something else, anything else.
If you keep dreaming about this, you might remember it, and you're not ready.
I'm not ready to talk about this. Oh, God, please dream about something else.

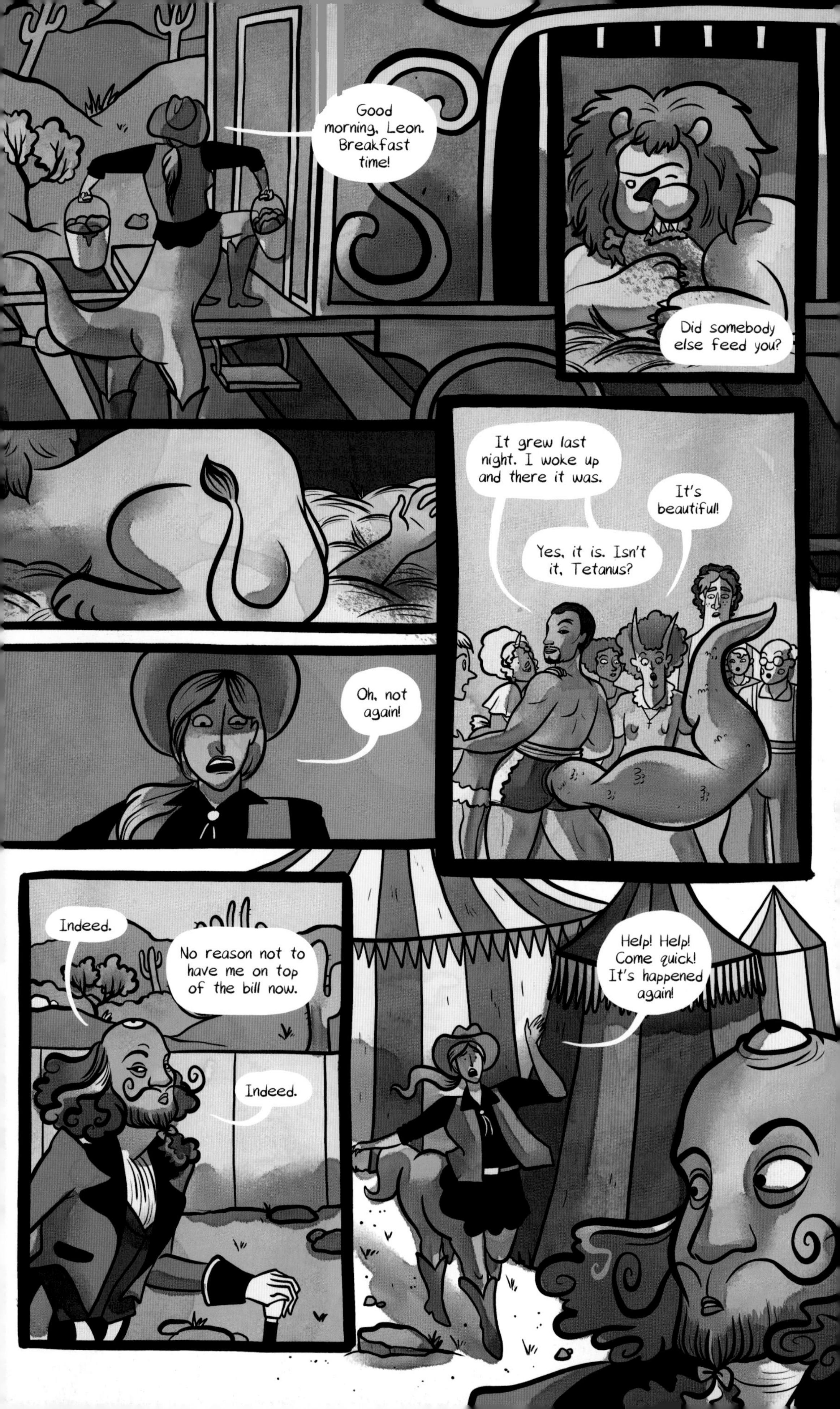

Good morning, Leon. Breakfast time!
Did somebody else feed you?
Oh, not again!
It grew last night. I woke up and there it was.
It's beautiful!
Yes, it is. Isn't it, Tetanus?
Indeed.
No reason not to have me on top of the bill now.
Indeed.
Help! Help! Come quick! It's happened again!

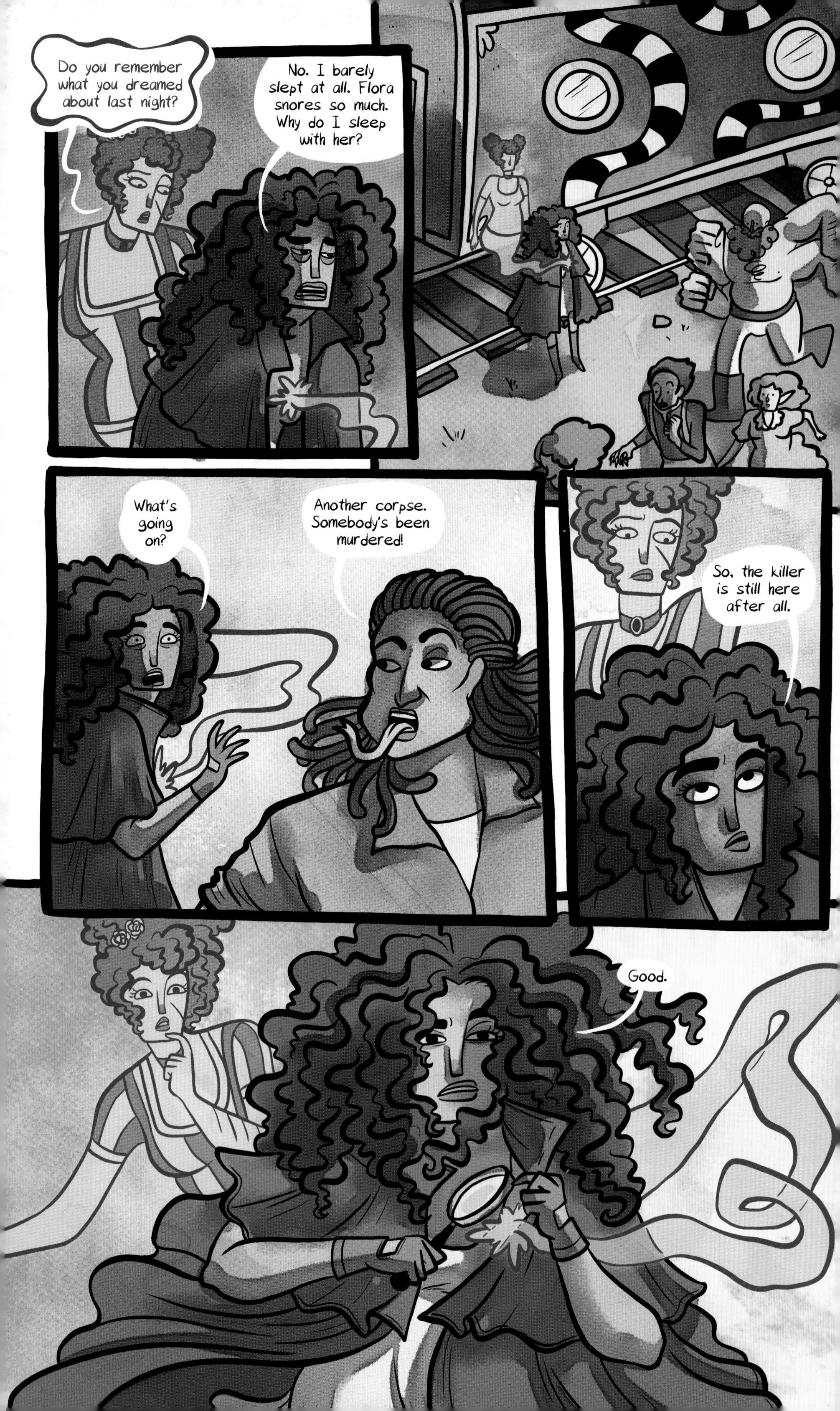
Do you remember what you dreamed about last night?
No. I barely slept at all. Flora snores so much. Why do I sleep with her?
What's going on?
Another corpse. Somebody's been murdered!
So, the killer is still here after all.
Good.

End of Book Two

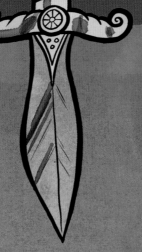

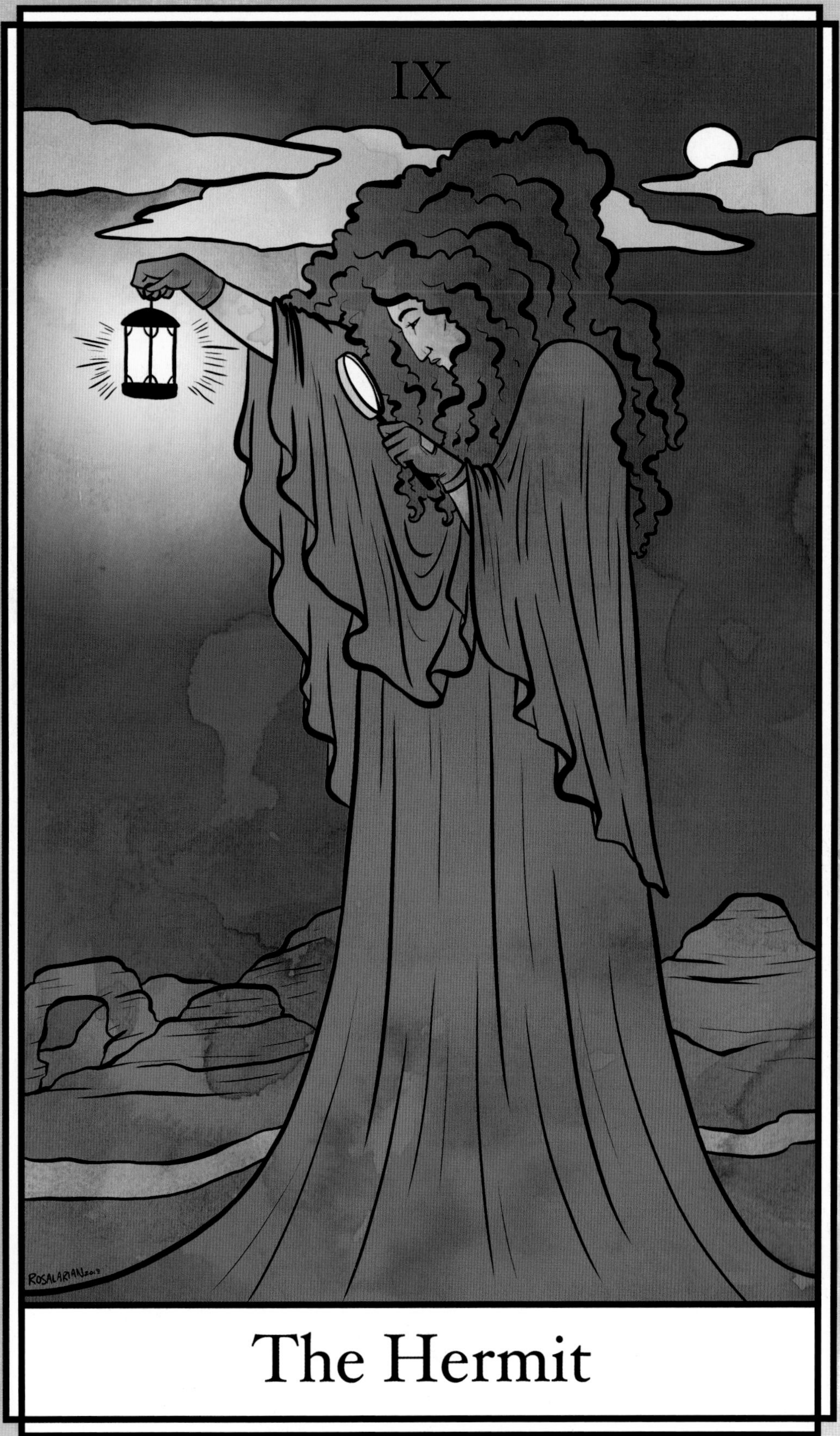
IX
ROSALARIAN 2013
The Hermit

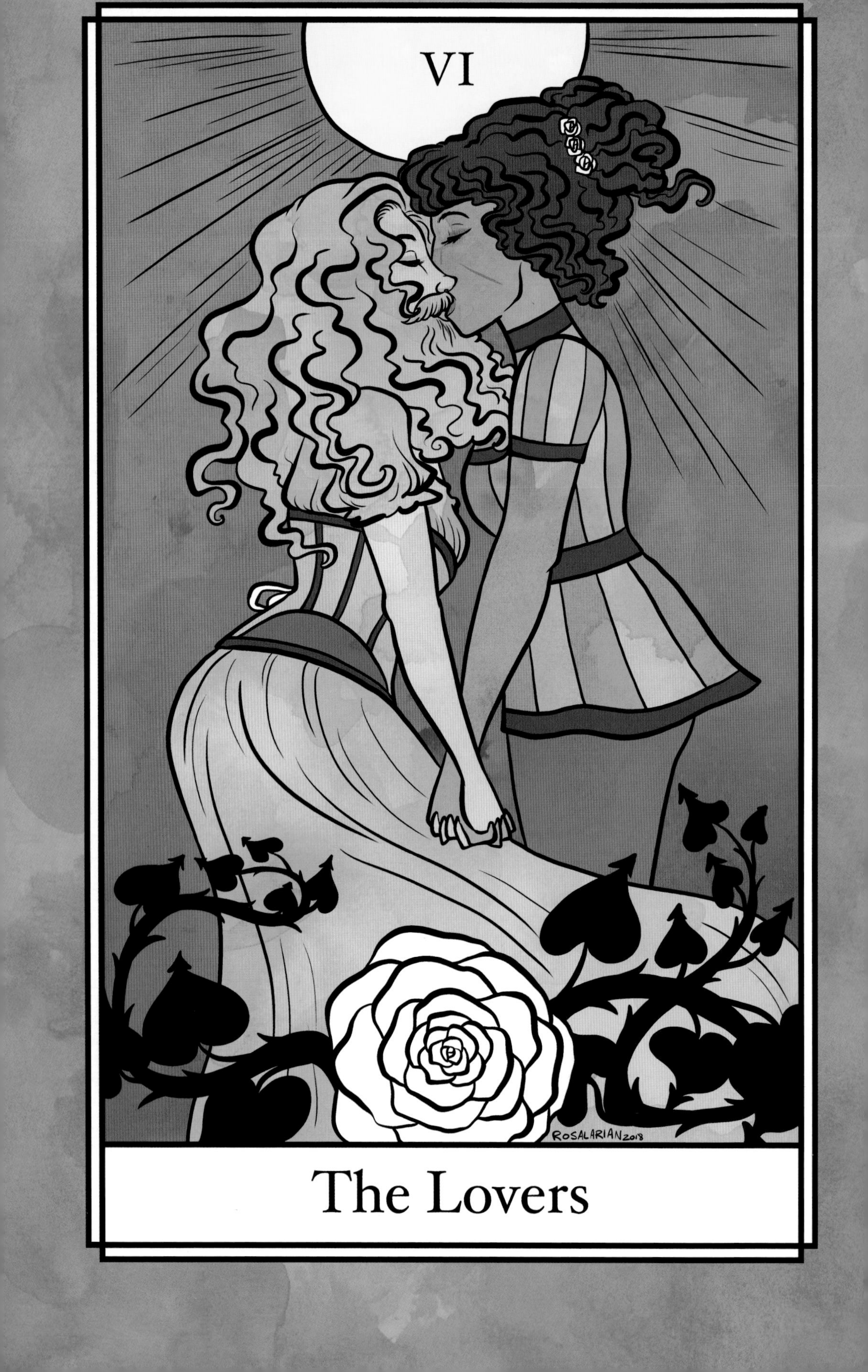
VI
ROSALARIAN2018
The Lovers

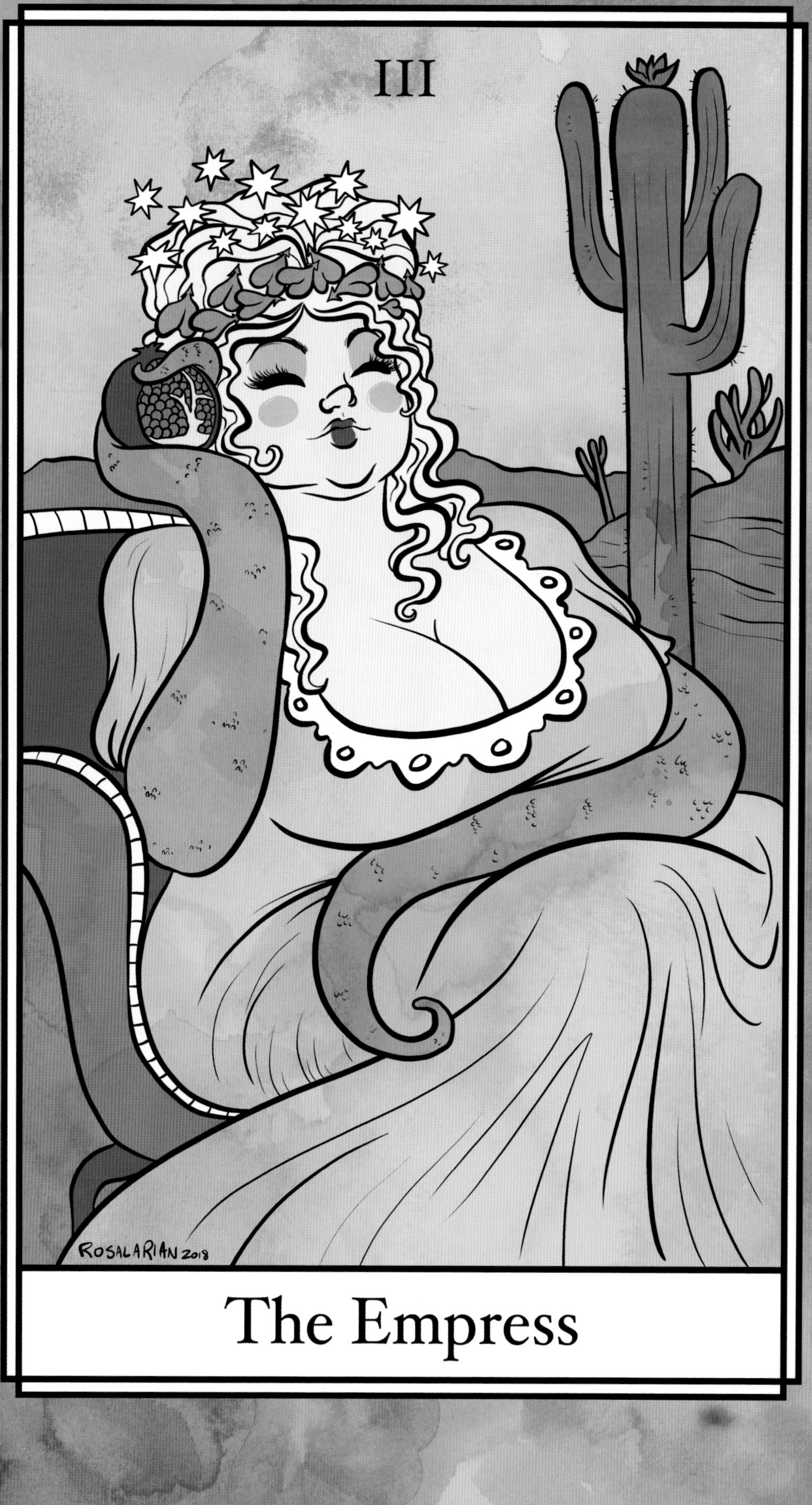
III
ROSALARIAN 2018
The Empress

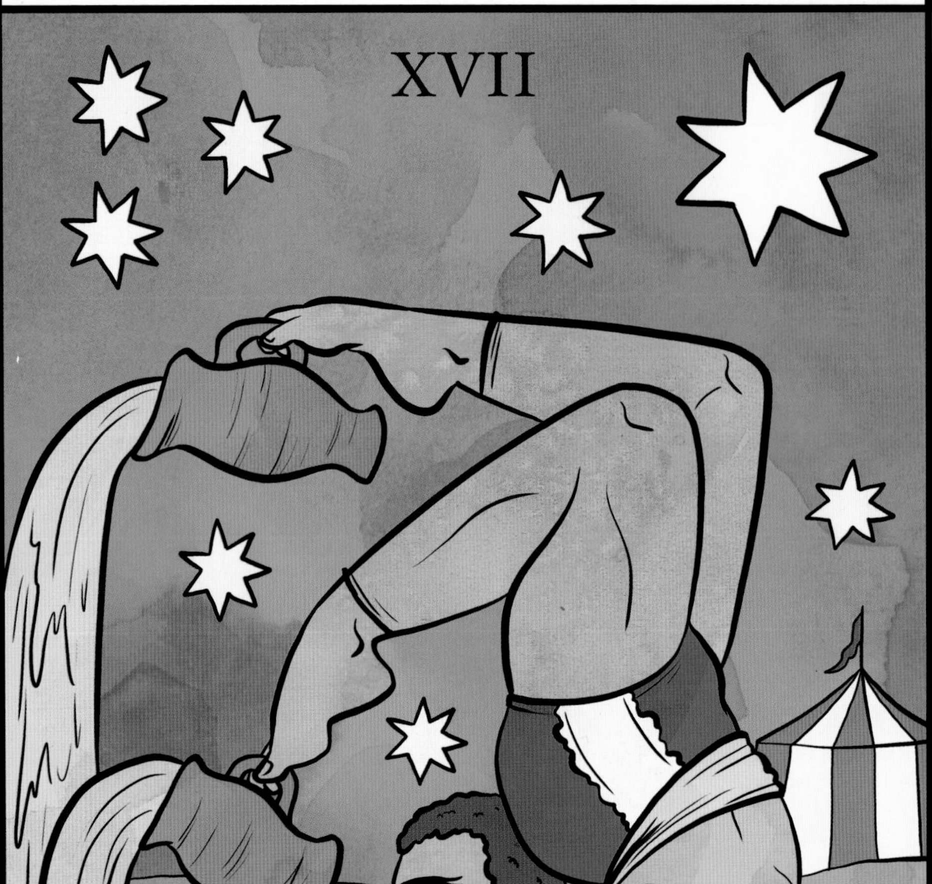
XVII
ROSALARIAN 2018

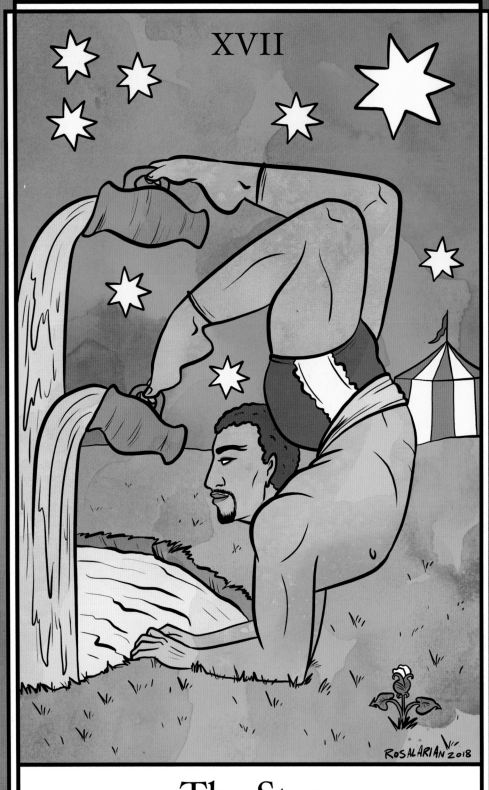

The Star

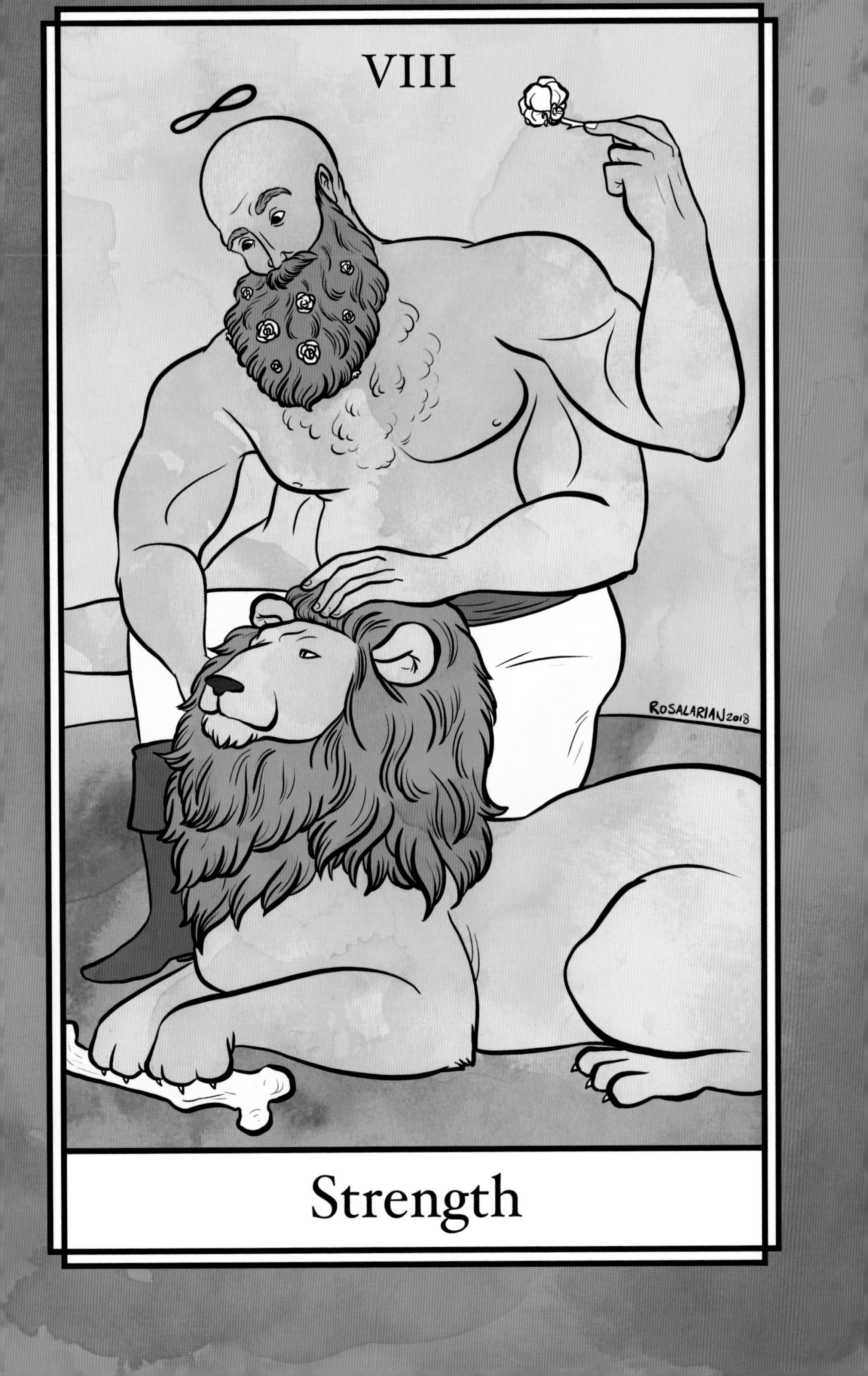
VIII
ROSALARIAN 2018
Strength

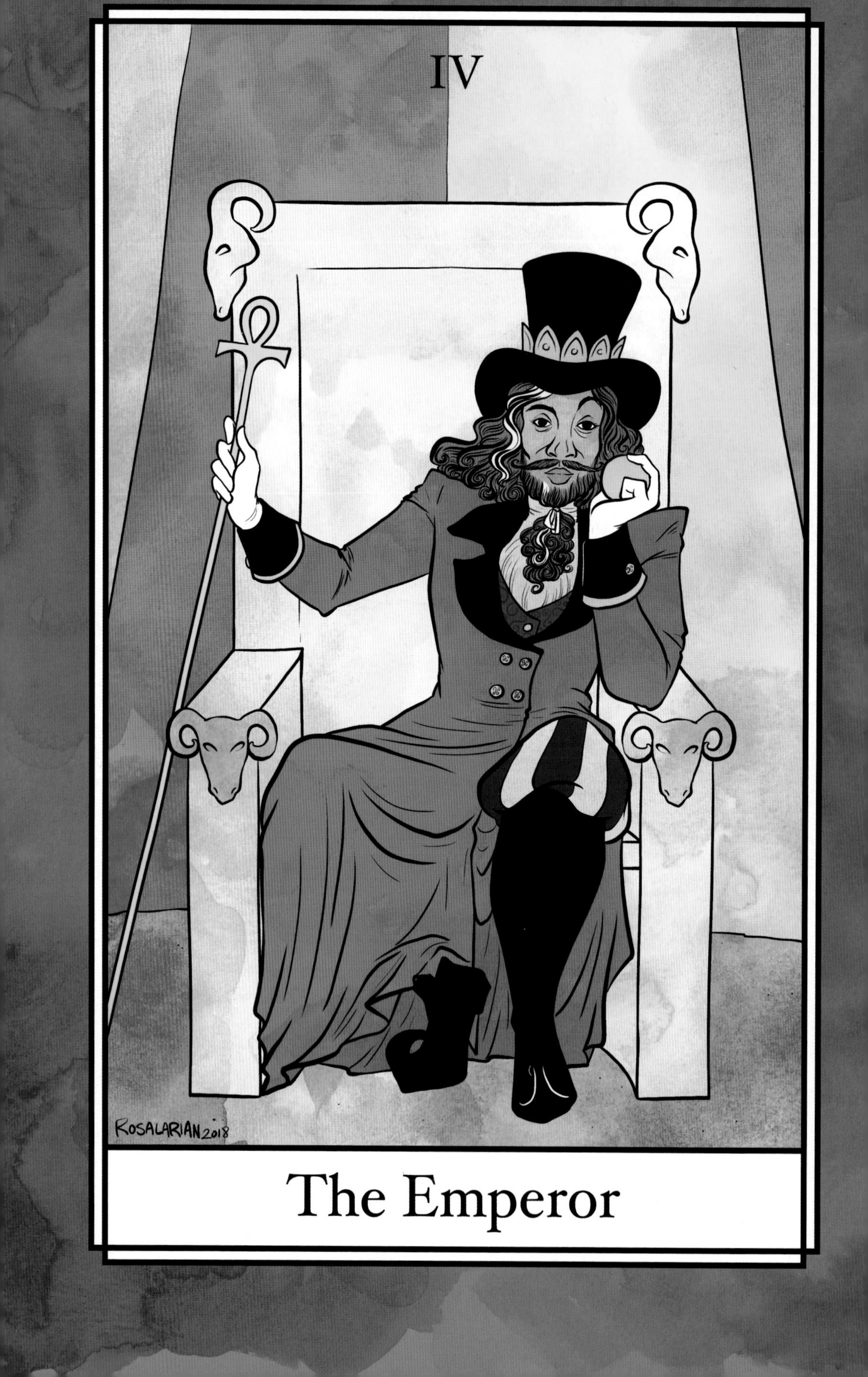
IV
ROSALARIAN 2018
The Emperor

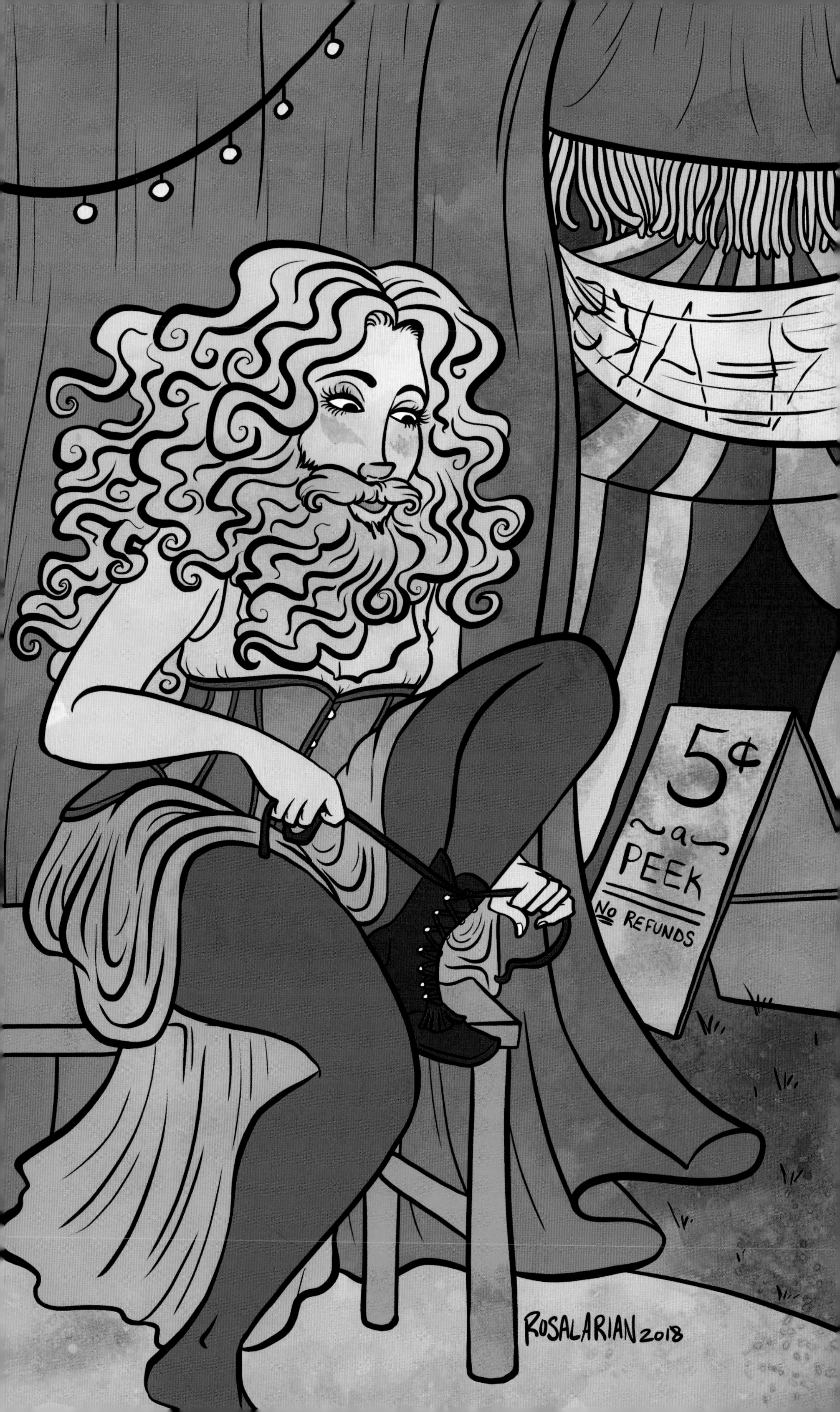
5¢
~a~
PEEK
No REFUNDS
ROSALARIAN 2018

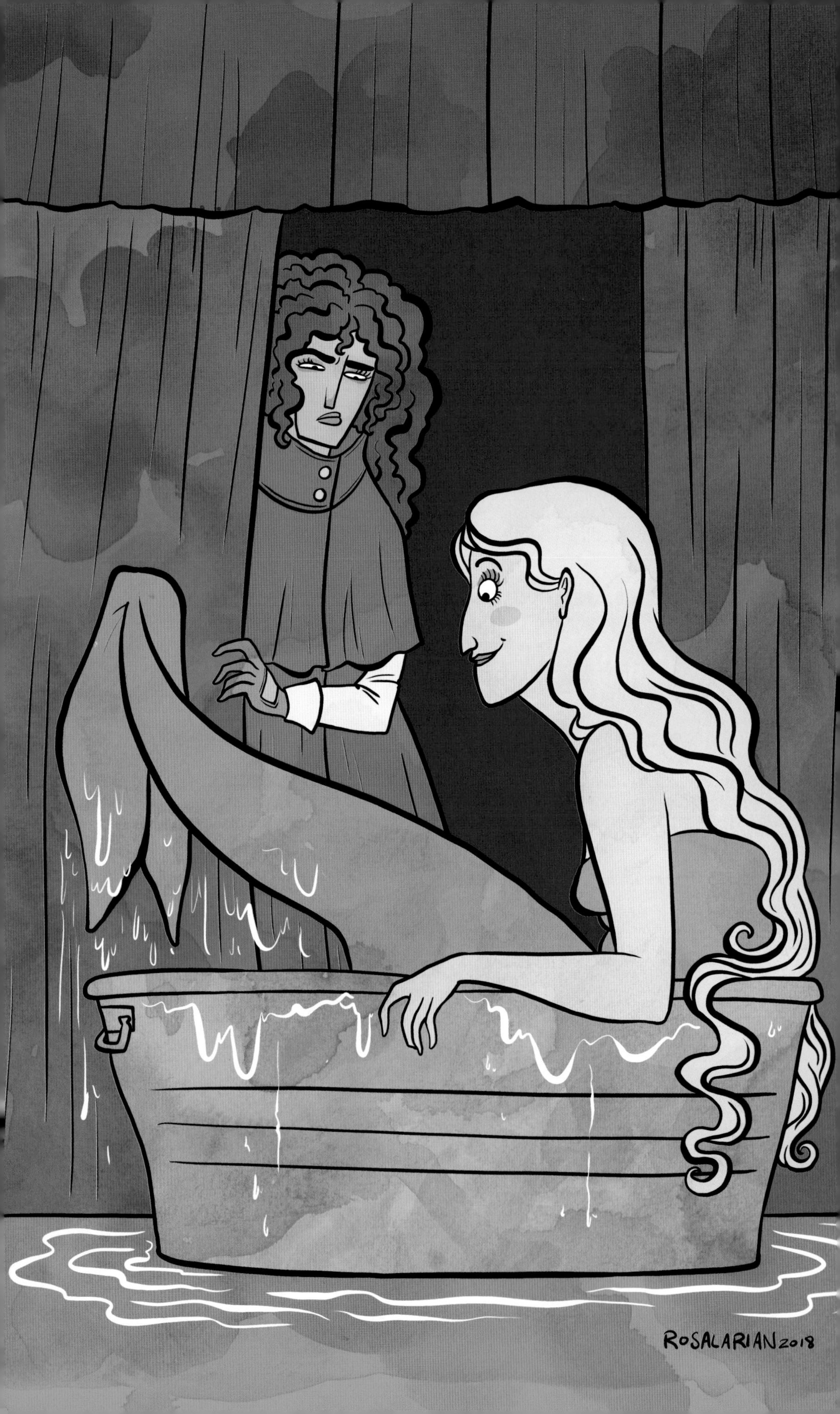
ROSALARIAN2018

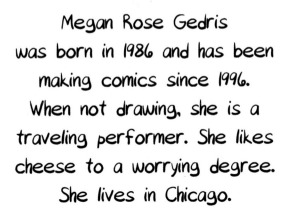

Megan Rose Gedris
was born in 1986 and has been
making comics since 1996.
When not drawing, she is a
traveling performer. She likes
cheese to a worrying degree.
She lives in Chicago.

See more of her work at
rosalarian.com

GAZE UPON
THE
MONSTROUS
VISAGE
OF THE
ONE
HEADED
GIRL